Imara has lived a life s   wasn't
shunned, just never ac__   d of a
seventh child, she had had the bad taste ~~to be born~~ a girl.
Her father's family had no use for a girl, so she was sent to a
city where the populace didn't use magic.

Now that she is grown and entering college, she has chosen
the best magical college in the country. It just happens to be
located in her birth city.

When family begins to encroach on her education and someone threatens her life, can her new familiar do as he promised and keep her safe, or will Imara have to use what little
magic she has learned to keep herself alive? Either way,
things are going to be unpleasant.

Shape Shifting 201

Imara made it through her first term without too many issues, but now that she is in the second term, a magic-draining fiend is stalking the students, and her familiar is bored
with guiding her through the early stages of magic. He has
taken to giving her misinformation to see if she can use her
own judgments. It is a challenge she doesn't really need.

XIA agents are taking courses at the college, and one of them
ends up next to Imara during her ethics course. A few conversations lead to a lunch date, and now, she must determine if a social life is worth more than her scholastic one.

Mr. E just likes going on lunch dates. The servers swoon over
his cute fuzziness. He is no help at all.

Sky Breaking 301

Sky Breaking seemed like a useful course, but its usefulness lay in the amount of credits that would count toward Imara's degree.

Once she is in the course, she meets the only other student, and they strike an unlikely friendship. Kitigan is a seer who has an interest in farming and apiculture, weather magic is part of that peculiar parcel.

After a series of classes that turn into tests, Imara is happy to head to Kitty's farm for a weekend away from school, and Mr. E wants to head out and ride some sheep. Everybody has something to do, including the trespassing werewolf pack that just moved in next to Kitty's family farm.

Imara has to walk the fine line between guest and defender while taking her Death Keeper skills for a spin. Her weekend is anything but relaxing.

Stealth Magic 401

Imara wants nothing more than to find a different course, but stealth magic gives her the credits she needs to stay on track, and there aren't any other options rearing their heads.

Stealth Magic is not what she thought it would be, and the idea of breaking into a home to rob an ancient artifact for her final exam was a little daunting. Luckily, Imara has friends who are going to help her through training, some old and some new.

Through some work with the XIA, she finds a tutor for her training and a place to do it. Ritual Space offers her a welcome, and the inhabitants set themselves to the monumental task of her training. The exam is getting closer and time is a factor.

Mr. E just likes chasing the enchanted bunnies of Ritual Space.

Spell Crafting 501

Imara's life is going according to her plans. She has her boy-friend, her kitten, and is about to earn her degree in Mage-craft and graduate. Once she has that degree, she has the right to request an application for a commercial magic license. It is the goal she has been working toward all along.

A shadow begins to haunt her during the day and stalk her when she is away from the college. She doesn't know what it wants, but it follows her with a purpose she can't fathom until she finds the identity of her stalker.

By the time she learns that it is Mr. E the stalker is after and not her, the trap has already closed.

Surrendering Magic

Bara has lived her life knowing that she is going to have to spend every waking moment learning or go mad, and even though she has a boyfriend, friends, and distant family . . . her future is bleak.

With a family letter, she sees her chance to grasp a future, even without magic in it. She has a chance to step into the human world, and with the blessing of her boyfriend and her friends, she decides to go through the extraction of the cursed magic she was born with.

The next morning starts far too early, and a cat in her room wakes her and urges her to get ready. When she's prepared, they step through a portal and end up in a place Bara wasn't expecting. Ritual Space. Her trials and surrender are going to take place in the safest area in the world. No magic will escape it, and nothing harmful can enter without the consent of the proprietor. It is the safest place to lose herself, so she begins the process of losing everything she had been taught to love and fear.

No pressure.

The Hellkitten Chronicles Collection
Copyright © 2024 by Viola Grace
ISBN: 978-1-990635-40-3

©Cover art by Angela Waters

Published by Viola Grace

Look for me online at violagrace.com.

Soul Casting 101
The Hellkitten Chronicles Book 1

VIOLA GRACE

Soul Casting 101

THE HELLKITTEN CHRONICLES

Imara needs a familiar, but what she ends up with is the toughest kitten in the magical world.

Imara has lived a life separate from her family. She wasn't shunned, just never acknowledged. The seventh child of a seventh child, she had had the bad taste to be born a girl. Her father's family had no use for a girl, so she was sent to a city where the populace didn't use magic.

Now that she is grown and entering college, she has chosen the best magical college in the country. It just happens to be located in her birth city.

When family begins to encroach on her education and someone threatens her life, can her new familiar do as he promised and keep her safe, or will Imara have to use what little magic she has learned to keep herself alive? Either way, things are going to be unpleasant.

Prologue

Mirrin was exhausted but delighted. She had carried out her contract and given her husband what he wanted and a little more.

The nurse turned toward him, holding the dual burdens. "Mr. Demiel, here are your children."

Mirrin watched as her husband started forward and then paused. He growled, "Which one is my son?"

The nurse frowned. "Um, here. This is your son."

Mirrin reached out for her daughter. "Please give her to me."

Holding his precious son in his awkward arms, he shook his head. "Mirrin, you know we are not going to keep her. I have what the family needed. We have the seventh son of the seventh son. The lucky one. Our fortunes are going to turn, but in the meantime, we are not going to feed an extra mouth. You know that arrangements have been made."

"Desmond! It is just a little girl. What kind of harm could she do?"

The nurse was hesitating with the little girl in her arms.

Mirrin pushed herself up, her body protesting mightily. "Give her to me. She may leave tomorrow, but today, she is my baby. My little Imara."

"Mirrin, let her go. She is unlucky."

"You have your seventh son, Desmond. Our contract is over. I am taking our daughter to Sakenta, and then, I am leaving."

Her husband was shocked. "What? You have seven sons to care for."

"My contract was to bear you your seventh son. I did that. I am not going to live with you screaming and ordering me around anymore. You wanted those hellions, you deal with them. I have my own life that I want to get back to." Mirrin

1

was somber as she stroked the pink cheek of her daughter.

She couldn't keep her girl. All children that she bore were the sole responsibility of the Demiel family. She was simply a conduit of her family's genes and their own debt to the Demiels. If she could keep her daughter, she would, but that wasn't in her contract.

Imara Demiel was going to grow up without the burden of a family history or being a ley-line mage. Her world was going to be wide open, and Mirrin hoped she lived long enough to see it.

Against all odds, Imara had been born before her brother in the same minute. She was the seventh child of a seventh child, and while the Demiel's didn't set any store by that, Mirrin knew that her family would cherish their new addition if they were allowed to claim her. The Deepford-Smythe family would keep an eye out for their newest member. They may have lost everything, including their family honour, but they loved their own.

Little Imara couldn't have direct contact with her mother, but the Deepford-Smythe family would find her and take care of her. Some way, some how, her daughter would know how much she was wanted.

The hospital was silent as Mirrin walked slowly to the nursery. She just wanted to hold her daughter one more time before she was taken.

Mirrin crept into the nursery, reading the names on the plastic cribs until she found the one that said Demiel. The blue wrappings adorned her son, so she stepped to the next crib only to find it empty. There was no tag, no baby.

"They took her away at dinner. Your people said they will care for her." A nurse stood there with a sad but kind expression on her face.

Mirrin dropped to her knees. "Gone?"

The woman came over and placed her hand on Mirrin's shoulder. "Yes, Mrs. Demiel. Your daughter is gone; now, let's get you back to bed."

She got to her feet, and as they left the nursery, Mirrin

kept looking back at the empty crib that should have contained a baby she should have been able to keep. Too many *shoulds.*

Mirrin hoped her daughter got the freedom and power that she had been born to wield, and she wished more than anything that her father never found out what she was.

The seventh child of the seventh child was just as powerful as a seventh son. With Mirrin and Desmond both seventh children, their seventh child was bound to be immensely powerful. Their seventh child was their daughter, and Desmond would never know.

Chapter One

"Imra, we need a calm-down at twelve B. There is a wild mix of something going on."

Imara looked at him with a weary gaze. "Come on, it's my last night."

"This is your job, Imra. Your last night to do it."

She made a face at Death Keeper Thomins and got to her feet. Most of the students in her high school were not fortunate enough to find a job at the repository of the dead. Being an Apprentice Death Keeper had let her save up, and when she was ready to apply, she had gotten into the most prestigious magic college for three provinces.

The next day she left for her new school to learn the basics of charms, spells and magic in general. For that night, she had to find out what was going on in twelve B.

She smoothed her cassock and lit the lantern outside the door. With a sense of finality, Imara hooked it onto her staff and walked through the repository, past the active graves until she reached what was supposed to be the newly silent.

Imara walked down the rows of those who had been retired by their families, their knowledge no longer required.

Her lantern illuminated the three specters floating above their resting places. "Good evening, lady and gentlemen. Is there any particular reason for your rising?"

She approached them and set the lantern on the grass. She folded her hands in front of her and waited.

Madame Gregoria Limack floated toward her and extended her hand. Imara mimicked her gesture and smiled as the specter made contact.

We worked out that you are leaving us. We wished to give you a proper send off. You have been a treasure to watch as you grew into the young lady before us.

"Thank you. I will be sorry to leave, but I am very excited

4

to go to Depford College."

One of the men floated forward and touched her arm. *We are excited for you, as much as we are able. We wish you luck, and we wanted to offer you a gift.*

She blinked at Mr. Frimaldi. "Thank you for the thought."

Mr. Exeter grinned and touched her shoulder. *We managed to arrange it with a little help.*

"Well, Imra, you seem to have made an impression on our guests."

She turned to see Thomins approaching. He was grinning, and he had a small object in the hand not holding the lantern.

"You are in on this?"

"They asked me when we were moving them. They wanted to give you something and forced their families to chip in. It was hilarious." As a Death Keeper, he always sided with the guests. They were the ones he had to work with, after all.

She stared at the spectral and physical gathering around her. "You threatened your families?"

Madame Leemra laughed silently. *We did not give them all our secrets. They may have decided to retire us, but that does not mean we have been drained of all knowledge. We are not leaving until we are good and ready.*

Imara sighed. "You didn't have to do anything."

Thomins smirked. "They wanted to. This is a letter to the Dean of the College. There is also a small box with a letter in it. They are yours with the compliments and best wishes from our locals."

She took the gifts and looked and them with stunned amazement. "Thank you. Thank you all so much."

They converged on her and caressed her cheeks and arms. She caught the thoughts, the well wishes and the flashes of them sending their children and grandchildren off to college. She was their chance to live a little past the veil of death.

Silently, she promised to check in with them whenever possible. They laughed at that. She was going to be getting on with her life and that was good. Life was for living, and for *the* living. They were just happy that they could force their descendants to contribute to their going-away gift.

The party lasted for an hour, and then, the inhabitants of twelve B retired for the evening, their energy spent. The copies of ancient mages retreated to their soul stones and rested in the monuments that held them. A living life was reduced to a six-inch wide by three-foot high pillar of stone with the gem embedded in it.

As an Apprentice Death Keeper, she had had to monitor the energy level in the stones and keep them clean. Planting flowers around them that bloomed and glowed in the darkness was something she did on her breaks. Apparently, it was appreciated.

She wished she could do more for them than tend their tombs, but that was the job, so she did it.

When they all winked out, she picked up her staff and lantern, holding the gift with the other hand.

Thomins was grinning at her. "There were others who made their families contribute, but they have faded already."

"Why?" They returned to the office next to the parking lot.

"Because for a moment when they met you, they saw someone with potential for a future that they wanted to contribute to. They do not get many opportunities to participate in the living world."

Imara nodded. "I know that, but why me?"

"Madame Ikohn is one of your ancestors. She needled the others into participating since she could not address you directly." Thomins dropped that little bombshell casually.

"My . . . I did not think I had family here."

He chuckled. "She was born here and moved when she married. She was a contract bride and returned to her family when the contract was fulfilled. I believe she was deputy mayor for a decade."

Imara's mind was spinning as they extinguished and stowed the lanterns. She set the staff in its slot and looked at the objects in her hand. The letter addressed to the Dean of Students was a heavy, cream-coloured parchment with a black wax seal. She didn't recognise the family mark, but she would deliver the letter.

The box that was only slightly larger than the letter and was black and purple, carved with glyphs and humming with power.

"I don't think I can accept this. It looks old."

Thomins grinned and sat with his feet up on his desk. "They ordered the family to give it to you, so it is yours. I have a record of transfer if anyone requires it."

"Which family is it from?"

He chuckled. "You will have to open it and see, but it is the end of your shift and you need to be getting that transport to the college."

"I am driving. It is only two hours away."

"Then, you had better be going. It has been fun having you here, but your destiny lies with the living. I have been around long enough to know that. Life as a Death Keeper is not for you."

She walked over and extended her hand. "Thanks for all that you have shown me, Thomins. You truly have a knack for soul manipulation that is enviable."

He gripped her hand and grinned. "You were definitely grasping the basics. I have high hopes for your future studies. Don't be a stranger."

Imara nodded and swallowed the lump in her throat. "Thanks. I will keep you posted on my progress."

"Do, or I will call the school myself. I am fairly sure that I am going to be inundated with status requests from the occupants here. I am going to need every tidbit of your life that you can share."

She laughed. "They are relentless."

"They are, but stimulation is good for them. It makes them last longer."

She looked through the window at the carefully organized repository of mind imprints held together inside painstakingly enchanted gemstones. The soul might be gone but the mind remained, and the minds needed stimulation. She had unwittingly provided that stimulation with her tales of high school and her boarding house.

Her life had become their link to the living world. She was going to miss being that bridge.

She sniffled as she drove from the boarding house to her new—temporary—home at the college. The box was on the passenger seat next to her, along with the letter.

Her bags were in the back seat. A few weeks of clothing, notebooks and pens were all that she owned.

Dawn was a thing of the past, and she would be reaching the college in minutes. A nervous clenching of her stomach reminded her that she hadn't had breakfast, or dinner for that matter.

Her first stop was the office of the dean of students, and after that, she was heading straight to registration.

Chapter Two

The parking spot she had been assigned was at the far end of the universe from any of the class buildings. It wasn't great, but it was secure.

Imara tucked the letter into her jacket and zipped the box into her backpack. Her suitcase had excellent wheels, and it would make a lot of noise but remain intact wherever she dragged it. It was her big splurge purchase, aside from tuition and lodgings.

She locked her car, checked the map on her phone and went to deliver the letter.

Senior students and freshman were beginning to arrive on campus. She passed nearly a dozen as she hauled the rumbling case across the sidewalks and pathways.

The soil under her feet contained magic. The college had been built on a wave site, and the ancient magic still simmered below the surface. This was where she would learn to hone the skills she had been born with.

The feeling of walking through somewhere she had always been meant to be was strange. Sakenta had been a great place to grow up, but the lack of magic use in the population was a stark reminder that she didn't belong. Each and every day she was thankful for the guidance counsellor that had put her in touch with the Death Keepers. It was a small outlet, but it had been welcome. Her first experience with using magic had been talking to the dead. It was not a normal introduction, yet it had confirmed her desire to seek out more information and education on the subject. She was destined for magic.

Anticipation was pushing past her hunger. The dean of students was located in the same building as registration, which meant that there was only a small diversion necessary.

She crossed the inlaid marble floor, passed the registration tables for first years and walked up two flights of stairs to the dean's office.

Behind the heavy door, she found a young man seated behind a desk, and he appeared irritated as he set his phone down. "Can I help you?"

She reached into her jacket and pulled out the letter. "I have this for the Dean of Students."

The young man with the dark brown hair and deep green eyes smiled. "I will give it to him."

Her fingers tightened. "I think I am supposed to deliver it myself."

"You have brought it to his offices. That means you have delivered it. Give it to me, and I will send it through."

She didn't know what that meant, but she extended the heavy parchment to him.

Without looking at it, he opened a small, flat box on his desk and he set the letter inside. He closed the box while smirking at her, and the glyphs glowed. "There, the dean has it. You can be on your way."

She opened and closed her hands, turned and hauled her stuff out of the room, feeling as if something was undone.

Ah well, there was registration, checking into her room and getting a meal to do before she could spend some time focusing on what she had left undone.

The young man named Anton had given her excellent directions on how to find Reegar Hall. The pity in his eyes was something she could have done without, but as long as the place had space for her to sleep and study, she had what she needed.

Going to magical college on a budget was not going to be easy.

Imara looked at the exterior of Reegar Hall, and she wrinkled her nose. Where the other buildings had ancient brick and stone, Reegar was all concrete and cracked mortar. She walked inside and was greeted by a chipper redhead who seemed relieved to have something to do.

"Hiya, are you lost?"

"No. I am one of the students assigned to Reegar."

"Oh. Oh!" The woman pumped her hand happily. "I am the Resident Advisor for Reegar Hall. My name is Bara. Bara Wilmington."

"Imara Mirrin. First year."

"Right, of course. Do you have your food card?"

"I do. It is in my pack."

"Well, get it out and I will seal it to you. It is best to do it right away. Folks tend to lose them, and it costs a fortune to replace them."

Imara fished around in her welcome envelop and pulled out the two-by-one inch card. "Got it."

"Great. Give me your wrist." Bara plucked the card from her fingers and took her left wrist. With a bit of pressure and some muttered words, the card sealed itself to Imara's skin. It became as flexible as a tattoo but only visible when the light skimmed across it.

Bara smiled. "I specialise in bio-manipulation magic. If you take any shifter courses, let me know. Now, come this way. You are the only confirmed booking this year, so it will be just us in the entire hall."

"Why?"

"It isn't the most prestigious, and Magus Reegar was an insane genius who is said to haunt this hall."

Imara followed her own personal RA up the steps and down the hall to the rooms. "That is probably why they suggested it to me. I have met a specter or two in my life."

"Really? How many?"

"Two hundred and thirty-four, give or take." She hauled her bag along after her and looked at the plain, uninspired decoration. It was as if someone had forced the building to be bland.

Bara paused and looked back. "That is a weird coincidence."

"Not really. I knew about the haunting and the price was right. One was an enticement and the other wouldn't scare me off. Guess which was which." She grinned and hoisted her bag up next to her.

Bara waved her arms. "You have your pick of any of the rooms. It will key to you and your familiar when it arrives."

Imara paused. "My familiar?"

"Yes. Your registration indicated that you were taking the Soul Casting course. A familiar is a requirement." Bara frowned. "You do have one, don't you?"

Imara felt her heart sink. She had looked forward to taking that course. "No."

"I am sure you can work something out. The practical part of the course is a few weeks in." Bara reached out and patted her arm.

Imara looked down the hall and took a deep breath. She let her instinct be her guide, and she gripped her suitcase. With a slow exhalation, she sent the luggage down the halls on its wheels. It careened from side to side, twisting and rolling to a stop in front of the door on the left at the end of the hall.

Bara nodded approvingly. "That is a good choice. It has windows that open if you are doing any light spell work."

Imara walked to her new door and pressed her hand against the door handle. It fought her for a moment before it opened, and she looked at her new domain.

The luggage rolled inside as if it knew home when it saw it. Imara turned to Bara. "I suppose I am home."

Bara nodded. "Please. Settle in. I will be on the main floor if you want a tour."

Imara gave her a short smile. "I will be down in a few minutes. This won't take long."

The door swung closed in Bara's face. Apparently, the hall wanted her to settle in as well.

Imara looked around and sighed. The décor was bland, but it was neat and clean. The bed was a double, covered with white sheets, a polar fleece blanket and fluffed pillows.

The bookshelf was empty, and the desk was plain but pristine. The chair had four legs instead of rollers, and the floor was smooth cement.

She needed a small carpet. That much was certain.

Imara opened her luggage and put her books on the shelf. Her clothing was all foldable, and it slid into the dresser next to her closet without any trouble. There was plenty of room to hide a body in the empty drawers.

"Wow, this is better than I thought."

"Thank you, I do try, but I am restricted by the college from doing anything else." A man walked through her wall. His clothing gave no hint as to his date of death, but his vibe was definitely that of the dead.

She smiled tightly. "Magus Reegar, I presume?"

"Yes. You are the new student."

"I am. Imara Mirrin."

He extended his hand. "That is not your full name."

"No, but you can call me Imra." She placed her hand next to his and let him close the gap between them.

The peculiar cool touch of a ghost was augmented by the crackle of active magic. That wasn't right.

She flexed her fingers when he withdrew his hand. "You are not a standard ghost."

He grinned, his mustache turned up with his lips and the slicked-back hair gleamed in the light streaming in through the window. He almost appeared solid. There was only the hint of translucence through his grey wool suit.

"You are correct. I died in this building by another's hand."

"So, your power came with you."

He chuckled. "I knew you would be a good fit here. You have the run of the building."

"Excellent. Please don't come in without knocking. I am a woman living alone, and I don't need to worry about warding myself from nocturnal specters."

"I was expecting a little more trepidation."

She chuckled. "It takes more than a magical man without a body to creep me out. I am here to learn and get an education that I can work with."

She watched his dark features as he eyed her up and down. She took in the clothing from another era that wasn't quite at odds with contemporary garb. He had been a sharp dresser, and even the creases in his trousers had made it into the afterlife.

"You are here because it is inexpensive, but I trusted my instincts when you applied for residency here. I did nothing to interfere with the application. They might have called me mad, but aside from one day where I didn't trust my own judgement and ended up haunting my own hall, I have always gone with my instincts. I will offer you what help I can, but you are right. You are here to study. I will respect that and make sure to knock. Welcome to Reegar Hall."

He disappeared as suddenly as he had appeared, leaving Imara alone in her room.

"That was interesting. He even had an audio presence. That was definitely different."

Talking to herself was par for the course. It didn't matter who was around, but there was usually something or someone listening.

Her stomach growled loudly, and she grinned. It was time to put it to rest.

Brunch was left on her agenda, and then, she was heading to the bookstore. Half her books were online, but the other half were beginner enchantment books.

Coffee and books were in her future. That much was certain.

Chapter Three

Bara was an excellent hostess, and she seemed exceptionally happy to have another body in the building.

"How many folks can fit in Reegar Hall?"

"Fifty. He only accepts the ones that he thinks will do credit to the hall."

Imara grinned. "Which is us."

"Precisely. Cappucino?"

"Three is usually my limit, but sure." Imara watched as her companion fired up the machine once again.

The outfitting of the study area was incredible. The true passion of Magus Reegar was displayed in the in-house library and snack bar.

The bagel had stopped the gnawing hunger; the fruit salad had given her a burst of energy. Now on her fourth coffee, she was going to be able to head straight to the bookstore to get the last of her supplies.

Bara sat across from her again. "So, what are you going to do about the familiar?"

"Can't I just get a pet?"

The coughing and spluttering that Bara engaged in was enough of an answer.

Imara sipped at her drink. "Not a good idea?"

"Not unless you want to explode a bunch before you find one that can hold all your power. That is what the familiars do. They act as a repository to keep your essentials safe while the rest of you is playing with spells."

Bara wrinkled her nose. "See the dean of students. He can look into your family lines to see if you have any familiars available."

Imara leaned forward. "Family lines?"

"Sure. At some point, most mage families have made familiars for their children. Or, they have had them made."

"Damn. Well, I guess I am going to have to drop a class before I even get started." Imara heaved a deep sigh. "That sucks."

"Seriously, check with the dean. He has all the records for each student." Bara bit into a muffin and looked up in surprise when a loud knock sounded. "Whaff vah hew?"

"Should I get it?"

The RA swallowed hard and shook her head. "Nope. This is why I get to live here and get a stipend. I will be right back."

Bara brushed her fingers on her jeans as she crossed the room and headed for the hallway leading to the front door.

The expression on her face could only be called bemused when Bara returned with a blue-tinged man trailing after her.

"Uh, Imara, it is for you."

The man was carrying a briefcase, and he looked at her intently as he approached. "Miss Mirrin?"

She got to her feet to greet him. "Yes."

"I am Yringar Mornwalker, dean of students."

"Oh. That is funny. Bara was just saying that I should speak with you." She extended her hand.

The prickle of cold ran up her arm as he returned the greeting.

"Ms. Wilmington, may we have the room please? I have a great deal to discuss with Ms. Mirrin, and I believe discretion is paramount."

"Of course. I will wait outside the door in case Magus Reegar authorized anyone else this year and didn't mention it."

Bara smiled and flicked some of her red tresses over one shoulder. She headed for the hallway, and Imara was alone with a strange, blue man.

He smiled tightly and took the spot in the comfortable chair, swamping it with his size.

Imara couldn't help but stare. "You are . . . not human?"

He grinned. "I am supposing that you have not met many extra-naturals in your life. I am a mixed-heritage frost giant. Now, I am here to discuss your inheritance."

"My what?"

"Your mother's family has set aside some funds for you, as well as books and a familiar."

Imara blinked. "I couldn't be that lucky. What familiar?"

"It has been in the Deepford-Smythe family for generations. Twenty generations to be precise. To be honest, I was shocked when I received that letter this morning. It took some doing to find your pedigree, but now that we have it, you are going to reap the full benefit of your connections."

He popped the clasps on the briefcase and opened it, pulling out a sheaf of papers four inches thick and studded with file folders and tabs.

"First, as you are an *Unknown,* we will go over your family histories and attachments. When that has been settled, we will get into your inheritances. You have several that have been given to you based on your mother's side of the family. They didn't have much money, but they did have power. The histories are now yours to go over at your leisure. I am sorry I took so long, but there were a lot of documents to copy."

He handed her the first folder and smiled. "You know your status?"

Imara held the file that she had dreamed of since she was a teen. "Yes. I know that I was the extra in a contract bond. My brothers remained with my father, but there was no need for a daughter. I was sent to Sakenta and raised by the state and a family trust. My situation was to remain unknown to family until I became an adult. I was also considered to be unlucky."

"Only by your father's family. In your mother's notes to you, you were the lucky one. You were born seventh as the child of two seventh children. You are exceptionally lucky."

He fished out a folded sheet of paper. "Here is your family tree. You will need it for genealogy courses."

Imara's mind was whirling as she got family histories, lists of local relatives and an appointment card to meet with the Master of Familiars on campus. He would set her up with a link to her family beast.

She was hungry again by the time he was finished, but

getting her familiar now took precedence to her belly.

"There are a lot of masters on the campus."

He smiled brightly and chuffed a laugh. "There are. We can't have folks being taught by just anyone. Everyone working as an instructor here is a master in his or her field. Thamus is the Master of Familiars. He teaches the higher levels how to create their own familiars. He also manages the inherited-familiar program."

"Right. Where do I go for that?"

"I will take you there. I believe you have enough to absorb for one day." He nodded. "Keep the appointment card to present to Thamus. He is a stickler for formalities."

She looked at the mountain of documents. "May I take this too my room before we go?"

"Certainly, but you do not need to remain here. There is a stipend allocated for your residence here at the college. It will fit you into a more . . . suitable location."

Imara looked around. "I like it here. It suits me. As long as my familiar is content with the space, I won't have anything to complain about."

"Are you sure?"

Magus Reegar floated into the room. "She said it suits her, Yringar. Leave her be."

The dean tensed. "I didn't know you were strong enough to skulk around here, Reegar."

Magus Reegar was nearly opaque as he approached them. "Ms. Mirrin gives off all kinds of energy. Forming something visible is child's play in comparison to what I am now capable of, just with a few hours of her under my roof."

The dean looked ill. "You are feeding from her?"

Imara held up a hand to forestall the conversation. "I give off waves that are useful for the disembodied. I am looking forward to learning shielding techniques. I can still power Reegar if he asks after I can put a cork in the fountain, but until then, he can hold conversations like a normal person and even read a book if he so chooses."

She got to her feet with her armloads of paperwork. "I will be right back."

Her desk received the paperwork without even shuddering, which was a miracle given how flimsy it had seemed on first inspection.

She clutched the card with the details of her familiar assignment and returned to the lounge.

Reegar was in the stacks of books and looking for his favourites.

She smiled at the giant who was waiting for her. "I am ready to go now."

"Good. I will take the time on the journey to ask you about your family name and why you don't use it."

She smirked. "Good luck with that."

They walked out of Reegar Hall, side by side. The walks were filling with new students and returning seniors. Whatever the other pedestrians were, they gave the dean a wide berth.

"Sir, if I may ask, why are you working at the human magic college?"

He smiled. "My people skills."

"I am guessing you don't have to use them often."

"No, but they are available when the need arises."

She grinned. They passed the main administration building and turned down toward a path leading to large, wide structures and open fields.

"So, Ms. Mirrin, why don't you use your family name?"

"Ah, well, that is just because my mother's family name gave me too much trouble when I was young and my father's family didn't want me. I chose my mother's first name as my last because it seemed that she was the first person in my life who wanted anything to do with me. She made sure that I was given to a good institution in Sakenta, and they raised me with an eye to my future. Unfortunately, my family name made them treat me with odd attention. The Smythe name was on the front of the boarding school and nursery after all."

"So, when did you change it?"

"When I was changing from junior high to high school. I changed my name and had them set me in as a new student from out of the city. I changed boarding homes as well and started over."

"They allowed this?"

"Of course. I was an excellent student and a credit to the contract breeding that the Deepford-Smythes engage in. They want me to be successful, so they are paying the bills for the most part."

He nodded. "I read that in the letter. Your Great Aunt is very proud of the work you have done to send yourself to college, but she has decided it is time for the family to truly step in."

"I was given to believe they were broke."

"They are, but there are family discounts to be had. There was a trust for you that wasn't activated because of the name change. That is being rectified as we speak."

"Excellent. More money means more courses."

"Oh, your courses are all complements of the college. The Depford of Depford College is one of your ancestors on your mother's side." He shrugged slightly. "It is all in the files."

She rubbed her forehead. "This is all a little much."

"Don't worry. Your familiar will be able to relieve some of that pressure." He chuckled. "Here we are."

They paused in front of a large blue barn painted with containment glyphs on every eave and every peak. It did, indeed, look like the right place. Whatever was conjured in that building would stay there unless it was deliberately set free.

She clutched the card with her familiar information and stepped up to the wide, black, double doors.

"Here is where I leave you. Simply hand the card to the first mage who asks you your business. They will handle it from there."

Without another word, the dean of students turned on his heel and left her at the base of the steps. It didn't fill her with enthusiasm for what came next, but if she had to, she had to.

Chapter Four

Standing in the foyer, she could see hundreds of containment glyphs covering the walls. They were slightly different from the ones used at the repository for the dead, but the theme was the same. Nothing gets out.

A young woman with glasses that had slid to the tip of her nose looked up with a smile. "May I help you?"

The ferret on the young woman's shoulder sat up on his hind legs in joint inquiry.

Imara extended her hand and gave the woman the card.

After a short glance at the card, the woman jumped to her feet and bobbed a short bow. "Please excuse me."

Imara looked at the portraits of mages and their familiars. Fierce mages were accompanied by fiercer beasts. It looked a little overwhelming to her, and she was about to skip the entire process when a voice called out to her.

"Imara Mirrin?"

She turned and blinked in surprise at the only figure that had appeared on campus wearing mages robes. "I am."

"I am Master Thamus. So, Yringar ran off? Typical. He will never live down the time he was working with the shifting class and got stuck in the body of a wolf. We had to house him here for weeks before the Shift Master came back from his sabbatical." He came forward and extended his hand to her.

She took in his healthy, tanned good looks, dark hair and rich pumpkin-coloured eyes. He was the epitome of magical health, and the embroidered robes that he wore added to the aura he presented.

Imara extended her hand and felt the power in his grip. "Pleased to meet you." She ignored the rest of the statement. It didn't pertain to her anyway.

"So, you are here to get your familiar?"

"Apparently." She gently tugged her hand free of his.

"Please, come this way. I will explain to you how this is going to work and what your familiar actually is."

"I would be delighted to learn."

He reached for her hand, but when she didn't extend it, he nodded and led the way.

They passed a wall of aquariums, a hall led to the sound of screeching birds; she could hear and smell animals all around her. It was an assault to the senses.

Thamus led her in what seemed like a huge circle, but he finally turned down a hall that ended in a quiet room.

A gateway made of wood took up one wall. There were cushions in the center of a power circle and a low table waiting for them.

"Please have a seat. Are you comfortable with your grasp of what a familiar is?"

"Not particularly. It wasn't taught in Sakenta. We knew about the wave, but nothing more of magic was taught than that."

Master Thamus settled his robes around him in a dramatic and well-rehearsed fashion. "Well, in that case, I will give you the broad strokes for the type of familiar you are about to receive."

She nodded, and he waved his hand. A teapot lifted into the air from a sideboard and floated toward them. A stream of water was pulled out of a pitcher, and it cascaded in a column to meet the pot. Leaves from another container tumbled along.

It was a charming show, but she wished that Thamus could talk at the same time.

When he was using magic to heat the pot, he finally spoke. "While most mages take on a familiar as they advance in their careers, some inherit their familiars. These beasts are actually thinking magic users, bound in an animal form."

The pot lifted and tipped, filling two small cups.

"That doesn't sound pleasant for them."

"It isn't, but it is their fate. Families bound together. Hellhounds and mages linked by blood and power around the world."

"Hellhounds are people?"

"Mages who draw power from the demon zone."

She was nervous. "Is that why I am here?"

Thamus shook his head and sipped his tea. "No, your family is linked to a penal familiar."

"A what?"

"Your family and others were victims of an ancient mage. He killed several elders, and when he was caught,, he was put into service as a familiar for the eldest member of each family without a familiar, in rotation. The previous mage who had this familiar just passed last month. He is now up for claiming."

"I won him?"

He chuckled. "If you like to think of it that way. He can be an incredible assistant or an unbelievable burden. The choice is yours."

"What is his shifted form?"

Thamus smiled. "That is up to you. At the moment that the gateway opens, it will touch your mind and find the kind of beast you want your familiar to be. He will become that."

"So, he has no choice. If I want a goldfish, he becomes a goldfish."

"Not very useful, but yes. Think of what you want as companion, study guide and assistant, even mentor. That will be the form he takes. Now, drink your tea. It will help the gate reach your thoughts."

She reached out and picked up the cup. It tasted like drunk marshmallows. She finished it but wasn't happy about it.

Imara set the cup down with a click. "Done."

The pot filled it.

"Good. Do it again."

"What?"

"When your mind is ready, the portal will open. Until then, keep drinking the tea."

She made a face. "Why couldn't it have been coffee?"

"Because you can't hide herbs in coffee." He smiled

politely. "Everyone expects herbal tea to taste peculiar."

She lifted the cup to her lips and slammed it back before setting it down. "How do I take care of it?"

"Well, his animal instinct will be strong, but when you need it, his human mind will spring to the foreground. He can eat what you eat, but figuring out the cleanliness routine will depend on what animal you choose."

She had been to one shot party before going to college, and the tea turned into an endless line of shots. Suddenly, the fish made sense. If she kept this up, her back teeth would be swimming.

"Tell me about yourself. What was your school like? What about your home?"

"Is this necessary?"

"You need to think of the moments when you felt you needed a champion. Those are usually the places where the need is formed." Thamus smiled gently. "That is what the gateway is looking for so it can shape your familiar into something you truly want."

The light crackling of energy touched her thoughts.

"Whoa. I think something is happening."

"Keep drinking and talk to me about the worst moment in your life."

She felt the world fuzzing away at the edges, and she started to speak. "I had changed schools and was having my first day as the new me. No friends, no one I knew, and a new part of town. The new boarding house was austere and there was nothing living near it. The entire aura around my new neighborhood was static. Nothing grew. I wanted something of my own that had the potential to become something amazing. I wanted something I could touch and cuddle when I needed it. Something small, something cute. Something forever."

With every word, the prickling in her mind grew more intense, and as she finished her sentence and looked at the portal, fire blazed.

"Your familiar is about to arrive. Please extend your hand."

Imara kept her gaze on the portal and extended her hand. She felt a small burst of pain and heard chanting. Her focus was on the shadow forming in the swirling flames.

The vortex widened and the shadow grew larger. Imara pulled her hand away from Thamus and extended it toward the approaching figure.

Tears pricked her eyes as the creature came into focus. He was exactly what she wished for.

Trapped in his crystal cell, he flexed his fingers as he waited for the call. He was nearing the end of his sentence. Once he was free, he would be able to choose a dignified death or a new life under the aegis of the Mage Guild.

The families that he had harmed had been paid in labour, protection and guidance. Nearly a thousand years of servitude had been enough for him to consider his options and the evolution of magic.

The Mage Guild had come to his conclusion that magic obtained from the demon zone was not healthy for those around the mage using it. They had placed locks on everything related to demons, and now, he was in a world where his fondest dream had come true. He wished he could have been born a few centuries later.

The pull of magic came just in time. He had been getting bored and nothing good came of getting bored.

The crystal opened, and he stepped free, heading for the platform where he would become the beast that his mage wanted. He had been wolves, lions, a unicorn, and even a small dragon. He wondered what magnificent incarnation he would take on next.

With a deep breath that took in no air, he walked forward and let the magic shape him to his new mage's will.

"Mew." The tiny black kitten made the small sound, and then, it blinked in surprise at its own voice.

"Mew. Mewmewmewmew."

She smiled and extended her hand, noting the blood on her fingers. He lifted his tiny head up and licked at the crimson drops.

Thamus's voice was strangled, but he stated. "And bound by blood, he shall serve you until the end of your life or his."

She looked down at the tiny kitten with the huge orange-gold eyes. "Hello. Uh, Thamus, does he have a name?"

"His name will be disclosed to you in time. When you are better able to deal with it, you will receive everything you need to know about him. For now, name him as you would a pet."

She watched the tiny pink tongue lapping at her fingers and felt the scrape of needle-sharp teeth. When he drew back a little, she reached out and grabbed him around his ribs.

"He is so tiny." She couldn't stop smiling as she cuddled him against her.

He let out more of those small and indignant sounds, but a rumbling purr started up as she stroked his small body.

Thamus was shocked when she looked at him. "You made him a kitten."

"Yeah. I always wanted one, but I was never in a home that could have one."

"He is a black kitten."

"Yup. I thought that black had the most dignity."

Thamus pinched the bridge of his nose. "Right. Well, I will register him as your familiar and give you the books you will need to study how to make your partnership more effective."

"Oh, good. I am in the Soul Casting class, and I needed a familiar for that." She rubbed her chin against the top of the kitten's head.

"Contact my office when you have a name for the registry. Naming him will help you focus, and focus will increase your power."

"I will think about it. Can I just go now?"

"Certainly. My assistant will have the books at the front desk. Pick them up on the way out."

She knew a dismissal when she heard one. Imara got to her feet with her new companion in her arms and left the Master to do whatever he was working on next.

She had her kitten, and he was curled against her and purred happily. Now, she needed the instructions that went along with her new companion.

How difficult could it be?

Chapter Five

"**O**kay, since you won't answer to anything I want to call you, you are going to pick your own name." Imara finished attaching the last sticky note to the wall of her room.

The fluffy black kitten weighed less than a pound as she moved him past the letters. "Just paw the one that you want. I will spell it out."

She moved him past the first layer and in the center of the second; he pawed at the M.

"Right. M. Okay. Next letter." She moved him past the letters again and was becoming despondent when he struck out at the R.

"Okay. M.R. Wait, you want me to call you Mister?" Imara turned him to look at her.

"Mew."

Chuckling, she was going to set him down when he flailed his little paws with their needle-sharp claws at the wall. Either he saw a moth or he wanted to go again.

"Right. Mister. Here we go." She held him and cruised him past the letters again. He attacked the E.

"Meowwwww." He was triumphant.

"Mr. E. Mystery?"

"Mew." He lifted his head high with his paws folded against her fingers.

"Well, either one is better than here, kitty-kitty." She winked at him and set him down.

He scampered away to explore the confines of her room with feet that looked too big for his body. There was a dorky charm to him, as there was to all kittens.

Bara had taken one look at him, squealed and ran out to get him supplies.

Imara had been amused, but Bara was one of those women who really enjoyed cats. Magus Reegar hadn't shown up yet, so it was a question as to how he was going to react to the new arrival.

Imara looked over at the mountain of paperwork, the textbooks she had picked up and the notebooks willing her to fill them. "So, should I study or learn about my people? Decisions, decisions."

Mr. E leaped into the air and landed neatly on the pile of documents. "Mew."

"Well, I am supposed to be following your advice, so sure. Tell me what I should read first."

She eased him from the top of the pile and spread out the folders. The kitten stalked back and forth on them before pawing at one.

Imara opened the file and read the documents inside. The heir contract that needed to produce no more or less than seven sons was detailed as to requirements, and the ability of one or both parties to dissolve it the moment that the seventh living child was born. It included the disposition of any female children to Sakenta. Girls weren't part of the contract. The Demiel family was after a seventh son of a seventh son. They needed an infusion of luck to go with their cash.

The next document was the settlement that Mirrin Deepford-Smythe Demiel had received when she left her husband and children.

The condition of the contract that concerned daughters was rather cold. It was a short addendum that indicated any daughters born to the mother were to be given into care and raised away from the families. No contact between parent and child was to be allowed or encouraged until the daughter in question was an adult.

If more than three daughters were born, the contract was void and both parties would dissolve their union.

Imara sat back and wondered about what would happen if the father engaged in any activity out of the marital union.

A thud got her attention. "What are you up to now, Mr. E?"

Her backpack jerked and twitched. She sighed and finished opening the zipper. A set of rich gold eyes looked up at her from the shadows. "Mew."

She reached in for him, and his little claws hung onto something. The box clattered to the ground a moment later.

Imara blinked. "You wanted me to get that out?"

He waved his paws toward the box.

"Right. This would be easier if you could talk, but I guess I am going to have to work on that."

He gave her a short nod. Nice to know that there was something she was missing. She already felt completely overwhelmed.

Imara picked up the box, and it flared blue in her hands. She nearly dropped it. A small crack appeared along one side of the box, and she used that opening to pry the lid up.

A letter was lying in the box. She slipped it free and examined the heavy parchment and thick seal.

It was addressed to *My Dearest Imara.*

The handwriting was feminine and the seal was that of the Deepford-Smythe family. If she wasn't mistaken, this was a letter from her mother.

She cracked the seal in half and read the letter.

Mr. E crawled into her lap and purred as she sniffled and smiled through the document.

It was simple. If she was reading it, she was an adult and at college. Her mother wanted to start a correspondence with her via the letterbox, but she understood that a student had a lot of pressures in the first few weeks. She could wait until Imara had her feet under her before they met face to face.

Imara carefully folded the letter, and she tucked it into her bag. She wanted it where she could find it if she wanted to read it again.

With a sigh, she picked up Mr. E and rubbed her face into his kitten fur. He started to purr, and she laughed and exhaled hot air onto his skin. He jolted in surprise, and then, his body rumbled violently with the increase of his purr.

She exhaled again, and he went limp in her hands, his eyes blissfully closed.

"What is that?" Reegar floated through the wall and

glared at the kitten.

"This is my familiar. His name is Mr. E."

Magus Reegar moved close, glaring at the small bundle of black fluff in her arms.

"He is powerful."

"Apparently. Did you have a familiar?"

"No. I never saw the need. My interest was in potions and spell work, not animal husbandry."

"And bending humans to your will."

He muttered, "That was more of a hobby."

A knock at the door announced Bara with all the cat supplies her vehicle could handle.

"I haven't had so much fun in years." Bara grinned. "I love shopping and finding things. Do you think this is enough?"

"I think it is fine. So, I can use the fridge in the lounge?"

"Of course. Registration is fizzling out. We are on our own for the term. Oh, and I bought him some beef. I hope that's okay. You did say that he could eat people food."

The kitten in her palms came alert at the word beef. He made murping noises and ran to Bara, searching through the bags at her feet.

"And I have lost him. Mr. E, rein in your enthusiasm."

"His name is Mystery? That is so cute."

The look the kitten gave Bara could have curdled milk. It appeared that being cute was an affront to him.

Bara grinned and unpacked several of the bags, setting the food aside so that she could refrigerate it. Toys, a soft bed, a grooming kit and a litter box and litter.

"Wow, you got everything but a toothbrush."

Bara snickered and plunged her hand into a bag. A toothbrush with a tiny and narrow head emerged. "The toothpaste is flavoured like salmon."

Mr. E popped up on his hind legs and pawed toward the tube.

"Well, I guess I should go to find something to eat and feed him before I organize my books for tomorrow."

He waved his front paws in the air, and Imara snatched him up with one hand while grabbing the bag of food in the other.

Bara remained in her room and started arranging things, humming to herself.

Reegar shook his head and came with them. "She was excited by the idea of an animal in the hall. Apparently, she always wanted a pet."

"You are looking rather fit."

He snorted. "I haven't had this kind of influx of energy in decades. You are very powerful."

"Yup, with no control. It is a lot of fun."

"I can only imagine what it would be like when you were around the dead."

"Well, I was able to make a good living at it just working part time as a death keeper's apprentice." She smiled. "You would be amazed at how much two days a week with the dead can bring."

"Are funds a concern for you?"

"They were. I have enough for now. It will get me though the next few years. After that, I had better find a source of income in short order."

He blinked. "Can you not simply return to your family home and seek a position at your leisure?"

"No. I am an unknown. A discard after a contract. My family and I have no connection. I am truly on my own. I will succeed or fail on my own merits."

"So, it is in your interest to study hard and not engage in the normal frivolity that the college seems to bring out in the young?"

"That is correct. It is the same reason that I got Mr. E. I need him for my courses. A familiar is a prerequisite."

She set the kitten on the floor and unpacked the groceries into the fridge in the lounge. She kept out the enormous steak and set it on the counter.

A little bit of rummaging yielded a cutting board and knife. With practiced motions, she minced up less than a tenth of the meat, segmenting the rest and stowing it in the freezer.

"Here you go. Now, table or floor?"

He made a mewling noise and reached for the small plate.

She scooped him up and put him and the plate on the tabletop. The small smacking noises made her smile as she set about throwing together a quick stir fry for her own purposes.

When Bara appeared, Imara asked, "Care for some?"

"I could smell it down the hall. I thought you would never ask." Bara got two plates down, and the meat and veg with spices and sauces was split down the middle.

They sat near the fuzzy blob of black that was still making inroads on the beef and shared a meal.

It was her first dinner in her new home, and for the first time in a long time, it felt like she was right where she was supposed to be.

Chapter Six

Sleeping in was not an option. Small, fuzzy paws smacked at her face in a playful staccato.

"Mr. E. Get off."

"Mew."

She sat up and looked out her window. There was no light. "You have to be kidding."

He bounced away, standing next to the door. "Mew."

She grumbled and got out of bed, stumbling to the door. The moment she opened the door, he darted through it, stopped and meowed back at her.

Wearing nothing but a long t-shirt and her panties, she stumbled down the dark hall until she heard the distinct but subtle chime of her alarm. She had left it in the lounge.

"Dammit!" She ran forward and grabbed her phone.

Mr. E jumped up and stood on the table, making little squeaky sounds. She checked the phone and winced at the time. She grabbed him and cuddled him. "Thanks for that. I only lost a few minutes."

He lifted his head proudly. She tickled his head with her fingers and the purr commenced. Time to get ready for class.

Mr. E had an uncanny knack for sitting quietly on her shoulder. The women who saw him cooed and even the men gave him fond looks.

The History of Magic class was full. It was a basic course that could be passed by anyone with a working attention span from elementary school.

Imara announced her name for attendance and didn't have to do anything else but listen to the lectures on the suspected waves of magic and the effect they had had on early man.

Elves were an alteration of human physiology, as were

34

shifters, but it was suspected that mages were exposed over and over before finally absorbing the magic that was being dumped into their geographic location.

Imara took notes, made note of the assignment and got up with the rest of the class. She must have startled Mr. E because he dug his claws in.

She trooped to the dining hall with her compatriots, and she began chatting with a few women who wanted to know about Mr. E. He loved the attention and loved having his own burger and fries for lunch.

Imara opted for a salad and a set of chicken fingers before she settled in to eat before her familiar could finish his burger.

One of her new companions asked, "So, what can he do?"

She looked at the kitten, who was happily munching away at his meal. "Well, he can put away food at an alarming rate, and he has excellent senses."

He looked at her with a piece of cheese on his little, black nose. "Mew."

The entire table laughed.

She removed the cheese and scratched his head. "Sorry that you got stuck like this."

He gave her a sober look from his bright eyes and slowly nodded.

The frustrations of having the instincts of an infant cat were becoming a secondary memory.

His mage's sincerity was not in doubt. She hadn't betrayed what she knew about him. As far as her companions knew, he was simply a small feline.

He finished the meal she had presented him with and returned to her, cuddling against her chest while she ate. His full belly made him awkward, but he knew she would take care of him if he rested.

One day with his new mage and he still didn't know what she wanted out of life. The others had presented him with a list of demands, but she simply seemed to crave companionship. He could do that merely by remaining the small creature she had chosen him to be.

In all his centuries as a familiar, he had never before had a mage who didn't want to tap into his power immediately. The previous incarnation of servitude had demanded that he start helping with the increase of power immediately and that mage power continued until he died. Eight decades of propelling Magus Yuman Smythe to success in his field of potion design while wearing the body of a raptor had been exhausting. This time, he was actually going to enjoy his punishment. Mage Imara Mirrin had power and no idea what to do with it. If he was careful, he could make her into the strongest mage of her age.

He let out a deep sigh and slumped bonelessly to the table. Life as a kitten might make him small and helpless, but it came with protection offered up by his own mage. It was a strange turn of affairs.

He flicked the tip of his tail lazily as he wondered if there was going to be dessert.

Imara tucked Mr. E into her sweatshirt and zipped it up so she could carry her books. It was time for her Soul Casting class.

When she crossed the college and entered the Wayforth building, she was surprised to find only five other people in the lecture hall.

She was comforted by the fact that all of the other students had an animal with them. It appeared that she was in the right place.

Imara took a seat and settled the unconscious Mr. E into a more comfortable position.

The instructor came out, and the power that surrounded her was stunning. "Hello, I am Magus Deepford, and I am here to teach you how to cast your soul into the universe and bring it home safely again."

The magus's familiar was an elegant black panther that paced next to her with haughty grace.

"Does everyone have their familiar?" The magus looked around, and her gaze focused on Imara. "Do you have yours?"

Imara unzipped her sweatshirt and pulled out Mr. E. "Got him."

The magus smiled. "Good. He's adorable. Have all of you bonded to your familiars?"

Only one of the students raised their hand.

"Right. Well, we will cover that next week. This week is about the history of familiars. We will cover the reason that we use them and what they can do for us. Once you are aware of the capabilities, you will be tempted to use them. I can assure you that the restrictions of how you can use your familiar are strictly enforced. The Mage Guild hands out punishments to students on a regular basis. They do not make exceptions for youth or inexperience. You will have to take responsibility for everything done using your familiar, no matter its origin."

She looked at the students, one by one, making eye contact and waiting for acknowledgement.

"Now, pull out the textbooks, and we will begin with the first recorded history of a mage using a familiar to extend their own power."

Imara flipped to the first page in the textbook and got her notebook ready. During the lecture, she made notes on things to check up on, including the first familiar and the first hellhound.

The origins of the hellhounds were fascinating. Low-powered mages tapped into the demon zone to increase their energies and ended up bonded to the energies. The bond became genetic after two generations, and after that, there was no going back. Those born to hellhound families were bought, fought and traded amongst the mages until they formed an uprising.

That was the end of the first lecture.

"So, I want you all to identify the players in the uprising and have a list of five ready when we convene again on Thursday. Have a nice two days. Dismissed."

Mr. E had made his way to her shoulder, and he was purring in her ear as she cleared up.

She bagged up her books and slipped her pack over one shoulder. Mr. E adjusted his position, and they left the class in silence.

She wanted to stop and chat, but she had studying to do. There would be time to meet the other would-be mages later.

Bara was at a table in the lounge with her own stack of books. She grinned when Imara staggered in.

"Rough day?"

"I think Mr. E ate his body weight in a cheeseburger and fries."

"You shouldn't let him eat that. He will get sick." Bara was concerned.

Mr. E hopped to the table and flattened himself on the table with a deep purr.

Imara shrugged. "He picked it."

She set her bag down and started pulling out her books and her laptop.

Bara smirked. "Use your student id and the password is ReegarHallRocks."

Imara grinned. "I am guessing we have a fast network?"

"You can stream anything you like. It is wide open, and there is a printer on the network. It is in the kitchenette, next to the fridge."

"I didn't notice it."

"Magus Reegar had it installed. He wants you comfortable." Bara chuckled. "I am enjoying his sudden attention to the modern era."

"I think he just wants to learn to use the internet himself. There is a lot of fey porn out there." Imara grinned as she signed in to the network.

Reegar appeared and took the third seat at the table. "I don't know what that is, but it sounds fascinating."

Bara snorted. "Well, Magus Reegar, I am sure you have seen worse in your time. But, if you want to order a computer, I will help you choose one."

Reegar inclined his head. "Thank you. I will check with the college administration first to see if they can help, but if it doesn't work, I will come to you."

Imara watched as he reached out to pet Mr. E. "You are definitely more solid today."

"Thank you. I feel more alive than I did when I was up and in my own body."

"My pleasure. This used to be my part-time job."

Bara blinked. "How did that work?"

Imara set up her homework station and looked at the RA of Reegar Hall. "Ah, well, I took an aptitude test in high school. I needed an evening job, and Sakenta believes in aptitude application of talent. So, I was assigned to shadow the Death Keepers at the main repository, and a week later, they offered me an apprenticeship at an excellent rate for a teenager. Three years of evenings helping folks speak with their dead managed to pay for college."

"So, you made them stronger?"

Imara sat back and rubbed the back of her neck. "A ghost, or disembodied spirit, loses cohesion over time. If their tether isn't perfect, they will degrade much more quickly. When you have degradation and a strong ghost, you can have all kinds of spectral phenomenon."

She reached down and grabbed a bottle of water from her bag, cracking it open and taking a sip. "My job was to maintain the anchor points that held the tether and warn anyone if they were cracking, clouding or degrading. Speaking to the dead to check their status was part of the job. I thought everyone could make the ghosts stronger when they needed to. Apparently, it is a weird connection that I have to those who are no longer flesh."

"Wow. All I did was mow lawns all summer. Do you have an open mind?"

"Yup, and an open power-generating body. So, I need to find some warding spells or, at least, control."

"I can help you with that. So, did you want to order in or are you willing to try whatever I make in the kitchen?"

Imara smiled. "I am willing to try whatever you come up with. I haven't had much experience with delivery. The boarding house owners didn't want any strangers on their property."

"You are kidding." The woman's astonishment was nearly palpable.

"No. Whatever you choose is fine. I will chip in if you choose delivery." She nodded and got into her books, checking on the assignments and working on her histories.

When Mr. E crept onto her laptop and looked at her with a murp in his voice, Imara cursed and lifted him up, setting him aside and removing the characters he had just created.

"You are no typist, Mr. E. Wow, did you lose weight?"

He murped again and looked smug.

Reegar snorted. "He was fat and then he was thin. He is using his own magic to alter his body."

She picked up her little buddy and cuddled him. "I think he reset himself to summoning specs."

"You know he is powerful."

"I do. It was non-negotiable." She scratched lightly under the kitten's chin and watched as he closed his eyes, and the purr got louder.

Imara glanced around. "Where is Bara?"

"She went to answer the door. There was a parade of delivery vehicles dropping off parcels."

Imara could feel the prickle of magic as Bara returned with a barrage of bags floating in the air behind her.

"My treat. Pick what you like and we will keep the menus on speed dial." Bara worked her fingers, and a wide blanket covered the floor. Bags opened, plates and cutlery flew around, and in moments, a picnic was ready for a small army.

Bara settled on the floor and waved at the expansive selection. "Take a seat and enjoy. We are the closest thing to sorority sisters that we will have. Consider this a rush party."

Imara had no idea what that was, but she set Mr. E on the ground and settled into the picnic space. "Well, then, sister, shall we dine?"

Chapter Seven

The droning sound woke her for the sixth night in a row. She nudged at the kitten snoring on her abdomen and tried to wake him.

"I told you, you are too small for a pizza." She rubbed his swollen belly.

He squirmed on his back, all four paws in the air. She chuckled and checked the time. It was just after two in the morning.

She sat back and stroked his belly as she pondered her first week of school. The history class was interesting, and she had already prepared all the reports listed on the course outline.

Her financial-planning course was fun. She enjoyed the numbers and the absolutes of where they went.

Herbology was a tricky course. She had never taken much interest in the properties of plants, but now, it was a lot more than picking the right spices for dinner. She had found that it was taking a lot of her concentration to keep track of what each plant did at what point of the lunar cycle. The possibilities were staggering.

Reegar was surprisingly helpful. He not only had a grasp of herbology, but he also had found the ritual that would ease communication between Imara and her familiar.

The next day in class, in front of everyone and their familiars, she would bind her mind to Mr. E's and finally confirm his identity once and for all.

He could be either Edan Stormborn or Eadric Hellborn. Both led rebellions against the mages regarding the use of demon energy. Both had been brought up on charges when they were captured and disappeared from history.

She had asked the fuzzy monster, but he wasn't telling. He looked smug and then chased his tail the moment she

41

asked. She smiled and laughed instantly, forgetting the question.

Cute and cuddly was the most devastating thing she had come across so far. As she played with him quietly, his eyes opened and he burped. Instantly, he went from roly-poly to his normal slim and dorky.

She chuckled and he got up, curled himself in a ball on her stomach and started sleeping again. He might have been a great and deadly mage, but right now, he was freaking adorable.

Imara settled, made sure her alarm was on and braced for what the next day was going to bring. She was going to do her first, actual, deliberate magic. Was there a word for excitement and eagerness mixed with terror?

"Ms. Mirrin. Are you clear on the protocol?" Magus Deepford checked on their placement in the warded circle.

"Yes. I reach for him and he should reach for me and we meet in the middle."

"Without moving."

Imara sighed. "Right. Ready for this, Mr. E?"

"Mew."

Magus Deepford chuckled. "That is still the cutest damned thing. I have never seen anyone with a kitten for a familiar."

"You haven't?" Imara was suddenly a little nervous.

"No. Most mages pick a more impressive creature as their familiar. Go ahead."

With that resounding endorsement, Imara looked at Mr. E and reached out with her thoughts. His orangy-gold eyes locked with hers, and she felt a prickle in her mind. The prickle became a tunnel, and soon, she heard thoughts around her that weren't hers.

Welcome to my mind, mage.

Not a mage yet. I am still a Death Keeper's apprentice.

You are much more than that.

So, who do I have the honour of communicating with?

You have narrowed it down to two choices. You are

correct. I am indeed one of them.

Which one?

I will let you know at a later date. For now, know that we are indeed bonded until the end of your natural life.

Oh. Goody. Imara sat up straight and nodded to her instructor. "All done."

"Let me just check." Magus Deepford probed at Imara's mind, and after a surprised jerk, she nodded. "Right. Excellent. Ms. Harkness, you are up."

Ninya Harkness, whose dreams included becoming a captain in a Mage Guild outpost, stepped forward with her hawk, Hector.

Hector eyed Mr. E, but as she gathered her kitten, Imara heard a low growl coming from the tiny body. He wasn't going to back down, and Hector finally looked away.

Impressive.

He always was a lesser mage. Every time I have run into him during my incarceration, he has retreated.

That bore thinking about, but Imara sat back in her seat as Ninya mumbled and chanted, trying to weave the connection.

Imara didn't have to do all the chanting; her skills with the dead were honed enough that she could reach out to another soul who was reaching back.

She cuddled with her buddy as the rest of the class bonded with their creatures.

When the bonding was done, the mage and the beast looked at each other with new eyes.

It was quite jarring when the door to the hall was banged open and a woman strode in toward the front of the class. "Where is Imara . . ." She checked something written on her wrist, "Mirrin?"

The entire class was staring at the interloper.

Imara got to her feet, and Mr. E hopped to her shoulder. "That would be me."

"You have stolen my familiar."

Imara could feel Mr. E stand up and bristle. "He disagrees."

"I am the Deepford-Smythe heir, and he is mine."

Imara stepped toward her, aware of their audience. "Could we discuss this in private?"

"No. Claims must be acknowledged by witnesses. He is mine, and I will have him."

Magus Deepford stepped forward. "Laia, this is unseemly. What are you talking about?"

"I went to the familiar center to get my familiar, but the one that was to be delivered to the seventh of seven was already taken. It took a week of bribing and asking the right questions, but I finally found out who got it. She did."

Imara held up her hand before the instructor could speak. "Your birthdate?"

Laia frowned. "What does that have to do with it?"

"Whisper it in my ear. I will tell you mine. I have a right to him if what I suspect is true."

The woman leaned forward and whispered her birthdate. Imara returned the favour with, "Imara Deepford-Smythe out of Mirrin Deepford-Smythe by Desmond Demiel, Seventh of seven by both parties."

Laia blinked and leaned back. "They didn't tell me that."

"I am fairly sure that no one thought of it. Now, do you still have a legitimate claim?"

Laia blushed hot and looked down. "Um, no. I will go and get the next familiar on my family's roster. I apologize for the interruption, cousin."

Imara stared at the pretty blonde with the red face. "It is fine. I can authorize the dean of students to show you the family documentation. If you would leave now, the rest of the students would like to bond with their familiars."

Magus Deepford smiled. "If no one objects, she will need to know how to do this herself. Laia needs to witness the bonding."

Renee and Able nodded that they didn't object, and soon, the class was back in order as the ritual was repeated over and over.

When Magus Deepford addressed them again, she was grinning. "Excellent. Now, next class we will start the beginning focus and rituals of being able to give custody of your soul to your familiar. Dismissed."

Imara exhaled and got to her feet, grabbing her bag. Laia gripped her by the arm. "I am sorry. They just told me that someone else had claimed him. I didn't know about you."

"You still don't. Like I said, I will contact the dean of students and you can look me up."

"Couldn't I just ask you? I mean, we share family."

Imara chuckled. "No, we aren't. I am unknown. I am on record but have never met a relative, until now."

Mr. E let out a small, "Mew." It was a burst of sound that hung in the air between them.

"Mr. E says that it is time for dinner. Would you like to come with us?"

Laia blinked. "Really? I mean, that would be great, but I am meeting some cousins for dinner."

Imara sighed. "Ah. Of course. Another time."

Laia nodded. "Another time. It was weirdly nice meeting you, Imara."

"You too. Good evening." She slung her bag over her shoulder and left the lecture hall. Huh. She had just met her first blood relative face to face. Laia had not spit in her face, so that was something.

The paths between the hall and her classes were burned into her memory. She walked home with a long stride and an urge to talk over what had just happened with Reegar and Bara.

Her mental exercises were stopping the leak of power that she engaged in wherever she walked. The ghosts on the quad stopped rushing at her for power boosts, and she was finally feeling positive about her chances of making it through her first term.

Her Herbology exam was already under way. She had to select six plants that would produce a power and health-enhancing potion when properly enchanted by a master potion maker. That was the exam. She had to pick her herbs that would create the proper potion and drink it herself to test its veracity. There was nothing like putting the pressure on to make sure that the students payed attention.

Ten more weeks and she would know if she had chosen the right herbs and plants or if she was going to turn green and puke.

Reegar was waiting when she came in. "Congratulations on your bonding! Bara will be late. She left a cake in the cold box."

"She didn't have to do anything. It is my day to cook."

"She wanted to. It was your first spell work. It deserves to be celebrated." Reegar offered her his arm and escorted her into the lounge.

"We didn't do anything. I touched his mind, he touched mine. There is now a tether between us. That's it."

"That tether is going to power everything you do in the next few years. It is an important moment."

"I will trust your judgement on that. You seem perky today."

He chuckled. "I contacted a friend via email. He responded. It has been nearly a century since we last spoke, but he is there and I can talk to him."

"What does he think of your contact?"

"He responded and is on his way here to meet me." Reegar laughed. "For the first time in a century, I will have a guest that I have actually invited."

"I am excited for you. Did you want me to work on a focus stone?"

"I would rather that you went into the library and charged one of my books. Something personal to me that won't sync itself to other specters."

"Sure. I have a few hours tonight. I am caught up on my homework."

"Good, but first . . . cake."

Imara giggled and patted his nearly solid arm. "I like the way you think."

Bara came in while Imara was bleeding off her extra energy into a book of masculine erotic etchings from the Victorian era.

"Imara, what are you doing?"

"Giving Magus Reegar a touchstone—of sorts. I mean, I am not going to touch it, but he wanted something to use for emergency power if I wasn't around. He has been so helpful, I said sure."

Bara grinned. "I see you enjoyed the cake."

Imara snorted. "Mr. E decided it had been a while since he had seen cake. He attacked it and is now sulking, after his bath."

Imara looked to her familiar seated on the table and swathed in a wide wrap of towels. He looked like an angry rat, and bathtime had shown her what the communication between mage and familiar could be. There was a lot more cursing on his part than she had imagined. Her mind had been painted scarlet with irritation. He hadn't even let her brush out his fur afterward.

Bara covered her mouth as she giggled. "He looks unimpressed."

"I am unimpressed. That looked like a great cake."

"Aww . . . you didn't get to have any?"

"Nope. He dropped right onto it without any hesitation."

"Too bad. It was from your family."

Imara paused. "What?"

"Yes. It arrived this afternoon. I didn't have a chance to tell Reegar anything other than that there was a cake in the fridge. He must have assumed I bought it. Congratulations by the way."

"Thanks." The book she was working on glowed softly, and she closed her hand. "I think I am going to do some more studying in my room."

"Don't you want dinner?"

"No. I am fine." She looked at Mr. E and beckoned. "Coming?"

He narrowed his eyes and stalked out of his towel cocoon. She didn't laugh but cuddled him against her chest, picked up his brush and headed for their room.

Family had sent the cake. It reminded her of the box and the letter she had yet to write.

I am sorry I ruined your cake. I just had the urge to jump so I did.

It is fine. Cake can be distracting. You did remind me of something, though.

What was that?

I need to write to my mother. Sulking about my situation won't make it better. Only by taking action can I change my circumstance.

You got all that from my leap into icing?

It was a very profound leap.

He pressed his head against her shoulder, and she brushed him out until his black fur was silky and smooth once again. When he was asleep in her lap and she was seated at her desk, she pulled out sheets of paper and began to compose a letter to her mother.

She scrapped several drafts before beginning the letter with, *Dear Mother. I performed my first conscious magic today.*

Imara took a deep breath and kept writing.

Chapter Eight

Two days after the bonding, Imara got another parcel. She got back from her herbology class and found a box on the step outside Reegar Hall.

"Weird. Huh, it's for me." She flipped the box in her hands and noted the popular website logo on the packing tape.

Mr. E thudded on top of it a moment after she turned it around. *Notgood, notgoodnotgood. Don't touch.*

"What?"

Get Reegar. Mr. E was perched on the box, fully fluffed with his back arched.

Imara frowned, but she entered the hall and called out, "Magus Reegar, I need some assistance here."

Reegar walked toward her, smiling brightly. "Imara. How lovely. My guest was wanting to speak with you."

"That sounds delightful, but first, I need your help. There is a parcel on the doorstep, and Mr. E won't let me near it."

Reegar scowled and walked to the door. He opened it and looked down at the angry, miniscule cat and the box he was standing on.

"Well, I can't do anything myself, but the timing is very lucky. Let me get my guest."

Imara stood with her pack on her shoulder, looking at the box with the new accessory made of fur. "Right. Thank you."

A moment later, Reegar walked down the hall with a creature made of shades of grey and silver.

The elf was dressed in rich charcoal tunic and trousers with a wide sash at the waist. The boots were matte, and if he stood in the shadows, he would nearly disappear. Well, most of him. The silver of his hair blazed like a beacon.

"It is an honour to meet you, Imara Mirrin."

She inclined her head. "I will return the greeting as soon

49

as we get the parcel sorted so my familiar can engage in his normal evening food orgy."

Reegar pushed her back against the wall with a gentle hand on her shoulder. "Don't touch it. Liirick will take care of it. Won't you, Lee?"

"This is a nasty piece of spell work. Did you handle it?"

She looked at her hands. It had been a cold day, so she was wearing gloves. "By the corners."

The elf knelt and used the edges of his sleeves to lift the box and the familiar up, bring it within the building. "Ree, where is your lab?"

"Follow me."

Magus Reegar led the way down a hall that he had pronounced strictly off limits to her until she was a second year.

"So, you are Liirick of the Dark Shadows?" Imara trailed behind them.

"I am. You may call me Lee."

"I just finished a report on you for my history class. I had no idea you knew Reegar."

"He and I were friends for all of his years. I was a guest lecturer here, and he and I met socially after. The Guild was not pleased, but he remained my steadfast companion whenever I was in town."

The relationship and Reegar's delight in being physical gave her sudden understanding. "I am glad you were able to reconnect."

Lee glanced at her, and she noted that his eyes were a dark pewter and they twinkled with amusement that belied his age. He was over six hundred and had come in to help many human settlements when the waves of magic broke and spread across the world like ripples in a pond. He had helped them adjust and trained the mages that had gone from simple lives to being able to manipulate the world around them. Fey and mages like him had saved lives and helped get the one-percent mages to safety.

"So, you wrote a report on me?"

"Yes, well, you were one of the mages I focused on. Having folk like you finding the single mages in larger communities and getting them to safety is what made the Guild possible." She held her breath.

"Yes?"

"What is a wave like? There hasn't been one in decades."

Lee grinned. "I think that can wait until after I disable this curse."

"Oh. Right. Is that what that is?"

"Yes. It is keyed to your blood, so as long as you don't make contact with it, it is fine for me to handle. You were lucky I was here."

She wrinkled her nose as they entered the lab. "Yeah, I have that kind of luck."

Lee set the parcel down on a worktable, and he got forceps and blades.

Mr. E scampered over to the edge of the table, so Imara let him resume his post on her shoulder.

Reegar went to a cabinet on the wall, and he opened it, removing a few bottles of coloured liquids before walking over to the table and setting them down.

"Thank you, Reegar." Lee smiled briefly and began the careful work of slicing into the box.

Imara pulled up a chair and watched the procedure from several feet away.

The box was opened; the folded paper that had kept it in place was carefully removed and set into a large copper bowl.

"Hmm, I would guess that this is a fourth-level charm and not the first curse that this person has sent. The blood that has marked it is strange."

Imara perked up as Lee gave a running description. "Strange?"

"It is your blood, but it is male. It has to have come from a close relative, but the strange thing is that the blood itself is the curse. I have nev—wait, I have seen this once before. Do you have siblings?"

She wrinkled her nose. "Several. At least seven."

"How many cousins?"

"I have no idea. I met one a few days ago. She seemed

nice."

"This is definitely male blood. An unlucky child."

Imara went cold and then hot. "You don't say."

"Yes. This kind of charm only works with the blood of an unlucky one. So, your brother's blood mixed with that of the cursed blood from the same family and you have an excellent curse."

He used the forceps to lift out a small bundle of fabric marked with glyphs. He set it into the bowl, on top of the paper. With the contents of the box disposed of, he shredded the box and set it in the bowl around the edges.

"You must be hell on Christmas presents." Imara observed.

Lee grinned and Reegar chuckled. "He brings the surgical kit to the tree."

Lee sighed. "I have not celebrated the holidays since you passed, Reegar."

Reegar's form fluctuated as he was overtaken with emotion.

Lee carefully unstoppered the bottle with blue solution, and he drizzled it over the contents of the bowl. "This is a negating solution. It takes apart the blood on a cellular level and is not something you want to touch to your skin."

A dark bottle with an arcane label was opened next. "This will attract the curse and hold it so we can destroy it."

"Right. Makes sense."

A single drop fell from the bottle, and Lee stepped back as a stream of flame shot upward.

"Got it. Imara, can you light a match?"

He was standing with his hands to either side of the bowl, so she struck the match.

"Now, insert the match so the flame is above the blue stream of fire."

She followed his direction and eased the eighteen-inch wooden match past his hands and into the small flame in the center of the bowl. The explosion was sudden, and Lee grabbed her and put his body between her and the violent explosion.

Imara hadn't seen a magical shield before, but she was wrapped in one as the echoes faded. She looked down to the generator of the shield, and her kitten looked at her soberly.

I told you it was dangerous.

Thank you.

I do not wish to see your promising career end quickly. I have faith in your ability to be a great and troublesome mage.

She grinned and scooped him up, cuddling him.

"Thank you as well, Liirick. You have a lot of skill at unraveling curses."

He chuckled. "I have been taught by the best. The DeMonstres are friends that I spend a lot of time with."

Reegar set about cleaning up after the explosion. "Well, this is not how I anticipated your first visit, Lee."

Lee moved to the specter and wrapped his arms around him. "I came to see you. Whatever comes up, I am just delighted to be visiting."

Imara smiled and returned to the entryway, gathering her backpack and hoisting Mr. E to her shoulder.

She carefully removed her gloves and tossed them in the trash.

The tea party set in the lounge was amazing. Reegar had gone all out.

The specter and the elf returned to the lounge, and Liirick poured her a cup of tea.

The steam was disconcerting. "How can it still be hot?"

"I have educator status at this college. I have free rein to use magic for any purpose. That includes keeping the tea hot and the sandwiches cold. They are from a bakery in town that has been around since the start of the college. It was a trip through nostalgia to come back here."

The elf prepared a plate for her and extended his arm. "For your valiant defender."

Mr. E murped proudly and hopped to the table, diving into the sandwiches with his amazing appetite.

"He eats on the table?"

She smiled. "When he can make the jump from the floor

to the table without magic, he can eat down there. Until then, he eats where I can keep an eye on his intake."

"You are worried about his diet?"

Imara chuckled. "No, I am fascinated by how much he can eat."

Lee sat back and Reegar joined them. "What are you two discussing?"

"Mr. E's eating habits."

"Ah, a fascinating subject. I have never observed a familiar eating as much as he does or eating human food, for that matter. But, I have not actually met an inherited familiar with a penal aspect."

Mr. E growled at him. Apparently, he was sensitive about that designation.

"I don't care what they say about him. So far, he has been a great familiar. Doesn't even peek on me in the shower."

He continued to devour a thin ham sandwich.

Lee chuckled and Reegar sat next to him. Their hands were close on the table. It was sweet.

Reegar sighed. "This was my favourite bakery. I will miss the flavours."

Imara blushed a little, but she felt it necessary to say, "Have you tried skelping?"

Reegar blinked. "What?"

Liirick cocked his head. "What is that?"

"It is a slang term for possession for pleasure. Reegar would place his specter within your body, and what you can experience, he can experience. It isn't just electrical impulses that give a simulation of life but uses a living body to feel. You have to agree, of course. You could propel him outward in a moment if you didn't. Life always wins.

Reegar looked to his ex-lover and raised his brows. "If you were willing, I would love to try, but I am a little too solid for that."

She coughed delicately. "Bleed off your extra energy into metal or stone. You will be intangible once again."

Lee was grinning. "You want to be inside me?"

Reegar chuckled. "In the worst way."

Imara reached for a plate and picked out a few sandwiches. "If you two are going to get reacquainted in public, I am going to grab some snacks and head to my room. I will be back for Mr. E in a moment. Don't do anything of the naked variety until then, please."

Reegar held up his hand. "Do not leave. Aside from our flirting, Lee has too many manners to make a lady feel uncomfortable."

Lee shrugged. "He is not wrong. You are here for the next three years. That is plenty of time to play at our leisure. I can probably arrange three or four lectures per term and come in on weekends around that schedule."

Imara blinked. "I think I would like to attend some of those lectures."

"You might not be able to attend until you complete your first term, but I can always let you know what you missed in a private tutorial."

"That sounds pleasant. I would like to know how to recognize a cursed object. I had no idea what you saw when you looked at the box."

Lee looked at her and cocked his head. "You are warded."

"Yeah, I had to do it to stop the leak."

"It is the wrong type of ward for you. Instead of helping you, it has blinded you. If Reegar will assist, I can make you a charm that will appear the same from the outside but leave your senses free."

Mr. E got up and walked over to sit in front of Reegar.

"Lee, what is he doing?"

The rumbling purr and sudden rise to his hind legs made Imara cover her laugh with her hand.

Reegar's voice was strangled. "What is he doing?"

Lee smirked. "He is giving you big kitten eyes."

"Spells and stars, that is adorable. Yes, yes, of course I will help."

With a cheerful murp, he turned and trotted back to his plate. Imara covered her face and howled with laughter. It was nice to know that it wasn't just her that he could wrap around his fluffy paw.

Chapter Nine

The letter exchange with her mother became a regular feature of her life, but she had to cut back after midterms. She hadn't done as well as she had hoped, and there had been two more cursed boxes on the doorstep. Reegar had called an instructor to take care of the parcels, and the person leaving them had yet to be identified.

The small amulet she wore tucked into her bra was preforming exactly as Lee had described. She could see out, but they couldn't see in. Her stray energies were also contained but that was more meditation and practice than anything else.

"Enough, Imara. You have been studying for weeks; you are ahead of everything except Herbology, and you need to get out and have some fun."

She looked at Bara briefly and turned back to the textbooks and research books on the history of magic. Reegar had brought in more books from somewhere, and she hadn't had to spend any time in the college library.

"I don't need fun. I didn't budget for fun."

"I will pay. There is a fey orchestra playing in the quad tonight."

Imara smirked. "That is a lie. It is a goblin rave. I might have my head in my books, but I did look up and see the posters."

"Half-goblins. Their voices are supposed to be incredible."

"Why does it have to be tonight? I was just getting in-depth on the third century when that wave hit. It is the first recorded instance of trolls and giants."

"Fascinating. Come out and have fun. Just for a few hours, you can pretend to be a normal student. Come on . . ."

Her whine was what did it.

56

"Fine. Fine. I will come with you, but I am wearing this. Oh, and Mr. E."

Bara frowned. "I don't know if he will like the sound."

Imara saw the logic in that. "Mr. E, do you want to go to a goblin concert?"

He gave her a slow blink and rested his head on his paws. He was content where he was, sleeping on her backpack and guarding her snacks.

"So, that's a no. Well, I guess I can spare an evening."

She looked at her paperwork and memorized what was where.

Once she had a good idea of where she had left off, she stacked everything together and brought it to her room. She returned to the lounge, and Bara appeared surprised. "Ready?"

"Sure. I am not going for socialization, so makeup is not necessary. This is an open party, so a skirt isn't necessary. I am fine in jeans and a sweatshirt."

"Right. Okay, come on, dinner is on me."

Imara grinned and gave herself a quick pat down to find her wallet. She had her ID, so she was all set.

"Excellent. Lead on."

Bara linked arms with her and hauled her out of their home and into the night.

They made their way to the gathering throng, and Imara grinned. "Food carts."

"Well, I am not taking you to the dining hall. Come on, those little donuts are calling me."

Grinning, Imara went to experience the depths of junk food before she stood and listened to her first concert.

Sharing small portions with Bara was surprisingly fun.

"So, why did you choose Reegar Hall?" Imara mumbled it around a mouthful of fries, cheese and chili.

"Same reason as you. Finances. Reegar Hall needed a resident advisor to continue to be considered part of the college, and I needed a place to live when my original hall was over capacity."

"That can happen?"

"Sure. I was on a waiting list for housing and told to check in when I arrived. When I arrived, Leethan Hall was full and I was out on my ass. The housing advisor recommended my asking for a placement at Reegar Hall, and Magus Reegar agreed. I had a place to live and a master mage to point me in the right direction when he was feeling sociable. It has been a comfortable few years, though I haven't been able to get any folks to come over for an evening. No one is interested in dealing with him."

"He seems pretty cheerful to me."

"He has been able to interact with the physical world for the first time in nearly a hundred years. Of course he is cheerful." Bara snorted. "Seriously, though. I am happy that you signed up for us. I was spending more time in the library than at home, and I love the library at the Hall."

"It is thorough. I like studying there. It is so quiet and Reegar is very helpful."

Bara moved closer to her, "Is there any progress on your stalker?"

"Is that what it is? I thought I had a personal terrorist or a mail-order assassin." Imara grinned. "The afterlife isn't too bad, and Mr. E would get to get another mage assigned to him."

Bara was shocked. "You hold your life so cheap?"

"No, but I am not afraid of what happens next after we leave the physical world. Specters are just another phase of existence."

Bara tossed the empty container and wiped her hands on a napkin. She flicked her fingers, and flame took the napkin.

"I wish I could do that." Imara sighed.

"It is a third-year spell."

"Excellent. I have passed a few of the equivalency exams, so I am going to start using the fun stuff after this term." Imara looked around and watched the variety of humans mixing and mingling in the quad. The band was setting up and getting ready to start their set. Imara had never seen a goblin in person before, but only two of them were pure.

The four-armed drummer was practicing a few beats; the

six-eyed keyboardist was checking his equipment and the two nearly human guitarists were in conversation. The base player was human. Well, he was mostly human. His skin was greenish and his ears were pointed.

Bara murmured as they joined the crowd. "What equivalencies?"

"I am a third-degree necromancer, second-degree enchanter and first-degree potion master." Imara grinned. "I had some time on my hands before the exams."

"How long are you planning to be in school?"

"Three years or less. I need to get out and make a living." She shrugged.

"Wow. That is quite the career path. What do you want to do?"

"I want to get into necromancy or possibly the spectral arts." She grimaced. "I have to decide soon. The next thing I know I am going to be out of my first term and I will have to make up my mind."

"I thought you had more of a budget for classes than that."

"I have enough for five years, but I don't want to spend that time here."

"Why not?"

"Because that money will get me an apartment and a wardrobe to start a new life. Mr. E eats a lot."

They had to stop their discussion because the band started the concert, and Imara was rapidly going deaf with a grin on her face.

An hour later, her hearing was a thing of the past, but she was still smiling. The music had moved her and had decided her on one of the courses she wanted to tackle. If there was still space, she wanted to take Sound Magic Theory. She wanted to know how someone could move her with just sound, strings and a beat.

They were near Reegar Hall when she was struck.

A shadow separated from a nearby hedge and charged for her. There was a body behind the shadow as it collided with her. Pain shot into her arm, and the impact dropped her into Bara. They fell to the ground, and everything went scarlet.

Bara was yelling and trying to get her to sit up. Imara helped as much as she could, and Mr. E met them on the way to the Hall.

He climbed her body while Bara was walking her to the building, and he tasted the impact spot on her arm.

She is going to die.

Imara couldn't answer. She was wracked with agony as Reegar took over her maintenance, lifting her into his arms and carrying her to the lab.

It took twenty minutes of Reegar barking orders and Bara applying a series of treatments in turn, for Imara to be able to speak.

She could feel the fury of Mr. E in her blood. He was on the hunt. "Mr. E is hunting."

"I am glad you are back with us. I have managed to reduce the effect of the poison, but I have had Bara put a call in to the main office. Unfortunately, there are several idiots who are taking up the healers that you need. We can't identify the toxin completely without them."

"Threbesh demon blood. They stabbed me with demon blood." She gritted her teeth and relayed what Mr. E was telling her.

Reegar sighed. "Good. That is an easy fix. Where is he? He should be with you."

She closed her eyes as Reegar started barking out orders to Bara. She sought out Mr. E, but he was busy. His mind was full of rage and ancient hate.

She opened her eyes as Bara applied a poultice that smelled like sulfur and mint. "Uh, Mr. E is busy right now."

Eadric the Hellborn crouched low to the ground as he faced down his opponent.

You think that that feeble body can take me, Eadric? I have waited centuries for you to be given a form that matched your skills.

Eadric circled to get an attack position on the ferret with the bad attitude. *I see your mage chose a form that matched your soul. I have rarely seen a better match to personality, Kemeer.*

So, you recognized me? I thought I had managed to hide rather well. The idiot who inherited me was easy to control.

That is not our place, Kemeer.

It is what I want. I have used her to gain what I needed to destroy your mage, and when her heart beats her last, you will be returned to wait for decades until you can be assigned to the next generation. In the meantime, I will gather power and bring the mages back to the top of the food chain.

That is why you were made a familiar in the first place, Kemeer. He growled and gathered himself.

Eadric felt a surprising burst of power coming from Imara, and he used it to effect.

Kemeer may have thought he was getting a kitten, but in a wave of energy, Eadric took on the body of a black tiger, stepping calmly on the small, squirming body until it cracked.

The woman sitting in the corner, dressed in black and holding a blade, came to her senses. "What? Kimmy, where are you?"

Eadric resumed his kitten form and left the way he had come. Kemeer wasn't dead, but he was crippled. He would need attention, and there was only one place his mage could take him.

Eadric bolted back to Reegar Hall to be with his mage while she recovered. He wasn't sure if she even knew that she had sent her strength to him.

The door to the hall cracked open at his approach, and he streaked toward the lab without hesitation.

Imara was slumped in a chair, face pale, lips blue, while Bara was working on her. The young mage applying medical assistance was crying. "It isn't working."

Eadric hopped up onto Imara's lap, and he pressed his head against her ribs. His purr was deep, and he hoped that it was enough. He put all of his power into his mage and tried to stop the leeching of her soul through her open wound.

Hey fuzzy guy. Did you get it done?

He is incapacitated.

Why?

He sighed against her chest. *He hates me. He is one of those I was fighting against, and his crimes against the un-powered populace landed him in the inherited-familiar system.*

So, he kills me and he sends you back to storage?

And he has a clear run at bringing the mages back to power. That is his end goal. He considers mages to be superior to pretty much everyone else.

He could hear Bara muttering, "It is working."

So, who was he?

The familiar to the receptionist at the familiar facility. He saw me the moment you carried me to the desk to get the materials.

Does his mage know?

No. He had her within his control. She was the one who attacked you. When she takes him in for medical care, we will learn where she got the blood for the curses.

I will let Reegar and Bara know. What was the name of the familiar?

Kemeer. His mage calls him Kimmy. He is a ferret.

Right. I hope I can enunciate. Her chuckled in their link made him relax a little. She was a good mage and had the potential to be a great one.

Imara lifted her head. "Person responsible is a ferret named Kimmy. Kemeer the archmage is the familiar of the receptionist at the familiar center. He hates Mr. E and has been taking control of his mage in order to kill me and destroy Mr. E for this generation."

Bara looked at Imara, "Familiars don't take control of their mages."

"This one does. Read your history. Kemeer wanted to

raise the mages above all others, and he was willing to use whatever he could to accomplish it. Demon-zone energy was one of those things." She spoke in a rush. She could feel darkness pushing in on her again.

"Right. We need to get you to the infirmary, but I can't carry you."

"Get me on my feet. Mr. E will help me walk there. This can't be done in the darkness. If I am not coming out of it, I want to make sure there are witnesses to my death that will record it. If it is Kemeer, he needs to be stopped."

She squirmed out of Bara's hold and sat on the edge of the chair. With a few deep breaths, she levered herself to her feet; Mr. E was draped around her neck, still purring.

Bara was frowning. "You need to sit. I am sure they will be here soon."

"I am not. I will walk toward the infirmary, and if they turn up here, Reegar can tell them where to go." She took a slow step and then another. Reegar watched over her as she moved at a slow pace toward the door.

Reegar finally announced. "I am not going to let you die on the lawn. Hold tight to Bara when you step out the door."

His words were weirdly ominous, but Bara stepped to her side and held her hand as they stepped across the threshold.

A tunnel of light rushed to greet and engulf them. When the light faded, they were standing in the entry hall of the infirmary.

The folk waiting to be seen were drunk, drugged or had minor fight injuries.

Bara tried to get someone's attention, but Imara had used up all her strength. She sagged against Bara, sliding toward the ground.

A deafening roar made all the conversations stop.

Imara smiled as the noise repeated and she hit the floor. In seconds, hands lifted her up and Bara was explaining the situation and the initial treatment that had been administered. She was rushed past the waiting area and into treatment.

"So, you had excellent urgent care, Ms. Mirrin. The idea was right, but the ingredients were no longer effective. They had degraded over time and could only give partial relief."

The healer at her side made notes in her chart. "We don't often see blood poisoning of this variety, but your friend was able to direct me to a familial match on campus. He agreed to donate a few pints for you."

A shadow fell between her and the light. A male voice chuckled, "And they didn't even give me a cookie."

The healer cleared his throat. "I will leave you to get acquainted."

She glanced to her left, and an IV drip was still providing her with blood. "I am guessing that you are one of the Demiel men?"

He extended his right hand to hers. "I am Luken Demiel. I believe we are twins."

"Imara Mirrin, and yes, we are."

"You know, it was the strangest thing. I was in the waiting room with a buddy who had picked a fight with the drummer from the concert and a woman came out and asked if there were any Demiels around. I raised my hand, and the next thing I know, I found out you needed help and I volunteered."

"Just like that?"

He carefully settled on the edge of the bed. "Well, your familiar did put his claws to my throat and growl at me. I got the feeling that he would have taken the blood by force if he had to."

Imara looked around and saw Mr. E, sitting watchfully on her thighs, his tail flicking.

"I have never been threatened by a kitten before. It was an interesting experience." He smiled.

She saw an echo of her own face in Luken's. "He's an interesting individual."

"I can see that. He is an inherited familiar?"

"He is. Our mother's side of the family wasn't fussy about gender when it came to the seventh child."

Luken nodded. "My career path doesn't require a

familiar, so you are welcome to him. He is a little runty for my taste anyway."

Mr. E got up on his tippy toes and hissed.

Imara extended her hand to him and stroked his fur, careful of the IV. "He is exactly what I needed, exactly when I needed him."

His mind touched hers, and she reciprocated. She chuckled. "I wouldn't have it any other way."

Chapter Ten

Exams rushed in around testifying and having Mr. E examined from nose to tail. Imara spent most of her time in the lounge and library.

Reegar had been visited by every necromancer in four counties, but none had been able to figure out how a man dead for nearly a century had created a gateway across the campus. It should not have been possible, but then, they didn't take into account that Imara had charged up every bit of gay erotica in the building with enough power to make him nearly corporeal. That was a lot of erotica, but it had taken the heat off her activating ghosts on the campus.

Weeks of carefully nurturing her plants was now down to the final exam. Imara carried the tray of plants into the exam room along with the other students. The normal jovial atmosphere was tense.

Their instructor examined their trays and confirmed that the herbs they were holding were theirs and theirs alone. Each plant was tagged, each tag was enchanted and each pot was warded. They were as secure as they could be.

"When we started prepping for this exam, I told you that the goal was to create a formula to enhance power and health. Two of you have most of the proper ingredients. The rest of you are going to have an interesting day."

Imara stood by her workstation as the door to the class opened and fifth-level potion masters walked in with their mortars and pestles.

"Al right, students. Pick the ingredients in the correct quantity and hand them to the potion master."

The woman in front of her had quirked lips.

Mr. E started to whisper in her mind, and she followed his direction, plucking only a few leaves off each plant, holding them together before plucking more.

When they were done, she inhaled the fragrance and thought about it. Mr. E was silent.

She needed more mint. Her power ran hot, and she needed cooling.

Her potion master was grinning as Imara put the ingredients in the bowl. "Go to it, madam."

Imara's was the last potion master to get to work, but she muttered and whispered quickly. She was the first finished. "Done."

She took the mortar and tipped it, dripping the liquid into a vial. There was barely a handful of drops in it.

The potion master corked the potion and handed it over. "There you go. Good luck."

Imara set the small bottle in front of her, and she waited for the rest of the class to finish. The instructor came to her, opened the vial and nodded. "Exit the classroom and go to the left. When you are there, you will be taken to a cubicle where you can take your potion."

"Yes, Magus." She nodded and took the vial, holding it in her fist so no one could see how small the sample was. As she passed others, there were huge salads of herbs being crushed into potions.

She had her tiny sample, and she hoped it was enough of the right things.

Out the door to the left, there was a fey with familiar features and more behind him. He winked and gestured for her to be quiet.

"Come with me, student."

She followed him to a cubicle, and he gestured for her to take a seat on the lounge while he perched on a high stool. "Take your potion whenever you are ready, student."

She dragged in a deep breath and uncorked the vial. She was about to tip it toward her lips when she paused. Not all herbs were designed to be taken internally. Two of them were in her potion. She turned to the scar on her arm from the stabbing, and she poured the drops onto that mark. She rubbed it in and washed her hands with the last of it. A bright tingle ran through her fingers and worked in her arm.

Heat and power started to pulse in her veins, and she sighed deeply. "That feels better. I was starting to feel it when it rained."

"Pass. You have passed your Herbology course with a Excel grade. You are now able to take any mage or potion courses in the future."

"Why?"

"Because you know how to listen to the plants and be wary of what they can do. Ignoring basic chemistry is how most potion mages suffer injuries. So, you are free to go. Enjoy the power and the health."

"It will only last a few weeks."

He grinned. "The power, yes, but the health and any repairs made to your body will remain. Your arm looks much better."

She glanced down at the stab wound, and her eyes watered when she could only see the faintest outline of the blade mark and that was still fading.

"Right. Thank you, observer. Have a good day." She nodded and passed him, walking down the hall that he directed her to.

Behind her, she heard an explosion and shouting, so she was guessing that one of the other students wasn't getting a top grade.

Whew. Thanks for the guidance.

I was only reiterating what you had been practicing. Quantity doesn't mean more power, it just means less control. You knew that. You just needed reminding during the practical application.

Mr. E purred into her ear, and she giggled. *Why do you do that?*

It is why you chose this form for me. You need comfort, and a kitten is the best means to deliver it. I have no problem with that.

Your ego can handle it?

My ego can handle a lot.

Good to know. She left the Herbology building and headed for home. She had one more exam to study for, and it was going to make or break her career options. Soul manipulation seemed to be what she was designed for, so she wanted to get an Excel in the Soul Casting course. It was simple; she had to park her anchor in Mr. E and send her soul to one part of campus, retrieving information that would only be found at that spot. Once she had it, she needed to return to her body and tell the class what she had seen.

She was going to need to practice a few times more if she wanted to be able to stuff herself back in her body with any kind of speed. Her issue was extra energy and bleeding it off in an appropriate manner.

Bara and Reegar were helping her practice, and Luken even came by now and then to lend a hand. Their relationship was a strange one, but they were both making careful strides to knowing each other.

If Imara didn't know better, she would think that Luken and Bara were developing more than a casual relationship. She grimaced. It was a brain bender for another time. If they did get together, it wasn't her business.

That night, she was going to scatter herself around the campus and try to stuff herself back into her body in under five minutes. This was going to require pizza, lots of pizza.

"Ms. Mirrin, you are up." Magus Deepford tapped a folded document against her open hand.

Mr. E was at full attention on her shoulder. He was ready.

Imara took the stage, and she knelt in the control circle. Magus Deepford handed her the document. "Whenever you are ready."

Mr. E jumped to his spot in the circle, directly in front of her, and he nodded.

She cracked open the seal on the exam, and it said, *Find the person in scarlet on the third floor of the administration building and read their nametag.*

She nodded to the teacher and stated, "Start the clock."

She locked her gaze to her familiar's, parked her soul with him and took the rest of her mind on a journey through the campus.

She found the offices on the third floor and flashed along until she located the man wearing the scarlet shirt with the nametag. She chanted the name to herself as she turned and headed back to the Wayforth building.

Her excitement had charged her, so she activated a few ghosts that Reegar had enticed for this purpose. They caught the extra energy and had a physical presence for a few hours, but it let her squeeze back into her body, pulling the link back from Mr. E's protection and opening her eyes.

She wrote the answer for the instructor, her hand shaking. When it was done, she handed the paper over and said, "Time."

Magus Deepford stopped the clock. "Forty-five seconds. Well done, Ms. Mirrin. Well, that is well done if you have the right answer."

She looked at the answer and chuckled. "*U R Name* is the correct answer. Most students choose the woman in red, by the way."

"It said scarlet, I went for scarlet."

"I can confirm the well done. You have passed with an Excel grade."

Imara's shoulders slumped in relief. "Thank you."

"Don't thank me. Now, get out of here. It is time for the next student. Mr. Dillwell, please take the stage."

Mr. E jumped to her shoulder, and she resumed her place next to the others who had completed their exams. A few discreet high fives went around before Dillwell finished his exam. He did it in three minutes and forty-five seconds. It was a passing grade, and his relief was evident.

Ninya turned to her and asked, "We are going out to celebrate after this. Will you join us?"

Imara grinned. "I would love to but have some friends that I am getting together with. Thank you for the invitation; I am looking to be more sociable in the second term."

She said her farewells and listened to Mr. E's triumphant whoops and chortles as she left the lecture hall and headed for the open air.

She had passed. Every first course had been passed with high marks. She was ready for the new courses of the second term. She was a giant leap closer to her new life and being giddy with relief didn't cover it.

She could hear the pounding of the music before she even reached Reegar Hall. The drab, grey building was pulsing with energy, and when she entered the familiar space, the laughter and high emotion of the specters she had overcharged was everywhere.

Bara greeted her at the door. "I am guessing that you passed?"

Imara nodded and hugged her friend. "I passed!"

"Good, then we aren't throwing this party for nothing." Bara hauled her into the lounge where Reegar and Lee were hosting a modest buffet with a huge *Congratulations* banner over their heads.

Luken walked toward her with a huge cake in his hands, a tiny sculpture of Mr. E had been depicted in sugar. A pathway had been drawn on the cake and the first five blocks after the start block had been marked with her grades. The end of the path was twenty marks away, and she dragged in a deep breath.

"Wow. Thank you." She kept her senses trained on Mr. E, but he didn't seem inclined to leap on this particular cake.

"Well, blow out your familiar and we can tuck in."

She giggled and leaned forward to blow out the candle protruding from the kitten sculpture.

When the small plume of smoke curled upward, the specters and her friends cheered. Luken set the cake down and the party began in earnest.

Reegar and Lee started the dancing off, engaging in the moves of Swing as if they had danced together a thousand times before.

Imara kept the power flowing to the party as she sat and had cake with Luken and Bara.

"So, Luken, you are a third year?" She smiled at him.

He blushed. "How did you know?"

"Your aura. You have the mark of learning on you, but it

is the mark made by picking up knowledge you didn't particularly want. Mandatory classes."

"Aura?"

"Well, soul print is more the thing. I can see power, emotion, energy, but only in a few situations when I concentrate."

"Wow. Nice. I wish I had something like that. I am stuck with standard spell casting."

Bara perked up. "Really? What is your favourite spell?"

Imara eased away from them with her fork busy providing her with all the cake she could want. It was damned good cake.

The ghosts were having a rave, and she was right in the middle of it. A few came to say thanks for the moment of clarity and others questioned her on her family lines. She found polite comments for all of them and eased out of the hall, taking in the evening air.

"It sounds like quite a party in there."

Imara looked at the woman standing in the shadows. "It is. Would you like to come inside?"

"I have not been invited."

Imara grinned. "It is my party; I am inviting you now."

"What is it for?"

"I survived my first term at the college with excellent marks. If I can maintain it, I can fast track myself into a career in a couple of years."

The woman tilted her head. Imara still couldn't see her.

"Is it wise to rush an education?"

Imara chuckled. "I won't stop learning just because I graduate. I will simply have the prerequisites to pay my own way in the world. I need to work, and I want to work, but I have to get credentials to be able to do what I want to do."

"You are a young woman with a path in her mind. Is that your familiar?" The laughter in her tone was unmistakable.

"Mr. E, this is a strange lady in the shadows. Strange lady, my name is Imara and this is Mr. E." She could feel Mr. E stretching from his comfy spot draped around the back of her neck. He made a cute murp sound, and the woman chuckled.

"I am the Chancellor of Depford College. My name is Mirrin Deepford-Smythe. I am your mother and very glad to see you."

Imara stared at the face that looked like she would in thirty years. "I am pleased to meet you."

"Ah, my baby girl. You have no idea how happy I am to finally be able to touch you." She extended her hand and Imara took it.

The delivery room, fighting to hold her daughter and announcing to her husband that their contract was at an end. The rush of emotions was intense and bittersweet. She knew that Imara would be fine. She had the luck of two families behind her. She would grow strong, and when she was an adult, Mirrin would find her again.

Imara staggered when her mother released her hand. "You gave me your memories."

"I did. It was faster than explaining."

"I think I get it. The Deepford-Smythes are broke?"

"Not now, not anymore. You brought luck to the family line the day you became a death keeper."

She thought back. "Is that why the Dean of Students came on my first day?"

"Yes, your great-great aunt sent a letter and entailed her unclaimed estate to you. Didn't they tell you?"

"No. It wasn't mentioned in the documents."

"Ah, well there is a trust that will kick in when you graduate. It is a nicely sized bit of funds with a chunk of property in downtown Redbird City. Is that really the fearsome familiar?"

Mr. E lifted his head as she reached for him. When Mirrin scratched his head, he purred and leaned into her hand.

"Yes. He became what I needed, and I needed someone to care for who would offer me comfort. I take care of him; he takes care of me."

"I am glad that you have each other. You wrote that you

met your twin?"

"I did. Luken is inside."

"He is a sweet boy, but you are on different paths. Don't forget that. He cannot go where you do, but you will always be twins."

Imara sighed and turned, hugging her mother tightly. "I know. I know where my path is leading, and Redbird City fits into my plans."

When Imara straightened, she wiped the tears from her eyes. "So, did you want to come into the party? If you have never seen an elf and a specter cut a rug, now is your chance."

Mirrin laughed. "I can't resist an invitation like that. Please, introduce me to your friends."

Mr. E sat up straight as if trying to make a good impression, and Imara led her mother into her party.

It was a great end to her first term, even if most of the party was more dead than alive; they were her chosen company.

Mirrin watched Liirick trying to teach Imara to swing dance while her familiar consumed the cake.

"So, Reegar, do you regret taking her in?"

"Ah, dearest Chancellor, I don't regret it for a moment. She understands the needs of the dead more than we even do. She has crafted a trust fund for me for a few years after she leaves, so that I will never be without the ability to become physical in my own home. How thoughtful is that?"

Mirrin eyed her youngest son and the woman he was flirting with. "What about her?"

"Bara is a legacy to my hall. She enjoys the library and that is all that I need to know most days. The addition of your son is causing a bit of a stir, but she is nearing graduation and will need to choose her path. If she wants to further her education, I am still here."

"What about next term? Will you take in more students?"

"I will take two more in. I am going to choose carefully."

"Good. Perhaps we can arrange to change your façade as well."

Reegar smiled. "It is a thought. I will bear it in mind. I am beginning to like hosting students."

"It only took eighty years. Not bad."

"Mirrin."

"Yes?"

"Thank you for coming. I wasn't sure you would when I sent the invitation."

"Thank you for inviting me. She didn't mention it in our last letter."

"She didn't know. This was our party for her. She has made an impression on those around her, and this is her reward. If the reward has to come from the dead, so be it."

"She is that powerful?"

"Getting stronger every day, and I am happy to be here to see it. She hasn't given me life again, but she has let me come to grips with what I was missing by not engaging with the world I am still present in."

"That is quite the gift."

"And she gives it without knowing. So, be proud of your daughter and send her a card in that enchanted box of yours. If her brothers are anything like her, you should be very proud."

Mirrin chuckled. "I will. I knew the moment I held her that she was going to make a mark in the world, and I just hoped that she would be happy doing it. Today was a huge leap for her, and I am delighted that you are there to catch her on the other side."

There was a lot of meaning in those words as they hung in the air between them.

As Imara's enjoyment expanded, the ghosts got stronger, and soon, the entire spectral population of the college was bopping and twirling. Mirrin watched her daughter's effect and wondered at the luck that had brought them together again.

Then again, with a seventh of seven involved, luck was always a factor.

Shape Shifting 201
The Hellkitten Chronicles Book 2

A would-be magus with studying on her mind must deal with a possible suitor and her feisty hellkitten.

Imara made it through her first term without too many issues, but now that she is in the second term, a magic-draining fiend is stalking the students, and her familiar is bored with guiding her through the early stages of magic. He has taken to giving her misinformation to see if she can use her own judgments. It is a challenge she doesn't really need.

XIA agents are taking courses at the college, and one of them ends up next to Imara during her ethics course. A few conversations lead to a lunch date, and now, she must determine if a social life is worth more than her scholastic one.

Mr. E just likes going on lunch dates. The servers swoon over his cute fuzziness. He is no help at all.

Chapter One

The persistent tapping on her nose and lips brought Imara out of a sound sleep. She spluttered. "What?"

You are going to be late for your first day of winter term. You have forty-five minutes to shower, get dressed, eat, and get across the campus. The close-range kitten face was cross-eyed as he smacked her face with his tiny paw again.

Damnit.

Exactly. Forty-four. The clock is ticking, and you don't know time magic yet. Get rolling.

Imara got up and dumped Mr. E to the floor, stumbling past him to her bathroom. He might be six inches tall, but he was right. She needed to get moving.

Brushing her teeth in the shower caused a soap and toothpaste confusion. It was enough of an issue to wake her up completely, and she left her room with a wet head and a disgruntled kitten five minutes later. He was not a fan of her lack of enthusiasm for a hairdryer.

Reegar had a travel mug of coffee waiting for her. He handed it to her with a jaunty bow. "Your pastry is in the box on the counter."

"Thanks. Immit Hall would have to be on the other end of the freaking campus."

"You will make it. I have seen you run to beat Bara to the remote control. She made your coffee."

Imara wanted to snark at him, but the blueberry pastry was taking up her mouth. She grabbed a second, checked her bag and that she was wearing shoes, and had actually gotten dressed. Some nightmares didn't need to be dragged into reality.

She jammed the second pastry between her jaws, checked for Mr. E, and charged out the door with her coffee cup in her hand.

The first course of the winter term was Shape Shifting 201. It was just the thing to bring misery to a Monday morning.

She jogged and chewed her way through the campus, the mild weather was the gift of the weather mages. It was always temperate if on the cool side.

The coffee was screamingly hot, and the sudden pulse in her lips confirmed that pain was as good as caffeine to wake her up.

Imara finally made it to Immit Hall with three minutes to spare. She found the lecture hall and sat at one of the four available tables. She smiled and nodded as Mesook Mnara waved at her. They had shared the financial-planning class last term, and Mesook had mentioned her desire to take this course.

Imara pulled out her notebook and pencil. She surmised that Mesook had made it off the waiting list.

She took a final slurp from her thermal mug, sealed it, and tucked it into a side pocket of her bag. When she straightened, the instructor wandered in.

Mr. E whispered in her mind. *Well spotted. That isn't a normal lynx.*

The cat paced back and forth, getting closer to the tables and the very still students.

The mage snarled and swiped at the students, one by one. Imara looked at the incoming paw and extended her own hand to meet it.

At the moment of impact, the lynx changed into a man wearing loose, dark, cotton clothing and a smile. "Well done, Ms. Mirrin. I was told to watch out for you."

"By whom?"

The instructor chuckled. "I will leave you guessing on that matter."

He turned and walked in front of the class of seven. "Hello, I am Magus Korian Yassur. You may call me Instructor Korian."

He faced them and nodded to Imara. "So, what did you

see that they didn't?"

"Your form was too large, you made eye contact with more than one of us, there were no postures or behaviours visible that would have indicated you were threatened or hunting. Simply put, you were not acting like a cat."

With every phrase, his eyebrows raised a little higher. "Well, that is encouraging. Are the rest of you aware of what she just pointed out?"

Mesook raised her hand.

"Yes?"

"She pointed out that the shape isn't enough. If you want to be convincing, you have to know the animal you want to become."

Korian nodded. "Correct. This course is partially about the magic you will need to know but mostly about how to research what you need to be convincing."

He gestured, and the lights dimmed. "Let's see what happens when folks get it wrong. If you cannot stand thinking about the errors, this course may not be for you."

Imara watched as an image was projected on the walls behind the instructor.

The picture of the twisted creature lying on the ground was difficult to make out until she located the fingers and worked her way back to the arms. It was a combination of dog, cat and a bit of fish, overlaid on a human structure.

"This was a student two years ago, who had not decided on the beast she wanted to change into. In this very building, she twisted into this and passed away. Her lack of clarity cost her her life."

The light flared, and another image was displayed. A bureau was sitting quietly against the wall. Imara stared, and slowly, a wave of horror overtook her. The pattern in the wood was that of a face, screaming in agony.

"This student chose this form as a joke, but as it was inert, he was found ten days after his transformation. He was in the main hall of his dorm, and no one noticed him."

Imara winced.

"Here is a student who wanted to play with size. He was

eaten by his roommate's familiar."

A dead rat was on the floor with blood smears around it.

"Another who wanted to take the form of a large animal but chose the wrong location for transformation."

An elephant trunk flopped out of what seemed to be a broom closet.

Two students got up and left the class.

"Good. That narrows the field. Now, the form you need to build toward should be comfortable, sensible, and of a reasonable size."

Korian walked around the room as the lights came up. "Now, we are going to discuss the anatomy of a shape shift. Many folks think that it is a painless process, but you are reshaping skin, muscle, ligaments, and bone, not to mention the burning itch of growing fur."

He paced around, lithe and restless. "To shift your shape, you need to know how long the claws must be, how many feathers and in what configuration. Instinct will not guide you here. You are designed to be human."

He took a deep breath and centred himself, facing them. "The first things we will learn are simple shifts. They are easily confused with glamour, but we are physically changing the hair, skin, and eye colour. Until you shift back, you will look like someone else."

Korian's smile was full of anticipation. "Now, let's learn about what makes the pigment in your hair."

Imara felt Mr. E settle on her feet, and there was quite a bit of snuffling and snoring as she listened to the instructor for hours.

She took copious notes and asked questions along with the other students. When the class was over, her mind was groaning and she wanted to get started on a few small attempts at magic under her belt. After the last few weeks between semesters, she was more than eager to start again.

When she got ready to stand, Mr. E clawed his way up her body and sat proudly on her shoulder. *You seemed to enjoy the class.*

The instructor was watching as she stood, and there was

something in his gaze that indicated he wanted to speak to her.

She walked up to him with her familiar digging into one shoulder and her bag pulling on the other. "Instructor Korian, thank you for the class. I am eager to get started."

He smiled. "Ms. Mirrin, I have been briefed on your situation. I must say, that given your family history, I was surprised to see you in my course."

"Why is that?"

"It is not the sort of thing that your brothers have shown an interest in. I went to school with your eldest brother."

His expression made more sense to her now.

"Ah, I don't have anything in common with my siblings. I have only met one of them that I am aware of."

"I thought you had . . . I mean the family appears very aware of you."

Imara smiled. "They may be, but I am not aware of them. So, I am looking forward to the next class. You are an engaging instructor."

Korian's dark cheeks flushed. "Thank you. You have an aura of power that makes it hard to concentrate on my words."

Imara blinked rapidly. "Um . . ."

"And there I go again." He smiled slightly. "I will see you next week."

"Right. Thanks again for the lecture. It left me with definite food for thought." She nodded and left the lecture hall.

He is attracted to you.

She snorted. "Yeah. I got that much. I am guessing it has more to do with my father's family than with me personally."

The long hike across the quad was just what she needed to clear her mind. Knowing that there was food waiting in the fridge to make a sandwich put a spring in her step.

You mustn't sell yourself short. You are an attractive woman, and if I were a thousand years younger and in a human form again, I would have seduced you already.

"Like hell. I have a plan, and you and other guys don't fit into it. There is time enough for that sort of thing when I finish school and have my own shop."

You really do have a focus, don't you?

"I have worked on it for over a decade. This is my path, and I am going to walk it. Stupidity with men can come later."

She heard him chuckle in her mind. She kept her echo from him. She wasn't in the habit of dating mass murderers, so he would have been off her list regardless of his own inclinations. Her dear little familiar just wasn't her type.

Chapter Two

With a sandwich and coffee at her side, she hit the library with a vengeance. Reegar was helpful in finding the books that were on her syllabus, but she still needed some basic anatomy information, and for that, she had to decide what she wanted to become.

She sat back and exhaled, looking at Mr. E, asleep on the *Tome of Transformation*. "So, should I be a cat? Dog? Land squid?"

He opened one eye. *You need to pick something you have always wanted to be.*

"I just wanted to be a proper mage."

Go to the roof, listen to the wind, and close your eyes. Think of the impulse you want to have, and that is your shape. Got it?

"You are exceptionally smug for someone who licks their own backside." Imara got to her feet and, nevertheless, did as he said.

She passed Reegar and headed for the stairs that would take her to the roof.

"Did Bara speak to you?"

Imara paused. "No."

"There is a term mixer that she wanted to drag you to. She mentioned that you should eat, as drinking might be involved."

"Oh. Right. I had a sandwich."

He smiled. "Good."

She nodded and watched the spectre walk into the library to enjoy touching the books again. It was one of the perks that the dead felt being near her. She made them nearly human again.

Imara smirked as she walked up the stairs. She leaked

magical energy and no one complained. It was a nice side effect of being the seventh child of a seventh child from a family who had a lot of necromancers in it. Power across the planes of existence seemed to be a river that had found an estuary in her.

By the time she made it onto the roof, she had her mind back on the task at hand. She wanted to concentrate and let the world around her speak, but all she could hear were the chattering of students on the ground.

She walked to the rail and looked down, focusing on the feel of the wind and the scent of the air. Lifting her head, she looked at the treetops, and a slow smile crossed her lips.

She relaxed and let her senses guide her. She turned her head when she heard noises and noted the pattern that her motions were taking on. The more relaxed she was, the more birdlike she became.

With a deep sigh, she made up her mind. If it had to be a raptor, it had to be a raptor. She just needed to figure out which one.

She skipped back into the library, picked out a book on bird transformations and walked back to the table where Mr. E still had his little black kitten nose covered with his tail. He was a ball of fluff.

She set the book down firmly, and he jumped, hissing and bouncing until he fell off the table.

Her giggles lasted until he climbed her jeans to regain his position on the table.

With a gentle grip, she scooped him up and placed him back in his nap spot. "You could have just asked me to pick you up."

You could have set that book down quietly. So, have you decided?

"I did, but you aren't going to like it." She lifted the book and directed the cover to where he could see it. *Raptors of the Magical World.*

He sighed and cleaned one of his paws. *I thought so. You have a definite predatory air about you.*

"I do not."

He gave her a bland look through his tilted eyes and walked toward the edge of the table.

She snagged him in midair and set him back in his place. He gave her a smug look. *See?*

"Yes, I see, but I didn't catch you with my feet. That is what I am looking into."

He resumed his bath time while she started flipping through the images of birds and their descriptions of how they had been linked to the magical world.

She didn't know what she was looking for, but she would know it when she found it.

She was nearly to the end of the book when she stopped. "Huh. That is . . . well . . . it's definitely a bird."

Mr. E sat up and walked over, peeping over her arm. *Good choice. Strong, powerful, intelligent, and associated with an ancient goddess. Well done, Imara.*

She took in the image of the griffin vulture and sighed. "Right. Time to get going on my anatomy lessons."

Bara's voice sounded behind her. "Oh no. You are coming with me."

Imara turned to look at her. "Did I promise I would go to this?"

"Yes. A week ago. I even got it in writing."

"Damn."

"Indeed. Now, get dressed, or I will use my new makeover spell, and I can't guarantee the results."

That was enough to send Imara scrambling to her room to put on jeans and a dark shirt, brush her hair, and apply a slash of lip gloss.

She returned to the study area a few minutes after she had left it. "Right. Ready."

Bara looked her over and sighed. "Right. Well, you made an effort, so let's go."

Halfway to the door, Imara turned back and called out, "Mr. E, are you coming?"

No, watching young mages get drunk is a memory I will keep in the past. If you need me, call on me.

"Right. Have a nice night and take it easy on the public

bathing. The cute gets creepy really fast."

He let out a small coughing noise, and she grinned.

She turned back to Bara. "Come on, let's get this over with."

Bara linked arms with her and hauled her out into the brisk evening air.

They walked for a few minutes when Imara asked Reegar Hall's Resident Advisor, "So, why are we doing this again?"

"Because you need to make connections of the social variety, Imara. Getting your grades isn't enough. When you leave college, you are going to need more than books. You will need folks you can call upon who have different specialities."

"So, this is mercenary?"

"Purely. Fun is incidental. You need to be seen having fun, and it is just that . . . an appearance of fun. Laugh, dance, enjoy yourself. Even two hours out might have benefits down the road."

"Wow. You are really selling this." Imara smirked. "What is your speciality, by the way?"

"I am still deciding. Reegar isn't in any hurry to turn me out, and I get a discount as long as I am resident there, so I am taking advantage of it."

Imara chuckled. "He likes the company."

"So do I. The last few months have been very alive in the Hall."

"For us you mean? Everybody else around there has punched through the veil a long time ago."

Bara grinned. "For us. The rumour is that Reegar has agreed to take in a few more students, but he is going to be very precise about who he lets in."

"Of course. It is his home, and he is in much better control now than he was last summer."

"That is due to you."

"Well, a side effect of me." She chuckled. "So, where are we going again?"

"To a party at the Echo Hall. There will be food, drink, and party magic. I just hope they don't mix the three."

Imara giggled and kept up with Bara as they made their way across the increasingly congested quad toward a building filled with light and music.

Her mind was filled with the details of what she needed to learn about flying as she met folks, shook some hands, and avoided others.

When she felt she had introduced herself to about sixty percent of the partygoers, she eased away from the crowd and analyzed the party.

Bara was speaking with a group of senior classmates, so Imara was free to scan the room at large. She spotted three people in a matter of seconds she was probably related to on one side of her family or another. Running into cousins and such hadn't really occurred to her. Sure, she knew that at least four of her brothers were still at the college, but the more distant relatives hadn't entered her consciousness.

The tingle of magic got her attention, and she turned to the doors that led to a wide patio. Not one to ignore a display of enchantment, she wandered outside and obtained a soda from a young woman sitting behind a makeshift bar.

"Are you a second-year?"

Imara blinked at the sudden question from behind her. She turned toward the man who asked it and shook her head. "No. I am not."

He grinned. "Excellent. Come with me. I need an assistant for the demonstration."

"I don't recall volunteering." She sipped at her orange soda.

"Would you please assist me in a demonstration of physical magic?"

"Who are you?"

The woman at the bar leaned forward, her blond braids with their bright ties swinging as she moved. "He is the light enchantments professor. Professor Breedwell."

Imara looked at his dark features and the amused sparkle in his brown eyes. "Sure."

He didn't press his luck. He took her hand and led her to an open tent where folks were lounging and engaged in casual magic. It was a bit beyond bending spoons, but they had to get up and get their own beverages, so the magic was for entertainment only.

"We have a volunteer!"

The crowd cheered. Imara pasted a nervous grin on her features and approached the makeshift stage.

The chair was ready for her, and a cursory check with a diagnostic spell told Imara that there was nothing magical about the carved wood.

"Please, miss, have a seat."

Imara took her seat and settled in.

"Now, miss, we just met out near the bar."

"Correct."

"Your name is . . ."

"Imara Mirrin."

"Well, I am Professor Breedwell, and tonight, we are going to learn about the details possible in physical magic."

The group clapped politely, but there was an air of anticipation to it.

The professor cast a warding spell, and that gave Imara the first inkling that the group didn't want to be disturbed.

"Now, we are going to see what use can be made of household objects."

Imara quirked her lips. "Should I be nervous?"

He smirked. "Yes."

Extension cords whipped around her wrists and held her tight. She took a deep breath and looked around the room for anyone who would keep this from getting out of hand. All the living faces were eager and nearly trembling with anticipation.

The faces of the spectres in the room were more concerned, and as her tension rose, so did her power output. They went from barely visible to solid, smiling at her as they slowly approached.

Words weren't necessary. If they ever wanted to see her back at Echo Hall, they needed to intervene.

"Professor Breedwell, these restraints are highly inappropriate."

He chuckled. "Don't worry. I do this every term. You won't remember a thing."

"We will." Five spectres stepped toward him and smiled.

"How did you get past the wards?" The professor looked irritated and nervous.

"We were already inside. This is a really bad idea, Poul." A woman in a delicate lacey gown with her hair twisted up and held by a series of carved fans smiled brightly.

"Do I know you?"

"Your grandfather did. Very well in fact. Did he ever get that mole on his lower back taken care of?"

The professor looked ill. "You are a ghost."

"Spectre. There is a difference."

A man in the audience called out. "What is the difference?"

Imara felt the tug on her senses as one of the spectres reached out and elevated him above the audience with the flick of his fingers. The man smiled and murmured. "Magic."

The room rioted with students trying to get away from the spectres who were giving a very detailed example of physical magic. Clothing flew, students flew, and the professor was hung by his ankles from the ceiling.

Imara was still tied to the chair as she watched it all.

The professor finally realized that she had to be related to the events. "Stop it."

"Great. Untie me."

The cords released, and she rubbed her wrists as she stood up. "They will gradually lose power, but if you want this to cease completely, drop the wards. I need another soda."

She felt the wards come down, and the crowd scattered. It seemed that this private party was over.

She gave the female spectre a small nod. "Thank you."

"Our pleasure, mistress. I hope this experience does not stop you from visiting again."

"Oh, no. This has been very entertaining. I believe you can put the professor down now."

The woman smiled slowly. "May I play with him a little?"

The professor's flushed face drained of colour.

"I think you can save that for another day. If he returns here, send word to me at Reegar Hall, and I can come and add some life to the events."

The spectres in the chamber grinned.

"Thank you, again. Please enjoy the party."

With that little pleasantry done with, Imara headed out to get another soda.

This party isn't so bad after all. She was grinning the entire way back to Bara's side.

Chapter Three

"You were right. I am having fun." Imara grinned at Bara. The waves of shock and scandal were making their way through the crowd.

Bara glanced at her, saw the grin, and excused herself from her conversational group. "What happened?"

"A professor asked me to volunteer, but the situation turned unwholesome, so I asked him to stop, and when he wouldn't, I sought alternative assistance."

One of the spectres walked into the room and bowed elegantly to the ladies before striding to his portrait and examining the plaque below.

Bara sighed, "You released some ghosts."

"No, I let some spectres enjoy the party. There is a difference." Imara chortled.

"You could have casted for help."

"Nope. There was a heavy ward around the area. I am fairly sure this wasn't the first time, but the audience was putting out some severely pervy vibes. I decided that I didn't want to play anymore."

"Do you want to stay?"

"Sure. The spectres are out and enjoying themselves, the display was broken up, and the professor had to beg for freedom. It is quite the party."

Bara sighed. "I am glad you got loose, but try and keep out of trouble."

"I try, but trouble finds me."

"Stop wearing a neon sign."

"Imara! I am so happy to see you." Mesook rushed up to her and linked arms. "You wouldn't believe what just happened."

Imara nodded to Bara and let her classmate drag her

away. "What?"

"Well, there are ghosts at the party. Real thinking and speaking ghosts."

Imara twisted her lips. "When they are mages and attached to a structure, they are spectres."

"Right. Well, a necromancer set them to attack one of our professors."

Imara blinked. "*Our* professor?"

"Yes. He is teaching the ethics class."

"Oh, good grief, he said he was light enchantments. That man has no business teaching ethics." Imara snorted.

"You know him?"

She chuckled. "We have met."

Mesook led her out to the rear gardens where music was playing, and light streamed from dozens of enchanted illuminated globes that bobbed and levitated over the partygoers.

"So, Imara . . ."

Imara felt her eyebrows lift. "Yes?"

"Have you chosen your beast yet?"

She blinked in surprise. "What?"

"Your beast, your shape-shifting animal. You are going to be a cat, aren't you? I mean you have one, so it is an easy transition."

"Uh, I don't think it will be a cat. Why do you ask?"

Mesook's expression was bashful. "I didn't want to pick the same creature and have you outdo me. I am going to try a family icon."

"Well, I am pretty sure you are safe. I don't have a family icon to change into."

Mesook smiled, and she sighed. "Right. So, Asian dragon for me then."

Imara was startled. "Are you sure?"

"Are you afraid I will get better marks than you?"

"No, I am afraid you will lose control and get stuck. That is a lot of square footage. They are huge. The instructor recommended changing into a creature nearly your own size."

"I think you are nervous about my choosing a more

impressive beast than yours. You keep your own council."

Imara nodded. "Fine. I will. I wish you luck with your creature. Remember, if you do want to practice, do it in a large area."

Mesook snorted and walked away, her shining black curtain of hair swinging against her lower back. The competitive side of her was a bit of a surprise. She had seemed perfectly fine in the herbology class.

She honestly hoped that they only had the two classes together.

Shrugging, Imara headed inside, passing a group of young women gathered around what looked to be a second-year student who was sobbing. Imara passed them and avoided staring. She found Bara, inclined her head, and mentioned that she was leaving.

"So soon?"

"I have had enough fun for one evening." She grimaced. "I want to leave before someone gets the plague or something."

"Ouch. Do you mind if I stay here?"

"Nope. Go ahead. I have some more zoological studying to do, and I am not sure what Mr. E is getting up to in my absence. He was a little too happy to be rid of me for the night."

Bara chuckled. "Thanks for coming out. See you at the hall."

Imara nodded and headed off, walking upstream through the crowd still entering the party. The night air had cooled considerably, and she shivered in the shock from the warm building to the cold quad.

She smiled slightly as she passed a few spectres near buildings in her path. They nodded in greeting and didn't ask her to speak to them. It was a politeness that she appreciated, as talking to spectres when the living were around was frowned on.

Approaching Reegar Hall, she could feel the magic pulsing inside the walls. Entering, she clapped a hand over her mouth as bubbles filled the air and appeared to be coming from the study area.

Magus Reegar was waving his hands with precise motions, and Mr. E was leaping around catching the magical bubbles that were floating out of a small portal.

Imara kept her hand over her mouth as her little familiar pounced from bubble to bubble, blinking as they exploded before he sat on his hind legs with his front paws stroking the air to catch the next bubble.

She must have made a sound because Reegar paused before resuming with a smile.

"He is giving the kitten in him a night to itself. If you are home, you will be pressed into tummy scratching detail after this."

Imara grinned. "Right. I will be on it. First, I am doing some research on my shape shifting. He can jump on my lap when he wants my attention."

"Excellent. I think he has taken in enough power from the bubbles. He will probably want a nap and then a cuddle."

She chuckled and went through the sparkling bubbles, taking up her position at the desk and getting back to her studies. Choosing a vulture as her beast was going to be difficult socially, but it felt right. She just had to find the details that would confirm her gut feeling. Time to study.

An hour later, with a purring kitten in her lap, she stared at her free hand and tried to compare the visible structure to that of a bird. It wasn't that different, but there would have to be the hollow nature taken into account during the shift. Unless she were a vulture nine feet tall, she would need to work on mass dispersal and return. It was more complicated than she wanted to go in her first form, but things were what they were. She would have to find a way to become her beast.

A sleepy voice whispered in her mind. *Why is it so important that you get it right the first time?*

"Because, Mr. E, I am making a form that flies. If I screw this up, I am going to be pavement pizza."

Keep rubbing my tummy.

She chuckled and pushed aside her diagrams and

sketches. Her watch pinged, and it was time for bed.

"Well, I guess that I have to head for bed. There is an ethics course in the morning, and I want to be bright eyed and . . . well, that's it. No tail required."

She scooped the sleepy kitten up and put him on the table. "Did you want to stay out here tonight?"

He purred in response.

"Fine, you know how to get in when you need to."

He purred again, his tail covering his nose.

She snickered and headed for bed. If he wanted to curl up with her, he could open the door. Nothing could stop a familiar from getting to his charge.

Gathering herself, she stepped into the ethics class and took her seat, not looking at Professor Breedwell. Mr. E sat upright on her shoulder, and he kept quiet.

She glanced at the other students and was a little surprised at the fullness of the course as well as the variety of ages represented. It seemed that everybody needed an ethics course now and then. Her familiar got a few stares, and several cooing sounds. He was remarkably cute.

Five more students arrived after she did, and when they were seated, the professor straightened. "Ladies and gentlemen, I welcome you to your first Magical Ethics class. We will learn all of the legal and moral ramifications of using and abusing your enchantments, as well as how to minimize the trouble with law enforcement."

Several of the older students chuckled. It was suddenly clear what they were doing there.

Imara smiled. She was in a class taught by a pervert, and she was surrounded by law enforcement. Well, that was certainly a stroke of luck. She took out her book and pen, settling in for the lecture. It was *definitely* a pretty good day.

Mr. E kept his own council during the lecture aside from the occasional snort when the professor said that the vulnerability of those you were with always needed to be considered.

Imara raised her brows at the professor, and he blushed.

It appeared he didn't practice what he preached.

What did I miss?

She bit her lip and tried to focus. *Nothing. I handled it.*

Then there should not have been anything to handle. I will check your memories.

Before she could do more than shift in her seat, he had found the details of the party, and his fur fluffed up. *That kind of charm was slimy when I was a mage. Now, his work is just tacky.*

Don't do anything.

What can I do? I am just a kitten.

There was a dark intent beneath those innocent words, and Imara frowned until he calmed down and his fur resumed its normal level of fluff.

By the time the lecture concluded, she had ten pages of notes regarding historical events which pointed to skewed ethics, as well as her assignment for the following week.

She scooped her work into a pile when the class was over and headed for the door. The man who had been sitting next to her paused and smiled. "Hi."

She looked at the man whose bearing screamed law enforcement, and she nodded. "Hello."

"Since we will be sitting next to each other, I thought I would introduce myself. I am Argus Dencroft."

She juggled her work and extended her hand. "Imara Mirrin."

He grinned and shook her hand. Mr. E growled softly.

"Is he your familiar?"

"Yeah."

"I have never seen a bound familiar before. Is he inherited?"

She blinked. The class was emptying around them. "Uh, yeah. He is. Mr. E, this is Argus. Argus, this is Mr. E."

She shifted her grip on her papers and books. "I haven't met a griffon before."

He stared at her, his dark gold eyes wide in his tanned face. He was gold and white from head to toe. His soul screamed that he was a griffon, and she was very attentive to souls.

"You . . . how do you know that?"

She smiled. "It is a conversation for another time. Right now, I need to put this paperwork down before I drop it. I am feeling a tectonic shift will occur at any moment."

He paused and then took her books. "Would you care for coffee?"

She blinked. "Um, sure. There is a nice café about a block away if you don't mind the walk."

He grinned. "I think that meeting you is something I should make time for."

The air went out of her lungs as his features went from interesting to devastatingly handsome. She blinked, blushed, and led the way to the café. Keeping ahead of him was her only way to maintain dignity. Mr. E laughing uproariously in her mind didn't help.

Chapter Four

Imara ordered for them both and waited for the coffee at the end of the counter. When she had their order, she paused a second before a patron shoved their chair back, windmilling their arms as they lost their balance. Imara went around the fall and made it to the table where Argus waited. Mr. E balanced carefully and chuckled when another patron wasn't as graceful.

"That was lucky."

She smiled. "You don't say."

"Yeah, if that had been me, I would be wearing the coffee." He sipped and smiled. "Perfect. How did you guess?"

"You looked like a *one and one* kind of guy to me."

He chuckled. "Funny."

"I know. So, why are members of the XIA here and taking courses?"

"We need to keep up our education if we want to be promoted. Ethics is a fairly easy course for us as we already have the training." He nodded to her paperwork. "You take thorough notes."

"Oh. Thanks. I would rather take down too much than not enough." She sipped at her ridiculously complicated latte.

"How did you know about my form?"

She blinked. "Ah, that. Right. Well, I have a primary focus that lets me see what is behind the physical."

He frowned. "I don't understand."

"I was a death keeper."

He still looked at her blankly.

"I see souls."

"Ghosts?"

She chuckled. "Not unless you are already dead. No. I see the motivating intelligence and energy that a living being possesses."

"Oh, so you can see through glamours?"

"Yup. That too." She gave him a small smile. "Isn't it weird for so many XIA agents to be in one class at the same time?"

He sipped at his cup. "Yes, this is very good coffee."

She nodded. "Right. So, how are you enjoying the college?"

Argus smiled. "Today has been a great day. It beats going to work."

"Where do you work?"

"Redbird City."

She set her cup down. "No way."

"Have you been there?"

She shook her head, "No, but it is in my business plan."

"You have a business plan?" He settled back in his chair and smiled.

"Of course. Why would I go to school if I didn't know what I would do afterward? I have done marketing studies, completed a business class, and am getting the certifications that I need to get my license for public magic." She ticked them off on her fingers.

He stared at her in surprise. "How old are you?"

"Nineteen. Well, I will be nineteen in a month."

His shock was evident.

She smirked. "You thought I was older."

"Yes. Yes, I did." He ran a hand through his hair. He sat straight again and seemed to reboot his brain. "What does a death keeper do?"

She smiled and explained how the people of Sakenta City dealt with their mages after physical life had fled. He asked question after question, and she answered them all. It was nice to have someone showing an interest in her talent.

They talked about the way Sakenta used the spectres as a resource for their families, and why it was a waste to ignore that much conscious power floating around. Argus was particularly interested in the fact that the spectres were aware of time passing around them.

Mr. E was sitting on the table, playing with a straw, when he suddenly sat up and yowled.

"Mr. E. What the hell?" She looked at him, and he gave her an unblinking stare with no commentary. Past the cute little ball of black fur, the daylight was turning orange. The afternoon was gone.

"Oh, damn. I am sorry, Argus, but I have to get going." She gathered her books and got to her feet.

"Imara, at least let me walk you home for all of the information you have given me."

Mr. E let out another ear-splitting yowl.

"I don't think that would be a good idea. See you next week in class, Argus. It was great talking with you."

Before he could answer, she bobbed a bow and left the café, Mr. E crawling up her arm as she walked.

Are you going to tell me why I did that?

Don't trust griffins. They have two natures and seldom direct both in the same area.

You are jealous.

He is too old for you.

She laughed the entire way back to Reegar Hall.

Using his calculations, everyone on campus was too old for her. Most weren't accepted until their twenty-first year. She and her twin were exceptions. They may have been separated at birth, but Luken shared her skills with books. He enjoyed studying as much as he enjoyed spending time with Bara over the holidays.

Having her twin dating a woman three years older wasn't a bad thing, but Bara seemed to have more than Luken Demiel on her mind. If there was a woman with less interest in finishing her scholastic career, Imara hadn't met her. Bara seemed to consider being a permanent student as an occupation. If she could afford it, Imara was cheering her on.

Back home, she checked her schedule for the next few days. She would be busy, but with the intensive classes at one subject per day, she had the next eleven weeks planned out. Classes in the mornings or afternoons, labs and homework in the evenings. It was the same schedule that she had engaged in during the first term, but the compressed classes were going to get exponentially harder.

She went to work on her ethics homework with a bright grin. Next week, she would get to see Argus again.

Her herbology course for second level was a mix of ages. The only folks in first year who qualified for the second course were herself and anyone who passed the exam. As far as she knew, that meant she was the only freshman student in the class. Everyone around her had their eyes on graduating.

Master Limokken was the instructor, and he looked them over before he pronounced, "This course is going to be graded on personal development with the final exam being eighty percent of the marks."

She tensed and listened carefully. Usually, she could get by by doing the homework in advance, but this wasn't going to be the case.

"Weekly, we will delve into different potions and poultices made from herbs. For the exam, you are going to grow your own plants with an eye toward forwarding their magic content. You are going to decide what you want your potion to do, and then, you will find the patch of soil on the campus that has the best magic content and, from there, grow your plants. If you don't start your plants in the next fourteen days, you won't have a sample before the exam. The details are in your course outline, so get to work and call me when you have something you want me to grade you on."

Imara looked around at the shocked faces of her classmates and headed to her workstation, her notebook in hand. She wanted to create a caffeine substitution for mornings, and this was as good a time as any.

With most of the other students still figuring out what they wanted to do, Imara and a couple of others got to work.

Mr. E supervised and watched her work from his perch on her shoulder. *You have come a very long way in a very short time.*

That is what I intended to do.

I know where the soil is. There was a smug tone to his voice.

She smiled slightly and sniffed at some lemon zest. *I believe I do as well.*

Where do you think it is?

Under the rim of the edge of the wave site. Since the campus is built on the site of an invading wave of magic, it makes sense that there would be some stored under the edge.

Sensible, but a little too literal.

What?

Where do you think magic is spilled over and over without dispersing?

The duelling ground?

See? You figured it out.

I don't know that the quality of magic spilled would be useful. I need magic that hasn't taken a shape yet.

Mr. E's rich tone was amused, *Are you sure I can't misdirect you?*

Pretty sure. I am going to find the site of the wave and get the soil there.

Good.

I thought you weren't supposed to misdirect me.

I would have stopped you before you followed my guidance. If I don't push you now and then, you will become dependent on me.

It was sound thinking. If they were ever separated and she needed to defend herself, waiting for him to tell her what to do might cost her life. Thinking for herself was a good habit to keep.

After two hours, the instructor made his rounds, and he checked on the potions. He looked over her notes and the progress she was making with the mortar and pestle and nodded. "Trouble waking up?"

"Something like that."

"Watch your ratios. You don't want to have undirected stimulation."

She looked over her notes and added a decimal place to the flower petals. She didn't need a potion that lasted as long as the flowers bloomed; she needed it for a day. With careful deliberation, she added sunflowers to the recipe. She would pass out the moment that the sun went down, but she would be bright and able while it was shining.

Imara worked until nearly the end of the class. With a look at the paste in her mortar, she realized what she wanted to do with it. She made a note in her book and made eye contact with the instructor.

He sauntered over and looked at the mash she was scraping into a jar. "I thought you were aiming for a potion."

"This will have more of a general waking rather than waking my digestive tract. The preparation will be applied to my temples, and that will spread the effect through my brain, or at least, that is the theory."

He nodded. With a flourish, he pulled out a sampling kit. He put a miniscule sample into a tiny flask and added a drop of diagnostic liquid.

"Well, you have magic, you have energy, and you have alertness. I give you a ninety percent for this first assignment."

She nodded and exhaled. "Ten percent because I didn't know what form it would take, right?"

Master Limokken nodded. "Correct. If I didn't know what you were aiming for, it would have been a hundred percent, but you had the word potion at the top of your page."

She blinked. "Right. Thank you, Master Limokken."

"Oh, and your familiar is welcome to help you find the soil. The years have shown that they don't do better than anyone else." He chuckled and left her workstation.

She sighed and set the jar down while she took her equipment to the sink. Mr. E was napping on her notebook, and she finished washing up, bringing everything back to her station and putting it away for the other students who took classes in the lab.

Mr. E was cleaning his paw when she finished, and she gave him a long look. *What is that about?*

One of the others got curious, so I defended your creation. I will accept a can of sardines in gracious tribute.

She stowed the container in her bag, and Mr. E hopped up onto her shoulder. With her station clear, she left the lab and went in search of the source of magic within the college.

Chapter Five

Wild magic usually left a distinct marker on the landscape, but the college didn't have any obvious signs of the wave coming through.

She was looking for the remains of a volcano in what amounted to a mountain range. Imara tried to look casual as she crossed the campus, her senses wide open and looking for a specific trace of something that shouldn't be there. When she only got touches from the population of the college, she pulled her senses back in. She was going to have to do some research, and the best books were home at Reegar Hall. She was lucky that Reegar just happened to have collected everything she needed.

Smirking to herself, she turned in place and started to walk back the way she had come. The collision with the man immediately behind her knocked her back and made Mr. E hiss.

She blinked rapidly. "I am so sorry. I changed my mind about my destination."

The man brushed at his clothing, and he nodded. "No harm done."

She paused and stared at another of her brothers. "Right. Well, excuse me."

She stepped around him and his friends, heading back toward home without looking back. She knew what she would see. His eyes were the same shade as hers, his hair was a touch darker, and his jaw was stronger, but he was definitely one of her siblings. She didn't know which one he was, so she kept going until she was in the hall with the door closed behind her.

I thought you liked Luken.

I do, I just don't know how the others feel about me.

Luken is the seventh son of the seventh son; he has the power he needs. The others might not be so charitable.

Right. Good plan. Your mother's family eventually became more interested in learning than destruction, but the Demiels have always been on the violent side.

She headed for the kitchen. *Were they on your list, too?*

I was getting there. The original Deepfords were a definite bunch of black souls, using demonic energies to gain power, land, and dominion over other mages.

Right. Anyway, I need to study to find the oldest structures on the campus. Any idea where I should start?

Start with the college memorial edition. It should have the list of oldest books.

She smiled and spoke out loud. "Excellent. I will start there."

He nuzzled her neck as she dropped her bag on the study table and helped her make a few choices from the library.

"What are you looking for, Imara?" Reegar walked in and watched her molest his collection.

"I am looking for a record of the oldest building at the college."

"Why?"

"I need to find the most magical soil on the property and use it for herbology. I don't want to use the mage's battlegrounds because there is focus and intent in that magic. I need wild magic. I want to find the source of the wave that sprouted at the school."

Reegar cocked his head. "There have been hundreds of attempts to find the source. It always evades those seeking it."

"Maybe they just haven't asked nicely."

He chuckled. "Perhaps that is it. I have a few books on the search."

"Look them up, please. I will need to start at the beginning if I am going to find the soil I am looking for."

Magus Reegar, spectre for decades and master of the house, headed off to find her the books.

While she waited, she got Mr. E his sardine and got

herself some crackers and cheese. His mind broadcasted happiness that only occurred when the kitten in him had full control.

She set out her notebooks and took out the alertness poultice. She sniffed it a few times and enjoyed the sensation of a waking mind.

Reegar came in with armloads of books trailing behind him, riding on a cushion of magic. Some of them looked older than the building she was in.

She looked at the stack set before her, and she took a deep breath, running her hands down the spines.

"What are you doing?"

"Trying to see if I get lucky." The faintest tingle ran through her left hand, and she pried the book out of the pile.

Reegar snorted. "That is a fictional account of the college. It was a history created by a previous student."

Imara grinned and settled in her chair. "Those are the best kind of stories. If I can get a clue, it will be worth the read."

He blinked and wandered back to the stacks of the library, phasing through a few of the shelves as he passed.

Mr. E climbed her leg and used her to boost himself onto the table. When he had curled up in a ball, she smirked and started reading.

The book was a novel nearly a hundred years old and written by an L. Ganger. *Hunted Moonlight* was the tale of a woman with blended bloodlines who was being pursued by a man with demon blood. They were both at the school, one as a student and one as an instructor. It was an amazing read.

She sniffled and sobbed during the book, finally getting to the ending where the couple forced their families' agreement by consummating their love in tasteful and obscure terms in the chancellor's garden, under a pear tree.

When she read the reference to the garden, she felt the tingle on her skin again. Right, well, that made sense and was a good place to start.

She set the book back in the pile and went looking for a

spell book on diagnostics. If she was looking for the source of magic on the campus, she was going to need a way to prove she had found it.

Bara came home with her arms loaded with supplies. "What are you up to?"

"I am just heading to the lab to make up some magic test strips."

"What?"

"Like an acidity test but for magic."

"Cool. Can I help?" Bara shifted her armloads of books and bags.

"I think you have your hands full. What are you taking this term?"

"Weaving. Magus Reegar said I could use the loom in the attic.

"Do I want to know why he has a loom in the attic?"

Bara grinned. "One of the students he scared away left it behind. I had better drop this stuff up there."

"You do that; I will get started." Imara continued her search, flipping through book after book until she found a few spells and potion recipes that would work. The thumping that was coming from the upper floor was enough indication that Bara wasn't going to be coming down anytime soon.

Reegar appeared at her side. "Would you like advice?"

"Sure. Let me just wake Mr. E up. If I let him sleep in the afternoons, he gets all cranky."

"How can you tell?"

She chuckled and passed the table where Mr. E still snoozed. She shifted the books to one arm and tickled him awake. "C'mon. I actually need you as a familiar."

He stretched, arching his small back with his fluff standing out at all angles. Half of his face fur was flattened, and he had a serious case of bedhead. She bit her lower lip and put him on top of the books with some blank sheets of paper before she headed to the lab.

What are you going to make?

Magic detection strips.

So . . . I can't shred this stuff?
She grinned and said out loud. "Nope, behave."
Setting up in the lab was fun. Mr. E perched on a tall stool, the books were open in front of her, and Reegar was telling her where to find the ingredients.

"I have never seen anyone combine those spells before."

She wrinkled her nose. "They seem right. Each has bits that I need for this to work."

"What if it blows?"

Imara laughed, "That is what Mr. E is for. He can at least repurpose my spectre so that I don't hang around and pester you. Then, he will go on to the next family member in line for him, or he will head to a different family. Either way, I am prepared for anything."

"I have never met anyone before you that had such a detachment for their life."

"I like being alive; I am just accepting that this isn't all there is." She took a deep breath, checked that she had all her supplies and equipment ready, and started to mix and chant with the white paper neatly settled next to the work area.

Hours went by with only gentle direction from Reegar and method critiques from Mr. E.

The light purple liquid was a small result for such a long effort. "Well, here goes."

With gloved hands, she picked up the small basting brush and painted the paper, front and back. The line with tiny clips was ready to hold the bespelled paper as it dried.

The small bowl of liquid covered twelve pages, absorbed quickly, and when it was used up, the light flashed brilliantly when Imara soaked the bowl and brush in the sink.

"Ouch. Okay, so it is water sensitive. Good to know."

Reegar laughed. "I thought it would be. A few of your ingredients are thirsty."

She snorted. "I know. I didn't think it would be that abrupt when they touched water."

The rest of the dishes were less violent. She was able to clear all the implements and put them on the drying rack without incident.

She checked the papers' progress, but they were still drying. "I am going to have to warn Bara about that."

"She has hung a few experiments out to dry, so I am sure she will be understanding." Reegar looked toward the line but kept his distance.

"I will have to remember to put gloves on before I move them." She muttered it to herself and double-checked her notes before closing her book and the others.

When everything was ready, she removed the gloves and draped them over the edge of the sink. "Okay, I think I am done for the night."

Good. It is past your bedtime.

She checked her watch and cursed. "Dammit. Why didn't anyone tell me?"

Reegar inferred her meaning. "You were engaged in creative spell combinations, I haven't seen that kind of enthusiasm in decades."

She muttered as she left the lab, dropped the books off at the study table and headed to bed. If she were lucky, she would get four hours of sleep.

Mr. E followed her, chortling in her thoughts. As she brushed her teeth, he snickered so she *accidentally* splashed him with water, and he hissed and skittered.

She apologized profusely and towelled him dry. She kept the part of her mind that he had casual access to calm with a hint of sympathy. The rest of her was snickering.

She only had one class left in the short week, so as long as she could get through the first class in household spell work, she would be fine.

She was snickering at herself as she fell asleep. She was going to get her butt kicked.

Chapter Six

"**D**omestic spell work doesn't involve any fancy chants or noxious potions. You use your mind, your power, and your control over the elements to keep your environment clean and under your control. In my class, it is easy to see the result of your study and focus. Your assignment is either clean, or it isn't." Magus Beelin paced back and forth in front of the rows of desks.

Imara held in her yawns as the instructor went on about what she expected of the class. She sat blinking in surprise when the class got practical in a rush.

"I want each one of you to come here and try and move this broom."

The class members got to their feet and shuffled to the area that Magus Beelin was pointing to. "Each of you will have thirty seconds to move the broom. Anyone who can do it is guaranteed a passing grade on the first test."

Imara hung back and tried to think of what she knew about telekinetic spells. There weren't any.

The timer chimed, and the first candidate shuffled forward. The mage strained from his place in line and tried to beckon the broom toward them. Nothing.

The next member of the class tried, and there was no success.

The minutes shot past, and soon, Imara was the only student who hadn't tried. The others were all seated and defeated.

The timer started, and Imara asked, "May I move?"

The magus quirked her lips. "Yes."

Imara walked to the broom and brought it back to the magus. The gasps and cries of the shocked students echoed in her ears.

Magus Beelin smiled, "Why did you walk to it?"

"It would have taken more effort to summon it."

At the nodded dismissal, Imara walked back to her seat, ignoring the glares of her classmates.

"That student has just proven a point you need to remember. The magic involved takes just as much from you as doing it by hand. The speed gained is a trade-off for your personal energy. There is nothing as draining as housework, and that includes those who can use an enchantment as well as those who work with their hands."

She set the broom back in its stand. "There are no spells for sweeping. The amount of control would mean you were stuck staring at the broom the entire time. Get one of those vacuuming robots if that is your only concern. If you want to sweep quickly, run a summoning spell for all dirt in your house and direct it to a bucket. That is not the first spell we will be working on, but it is on the list."

Magus Beelin raised her head. "The first spell work we are going to get into is stain removal. You are going to run into all kinds of substances here, and being able to clean your own clothing is important. From now on, come to this class prepared to get filthy so we can all work from the same baseline."

She waved her hands in the air. "Our classes will let you unclog a toilet, repair shattered glass, and get your room ready for your parents to drop in in under a minute. You will feel the strain, but you won't look like a slob."

The class chuckled and then sat back as the instruction began.

Hours later, Imara packed up her notebooks, put her pencil away and looked in satisfaction at the spot on her t-shirt that had been stained with oil an hour earlier. Spot removal was definitely something she could manage.

As she left her desk, Mr. E resumed his position on her shoulder. *I never learned to do that kind of thing. I guess it would have been useful.*

Learning how to take care of your own environment is always useful.

"Ms. Mirrin." The magus stopped her from leaving.

"Yes, Magus Beelin?"

"You have one hundred percent for the next test. Use the option wisely and study for the subsequent tests. The exam will be particularly taxing, so build up your stamina."

"Yes, Magus. Thank you."

"Don't thank me; you are the one who figured out manual labour would do the trick better than untrained magic."

"May I still take the test?" She asked cautiously.

The magus's smile was wide. "Hm, you do appreciate the education you are getting here."

"If I don't take the test, Magus Beelin, how will I know if I am ready for the next one?"

"Of course, you can take the test. I will even let you know how you did, but you will still pass, regardless."

"I would rather earn a passing grade."

The magus patted her on the shoulder. "You already did."

Mr. E purred and rubbed his cheek against Imara's. It was a signal to shut up and move along.

"Thank you, Magus. Have a good day."

"Have a good weekend, Mirrin. You have your work cut out for you."

Imara nodded and left the classroom. Removing the small spot of oil had exhausted her, and now that the weekend was looming, she had a nap planned before she tackled her homework.

The knock on her door was persistent.

"What?" Imara sat up and rubbed her eyes.

"Come on, you are getting off campus, and we are going out to dinner. My treat." Bara's voice was desperate.

Imara checked to make sure she still had her clothing on and opened her door. Bara was standing there, hair frazzled and her fingers wrapped in gauze and tape.

"Weaving kicking your ass?" Imara grabbed her shoes and put them on.

"Yes. I don't know how mages have done it for centuries." She sighed and slumped her shoulders.

Imara snickered as she stood. "They specialize. You are trying to specialize in everything. It isn't always going to work."

Bara groaned. "I know, but I have to try. It is a compulsion to try and get through all the course offerings, so I know where I want to direct my focus in the future."

"Right. Makes sense even if it is a little hard on you. Can I bring Mr. E?"

"We are going to be eating at a sit-down restaurant, so I would suggest you leave him here unless he can go invisible."

Mr. E was stretching on the pillow where he slept. *I can. The question is do I want to go out with two girls who are going to talk about me being cute and fluffy?*

Imara grinned. "Your choice, Mr. E. I want to grab one of those tester packs before we go, Bara. Nothing like a road test out in the real world."

Imara grabbed her bag and headed out of the dorm area, down the stairs, and down the hall to the lab. The vials of test strips that she had cut before her nap were all lined up with wooden pincers rubber banded to their exteriors. She settled one of the vials on the interior pocket of her bag and grinned at Bara. "So, you said it was your treat?"

"Yeah, can you drive? My hands are a little raw."

"Sure. Let's go."

With no sign of her familiar, Imara headed out with Bara and helped her open the car door. Bara acted as navigator, and they cruised through the gates of the college and into the town, resting in the valley below.

They parked in the lot of an Italian style restaurant, and Bara accepted her help getting out of the car. Her hands were in really rough shape.

"Maybe you should go to a medical centre."

"They would have a bit of trouble with my injuries. They are all psychosomatic." Bara made a face.

"What?"

"My fingers got sensitive, so I wrapped them up. I am not actually that injured beyond a few blisters."

Imara snickered as they headed for the building. "So, you are trying to dissuade yourself?"

"Yup. I know my triggers."

They waited and then followed a young woman to a booth.

Imara took her menu and looked it over. She casually mentioned, "You seem to have a good grip on your situation."

Bara grinned and peeked over her menu. "My entire family is nuts. Arming myself by learning what sets me off, what I need to learn, and how I get around my own neurosis is my permanent occupation."

"Wow . . . that is . . . wow."

"Yeah, I come from a long line of mad mages." Bara set her menu down. "What about you?"

"Ah, well, you have met my mom."

"Yeah, that was a little surprising. Explain to me how that is possible again?"

The server came and took their order. Imara ordered lasagne with a side of garlic toast and a salad, Bara opted for spaghetti with meatballs and the same sides.

Once they were sitting with their iced water and the menus were gone, Imara faced the resident advisor of her hall.

"So, why do you want to know the details?"

"I am really curious as to why you don't know your own mother. I know you told me, but I didn't pry. I feel like prying today if you are amenable."

Imara sat back. "Well, from what my mother told me, and what was in my file, the Deepford-Smythes were broke. Plenty of power but no money. The Demiel family had reached the end of their line for interbreeding, so they wanted a powerful bloodline to mix with theirs. Each family had a seventh child program running for extra power, and in the case of the Deepford-Smythes, they didn't discriminate against the females. They counted them all. The chancellor was the seventh member of her family, and my father was the seventh of his. A contract was signed to produce the desired seventh of seven, and they got married. I think you can guess what happened next."

"She wasn't happy."

"Nope. After each child, she was healed, and the next pregnancy commenced. It was dangerous, and she was treated like a farm animal. She hated it. When Luken and myself were born, the Demiels wanted me discarded as quickly as possible. As the eighth out of the seventh, I wasn't considered lucky. Luken got that particular designation."

Bara wove her fingers together and rested her chin on them with her elbows on the table. "What happened then?"

"My mother's family made arrangements to place me in Sakenta City. Since my mother was planning to divorce my father the moment that the contract was fulfilled, she had a plan for one of the twins. She was surprised that I was a girl but very happy at the same time. An eighth boy would definitely be unlucky, so I was taken away and put into care."

Their salads arrived, and a few minutes were spent as they munched their way through them.

Bara finally mumbled, "This is better than a soap opera. What happened then?"

"She divorced my father and left her seven sons. She took a teaching position at the college and worked her way up the ladder. She became the chancellor of the college by virtue of her skills, her time at the college, and her family."

"So, you grew up alone?"

"No, I grew up in one of the regulated placement homes in Sakenta. Folks have magic there, but no one uses it."

That was enough to redirect Bara's questions. For the rest of their time in the restaurant, Imara explained how she could grow up as she had without using magic until she was an adult.

"So, how is it you were able to qualify for the college?"

"I didn't say I didn't have magic, I just couldn't do the kind of thing that I am learning now. When I was a teen, I got a job at the Memorial Gardens as an apprentice death keeper. Talking to the dead isn't considered magic in Sakenta. It is necessary."

"This is amazing. You worked a night shift during school?"

"Yeah, it is a good thing that being a death keeper pays well. I was trying to save enough for college."

Bara grinned, "If you are the chancellor's daughter, you get free tuition."

"Only if I am legally claimed. I am not. She is the chancellor, and I am Imara. That is all we need to be, though one of my clients in the Memorial Gardens did send enough money to the college to cover my tuition until graduation. It is another reason I am in a hurry. I want to get into the job market and start using the one thing that I am really good at."

"What is that?"

"Dealing with spectres." She grinned and waved the last bite of lasagne in the air. "Even the master death keeper said he had never seen anything like my talent."

She ate the last bite and leaned back. "Thank you. That was delightful."

"My pleasure. Thank you for driving. So, have you heard about what is going on at the campus?"

"The women turning up powerless?"

"Yeah, that."

Imara scowled. "I thought that was just a rumour."

"Nope. One of the girls was in my enchanted textile class. She can't do anything. She had to go to the dean's office and have her classes suspended until she can use magic again. The weird thing is she doesn't know how it happened. She was at a party, blacked out, and woke up without the slightest drop of magic."

Imara shivered. "That is creepy. Didn't anyone see anything?"

"No one has reported anything. For now, they are treating it like a frat prank, but I am going to keep an eye on what I eat and drink at the parties."

Imara sighed. "You could just not go to the parties."

"Nope. This is part of my college experience. I want to live it to the hilt. Who knows, perhaps restricted socialisation is what drove my relatives insane?"

"Are you sure that you will go nuts?"

"If I don't take precautions, yes. It is in our bloodline and could even be called a curse. We are driven to do something at all times, and if we stop, the crazy soaks in."

"Wow. That is harsh."

Bara paid the bill and slid out of the booth. "I live with my family history just like you live with yours."

Imara smiled at the point of commonality and followed Bara out of the restaurant.

Chapter Seven

The weekend flew by as Imara immersed herself in her courses and practice. She got a notice that her business course was cancelled due to lack of interest, so that left her with free Mondays. She would just have to make up the course credit elsewhere. Her email to the chancellor requesting permission to dig in the garden had been sent off, so now, she had to wait.

With her Monday free, she practiced her shape shifting and worked on forming wings and claws. The head, neck and torso structure of the bird would wait until she had her instructor watching.

You are doing very well. You haven't had to use your emergency reversion yet. Mr. E was sitting and chewing on a very naughty claw. He had been working on it for an hour.

"I haven't transformed past the point where I could ask for help yet. I am pretty sure that when I get into that position, I am going to panic." She looked at her clawed feet poking out from beneath her bathrobe and the wings poking out of her wide kimono sleeves. Her body was urging her to complete the change, but she wasn't going to. Rushing a change was a very stupid idea.

It feels natural, does it not?

"Yeah, which is what scares me."

He looked at her with his eyes bright and tail lashing. *Why scared?*

"I have read the books about mages who got lost in their other forms, never to turn back to human. It is something to keep in mind."

You are further along than most would be at your age.

"It doesn't make me stupid." She flicked her hands and feet back to normal, sighing as the urge to shift faded.

No, I am learning that. You have the maturity of an old soul.

She laughed. "Not likely. The lucky ones are always fresh souls, or so the legend goes."

You don't know?

She barked a laugh. "Who would tell me? There isn't a counsellor who can describe the ins and outs of being a lucky one."

Reegar appeared in her open doorway. "What would you like to know?"

Imara tightened her robe. "You know about the lucky ones?"

"Of course, I have known two. What do you need to know?" He straightened slightly. "Where are my manners; would you like tea?"

She looked down. "Sure, give me a minute."

"You are fine. Bara is in class, and I don't care."

Imara paused. "Right. Okay. I am on my way."

She made her way down to the common area and watched Reegar prepare tea for her.

"So, what do you need to know about the lucky ones?"

She frowned. "Are they always the seventh of seven?"

"Generally. Both of the gentlemen I knew were."

"What about the child of two sevens?"

"That doesn't happen. Two seventh sons can't have a child." He tsked as if she were simple and carried over the tea tray.

She cocked her head. "What if one of the families wasn't choosy about the gender of their children and took the seventh daughter as their lucky one?"

He put a lump of sugar in her teacup and slowly poured. "The only family I know of that did that died out decades ago. It isn't an easy situation for the family and worse for the girls."

"Why?"

"She becomes an object to be traded. Her luck transfers to her children."

Imara frowned. "That doesn't seem very lucky to me."

"They are always taken care of, and all their children inherit a portion of their luck. Having lucky children becomes an extension of their luck." He put a splash of milk into her cup and slid it toward her.

"That sucks."

"Why so curious about lucky ones?"

"Luken. I want to know what I can about the birthright he inherited."

"Why?"

"Well, he is my twin."

"Oh, of course. Well, a true lucky one gains money, power, stature, and skill. Everything they do works out in their favour." He sat back. "One of the first lucky ones I met was an investigator in the Mage Guild. He was able to bring in everyone he went after, and he was not a man to bet against at the poker table. He couldn't get drunk but always managed to get just the companion he wanted for the evening. Your brother has a bright future ahead of him."

She quirked her lips. "Good thing that I am not the lucky one in the Demiel family."

He nodded. "It is a good thing indeed. I wouldn't wish that fate on anyone."

Imara sat back and sipped at her tea. It was just the way she liked it. "No, nor would I."

They sat in silence, and she sipped her tea. So, putting it about that she was the lucky one was going to have to remain a family secret. Hopefully, the cousin who wanted Mr. E as her familiar wasn't too chatty. Luken would get enough luck from their father's side. No one would think to look at her. She could keep her luck to herself.

Shape-shifting class was all about learning to change hair and eye colour. She went through the motions with Mr. E offering colour suggestions.

"Ms. Mirrin, you are not taking this seriously."

She smiled at him and batted her lashes. "Magus Korian, I am merely having fun with colour. I thought you would appreciate seeing rainbows on this gloomy day."

He looked at her carefully. "You have excellent pigment control. You have been practicing?"

"A little, with supervising mages standing by to stop me from anything stupid."

"I am happy about the supervision, but as I am unsure as to their ability to help you, I would recommend that you keep your experimentation to this class." Korian tried to glare the message into her, and she merely stared calmly back at him.

One of the other students let out a shriek, and he hurried to his side. Their class was down to four people, and Mesook wasn't one of them. The warnings must have freaked her out. Imara didn't blame her; shape shifting was dangerous.

Reversion charms had been their first enchantment of the day. The bands would transform with them, and each held a master pattern of the mage involved. It was a nice safety net.

Imara was relieved to know that Mr. E also had her template. He was a backup drive on four feet. Reegar had made him practice resetting her until they were familiar with the process. It had been a fun Monday.

When Korian returned to her, Imara was wearing long scarlet hair and lime green eyes.

"Fine. I understand you have grasped basic transformation. Can you change your height?"

Imara rose to her feet and looked down at him from eight inches taller than her normal stature. She pointed her ears for effect. It was a pity that her clothing didn't shift with her, but that was why she was shifting and not using a glamour.

"Walk."

She made a face and took a few careful steps, wobbling at the change in balance point. With a few more steps, she had the hang of it, and soon, she was striding across the display area of the classroom with confidence.

Korian flicked his fingers, and a flash and bang erupted in her path. Imara flinched back, and she could feel herself resuming her normal shape.

"If you were flying when that happened, you would drop out of the sky. That was a *seeming burst*. It forces reversion."

She was still facing twinges of magic running along her skin. "I am so glad you did that on purpose."

He reached out to pat her on the shoulder, but Mr. E bit his leg with a hiss and growl. Imara was startled, but she scooped her attack kitten up into her embrace.

Korian growled. "That hurt."

Imara's mind filled with images of Korian on fire and staked out and bleeding. Mr. E was so angry; he wasn't able to speak.

It wasn't the use of the reversion spell against her; it was the attempt to touch her that had set her fluffy defender off. Korian was attracted to her, and in Mr. E's mind, he had no business pursuing that particular avenue of interaction. He was her instructor, nothing more.

"You are not to touch me in anything but an instructional manner. Patting me on the shoulder or touching me in any way that he deems inappropriate will result in my familiar taking action."

Korian's skin darkened. "Ah. Well, I suppose that is appropriate. If that little bugger bites me again, he will see my teeth."

A bone-rattling roar echoed in the room, and its origin was the tiny beast in her arms.

Imara cleared her throat. "I believe that was *challenge accepted.*"

Korian looked at the kitten who hissed and swatted back at him. "Right. I will take that under advisement."

Imara cleared her throat. "As I have demonstrated the skills for this class, may I get next week's assignment and take my familiar to calm down?"

Korian nodded sharply. "That will be for the best."

He scribbled the assignment down and handed her the document. "Out, and he had better be in a proper temper next week. Contact is part of learning to shift."

She nodded and grabbed her bag, holding her hissing and spitting familiar away from him.

If you don't calm down, I am going to have to drop that

class.

He does not need to touch you, he wants to. I can smell it when he is close to you.

She grimaced and left the building. Mr. E calmed enough to climb onto her shoulder, which made carrying her books easier.

She took him home and dropped her books off, going out without speaking to him. He could have followed her, but he didn't.

Coffee seemed like a good alternative to aimlessly wandering the lanes and paths, so she headed for the shop near the edge of the campus.

After she got her order, she sat outside and picked her croissant to pieces. Dealing with lust wasn't something she was comfortable with, especially when it was someone who was alive. She had dropped Mr. E off because she didn't need his voice in her head while she figured out what she wanted to do.

Imara was into her second cup of coffee when a black SUV pulled up and disgorged three XIA agents. She recognized one of them immediately. To her consternation, he smiled and walked over.

"Imara, funny meeting you here."

"Hi, Argus. I didn't know that the XIA engaged in enforcement on campus." She wrapped her hands around her mug and tried to look casual while her heart was hammering in her chest.

A vampire wearing shades and a baseball hat came up next to the griffin, and a fey glided up on his left. The smooth tones of the elf were unforgettable. "Argus, won't you introduce us to your friend?"

She really didn't think she wanted to know those guys. The vampire looked like he ate horseshoes for breakfast, and the elf had enough muscle to pull out trees with his pinky. They made Argus look lithe in comparison, and his forearm was nearly as wide as her thigh.

They were all wearing black on black, the shirts tailored but snug. The XIA badge was carefully picked out in black and bronze with the logo of their particular extranatural affiliation underneath.

Argus scowled but remembered his manners. "Ivar, Lio, this is my ethics classmate, Imara Mirrin. Imara, these are the assholes I work with."

She grinned. "Pleased to meet you. Are you just passing through?"

"We had some appointments with the dean of students and some witnesses."

The men moved forward and took the empty seats around her table. The metal and wood creaked in protest.

Argus gave Ivar a glare, and the vampire got to his feet and lumbered inside.

Lio leaned forward. "So, Argus turns to jelly whenever he mentions taking the class. I am guessing you are the cause?"

She blinked. "I have no idea about that."

The fey had silvery features in skin so pale it was nearly warm moonlight. The delicate skin was stretched over wide musculature in a most disconcerting way. She didn't know much about fey, but he wasn't a proper elf.

He snorted indelicately and then made a muffled sound as Argus clapped a hand over his mouth.

"Ignore him, Imara, he is just hungry. We aren't normally up and about at this time of day, but the college insisted."

"So, you are here because of the magic drain? Why didn't they just send the guild?" Imara sipped at her coffee.

"The women affected have no magic. Therefore, they don't fall under the guild's protection." Argus scowled, releasing Lio's face when Ivar showed up with a tray full of coffees.

Ivar smiled at her, not showing his fangs. "I didn't know what you were drinking, so I got a selection."

The stack of pastries was the first casualty as Lio dug in.

"You didn't have to get me anything, but thank you."

She picked a cup labelled two cream and two sugar. Argus grinned and grabbed his own, then frowned. "Speaking of women under attack, why are you here alone? Where is your familiar?"

The fey was fascinated. "You have a familiar?"

She smirked. "Yeah. He bit my shape-shifting instructor, so now, I have to figure out a way to deal with that."

Argus beamed. "You are learning to shape shift?"

She grimaced as Ivar snickered. "Yes."

Lio asked, "What form have you chosen? Are you going to match your familiar?"

She let out a snort. "No. I have picked something a little bigger."

Argus filled his partners in. "Her familiar is a kitten."

The two agents chortled and drank their coffee while Argus leaned toward her. "What did you choose as your beast?"

She blushed. "You are going to read something into it."

He looked surprised. "I won't."

"Griffin vulture."

By the hoots of hilarity that her companions were letting out and the smug look in Argus's eyes, they had read something into it.

Chapter Eight

"I am strongly suggesting that you don't go out alone until the magic drain is found," Argus stated it at her door. "Keep your familiar with you when you are on campus."

"I like to have time alone. I am used to it."

"Tough. Being twitchy is no reason to be stupid. He has power, let him protect you."

She cackled. "Right, like he protected me from my creepy shifting instructor."

His face went from lecturing to steel. "What?"

"Mr. E says that the teacher smells like lust when he is around me, so when the teacher approached me, Mr. E attacked. It was a cute and fuzzy attack, but he still bit him."

She had never seen a growl pass over someone's features before. Muscles moved under the skin, and his lip curled.

"Uh, right. So, I was out on my own trying to figure out a plan of attack, so to speak."

"He tried to touch you?"

"Just pat my shoulder, but then, he said that shifting requires a lot of contact and that didn't seem right when he was instructing the rest of the class by pointing and using an illustration."

A full-body shudder went through Argus. "When is your next class?"

"Monday morning. I have a week to refine my approach." She smiled. "Thanks for the coffee. It was interesting to meet Lio and Ivar."

He chuckled. "They were enchanted by you."

"Yes, it was nice when Ivar mentioned that I was younger than his wallet." She wrinkled her nose. "I promise to use the buddy system around campus."

"Good. See you in class tomorrow." He bowed slightly and

left.

She exhaled slowly and watched him go. *Too old for you, too old for you, too old for you.* Her own mind beat her with the truth.

She leaned out to look around the corner of the building as he stepped into his vehicle. The flex of his muscles could be discerned, even from her distance. She exhaled slowly again and headed inside.

Mr. E ran up to her and climbed her leg, heading up to his perch on her shoulder. *I am sorry I lost my temper . . . Why do you smell like griffin?*

Argus and his team have been assigned to the investigation here at the college. They had a meeting with the dean and stopped for coffee. I was at the coffee shop, trying to figure out how to deal with Korian.

An amused chuckle ran through her thoughts; this time it wasn't her. *Did you let Argus know about Korian?*

Yes.

Oh . . . this is going to be fun to watch.

She didn't know what he meant by that, but she tried to think positive.

Argus was waiting in the hall when she arrived for the ethics class, and he smiled in greeting. They were the only ones there, and she was fifteen minutes early. She had no idea how long he had been waiting.

The snickering of her familiar was getting annoying.

The lecture was long, but the teaching assistant had their assignments graded and handed back by the end of the class. Imara sighed in relief. Getting ninety percent or higher was part of her business plan. If her grades were high enough, she would get an equivalence pass on certain courses. It was part of her accelerated graduation plan.

She glanced at Argus's paper and smiled. An eighty-six was nothing to sneeze at.

She folded her graded paper and tucked it into the envelope at the back of her binder.

"You are very meticulous when it comes to your notes,"

Argus commented as they got up after the lecture.

"Yes. I was once accused of cheating when I was younger, so now I keep track of each and every bit of information I get."

"Did you cheat?" He nudged her with his elbow.

"Of course not. I made an intuitive leap that made my teacher look bad. It was not a great moment for Mrs. Heckle's third-grade history class." She shook her head ruefully. "After that, I kept all my notes, tests, and reports."

"Wow. Third grade, huh?"

"Yeah. I am hardcore now."

Mr. E was purring happily at their banter.

"May I escort you to your home?"

She shook her head. "No, I am heading off for lunch."

He paused and asked politely, "May I join you?"

"You are going to look a bit odd in the cafeteria."

"We could go off campus. There is a noodle place a few miles away."

She made a face. "Do you mind if I work on the assignment?"

"No. That was my plan as well."

"Excellent. Do you want to drive, or shall I?" She grinned.

"My vehicle is nearby."

"Oh, good. Mine is parked in hell's half acre. Lead the way."

Argus grinned and took point.

Imara was face deep in noodles with Mr. E happily experiencing sushi for the first time when Argus dropped a conversational bomb.

"I would like permission to court you when your studies are over."

She finished her slurp on a cough. Her voice was a hoarse squeak. "What?"

Argus was looking at her earnestly. "I would like permission to court you when you have finished college and settled in your career."

"Um . . . are you putting dibs on me?" She stared at him

in consternation while the snickering from her familiar was nearly audible.

He cocked his head. "Something like that. I know you do not have time for a relationship, nor do I wish to be a distraction for you while you are studying."

"That is very thoughtful. You would be waiting for three years."

He shrugged. "Time isn't a problem, and I notice that you did not say no."

Her skin flushed. "Ah, yeah. That. Well, I didn't say no. That's true."

He smiled; his metallic eyes sparkled. "I will take that as your offer to consider it."

"You are happy with that?"

"Delighted."

Mr. E got up, stretched and wandered over to Argus, looking him up and down. The diabolical kitten reached into Argus's bowl and caught a pawful of noodles and chicken.

Argus didn't do anything as the kitten scarfed down the stolen goods.

What are you doing, you little maniac?

Testing your would-be mate. He is going to have to get used to me one way or another.

That can be accomplished without your digging in his food. I would have given you some of mine if you had asked.

This is more fun. I am enjoying teasing a large predator with you here to defend me.

That is it.

She leaned forward and scooped the black, fluffy serial killer up and spanked him, setting him back at his plate.

Argus grinned. "I bet he didn't like that."

I didn't even feel it. This body is all bounce and fluff. He flicked his tail in the air. *And you hit like a girl.*

She chuckled. "He is getting over it. So, how long have you been partnered with Lio and Ivar? Are all XIA agents so huge?"

"We are heavy hitters. We get called in for extranaturals who are rampaging or overpowering. Lots of trolls." He smiled.

"I have never met a troll." She slurped at her noodles then put a small portion in front of Mr. E with a selection of carrots and chicken. He didn't say anything, but purring commenced.

"Well, you sort of have. Lio is half troll, half elf."

She whistled softly. "That explains a lot. What about Ivar?"

Argus chuckled. "I think he ate a troll and it got stuck."

She giggled at the mental image and then sobered. "If we put off courtship for years, what are we in the meantime?"

"Friends? Companions? Classmates? If I get desperate, study buddies?"

She laughed. "Do I get to pick?"

"Of course."

"Friends then. Platonic and casual friends who can study together if you get desperate."

He grinned. "I will take you up on that if your familiar doesn't mind."

The low rumbling purr coming from the tiny body was answer enough.

Argus straightened and asked, "So, what did you get for answer three?"

She smiled and returned to her soup. "No action shall be taken against the powerless unless they have been armed by a mage."

"Ah, right. Okay . . . on to question seven."

She enjoyed studying with him and having endless cups of tea appearing while the old cups were whisked away. None of the staff even raised a brow at Mr. E.

Homework had never been so entertaining with a side of flirting. It was going to be a long few years.

Chapter Nine

Having members of the XIA roaming the campus at night cut down on the escalating incidences of draining, but it was the effect of Argus visiting her shifting class that made Imara feel safe.

Magus Korian had been star struck at a genuine mythical shifter sitting in on his class.

Imara had gotten down to business and fully shifted into her vulture. Argus had her extend her wings, and he had been very businesslike about telling her what parts of her form she needed to alter for flight.

Korian was hovering in the background, but with an actual flying shifter helping her with her scale, he didn't have anything to offer.

"Okay, now beat your wings." Argus smiled.

She flapped twice, and to her shock, her feet lifted off the ground. She was so surprised that she landed heavily on her tail feathers.

"It is fine. Everybody lands on their butt now and then. Come on; I will help you up, and you can glide to a tremendous landing on your stomach."

Before she could do more than shriek in panic and flap her wings, he scooped her up, and her claws were digging into his forearm.

With the rest of the class watching, he walked to the back of the auditorium, and her vision focused on the stage and the tempting prey of the small, black kitten.

She got her balance and focused, hearing the taunt from below. *Bring it on, baldy.*

She didn't shriek, didn't make a sound as she launched from her perch and glided toward her prey.

She hit him hard. The sound was a meaty thud, but

instead of perching on him, she used her momentum to carry him up and into the rafters.

Baldy? Really?

Oh, you heard that? I mean you are a lovely example of vulture nobility.

She perched and let him slip out of her claws. If he weren't a creature of magic, he would have been crushed when she snagged him.

She sat for a moment and watched the faces turned toward her. Only Argus was watching with a smile on his face.

Imara shook her head, looked at Mr. E and asked, *So, how do you feel about landing?*

He grumbled but got into a position where she could grab him.

She walked sideways, grabbed him, spread her wings, and began to flex and flap, lowering them at a predictable pace. She released her familiar a few feet from the ground and then dropped to the wooden floor.

Imara sat and breathed heavily as she took her human form again. The charm she was wearing generated her robe, and she sat on her ass and wiggled her toes in front of the class. "Well, that was fun."

Korian was staring at her, blinking in shock. "You . . . you made a complete transformation with only two classes."

Argus wandered up to her and helped her to her feet. She smiled brightly. "I had some coaching."

Korian nodded, and he shrugged. "Well, you have proved proficiency. You get the class credit."

"What?"

"The course aim was to achieve a secondary form that was functional and biologically sound. You flew, landed and flew again. That gets you a pass."

"Oh. Right. Well, thanks. I will just get changed and leave."

"That would be best. The other students still have a lot to learn."

"Oh. What about the final exam?"

"You just did it." Korian smiled and took a step toward

her, trying to reach out to her.

Argus moved, and Korian froze, retreating as he stared at the XIA agent.

"Right, well, I will file your passing grade with the college. You should receive a confirmation within the hour."

"Thank you, Magus Korian. It was an informative class."

She scooped up Mr. E and stroked him lightly as she walked to where she had left her day clothing. She pulled her panties and jeans on under her robe, turned her back and put on her bra before yanking her shirt on over her head.

Mr. E was watching to make sure that no one was peeping at more than her back for a few seconds. Once she was dressed, she pulled on her shoes and grabbed her bag and books with Mr. E taking up his accustomed perch on her shoulder.

Argus looked at her. "Would you like to get lunch?"

Her stomach churned and growled. She blushed. "How did you know?"

"Shifting shape always takes a toll."

"I want to change clothing first. I think I have my shirt on backward, and I have put on enough of a show for the day."

"Lead the way." He grinned.

She took off with a long stride, and he kept up with her as she made her way across the campus. Her body was energized, and she needed to use that energy or scream.

When they arrived at Reegar Hall, she invited him into the common room. "Wait here, and I will be right back."

Reegar looked up in surprise from the easy chair where he was reading his favourite spell book. "You are leaving him here?"

She smiled. "Just for a minute. I am just going to change clothing, and we will be on our way. Don't do anything weird while I am gone."

Argus glanced her way. "Which one of us are you talking to?"

"Both." She headed up the stairs and made a beeline for her room. Her bag thudded on the floor, and she sent her shirt and Mr. E flying, noting that it was inside out and he was excellent at landing on the bed. Her twisted bra was banished to the hamper, and her jeans followed.

She was dressed in a properly behaving bra, sweatshirt, and fresh jeans in under two minutes. She brushed her hair out and flipped it behind her, extended her arm to Mr. E, and her familiar was back in place on her shoulders when she finished tying her sneakers.

"Ready to go?"

Your purse.

"Thank you. You are an excellent familiar."

I know it.

She pried her purse out of her backpack and checked it quickly. There were money, keys, and her identification readily visible next to her phone, so she was good to go.

"Huh. I have a message."

She woke up her phone and listened to the message. She had clearance to dig up the soil she needed. She just had to make an appointment to be accompanied by a member of the chancellor's household.

As she walked down the stairs, she made the call.

Reegar and Argus were sitting and appeared involved in deep conversation.

With her appointment looming, she grabbed some plastic bags, a knife, and a spoon. They would help her do what she needed to do.

"So, what were you and Reegar discussing?"

Argus drove them off campus and out to the town again. "Just his enjoyment of you as a tenant. You seem enthusiastic about something. Good news?"

"Yeah, I get to go digging to get some soil that will hopefully let me pass my herbology course."

He blinked. "You have to find your own dirt?"

"Yeah. It is for the final exam, but plants take time. I have to get the plants under way as soon as possible, but the chancellor's office delayed in getting back to me."

"You need fancy dirt?" He glanced at her.

"I need magical dirt. I am pinning my hopes on the slightly risqué memoire of a previous student."

"Really?"

"Yeah, I am trusting my own magic and hoping for the best." Her stomach snarled again.

He chuckled. "Hang in there. We will be there in a moment."

"Where are we going?"

"Barbeque. You have just had your first shift, you need meat. Mage or not, your body has just had a shock."

He pulled his blue SUV into a parking lot and found a spot. The moment that the car settled he was around the vehicle and had her door open.

"Um, I thought we were pausing the idea of courtship for a few years."

He took her hand in his. "Just helping you out of the car, buddy."

She rolled her eyes while Mr. E snickered.

"Oh, can he come in?"

"Yes. This is a shifter-friendly establishment. The occasional ball of fur doesn't even faze folks."

The car door shut behind her, and he led her into the restaurant with his fingers woven with hers. It was more than the assistance of a friend, but she didn't want to fuss.

The air in the parking lot was full of the scent of barbeque, so Imara walked faster. Once inside, the server was friendly, told Mr. E what a pretty boy he was and took them to a table.

"Huh, this really is familiar friendly."

"Well, the college is ten minutes away. He probably isn't even the only one in here today."

She ordered a soda and water, he settled for green tea.

The menus were bursting with meat, but before she could make up her mind, Argus snagged her menu from her and shook his head. "Trust me on this. I will pick what you need. The first shift meal needs to be special."

Imara drummed her fingertips on the table. "Special?"

"Oh, yes. Just a moment."

He left the table, and she was sitting there with Mr. E still basking in the comment of the hostess.

A moment later, Argus reappeared and took his seat with

a smile on his lips. "It will just be a moment."

It was two minutes of stomach churning sounds before a server arrived and slid moist towelettes down before she delivered some riblets covered in sauce.

She grinned. "The rest will be out in a few minutes."

Imara tore open the wipe and grabbed a riblet. To her amusement, the server brought a small plate of shredded pork for Mr. E. He happily launched himself to the table while the ladies squealed and cooed at him while they went about their rounds.

Perhaps being cute isn't too bad.

Imara was halfway through the small tidbits of pork on bone when he spoke. *See? I told you so.*

Argus sipped at his tea. "Has that taken the edge off?"

Her stomach rumbled again. "A little bit. I no longer feel hollow."

"You had a mass dispersal. You are not going to feel great for a couple of days, and you will need massive meals. It is my honour to provide you with your first shift meal." Argus said the words with solemn formality.

"I thank you for the upcoming meal; now, please join me before I eat everything." She looked at the half dozen bits left on the plate, the clean bones stacked neatly beside them.

Argus picked up a wet nap and slowly cleaned his hands. He picked up one of the little bits and raised it to his lips.

The server arrived with a platter for two and set it firmly in front of Imara. Argus had a salad.

She looked at him over the display of ambrosia to her senses. "You have to be joking."

"No. You need this."

"Have some."

He grinned. "Thank you. It is up to you to share your kill, or in this case, your chicken and ribs."

"But . . ." she gave him an arch look. "The brisket is mine."

He inclined his head in acceptance, and the feeding frenzy began.

Chapter Ten

"Why aren't I full?" She looked down at her hands, still stained from the sauce after the two double platters. The soap in the bathroom wasn't up to the task.

"You lost molecular density. You lost mass to take your form, and when you shifted back, you didn't regain all of that mass. Basically, you forgot where you parked it. Your instructor should have shown you how to do it."

"I am not sure that he knows. He wanted us all to pick a shape that had nearly the same mass as our human bodies. I had to pick the one that called to me, but the others were pretty much matching their human forms."

"You did very well. Controlling the transformation is important. If you like, I can give you some instruction so that you can gain proficiency."

"That would be nice. Thanks again for the meal."

"First shift is a rite of passage amongst shape shifters. It is our only magic, so we celebrate it."

She smiled. "Yeah, I am getting that. Could you drop us at the chancellor's residence?"

"Certainly. Would you like help to dig?"

"I won't need help, but I wouldn't mind the company."

He grinned.

"Wait, don't you have to work this evening?" She bit her lip, worried that she was monopolizing his time.

"I don't need as much sleep as you do. I will be fine and up to class tomorrow." He smiled and turned with practiced ease through the twisting streets of the campus.

The chancellor's residence was nearly as old as the college and had ivy covering the exterior.

"Wow. This is neat."

"Haven't you been here before?"

Imara shook her head. "Nope. I have met the chancellor a few times, but I haven't been to the residence."

He parked in a gravelled lot, and they left the vehicle together, walking up the path to the ancient home.

Before they could knock, the door opened, and a young man stood in the opening. "Imara Mirrin?"

"Yes."

"I am Dresden Deepford-Smythe, the chancellor's assistant. I will take you to the gardens."

She sighed at facing one of her cousins. "Thank you."

The assistant emerged from the house and walked them around the building to the gated gardens. This wasn't a standard gate. The garden was guarded by a seven-foot stone wall that radiated magic. Dresden opened the gate for them and nodded. "You have two hours until the garden ejects you. I hope you find what you are looking for."

Imara nodded and stepped into the gardens, looking past the glowing and lush flowers and seeking the pear tree.

"What are we looking for?"

"A pear tree. I am looking for a pear tree."

As she walked, she dug blindly into her purse until she found the test strips.

Argus looked at the vial with interest. "What is that?"

"Magic detector. It hasn't had a field test yet, but I thought it might help."

She held the tweezers and flipped open the vial, selecting one out of the fifty little strips. She walked toward the large orchard section of the gardens and let one of the strips fall.

There was a minor flash on the ground, and Imara grinned. "Excellent."

"What did that prove?"

"There is magic. If it isn't magical, nothing happens."

He nodded. "Right. Can your familiar help?"

"I don't know. Mr. E, can you find the pear tree?"

He snuffled against her neck. *Fourth tree, two rows down. It was there when I went to school.*

She gestured, and they followed the direction of her tiny food-coma'd companion.

The pear tree was moving, but there was no wind. It was a good sign.

"I am going to drop another strip. You might want to guard your eyes."

She let one tiny piece flutter to the root of the pear tree. The flash of light nearly blinded her. "Found it."

Argus watched her cap the vial. "Where did you get those?"

"I made them for this purpose. I can dig here." She dropped to her knees and took out her bags, knife, and spoon. Mr. E kept his balance neatly.

"What are you doing?"

"I don't want to disrupt the appearance of the gardens, so I thought I would slice up the sod and peel it back before I dig out the soil."

"May I speed up the process?"

"As long as you keep the garden neat."

He extended his hand, shifted it to display large claws, and he sliced the grass in a one-foot cube that he carefully pried upward and set aside.

"There you go. Get spooning."

"Thanks for that." She took her spoon and the bags and collected a few pounds of soil. When she was done and the bags were sealed, she replaced the sod cut and tapped it down. It sank a bit but was otherwise fine.

As Imara stared, the soil filled up again and the turf fused into a pristine condition. "That was weird."

He chuckled. "Yes, it was. Shall we go?"

She nodded, and they followed the path they had taken through the gardens. When they stepped through the gate, it slammed shut behind them.

Imara jumped, and Argus turned slowly. "I am guessing our time was up."

She nodded. "That seems like a safe assumption. Well, thank you for the meal and the ride back."

He gave her a look. "I am escorting you back to your hall."

She wrinkled her nose. "Thank you. That is very thoughtful."

They walked back to his car, and she carefully kept the bags of soil on her lap.

"So, why do you need magical soil?"

"Herbology class. To make potions, you need herbs, and magical herbs make the potions more effective. Magical soil helps make magical herbs, and that increases the effect of the potions."

"Sensible. What exactly do those strips that you used do?"

"They detect magic. The stronger the magic, the more violent the reaction apparently." She got the vial out and used the tweezers to remove the strip. She put it on the dashboard, and nothing happened.

"Nothing is happening."

"Well, unless you enchanted this car, nothing would happen. However, if I touch it or you touch it, it would flare."

She carefully closed the container and attached the tweezer to the band.

The little piece of paper sat on the dashboard as he drove her back to Reegar Hall.

When they were parked again, she reached out and touched the strip with the tip of her finger.

"Damn! I should not have been watching that." She covered her eyes with her free hand. Sparks and shadowed rainbows were in her vision for several seconds.

"Have you tested your familiar?" Argus's voice was amused.

"No. I don't want to go blind." She muttered it, and Mr. E silently snickered.

She blinked and her vision stabilized. "Whew. That is better."

"Didn't you test it on yourself?"

"Nope. I know I am magical. I know you are magical. I sure as hell know that Mr. E isn't natural. That left your car."

He left the car and walked around to open her door for her. The first time it was weird; now, she just let him do it.

She gathered her bags, checked Mr. E, and swung her legs out of the vehicle before she realized she was still buckled. A bit of muttering and some fumbling later, she hopped to the ground and glanced at his grinning countenance. "You didn't see anything."

"Madam, I am an XIA agent, I am trained to see everything." He bowed, and they walked from the guest parking, across the quad, and over to Reegar Hall.

He was made of curiosity. "Where do you get the herbs that you plant?"

"I have already picked them from fields and public gardens around the college. They are at the hall, waiting for a proper receptacle."

"The building is very cold from the outside. Are you happy there?"

She chuckled. "I love it. There are only two of us there so far. I know that Reegar is being pressured to take more students on, so I am enjoying it while it lasts."

"Magus Reegar is a little strange. He doesn't smell like anything."

She chuckled. "That is because he isn't alive. He is a spectre."

"He was holding a book."

She blushed, "Yeah, remember when I told you that I turbocharged spectres? I can also make them solid with enough exposure."

"Can he wander freely?"

"No, he is tethered to his building, or within fifty feet of it, just like any spectre."

"Ah. He seemed so alive."

"He is living consciousness. He has the same hopes, dreams, and desires that he did when he was alive. His soul has probably been recycled already."

"Recycled . . . you mean reincarnated?"

"Same thing." She hugged the bags of dirt to her chest.

"So, there are two of him?"

"No. The soul has a body. Reegar's spectre is forever the same age with different experiences. He loves the same man he loved when alive and is lucky enough to have his lover be practically immortal."

"They have seen each other?"

"A few times. It is so sweet. With the internet, it is a whole new take on their relationship."

They approached the hall, and he walked her right to the door.

"Would you like to come in and discuss his afterlife with him?"

He chuckled. "No. I will see you in class tomorrow. Congratulations on your first shift, my friend."

He leaned in and kissed her cheek, turned, and walked away.

Her heart was pounding in her chest, and Mr. E was laughing uproariously in her mind.

She got into the building, went to her room, and dumped Mr. E on the bed. He lifted his hind leg and groomed his toes, looking at her with direct eye contact.

You are never going to make it three years.

She only needed two scoops of the soil, and the herbs stretched, flourished, and glowed.

"Damn. What am I going to do with the rest of this?"

Store it. That kind of power isn't something that you should waste.

"Right."

She got a canister and slipped the two closed bags of soil into it, marking it carefully with the words, *Enchanted dirt—do not touch.*

Why aren't you out with Bara tonight?

"I didn't want to. I wanted to get the planting done, just in case the soil didn't work."

You knew it would.

"I wasn't sure. I am never sure. Using luck to figure stuff out isn't reliable. Sometimes it leads me down a path that will benefit me in the long term but sucks in the short term."

So, you were worried about failing your herbology course?

"I am worried about turning myself into a large squid."

Ah. Well, you might need to see a therapist.

She grinned and picked him up, snuggling her face into

his fur. "Why get a therapist when I have you?"

He squirmed before settling and purring. *I despise being a slave to my baser urges. Scratch under my chin.*

She grinned and did as her familiar requested. With the lab tidied up, she headed up to her room for a well-earned rest. It had been a very full day.

Her dream of playing bongos turned into the sound of someone pounding on her door.

"Imara! Wake up!" A hand shook her shoulder.

She jerked awake, and her lights were on with Reegar staring at her with a frantic expression. "What? What's wrong?"

"Bara. Bara is the latest victim. She's downstairs."

"Shit." She got out of bed and jerked on her robe. Mr. E ran ahead of her as she stumbled down the steps.

Bara was sitting in the common space, tears running down her cheeks. Ivar and Lio were trying to question her while Argus was speaking with someone on the phone.

Imara stepped in, close enough to hear what Bara was saying but far enough to let the XIA agents do their jobs.

"I drank a soda, and then the world got blurry. I woke up, and I felt hollow." Bara wiped at her tears, her bandaged fingers moving with short jerks.

Imara wanted to do something, so she did. She rushed to the lab and pulled the ingredients for the reversion charm together. It was all she could think to do.

"Mr. E, can you grab one of Bara's bandages, preferably one that has touched a burst blister?"

I can burst it. Back in a minute.

In a handful of heartbeats, she heard a shout of confusion and a shriek of surprise.

Mr. E had done an excellent job. He brought three bandages in, and two of them were stained with white cells and blood.

She pressed the stained gauze into the paste she had prepared, and she poured magic into it, using as many time-bending chants as she could.

146

The mess in the bowl hardened into a scarlet jewel. She got some tongs and picked up the charm. "Stand back."

Mr. E stayed out of her way as she walked to the common room. Lio must have read her expression because he pulled Ivar away from Bara.

"Hold out your hands."

Bara sniffled and extended her hands, catching the charm in her palms.

"Repeat after me. Chrono-Key-Amber."

"Chrono-Key-Amber." Bara leaned forward, and the charm started to glow. "What is it doing?"

"It is resetting you by two hours. Your body will be like it was two hours ago. I don't know how long it will last, but you can repeat the call on the charm when it wears off, just don't drop the charm." Imara knelt in front of her, exhausted.

"How did you . . ." Bara trailed off and smiled, opening her hand and conjuring a ball of light.

"Shape-shifting reversion charm. I used your broken blister to reset you. It was all I could think of."

Mr. E brushed up against her and purred; she could feel him trying to support her with his tiny body.

Reegar was explaining what had taken place to the XIA agents, but Imara didn't care. She passed out where she was.

Chapter Eleven

Three worried faces were staring at her when she woke, and Mr. E was on her head.

"Hey, agents, why the worried faces?" She sat up, and Mr. E transferred to her lap.

Argus crouched next to her. "You fainted."

"I did not faint. I surrendered to exhaustion. There is a difference."

Bara was curled up in the chair, her chest moving evenly.

Reegar brought her a cup of tea. "Here you go."

"Thank you, Magus."

"That was inspired spell work. Where did you find the time charm?"

"Eberhart's Enchantments. It was theoretical. I am glad it seems to work."

Reegar walked toward the library and came back a few minutes later with the book in his hands. "Show me."

She set the teacup and saucer down and flipped rapidly through the pages until she got to the one she was looking for.

"Here it is." Imara handed the book back to him.

He took the book and frowned. "You should not have been able to do this."

"Why?"

"It is an immortality spell."

She looked over at Bara and then to the XIA agents who looked a little surprised. "Um, sorry?"

"Don't be sorry, but this shouldn't work."

"I guess I got lucky that it did." She smiled tightly and finished the tea.

"Yes, that would describe it. Bara is doing well. The charm you gave her is keeping her magic flowing, but we need to know who took it."

She looked to the XIA. "Can any of you track magic?" They shook their heads.

I can.

She looked at Mr. E. "Seriously?"

Of course. Would you like me to track Bara?

"Let me get dressed." She stood, and Argus moved to block her.

"Where do you think you are going?"

"Mr. E says he can track Bara's magic. He knows her well and knows me, so he won't be thrown by my scent in the spell."

"He can lead us."

"No, he can't. He is my familiar; he can only communicate with me." She glared into his metallic eyes. "Out of my way, buddy."

He stepped aside.

She ran back to her room, dropped her robe and pajamas and then pulled on her jeans and a t-shirt. Underwear wasn't necessary, she was on a mission in the middle of the night.

She yanked on her sneakers and headed downstairs. "Mr. E, lead the way."

Argus grabbed her arm. "You can come with, but let us go first."

"You can come with me. You won't be able to find Mr. E if he hits the shadows."

He paused, Lio nodded. "Right. Stay with at least one of us."

Mr. E yowled and pawed at the door.

"Agreed. Let's go." She nodded, and Ivar opened the door.

They sprinted after the tiny shadow as he sniffed out the magic trail.

Argus stayed next to her, and he muttered, "This is where she was found."

Mr. E circled the area several times and then yowled again. *I have it!*

The small bundle of fluff streaked off away from the shadowed space between buildings and ran into the open door of the house where the party had just been held.

Students were holed up in every corner of the rooms. Couples were making out, and some exhausted and disappointed singles were cleaning up with unsteady motions.

Mr. E was feeding her his senses, and he tuned out the smells of sweat, sex, and vomit. He was on the trail of magic.

They worked their way into the centre of the building where the ancient structure hosted a ballroom. The small bundle of fluff made a beeline toward the bar, and he crouched on the ground, growling with his tail lashing.

Lio and Ivar halted and waited for her to tell them what was going on.

She made eye contact with the woman behind the bar that was loaded with non-alcoholic drinks.

"It's her. She has Bara's magic."

As she spoke, the woman decided to act. She jumped over the bar and ran.

The agents were after the fleeing in a moment, and Imara collected Mr. E. "You did well, little buddy."

Thank you. She should not have messed with Bara. If the agents weren't here, I would have dealt with her.

"I am glad you didn't have to. Let's get back home." She cuddled him and made her way back through the detritus of the party and into the night air.

The path to Reegar Hall was longer than it had seemed on the way out. She walked past a few spectres and nodded to them politely. It was nice when they nodded back.

Watch out! There is—

She was hit hard in the side and knocked to the ground, sending Mr. E flying. The grass was crushed as she skidded to a halt and the scent of soil was in her nose.

She turned, and the bartender was standing above her, her chest heaving and fists clenched. "It was perfect, bitch. Everyone was looking at the men."

Imara tried to get to her feet, but the woman kicked her in the chest.

"The drink would have made this easier, but you have enough to keep me strong enough to start over."

Imara saw tendrils of darkness coming toward her and inhaled sharply just as a low growl came from her left. Acid green light flared, and a roar distracted Imara's attacker. Imara rolled rapidly to the side and got to her feet in time to see a giant panther tackle the woman and crush her throat in his jaws. The cat held her and shook her hard. The snap of her neck was horribly audible.

The cat let her go and turned to Imara, pacing toward her, his red eyes blazing and the green flames snapping around his silky black body. She leaned back, and he kept advancing, shifting into his kitten form and rubbing against her leg.

She whispered, "I didn't know you could do that."

I didn't either. None of my other forms had this option, but she was going to kill you, and my body transformed.

"I suppose that is a good thing."

You are alive. It is a very good thing.

The XIA agents appeared at the far end of the green space, running toward them intently.

She held tightly to Mr. E and watched Argus and the others as they slowed and walked carefully toward the body.

Argus asked, "What happened?"

"She knocked me down, kicked me and was going to do whatever she did to Bara, only without the sedation."

"What happened?"

She buried her fingers in Mr. E's fur. "My familiar stopped her."

Lio looked surprised. "Your kitten?"

"He's not a kitten. He's an energy projection with the soul of an ancient magus. He's registered if that is what you are worried about." She bit her lip.

Ivar was kneeling next to the body. "She's very dead. Her throat is crushed."

Argus frowned. "Go to the hall. We will be there when we have taken care of the body."

Lio nodded. "I will call it in."

She bobbed her head and walked briskly across the grass and toward Reegar Hall.

Magus Reegar met her at the door and ushered her inside.

He settled her on the couch in the common room, covered her shoulders in a blanket and got her another cup of tea.

You can let me go now.

She sighed and relaxed her grip. *I just wanted to hold you for a bit. I don't think I have ever been that scared.*

In that case, scratch my belly.

Imara sighed in relief and scratched his tummy. He curled in her arms, and she kept petting him while the vision of him killing her attacker rang in her mind.

"Bara's normal magic returned ten minutes ago. I took the charm from her and put it in the lab. She's gone to bed."

"Good. We found the culprit, and she's dead now."

"It was a woman?"

"It was. Black energy. I haven't seen anything like it." She thought about it. "I have seen a soul eater before, but its magic was more of a grey wisp."

"Black? Let me consult the library."

She looked at the stacks of books and got to her feet. "Maybe I can help."

"If it keeps you busy. You are in shock."

"Yeah, I would agree with that." She walked into the library and ran her hand over the ancient books on the shelves, letting her fingertips caress the spines.

She had made it through two-thirds of the books when her fingers tingled. "Got one."

"Ah, *Definitions of Power.* That is likely."

They took the book to the study table and opened it. She kept petting Mr. E as he purred and her blood pressure gradually reached normal levels.

The pages of the book turned one after another with a wide collection of information on power signatures and focuses. An illustration of black tendrils was suddenly front and centre.

"That's it."

Reegar looked at it and read aloud. "'Magus inversion. A mage who has suffered a severe psychic injury can begin to consume the magic of others in order to function normally.' It appears to be a nice word for psychic vampire."

A female voice spoke behind them. "There is no nice word for it."

Imara turned and saw the chancellor. "Magus Deepford-Smythe. I would say good evening, but it really isn't."

"No. I need to check your mind, Imara. I just have to confirm that you weren't the cause of the death. I need to see her last moments."

Imara nodded. "Go ahead."

Soft touches at her temples and she saw the evening on fast forward. When the replay was over, her mother slowly broke contact. "So, you were defended by your familiar. That is within the bounds of self-defense. I will report it to the guild, but they may still want to question you. It is fine. You didn't do anything wrong."

"Thanks. It is good to hear it."

Mr. E was still purring in her arms.

Her mother looked at her familiar and inclined her head. "Thank you for watching over my daughter."

Mr. E squirmed until he was sitting properly in Imara's arm, and he nodded his head formally.

Tell her that I accept her thanks and that you are worthy of protection.

"Uh, he says that he accepts your thanks." She smiled tightly.

Mr. E dug his claws into her arm.

"And that I am worthy of protection. Though he doesn't seem to think so right now." She flexed her arm and set him on the table.

Mirrin made a hesitant move toward her and then hugged her. "I am relieved you are all right."

"Thank you. Aside from it being your job, I am glad you are here. I needed a hug."

Reegar chuckled. "I would have offered it, but I have never been good at commiseration."

Mr. E licked his front foot and started washing his face. *I am an excellent soothing companion.*

Yes, you are, but there is nothing like a mother's hug.

He cleaned his fur, and her mother released her. Mirrin

smiled. "I will have Luken check on you this afternoon."

"That will be fine. I have an ethics class in the morning."

"Oh, Imara. Do you think you should? You have had a shock."

"My instructor is a douchebag, so I don't want to give him an excuse for a bad grade. I will go even if I take a nap during the lecture."

Argus came in and walked up to her, ignoring the chancellor. "Imara, are you all right?"

"I am fine, just a little shaken. Bara has regained her power, but I don't know what the situation with the others is."

Mirrin looked between them. "Have you met?"

Imara began blushing. "Ah, yes. We have. We share an ethics course and have gone to coffee and lunch a few times. He also coached me for my shifter class. We're friends."

Argus smirked as she babbled. "We have agreed to a delayed courtship."

Her mother's mouth opened and closed in surprise. "I see. I believe I am going to have to speak with your superiors to get a gauge of your character."

"Chancellor?" Argus was confused.

Imara decided to explain while Reegar was trying not to laugh. "She is my mother."

He stared at both of them in turn, and then, his lips quirked. "Well, that explains the similarities."

Imara sighed and picked up her familiar again. "I am a little tired, and the chancellor has confirmed my version of events so if you don't mind, I am heading to bed."

Argus inclined his head. "I will see you in class."

She smiled slightly and nodded.

Heading to her room seemed like the best thing for her to do. Hopefully, she wouldn't dream of panthers on fire.

Chapter Twelve

With the threat of the magic-sucker gone, the campus breathed a sigh of relief. Imara's name was kept out of the official reports, and no one on campus mentioned the familiar.

Life returned to the cycle of studying, tests, exams and spell work.

Tuesday lunches with Argus became a habit that they both enjoyed. The weeks flew by, and soon, there was only the exam left.

"So, one more class and I don't see you again?" She quirked her lips.

"You know that isn't true. I simply want to abide by your schedule, so let me know when you would like to go out for a meal or coffee, and if I am awake, I will be there."

She smirked. "Well, I do have time off between the terms. I will be starting again, but I have three weeks off after exams."

"So, after next week you have time off?"

"Yup, if the herbology exam doesn't turn me into something unfortunate."

"Are you worried?"

"Not really. After the way this term started, I have been practicing all of my magic skills and am confident that I can pass my courses."

He grinned. "I am confident as well. If I could read your handwriting, I would be tempted to cheat off your paper."

She laughed. "During the ethics test?"

"Yeah, it would be ironic."

She was still smiling a few minutes later, but it faded when she finally asked the question she needed to know. "Why did she do it?"

"Based on her journals, blog, and texts, she was assaulted the last term by someone at one of the frat houses. Her fury became the power that lashed out at others and women who were partying without drinking were tempting targets. She could dose them with what they thought was plain soda and simply corner them in the shadows."

"Did the others recover?"

"They are still recovering, but their magic is returning."

"That is a relief. One fatality was enough."

He nodded in agreement.

She twisted her lips. "So, since you have persistently bought my food, I thought I would get you something to re-mind you of me when you are back at work."

Argus leaned forward and raised his brows. "What is it?"

She reached into her bag and brought out a precisely wrapped box about two inches long and three inches wide.

"Here." She tucked her hands under the table.

"Shall I open it?"

"Please. It is just something small."

He took the box, and it looked tiny in his hand. He pulled back the neat bow and popped open the side to slide the box free. When he opened the box, Mr. E sat up on her shoulder.

The enamelled metal black cat with huge green eyes looked up at Argus with smiling lips.

He grinned. "Thank you."

Without another word, he attached the keychain to his keys.

"There, whenever you see him, you will think of me."

He chuckled. "You are pretty firmly entrenched in my thoughts."

"I hate to say that I am pleased about that. Have Lio and Ivar gotten over my age?"

He wrinkled his nose. "They are working on it."

"I will get older."

"I know, and I will be waiting. Your mother isn't pleased with our interaction."

She laughed. "She is just going to make sure that you aren't a serial killer. One of those attached to me is enough."

Mr. E let out a mew and purred.

"Well, you need to study for the exam, and I want to fly around the campus. I will see you tomorrow, Argus, and I will miss you when you leave the campus entirely."

"Then, let me take you back to your hall, and you can get on with your flight. See you tomorrow for the exam."

She nodded. "Yup. Let's go."

They got up from their table at the coffee shop, and Mr. E hopped onto her shoulder. It was amazing that he never got larger, but he was a projection of a kitten wrapped around a killer. It was best that he stayed the size that he was.

Their walk across campus was far slower than it needed to be, but she enjoyed it. The exams started the next day, and the rest of her week would be hell. This was the calm before the storm.

"Did you want to come in to do some cramming?" She quirked her lips as they approached the hall.

"No, I think I had better be on my way. I can't concentrate when you are around, my friend." Argus chuckled.

They used the words *my friend, buddy, dude, madam* to keep distance between them. It was working so far to remind them that nothing else could happen until she had graduated. They were holding tight to it.

When he left her at her door, she went in to face a pile of books; Bara's loom in the study area was clicking away as she laughed with Reegar. Imara watched them for a moment before she joined in and settled at the study table with the hum of her companions around her. She had an exam in the morning, and she wanted to knock it out of the park.

The Magical Ethics exam had been gruelling. For the first time, Imara begged off going out with Argus, and she crept home for some rest.

She could see him again after she ran the gauntlet of exams. Two more and she would be ready for a well-deserved rest.

Bara and Reegar made her a tremendous breakfast on the

day of her herbology exam. If she was going to have to drink her own potion, they didn't want it to happen on an empty stomach.

With her purse and familiar, she headed out to the exam lab, collected her pot of herbs from its secure locker, and she carried it to her workspace.

The proctors were watching the students, and four of them came over when she put her pot down on the table.

Her instructor checked the content of the pots using potions to test the magical transmission of the herbs.

Imara stood with her plants and watch the other students' offering be tested one by one. Only one student had zero magical effect in their herbs, the rest had sparks and crackling energy released by the testing potion.

When the magus stood in front of Imara, she wiped her palms on her thighs.

"What are those?"

She cleared her throat. "They appear to be apples on a rosemary bush."

"I see. And these?"

"Basil."

"No, the small objects."

She leaned forward and looked at the soft green leaves hiding the small curving items. "Bananas?"

"I see." He beckoned to one of the proctors, and a large vessel was wheeled over. The magus pulled off one of the apples with a pair of tongs and set it on the bottom of the vessel, clamped the lid on and poured the detection potion into the top.

Imara covered her eyes as a fountain of light poured out of the miniscule hole in the lid. It continued for several minutes and formed tumbles of pastel mists on the ceiling.

The instructor looked at her and nodded, "So, that is one hundred percent. May I know where you got the soil?"

"It was on campus, and there is a paper trail for my permissions." She looked at the avid students on her left and right.

"Of course. We will discuss it later."

He moved on and continued testing until the remainder of the students demonstrated their horticultural leanings.

When the exam was over, she scooped up her pot and watched Mr. E playing with the leaves.

"Ms. Mirrin?"

"Yes, Magus?"

"May I keep your exam project?"

She blinked. "I don't think that would be appropriate, but you can take an apple and a banana."

He smiled brightly and nodded. "Thank you. That is a lot of energy."

"Yeah. I lucked into a hint, and it paid off."

"I will be in contact with you for the location."

"That would be fine. It would be best if you could come to the hall. That way I can be assured of privacy."

"Of course. Excellent. I will be in touch. This is a phenomenal result."

He got his samples, and she got her mark. With a swing in her step, she only had to face the final exam. Domestic Magic.

She faced the room and tried to figure out if she had missed anything. She had unclogged a drain, removed a spilled potion and its effects from a carpet, pulled a cursed object out from under a settee using a rubber glove, and cleared crumbs out of a cupboard with a compression spell.

The timer chimed, and she had to stand while the instructor investigated the chamber.

"You missed the window, but you got the cursed idol under the settee without activating it, so you have passed, Ms. Mirrin. Excellent job."

Imara sighed in relief.

"Thank you, am I free to go?"

"Yes, yes. I have to reset this for the next student."

She was waved off and left the testing chamber that she had been assigned. There were five chambers active, and all had staggered start times. She was glad it was over and done with.

Imara was exhausted. Her focus for the term was over, and she had a few weeks of blank thought ahead of her. Good, bad, or ugly, she was done.

Reegar Hall had never looked so welcome. She walked in and headed for the common space only to shriek in shock.

"Surprise!" Bara and Reegar were flanked by Luken, Lio, Ivar, and Argus. Near the cake, Mirrin was standing with a present.

"I can't believe you did this again."

Reegar chuckled. "You are only here for another year and a bit, so I am making the most of it. Small parties are the best ones."

She chuckled and hugged her way through her friends and family. Argus held on just a bit longer than was appropriate, but she didn't comment.

The cake excited Mr. E. A black kitten sitting on a spell book took front and centre. *I have never been depicted in sugar before. I am perversely honoured.*

Imara chuckled, cut the cake, and the party got into full swing.

The XIA agents were interrogating Luken, trying to find out why he hadn't been a proper big brother to her. When he finally admitted—loudly—that Imara was his elder, Reegar turned and stared at her.

She shrugged weakly and smiled. "I am usually in a hurry to get my way."

Argus grinned. "I will remember that."

For some reason, she blushed.

Mr. E had badgered her into protecting his image on the cake, and he was guarding it like it was his baby.

Liirick arrived around sunset, and he brought takeout. The party continued into the evening, and after hours of trying, Imara got away from the crowd and headed up to the roof.

She was unsurprised when Argus joined her after a few minutes, but she didn't mind.

"So, no familiar?"

"He is playing with his new icing friend."

Argus sighed and walked up to her, wrapping his arms around her from behind and staring out over the college with her.

"You are a force of nature, Imara."

"Nope. I just have a focus. My life has been filled with an absence of hope, so I made it for myself. I am content with it."

"I am in awe."

"You are not. You are unsure because you haven't run into many women with this mindset."

He hugged her. "That too, but I am still impressed. I know where you came from, so to have your success is astonishing. I know you don't use magic to achieve it and that makes it all the more amazing."

"Well, I do use magic in the classes. That is what this college is about. I can't advertise myself as a spectral consulting magus if I am not a magus. I have to be registered with the guild, and that takes credentials."

"See? You have a plan to make something from nothing. You take my breath away."

He lowered his head to her neck for a kiss, and she smacked his forehead. "No shenanigans. Two more years."

He sighed. "Right. Two more years. You are just so sweet, lovely, intelligent, and powerful, I want to be with you at all times."

"Trust me, you are always in my thoughts, but I have my goals, and I will achieve them. When that is done, I can open my social options to include a partner." She patted his arm.

"As long as it is me, I can wait."

She grinned and watched the moon rising and the stars coming out. Argus kept her warm and simply held her as the sky performed just for them. The moment took her breath away.

Not all enchantments were magic.

Sky Breaking 301
The Hellkitten Chronicles Book 3

VIOLA GRACE

Sky Breaking
301

THE HELLKITTEN CHRONICLES

Her magic is coming along, her kitten is still deadly, and she is about to make an actual friend. Controlling weather is simple by comparison.

Sky Breaking seemed like a useful course, but its usefulness lay in the amount of credits that would count toward Imara's degree.

Once she is in the course, she meets the only other student, and they strike an unlikely friendship. Kitigan is a seer who has an interest in farming and apiculture, weather magic is part of that peculiar parcel.

After a series of classes that turn into tests, Imara is happy to head to Kitty's farm for a weekend away from school, and Mr. E wants to head out and ride some sheep. Everybody has something to do, including the trespassing werewolf pack that just moved in next to Kitty's family farm.

Imara has to walk the fine line between guest and defender while taking her Death Keeper skills for a spin. Her weekend is anything but relaxing.

Chapter One

Imara was curled up on the couch, doing some advanced reading for her next round of courses when Reegar wandered by. "So, your familiar is taking up hobbies?"

She blinked and stared at the spectre. "Yeah, he said he wanted to do something with his spare time. Why?"

"I had to help him with the welding tank. His paws couldn't turn the—"

She was up and out of her chair, heading down the hall with all the speed she could muster. When she got to the lab, she grabbed the frame and whipped around the corner.

She took in Mr. E in his safety gear and the objects he was welding together. It seemed better to wait until his foot was off the pedal that was controlling the gas before she spoke with him. "Mr. E, what are you doing?"

He was in prairie dog position, and as she asked, he pushed his goggles up to look at her with his adorable kittenish eyes. *I admired blacksmiths while I was a child, now that you have indicated I could entertain myself while you were studying, I decided to take up the hobby. It is more difficult with fur and my paws, but Reegar is helpful if bizarrely amused.*

Imara pinched the bridge of her nose. "I think he is wondering where you got the goggles."

Mr. E lashed his tail. *Bara obtained it for me, once Reegar explained what I needed.*

"Ah. Well, what are you making?"

He moved his small black body between her and his project. *I am just experimenting right now. I will let you know when I have something worth observing.*

"So, you want me to go?"

Please. You may call upon me if you need me, but I

believe you are doing fine with your studies.

"So, you are telling me to bug off."

I would never do that, my dear mage-in-training. But I enjoy the thought of making something with my own paws and minimal magic.

"If you get sparked, let me know. I will come running."

He let out a small purr, and his chin lifted. *Thank you. Enjoy your studies.*

She inclined her head and backed out the door, waiting until she heard him start up again before she snuck her phone around the corner and took a picture of her kitten with a blowtorch.

Chuckling, she glanced at the image for the next two hours while she went over the basics of weather manipulation.

Imara was sitting and studying when Bara burst in, "Imara, turn on the TV. Argus is on the news."

Imara closed her book and sat up, grabbing the remote and turning on the television. Bara grabbed the remote and flicked to a local station.

"Where are they?" Imara was watching footage from the previous night.

"There was a riot around Ritual Space. They have started to restrict bookings, and some wizard groups are complaining." Bara sat next to her on the couch.

They watched the XIA team round up the wizards who were disturbingly naked. Imara tried not to look, but the festively decorated bodies were hypnotic.

Bara snorted. "They were one of those *male magic is stronger* groups. I guess they pissed off the proprietor."

Imara wrinkled her nose as the Mage Guild bus pulled up and the men were handed off to those who would be able to deal with them. Epithets were fired from the arrested men to the non-humans that had cuffed them, but Argus and his team kept their cool in front of the camera.

The reporter tried to get them to speak, but the door to the space opened, and they excused themselves as the guild vehicle hauled the idiots off for processing.

The reporter smiled tightly and signed off.

Bara snickered and turned the television off. "Just thought you would like to at least see him this week. You two sure have an odd relationship."

Imara sighed and drummed her fingers on her book. "We are doing just fine. I am on a fast track through school, and he is dealing with whatever happens on his shifts. We connect when we can."

"From what I can see, you two don't *connect* at all." Bara looked idly down at her fingernails.

"None of your business, but I am a little young for him, according to him. I also have a business plan that we both want to see put into action. There is plenty of time for connections after that."

Bara sighed and leaned against the back of the couch. "You are so serious."

"That is my lot in life. On the other side, I am smarter than heck, have a few good friends, and a weirdly determined familiar, so I am feeling pretty good about myself." Imara opened her book and found her page. The smug smirk on her lips probably didn't become her, but she was enjoying the feeling of security that her surroundings were giving her.

A thought occurred to her. "By the way, how did Mr. E ask you for the goggles?"

Bara chuckled. "Reegar translated for him. Is he really using them?"

"Yeah. I think a welding shield would be better. He has a lot of fluff."

"Noted. I will keep an eye out. I am really enjoying the textile studies." Bara sighed happily.

Imara went back to her book, and Bara interrupted her again.

"Why are you studying across the board?"

Imara looked up and cocked her head. "How long have you wanted to ask?"

"Since last term."

Snickering, Imara tapped the book in her lap. "For what I

want to do, a business course is basically what I need, but to get my certification and guild membership, I need my degree. Learning what I can about other aspects of magic and its application can only help me in the long run."

"So, you still want to be an investigator?"

Imara corrected her. "A spectral consultant. Outside of the Death Keepers, the spectres don't talk to anyone. They can't."

"So, since you are a registered Death Keeper . . ."

"Technically an apprentice, but I am part of the guild."

"So, you can go right from graduation to consultant with a degree to propel you into full Mage Guild status."

"That is the plan. In the meantime, I am taking advantage of the largest collection of instructors and specialists on the continent. I have half the business classes already taken care of and am looking forward to whisking through the next three terms."

Bara gave her a long look. "Aren't you even tempted to delay just to experience college life?"

Imara shook her head. "Nope. I have been around enough partiers in my life to know that it might be interesting, but it leaves more regret than most folks want to admit. I would rather barrel through and save the regretful social situations for after I graduate."

"Are you planning on having any?"

Grinning, Imara turned back to her book. "I have every confidence in my ability to get into trouble, with or without my familiar."

"I have to say, I am glad to hear it. You are way too put together for someone your age. You make me look bad."

Imara found the spot where she had been reading about the effect of magic on thermal currents. "I don't. I just focus on my future. I have been planning it since I was four, so it is nice that I am finally here and my little self didn't know what a kegger was, so it wasn't in the plan."

Bara snorted and left her alone.

Imara got through two chapters before she felt a tingle and smelled scorched hair. She got up and had her glass in her hand the moment that Mr. E barrelled around the corner, the top of his head on fire.

She dumped the ice water on the flames and picked him up, removing his goggles and heading for the kitchen. A light tingle of magic ran through their connection, and she watched as the discoloured skin at the top of his head heal and then sprout fluffy fur.

He sighed and relaxed in her grip. *I didn't think I would catch fire.*

"That was silly of you. I am sorry, but you were designed to be a kitten, and kittens need to eat, sleep, and they are flammable."

He mumbled something about stupid mages and cuddled into her arms. *My head is still wet.*

Imara sat and rubbed the growing fur slowly with a kitchen towel.

The spectre of Magus Reegar materialized in the kitchen. "Was he on fire? There is a trail of singed hair from the lab to the entertainment room."

She smiled as Mr. E gave Reegar a narrow-eyed look. "He was. I don't know if he is finished with his project."

Reegar nodded. "I will turn off the equipment."

He disappeared, and Imara continued to soothe her grumpy familiar.

In his previous life, he may have been a homicidal mage on a mission, but now, he was her kitten, and he needed attention. She scratched under his chin, and his little body started a heavy purr. Yeah, he was a terrifying monster. She was lucky to have him.

Don't forget it. He gave a delicate yawn. *How are the weather magic studies coming?*

"They are fine. I think I am grasping the thermal drifts and how to use nature to magnify the effects."

Good. Prepare to be quizzed.

"What?"

In a volcanic habitat, how do you generate snow?

She blinked, and he made a mental ticking clock noise. Apparently, class was starting a few days early.

"You begin by locating a water source, and then, you check the temperature of the magma . . ." She continued to pet him as she worked her way through the options of the techniques she had just learned. It wasn't going to be the right answer, but it was an answer. That was a start.

Class was in session, and the professor was almost over his ouchie.

Chapter Two

Your suitor is definitely worthy of your attentions. The smug voice was laced with satisfaction from his position on his new perch.

Imara smiled and kept hiking. "I am glad you are enjoying it. I still have no idea what to get him for his birthday, whenever it is."

The new backpack was wide, sturdy, and had a shelf built into the top for Mr. E to park his fuzzy butt. She was his Sherpa through the campus, and he was enjoying the ride.

The summer session was in full swing, and the campus was nearly empty. Only the die-hard students were still attending. Half the faculty was on vacation.

The field she was walking through had a single pathway in it, and it was enough of a hint that she was in the right place that she didn't panic. The building that she was looking for had to be around here somewhere.

It is underground. Look for a large stone slab and stand on it for one minute. It will take you down. Mr. E seemed to have worn off his dizzy fun, and he was now taking her finding her course location seriously.

"How do you know that?"

I asked Reegar. He is a fountain of information. He shared a similar worldview to mine and is delighted to have me under his roof. I am one of his heroes.

"Oh, man. That isn't good."

I beg to differ. Despite my sentence, I had no idea that I had an underground cult following. It is heartening to hear that folks don't go for demonic intervention anymore.

"I don't think it was a trend that could have remained for any length of time."

It had begun to take on a cataclysmic pace. It had to be stopped, so I stopped it.

171

She wrinkled her nose. "And the guild obviously didn't disagree with your actions, or they would have sentenced you to death and not familial repayment."

Death would have been quick; this is an eternity of servitude. It is much worse.

"Thanks for that." She spotted the stone panel that he had described.

Imara, you are the bright spot in an otherwise tedious existence, even if your choice of forms for me could have been slightly more masculine.

She grinned and stepped in the centre of the circular pad. A click was audible, and the pad she stood on slowly lowered into the earth.

Weather control was about to begin.

"You won't need your familiar. It can wait here." The woman who spoke was distinctively green.

Imara set her backpack down, got out Mr. E's food and water and turned back to her instructor. "There, he is all set."

The dryad nodded. "Good. Now, the other student is this way. You will be working as a team."

"Other student? I thought there would be more."

"This is an advanced class, Ms. Mirrin. Few could make it through the selection process."

The structure they were in was stone. The walls, floors, and archways that led into other parts of the underground warren were all stone.

"Am I late?"

"No, you are on time. I believe the other student forgot to set her clock, but the Deegles have always been funny about time."

"Do I need my books?"

"No. You can read the theory after the lessons. It will give you more reference points then, and you won't overthink it."

Imara blushed. She had read all the texts twice. Her brain was whirling with situations and adjustments. She just had to try to tamp down those impulses when it came time to actually working with magic.

They walked down a hall, and a huge amphitheatre waited for them. There was one small figure sitting in the first row with glints of light coming from her hands when she moved. She moved a lot.

The dryad nodded to the other woman. "Introduce yourselves. I will set up the first lab."

Imara walked up to the other student and sat next to her. "Hiya. I am Imara, and it looks like we are it in this class."

The woman looked at her and nodded, her clothing dotted by orbs dangling from nearly every available surface. The woman smiled and extended her hand, covered in rings with small orbs on them. "I am Kitigan, but most folks call me Kitty."

Imara shook her hand in greeting and enjoyed the amused twinkle in the other young woman's eyes. "Pleased to meet you."

"You as well. I have heard interesting things about you." She quirked her lips.

"Nothing bad."

"Nope. I took a course on bookkeeping with one of your brother's last term. During a study group, he mentioned that you had joined the school."

Their instructor finished organizing herself and tapped her lectern. "Okay, ladies. Pleasantries are over. I am Weather Witch Annamaria Eckoak. You may address me as Eckoak. Yes, I am a dryad, but my father was a weather wizard, and it is a family skill. I am here to try and transfer natural talent into deliberate action. Sky breaking is a difficult skill to learn."

Kitty cleared her throat. "Sky breaking?"

Eckoak inclined her head and raised her hand. As she spoke, a cloud formed ten inches over her palm. "You are taking air, wind, water, heat, radiation, and anything else in the vicinity and inserting it into the existing weather pattern to assert your will. You are breaking the pattern and making another. You have to see where it is going and where it will end. The most important thing is to contain it. Now, I want each of you to come up here and try to replicate this particular effect. I want to see a storm in your palms."

Imara blinked. "What?"

"Storm in your hands, ladies. Now. Come here and give it a try." Eckoak gave them a slight and encouraging smile.

Imara walked to face her instructor with a dazed feeling. Her mind ran through all of the information she had absorbed over the last few days, and she held out her hands as Kitty joined her in front of the lectern.

She focused on finding water, but the air around her was dry. Deliberately, she didn't look at either of her companions as she spit into her palm to start things off.

Imara inhaled, exhaled, using her body as a heat source and her breath for wind. The tiny cloud began to form, and it flickered for a moment before dissipating and leaving her shaking and exhausted.

She dropped her hands to her sides and watched as Kitty cupped her hands together and blew softly. A tiny tornado formed, shooting upward before Kitty let it lose steam.

Eckoak looked up and made a *tsk* sound. "Sloppy but encouraging. Let me just grab that wind before it gets hostile."

Imara looked up, and against the stone ceiling was her little white puff of cloud colliding with the tiny tornado. Together, the systems connected and danced until they started to grow.

Their instructor extended her hands and beckoned. The weather system coiled downward until it rested in her palms. When she closed her fists, the issue was contained.

Imara blinked. "Wow. I thought I had let my weather system go."

Kitty nodded, sweat on her brow. "I thought so, too."

"You did, but moving air never stops." Eckoak continued to compact her hands together until they were flat. "That is why we are learning underground. Down here, it can be contained, but out there, you could kill someone."

Kitty swayed, and Imara reached out to hold onto her. "Easy." If she was honest, she needed contact for support as well.

174

Eckoak's lips quirked slightly, the first true amusement she had shown. "Now, what did you do wrong, aside from enrolling in this course?"

Apparently, the class had begun, and Imara had faltered at the first test. It was not a great start.

Eckoak watched the two exhausted mages stumbling back toward the entrance after four hours of focus and concentration. Her smile bloomed the moment that they were out of sight.

She closed up the auditorium and took the administration exit to the chancellor's home. She walked up the path and knocked on the door. When her friend opened it, Eckoak smiled. "Tea. Now."

"It's ready. I even included sandwiches." Mirrin winked.

Eckoak followed her college friend into the sitting room, and she smiled in delight at the spread that Mirrin had created for her. "This won't get her a better grade."

Mirrin chuckled and settled in her seat, pouring tea for both of them. "She gets what she earns, Koki."

Eckoak smirked. "She will do fine. She is a reader, isn't she?"

"I have heard reports that she might be making her way through Reegar's library."

"That would explain it. She made a pocket cloud on her first day."

Mirrin's hand shook when she handed over the cup and saucer. "She did?"

"Yes. She has focus and drive. Imagine what she could have done if she had been trained since childhood. It boggles the imagination."

Mirrin frowned. "She had a good education. My family saw to that."

"And yet, she was raised in a non-magical city barely touched by the Wave. It was sheer luck that she was offered the position of Death Keeper."

The chancellor shook her head. "It wasn't luck. My aunt is a Death Keeper, as are two of my siblings. They knew who they were taking on board."

"Well, well, well. Here I thought that you always played by the rules." Koki bit into the first sandwich. The thinly sliced salmon melted in her mouth.

"I did. None of us were in contact with her. My family simply looked out for its own and mentioned her aptitude to the right people at the proper time." The smile was that of the proud mother.

Koki sat back and sighed. "Well, she does have aptitude. Having read all of her files, she can do just about anything, so why is she trying to speed through college?"

"She has a plan, and she has a focus. If she wants to return to education later, I am all for it, but for now, she knows where she needs to be."

"How can you be sure? She's so young." Koki nibbled her way through another sandwich.

"She has nearly two decades of focus behind her. Personally, I think she came out of me knowing where she would end up. She had a career plan even then."

Koki laughed. "Did you regret being separated from her?"

"Every moment for the last two decades. I have kept my eye on her as best I could through family and guild connections, but the moment she got here, I nearly burst out of my skin." Mirrin grinned, "Reegar was a little put out at the beginning, but now, I think he actually looks on her as a niece of some sort."

"And now, you have roped me into the education of your offspring." Koki frowned.

"Hey, I made you tea, and those teeny sandwiches with the crusts cut off. You know how painful domestic stuff is for me."

"I accept that. The other student looks to be a good social match for her as well."

Mirrin held her hand up in surrender. "That was none of my doing. The Deegle girl is smart, and she has a lot of skills, but I have no idea what her personality is like. If she made it into the course and past your vetting, I am sure she is a worthy student."

"She is. If she and your daughter were one student, they would be exceptional. As it is, the two will manage to produce a decent storm by the end of the term, together or individually." The dryad watched her friend battle with pride and concern.

The seven sons that had applied to the weather magic course had yielded only two that she accepted. The daughter was almost made of different stuff. Imara was bright, cheerful, and determined. It was a change from the sullen entitlement of her brothers. Well, all of the brothers but the youngest, but he wasn't suited to weather work. There was too much fire in that boy.

"I have your room set up." Mirrin smiled as she refilled Koki's tea.

"So, the backyard, a tree, and the potting shed?"

"Yup."

Koki laughed and toasted her with the teacup. "Excellent. You are a sublime hostess for those in touch with the soil."

"Thank you. I do try. Do you think that Imara would mind me watching her lesson?"

Koki blinked. "I think she wouldn't even notice you were there. She has a brain for weather; she just needs to tune the rest of the world out. It will be difficult for her. She is desperate to move with the world around her."

"My fault. She needed more socialization. More friends."

"As you said, she made her choices. She is learning to live with them."

Mirrin looked out the front window and pursed her lips. "I want to help."

"Which shows that you are still her mother even if you couldn't raise her. Now, get over that and hand me another sandwich. If I have to teach your precious child tomorrow, I need some more sustenance." Koki smirked and watched as Mirrin went back to the kitchen for more food.

It took a lot to distract the chancellor, but Koki hoped that a small break from worry would be enough for her.

Imara needed more focus, and Mirrin needed less. Yeah, they definitely were related.

Chapter Three

The moment that Eckoak dismissed them, Imara retreated down the hall. Kitty walked in the same staggering steps that Imara figured she was using.

When they got to the entry vestibule, Imara collected Mr. E from the top of her backpack. He had slept the whole morning through.

"What are you doing next?" Kitty waited while Imara grabbed her stuff.

"I think lunch is in order. How about you?"

"The same. Did you want to go together?"

Imara blinked in surprise. "Sure. There is a nice diner a few blocks from here if you like."

Kitty beamed. "Great. I'll head up first and wait for you."

Imara chuckled and nodded, settling her familiar in the crook of her arm and her pack on her back.

Kitty headed up on the circular flagstone, and it returned to take Imara up in moments.

Out in the sudden warmth of the summer day, Imara swayed. Mr. E woke up with a yawn and a stretch.

You smell of sweat. It appears you got quite the workout.

"I did. Now, shush and get back on the pack."

He stretched and climbed her arm, settling in his little spot and curling up tight.

"You have a familiar?" Kitty was staring.

"I do. Apparently, he is an inherited familiar. Bloodlines and all that." She shrugged. "I honestly have no idea. I needed a familiar for one of my classes, and he is what I ended up with. His name is Mr. E."

Kitty laughed. "Such a formal name for a kitten. Why is he glaring at me?"

"He takes offense easily, but he is working on developing

178

hobbies, so I have hope for his personal growth." Imara could feel his indignation in their connection. She reached over her shoulder and scratched his chin. The small, rumbling purr started immediately.

"I have a bunch of questions for you."

Imara nodded. "I have one or two for you as well, but we can talk over lunch. I am starving."

They started the walk to the diner, and Kitty chuckled. "If it is about the balls, they are a family magic."

"How does that work?"

"It is a little embarrassing, but I can see through time but only as long as the orb will let me. Once I use one, it is burned out until I can reset or replace it."

"So, you are covered with them . . ."

"So, if I need to, I can check my future five seconds at a time."

"Is that handy?"

Kitty wrinkled her nose. "Not particularly."

They laughed at complicated family magic and made their way to the diner.

As she looked at the menu, Imara asked, *Mr. E, did you want anything?*

He was seated next to her, still on the top of the backpack. He looked over her shoulder, and his tail started lashing. *I would like a banana cream pie.*

Slice?

No, the pie.

This I have got to see.

You are going to. Order me some napkins as well. This is going to get messy.

Imara wasn't sure, but she thought that Mr. E was rubbing his paws together.

She exhaled and looked at her own selection. Cheeseburger with bacon and fries. Yup. She was playing to the old standards, but as a back-to-school food, it couldn't be beaten.

Kitty was biting her lip and glancing at Imara. "Do you know what you are ordering?"

"I do. You?"

"I can't decide. You go first."

When the server arrived, she cooed over Mr. E, who preened himself and let out a small *mew*.

Imara rolled her eyes and ordered. "Cheeseburger with bacon, fries, side salad, and a banana cream pie."

The server blinked. "A slice?"

"No, the whole pie, please. My familiar is a glutton."

Mr. E washed his little paw daintily in preparation for his food orgy.

Kitty cleared her throat and ordered a hamburger with a side of potato salad.

When the server was gone, Kitty gave Imara a thankful look. "I was terrified you would be a vegetarian."

Imara was flabbergasted. "Why?"

"I don't know. A lot of the women I have met here have been vegetarians, and I thought you might be one of them."

"I like how you describe them as a different species."

Kitty grinned, "They feel like that sometimes. My sister went veggie for a while. She was intolerable. My mom almost strangled her when she tried to liberate the livestock."

"Livestock?"

Her new companion blushed. "Yeah, I am from a farming family."

"What kind of animals?"

"You are genuinely interested?"

That was surprising. "Of course. I am new to this entire setting. I have been working to get through school my whole life, and it leaves very little exposure to other family styles or environments."

"Dairy and wool. Cows and sheep. Normally, they don't get along, but Mom's family were dairy farmers, and Dad's were shepherds. They consolidated, and now, we have a few hundred acres of useful animals."

"Which part of your family uses the orbs?"

Kitty leaned back as the server brought their drinks. "My dad's. He is also a glassmaker, and he makes the spheres for me."

"Not for himself?"

She rolled her eyes. "No. Since I was going away to school, he wanted me prepared to see my future at any interval. With the stuff I am wearing, I could probably get through a few months if I had to."

"Why so many?" Imara sipped at her water.

"Dads." Kitty shrugged as if Imara should understand.

She should understand, but there was no way she ever would. It was her father that had rejected her as a member of his brood, and it wasn't something that she could just give to the universe. Forgive and forget was difficult when she hadn't even been able to meet most of her relatives.

"Before you ask, I don't use them to cheat on exams."

Imara laughed. "I never thought you would. The instructors know about it, and most of the exams are practical. There is no advantage to knowing the future when you are just going to have to go through with it anyway."

Kitty looked at her with a stunned smile on her lips. "Exactly."

The food arrived, and when the pie was set on the table, Mr. E jumped right in. The cute noises he was making did not deter from the orgy of consumption he was engaged in.

Imara put some more ketchup on her burger and on her fries, picked up her food, and dug in. She had seen his cute feeding frenzy before.

Kitty grabbed her burger and dug in. They ate in silence as the tiny cat stomped and munched his way through pie.

A few people stopped by their table and took recordings of Mr. E wearing the pie before he ate it, but when Imara was done, Mr. E finished and worked at cleaning himself completely.

Kitty was halfway through her potato salad when Imara began to help Mr. E clean himself up.

"He ate all of it?"

"He did, but he hates getting wet, so I am going to dry towel him, and he can finish his grooming after that."

"How could it fit?" Kitty seemed genuinely astonished.

"Um, he isn't an actual kitten. He is an energy being in a kitten shell. He can eat as much as he wants." Imara finished wiping the cream off his paws, and he settled back against the sugar dispenser to suck his toes clean.

"But . . . he looks like a kitten."

"Yes, and he is supposed to, but he isn't. He is much more intelligent and devious than your average kitten. Also, slightly more homicidal."

Mr. E yawned and blinked at Kitty with wide green eyes. He was really putting on the cute.

"I don't think he is dangerous."

Imara remembered the sight of him transforming and attacking her enemy. "Yeah, you can think that, but wait until you have a snack that he wants."

Kitty chuckled and continued to eat.

Sitting back, Imara asked, "Why are you taking the weather magic course?"

"Farming folk. If I can create a separate weather system over the fields for just a day or even a few hours, it would make all the difference. You?"

"It is three credits toward my graduation and one of the only courses running over the summer term that I qualify for. I also thought it would look good toward guild membership."

Kitty nodded. "Makes sense. Have you tried to add a few community factors? I mean, if you are going for rapid guild membership, volunteering is an excellent way to get a leg up."

"Volunteering? Where?"

"The student office should have some information for you, but I volunteer to take the Mage Guides around the farm and introduce them to the animals."

"Are you a Guide?" In her circles, the thought of having a childhood organization that would assist with magical development was nearly mythical.

"I was. Now, I just volunteer. You never joined?"

Imara wrinkled her nose. "I was in a non-magical city. No Guides. We knew about them, but we didn't have them."

"Do you have a skill that you could teach eager little girls? If you do, I can help you get in touch with a local chapter." Imara's growing hope fell. "Nope, nothing special."

Mr. E loudly rattled the sugar container. *Death Keeping is not common. I think they would enjoy meeting spectres.*

Did you have the Mage Guides and Scouts when you were young?

No, but we did have schools that scouted for children with magical skills. They were brought in whether their families were in favour of it or not. He was being a very grim kitten.

Kitty pushed her empty plate aside. "You are talking to him?"

"I was. He reminded me that I am an apprentice Death Keeper. I could take the girls on a tour of the mage repositories if there are any around here."

"A Death Keeper? Seriously? Oh, man. None of the ones in this area have been willing to talk to the Guides. They say that young girls don't respect the seriousness of the situation."

Imara snorted. "Of course, they don't, but once they meet one of their ancestors, they usually smarten up."

Kitty was stunned. "You can do that?"

A blush started on her cheeks. "Oh, yeah. I have an affinity for death. I can have a conversation with most mages after they have passed. I mean, if they were properly laid to rest and their spectre released."

Kitty rubbed her hands together and grinned. "You are going to be very popular."

"I believe I am regretting mentioning it." Her palms were sweating.

"Don't worry. If you can get access, I can get you a volunteering credit." There was complete confidence in her tone.

"I will believe it when I see it. Now, how did you manage to make that tornado today?" Her change of topic wasn't subtle, but it was effective. They delved into the different techniques that they had used, and each learned a little something from the other. If it weren't for Mr. E snoring like a lumberjack, it would have been a really good study session. Laughter tended to break the flow of thought.

Chapter Four

"You want to what?" The voice on the other end of the line was shocked.

"I want to bring a group of Mage Guides to the repository after sundown so that they can speak with an actual spectre. It is an important step in their joining the magical community and not something that can be offered by someone who is not a Death Keeper."

"There is no availability for a staff member to take them on a *tour* of the dead."

"There doesn't have to be. I am a Death Keeper Guild member, and I can keep less than a dozen girls from running amok in a graveyard." She crossed her fingers.

"Give me your credentials, and I will get back to you if we have an evening available if I believe you can manage the visit. Don't hold your breath."

"Right. Apprentice Imara Mirrin of Sakenta. My number is—"

"I have it. Have a pleasant evening."

She winced as the click sounded in her ear, but it was hopeful. Thomins would give her a good reference, she was sure of it. She just needed to live up to her promise to keep control of the Guides. From what the Guide Master had said, they would be a handful.

He was rude. Mr. E was sitting on her desk and supervising her studies. He had jostled her into making the call, and now, he had the nerve to make a critique.

"He was a Death Keeper. They rarely work with the living. He will call back. Thomins said I was a natural and he would miss me when I left."

Did he want to sleep with you?

"Uh, no. When I started there, I was still a child. If he did, he would be a pervert, and I never got that vibe from him."

Hmph. Well, I still think that the idiot on the phone was ru—

The phone rang, the cheerful tune belted out of the slick rectangle, and after checking the number, Imara answered it.

"Hello?"

"Apprentice Mirrin, I apologize. Of course, we would be happy to have your group of *girls* come for a visit. Will you be waking the spectres?"

Imara grinned. "Yes. If you have any of their families or custodians who wish a consultation, I will bring a little more stability to some of the ones who are fading."

"Excellent! Yes, I will. Do you need anything?"

"Yes, please find a spectre who would be willing to answer questions about their situation. I would like to impress upon them that death is not the end. They will leave their knowledge behind."

There was a pause. "Right. That is . . . you have summed it up nicely."

"That was my job. I met with the families and took them to their spectres. I had to make it seem pleasant, and these girls will be introduced to it as gently as I can make it. May I have a date?"

"Name your day, and we will accommodate you."

"I will contact the Guide Master and call you back. Thank you so much. The girls will be on their best behaviour."

A few more pleasantries and they ended the call.

The next call was to the Guide Master, and the woman was so enthusiastic, she promised to get back to Imara within the hour when she had all of the agreements from the Guides' parents.

Imara exhaled and looked at her phone as if it was a snake. "Well, Kitty was definitely right. There is a demand for Death Keepers in the area."

There is a demand for you. You know that your skills with the energies of the dead are not normal, right?

She wrinkled her nose and scratched Mr. E behind his ear

until he let out a purr that rattled his little body. "I have suspected as much for quite a while. Now, quiz me on the types of clouds. We are having a test next week, and I want to be ready."

Shouldn't you be studying with Kitty? He narrowed his eyes as if he knew what she was going to say.

"I *am* studying with a kitty. No, she is busy with her apiary course. Bees are bees."

Two weeks after their first class, Imara was pretty sure that she had made another friend. Kitty had a great sense of humour, and despite her accessories, she was bright and had skills when it came to shifting weather.

Too bad. You need practice on your heat control.

"We are doing a lab tomorrow. The workspace is open, and we can let loose a little."

It was confining to have to wait until they had lab time in the underground complex, but it was probably for the best as neither of them was particularly skilled at taking their creations apart once they had gotten them going. There weren't a lot of places to hide in the lecture hall, but they had found most of them.

After a few minutes of studying, she looked at her phone and smiled.

It is the courtier, is it?

"Of course. It is our normal check-in time. He has had a good start to his night, and I am just about ready to pass out. It is the best time for a little technological contact."

The snort that came from Mr. E should not have been possible for such a small body. *I find it hard to believe that you are content to be distant from him. I can feel everything that runs through you when he is near. It is enough to make me blush.*

"You keep your assessments to yourself. We are waiting for any of that stuff. It would be too distracting if I threw myself into a physical relationship before my studies are done. I don't want to chance a pregnancy before I get what I want."

I thought that modern technology fixed all that."

She huffed and gave him a dark look. "Magic gets around that sort of thing, as you well know."

It has never been a concern of mine. My family was banished during my sentencing. The line died out during my fourth term as familiar.

"Oh, geez. I am so sorry, Mr. E. I had no idea."

He shrugged and curled himself into a small ball. *No reason you should have.*

The silence between them was heavy, so she closed her books, scooped him up, and carried him to her bed where she sat and stroked his ears until his body relaxed. No matter what the situation was, family wasn't easy.

"Ladies, today we are working on lightning." Eckoak was sitting on top of the lectern with a jaunty grin.

Mr. E was out in the vestibule with a book on metallurgy, so Imara didn't worry about what they were about to do.

Kitty gave her a worried look. "I am not sure about this."

Eckoak chuckled. "No one ever is. The bright spark is the first visible crackle of power for most elementals. Neither of you are elementals, so this is not going to be fun. I have heard that it hurts the first time."

Kitty snorted until she realized that their instructor was serious.

Imara nodded. "Right. How do we start?"

Eckoak smiled. "That is the spirit. Now, go and stand on those thick rubber mats."

Imara headed to the first of the mats, and she dried her hands on her jeans. This was not the moment to have any water involved.

At the far end of the chamber, a cage was wheeled out, pushed by a man with seriously messed up hair and a chalky complexion.

"Who is he?" Kitty asked it before Imara could.

"Tellfirth works with the Mage Guild when they send their officers on assignment. He's a medic. If you accidentally stop your own hearts, he can get you started and keep your heart going until more medical intervention can be arranged."

Imara's nervousness escalated, and a black streak moved past the cage to settle near her.

I am your first line of resuscitation, Mage. His black fur was spikey, and he was sitting a few feet away.

Eckoak frowned. "Your familiar is supposed to be in the antechamber."

Imara cleared her throat. "He is my first line of defense if I am injured. The medic can step in if my familiar steps back."

The dryad nodded reluctantly. "Acceptable. He just cannot assist you in your efforts."

"Don't worry. He is all in favour of my falling flat on my face; he just doesn't want me dead."

"Fair enough. Now, once Medic Tellfirth is in his Faraday cage, I want you to strike your targets with lightning. You have the rest of class to make one large strike. The target will let me know when you have engaged in sufficient vigour in your strike."

Imara glanced at Kitty when two large, glowing orbs rose from the floor and settled about sixteen feet in the air, fifty feet away. It was going to be a very long morning.

Imara focused for half an hour, and only managed to create a spark that travelled two feet.

Eckoak was leaning against the podium and sipping her coffee, not offering any assistance and occasionally laughing at them.

Kitty was sitting and chanting. It was her go to.

Imara looked at Kitty and her wealth of orbs then back to the target. Could it be that simple?

She looked at the orb and thought of it as a holding stone for a spectre. The power signature flared to life, and she nodded. "Right."

Another half hour had passed during her assessment, and Kitty was arcing lightning halfway to the target.

Imara raised her hands and charged them, holding them outward and calling the power from the target.

The energy rushed toward her, and she sent electricity back along the path. A crackle of lightning struck the orb, and it flared brilliant green.

She closed the link and sat down. Sweat was running down her spine, but Eckoak was grinning. One test done.

Kitty was still standing, her eyes focused and her hands forward. She had made a strike three-quarters of the way to the target, but she didn't trigger the target. She lacked power.

Kitty paused and flexed her fingers. The tips were bright red. She exhaled and looked at Imara. "I don't think I can manage this."

Imara smiled encouragingly and ran her hands through her hair before rubbing them on her thighs and back again. "I think you will get it. You just need to build up to it."

Kitty smiled and gave her a thumbs-up.

Imara waited on her mat while Kitty took off her shoes, walked off the rubber and rubbed her rings against her hair before buffing them against her thighs. She slowly built up her static charge, and when her hair was beginning to rise with the magical power, she stepped back onto the mat, conjured a small storm in her palms and then sent out a tremendous crack of lightning.

The target lit up and exploded.

Imara didn't cheer. She watched as Kitty stopped her storm and closed her hands, kneeling slowly. She drooped with fatigue, and when Eckoak moved toward her, Imara joined them.

Kitty lifted her head. "I did it."

Eckoak nodded and cupped her chin. "You did. Good call on the static. Pulling energy from nowhere to power lightning is usually very stupid. That is the reason for the medic. You two managed to get through it with some mild exhaustion. Well done, ladies, now go and get something to eat."

Imara helped Kitty to her feet, pausing to collect her shoes before heading for the door.

Mr. E ran ahead of them and was perched on her pack. She grabbed it with one hand and kept supporting Kitty as they got onto the lift.

"Come on, we are going to the Hall. I think you need a bit more than a sandwich."

Kitty nodded weakly. "Sounds great."

Mr. E sent a worried thought into Imara's mind. *I think I should run ahead and get Reegar to prepare something.*

Taking on more of Kitty's weight, Imara whispered, "I think that is an excellent idea."

He streaked off her shoulder the moment that they were above ground, and she watched his tail disappear down the path. She would have Kitty in a comfortable space in ten minutes if she could hold her up that long. She straightened her shoulders and hiked onward, with her friend stumbling gamely along.

Chapter Five

"**Y**our teacher should never have tried to get you to generate dry lightning. It was stupid." Reegar administered a draught to Kitty, forcing it down her though she fought the taste.

"It might have been, but we managed it."

"And she nearly drained herself of all vital energies in the process. I have seen this before, and it has had rather deadly outcomes."

Imara was manning the pot of soup that Reegar had pulled together. She watched the grumpy spectre taking care of her friend and fought a smile. "I knew I was doing the right thing when I came home."

"The draught will give her energy. Who is your instructor?"

Imara bit her lip. "Professor Eckoak. She's a very good elemental."

Reegar sneered. "Dryad. I know her. She was around the college as a student twenty years ago. She tried to plant a tree in my courtyard, and I sent her packing."

"Why was she here? The college is for mages, not extra-naturals."

"She evolved in her first year. Late bloomer. Her magic came on, and they didn't want to eject her, so they considered her an exchange student and waited to see if she would blend in."

"Did she?"

"No. But the issue of the tree was the only disagreement I had with her. I didn't hear much about her from the other building caretakers."

Kitty struggled to sit up straight. "What was in that vial?"

Reegar glanced at her. "It was the vitamin shot that I work

into all of Imara's food when she isn't looking. Nothing magical, just herbs and fruit extracts."

Imara suspected that he wasn't joking, but she asked, "Are you ready for some soup?"

"Yes, please. It smells great."

Mr. E came in, holding a metal charm in his mouth. He hopped up onto Kitty's lap and spat the charm out.

The light glow that came out of the charm was echoed in Kitty's eyes.

She blinked rapidly. "Wow, that feels much better."

She used her body to power the first strikes. It drained her. The harder she worked, the weaker she got.

Imara relayed the information to Kitty, and her friend nodded.

"Yeah, that is what it felt like."

She dished up some soup and put a plate under it as well as some crackers on the plate. "Here you go."

Kitty set the plate in her lap, and she got to work on the soup.

Reegar smiled. "How is it?"

"Excellent. Thank you."

"My mother used to make it for me when I was in school. Of course, she made it over a coal fire, but I think the essence of the herbs come through."

The thought of Reegar having a mother had never really occurred to her. Imara cocked her head. "Did you always like to cook?"

"Always. It was relaxing to do something so ordinary, so human." He smiled. "Everybody has to eat."

"True. I hadn't thought of that. Cooking wasn't something that I bothered learning." She shrugged. "There was always something to study. Food just showed up, and I ate it."

Kitty smirked. "I had to come when I was called, or I didn't eat."

Imara chuckled. "They had to feed me, or they didn't get paid."

Reegar glanced at her. "Was it awkward? You haven't mentioned your caretakers."

"It was rather cold. Even being here is warm and fuzzy by comparison, but then, I was always working toward a goal, and that didn't include them."

Kitty blinked. "You didn't live with your parents?"

"Nope. I am an off-contract birth. My father's family didn't want me, and my mother wasn't allowed to keep me. It all worked out." She said that in a rush when the stricken expression crossed over Kitty's face. "Really, it is all good. I have met my mother, and we get along very well. I have even met a few of my brothers. One is due here any minute, actually."

Kitty looked around. "Here?"

"Yup. Keep eating. He is dating Bara, and she has an early afternoon today. I am guessing he does as well because he is pulling up in the lot."

Kitty had just finished her restoring soup when Luken arrived.

Imara waved at him. "Hiya, Luken. This is Kitty. She is recovering from our morning class. Kitty, this is my brother, Luken Demiel."

Kitty looked from Imara to the young man standing beside her. "Well, he is definitely your brother."

Imara smiled. "Yeah, there is a resemblance."

Luken came up to her and nudged her on the arm. "This is my long-lost twin."

"I wasn't lost. I was merely misplaced." She laughed. "I found my way eventually."

"And I am glad you did. I wanted to see what my rugged good looks would be like on a lady. She isn't half bad."

Imara lifted her hand, held her thumb and forefinger apart and sent an arc of lightning from digit to digit. "I am not above zapping you, Luken."

He grinned. "Is Bara in?"

"No, but she should roll in in a few minutes. Her class is across campus, and it takes a while to haul all of her textile studies supplies home." She dismissed the energy and rubbed her palm on her thigh.

Luken nodded. "I will head out to help her. Nothing gets

more bonus points than helping a damsel in distress. Kitty, it was a pleasure meeting you."

"Pleasure to meet you as well." Kitty nodded and waved as he headed back outside.

When he was gone, Kitty stared at Imara. "He is a third year."

"Yeah. He got early admission. How did you know?"

"My cousin was in a class with him, and she had a huge crush. I have to admit, he's good looking."

Imara grinned. "He got the best side of the womb."

"Ah. Well, since I have my brain together for a moment, would you be interested in coming to my family's place next weekend? We have plenty of room, and my parents would love to meet you."

Imara blinked. "Um, why?"

We should go. I want to catch some shrews.

Imara looked at him. "Shrews?"

He yawned, showing his little white teeth. *They are all I can catch in this shape.*

Kitty smiled. "Yes, we have shrews. The yards are all hedged, so there are a bunch of small rodents around the property. We try and put up repulse spells, but they keep coming. So, Mr. E is interested?"

Imara sighed. "He is. I just am a little unsure of how to deal with a family situation."

Kitty blinked. "Don't overthink it. We could practice mantras and poses in the old barn, and when my mom calls us for dinner, we go in and eat. When we are tired, we sleep. When the weekend is over, we come home. Nothing more than that."

"Why?"

"Because I really get the feeling that you need to do something not related to studying. We can go play with the lambs and calves if you like. Generally, you will just relax and unclench."

Reegar was fussing near the kitchen, and he turned back, "It might not be a bad idea. I think that you need a little socialization."

Imara stared at him. "I need to study."

He snorted. "You are already done with the paper courses for this term. One weekend will do you good. You need to make more ties in the community than other students and your instructors."

"I have you and Bara."

He snorted again. "I am dead, and she is a career student. She isn't leaving here if she can help it."

Kitty was watching them and turning her head between them. "You are really a spectre?"

He bowed. "I most definitely am. Thanks to Imara's talents, I am solid and functioning within the confines of my territory."

"That's . . . amazing. What kind of spell does it?"

Imara looked at her. "Um, not a spell, just a benign energy output. I have an affinity for the dead."

Mr. E was sitting next to Kitty, and she was petting him absently. There was obviously something going on in her head.

Imara sat on the edge of the couch. "What is it?"

"I have a deceased member of the family that I would love to speak to. I know it is horrible to ask you to come for a fun visit and then ask a favour, but I haven't met someone who might be able to manage it before." Kitty looked down at Mr. E.

With a heavy sigh, she asked, "When do we leave?"

Kitty lifted her head and stared. "You will come?"

"Yes, I will. You will have to drive, but I will come. Is Mr. E going to be okay to come along?"

Mr. E hissed. *Where you go, I go. It's in my job description.*

Kitty nodded. "Of course. He will be welcome. Does he need any special food?"

Imara chuckled. "He does like pasta, and you have seen him eat dessert."

Kitty laughed. "I will tell my family to lay in a little extra."

"Good. Send me the location details, so I can let my boyfriend know. He worries if I am left to my own devices for too long."

Kitty grabbed her phone, and Imara's chimed a moment later. When Imara checked the screen, a text gave her the address, the location, and the GPS coordinates.

"That was thorough."

Kitty smiled. "Just in case you want to forward it to anyone. Better to discard some information than to not have it in the first place."

Kitty took one of her spheres off her necklace, and she dangled it in front of Mr. E.

"That isn't a good idea." Just as she finished the warning, Mr. E had batted the small orb out of her fingers and was chasing it around the carpet in front of the couch.

The kitten had once again won over the familiar, and it was a great thing to watch for an hour or so.

When Kitty was getting ready to leave, Imara asked, "So, what do I need to bring?"

"Yourself and clothing that you don't mind getting dirty. Farms are farms, and the best places to hang out and be quiet involve a little hike through woods and streams."

Imara nodded, and when Kitty was gone, she turned to Reegar. "I don't hike."

He laughed, dissipated, and she was left trying to find her familiar under the couch. A mage's work was never done.

Chapter Six

Imara held Mr. E on her lap as Kitty pulled her truck down a drive and the white fences that contained green meadows and distant large animals were on either side of the truck.

The kitten hopped up on his hind legs and looked out the truck window with his tail lashing.

Can I chase them?

Imara chuckled. "No. Stick to rodents and birds. If this weekend goes well, we might want to ask to come back."

His tail lashed. *Best behaviour then. Got it.*

Kitty grinned. "He dreams of chasing sheep?"

"I think he dreams of chasing elephants. His dreams are big."

Kitty nodded, and they spent the next few minutes drawing closer to the main farm.

"This place is huge." Imara was amazed.

"It needs to be. Cows are big, and sheep love to run."

The main house loomed up in front of them, and the cheerful white was dotted with a series of gleaming orbs.

"Oh, right. Family talent."

"Yeah, we can always tell where one of us is."

"Do you have a large family?"

"Our branch? No. but there are Deegles around the country." Kitty's rings flashed as she curved the truck in a slow arc and they stopped twenty feet from the main house. "We're here. Welcome to my home."

They exited her truck, and Mr. E was quivering with the urge to explore.

Imara whispered, "Be careful and keep our link open. Call me if you need help."

It was all he needed to know. The kitten streaked across the property and headed for the meadow that Kitty had identified as belonging to the sheep.

Imara sighed. "I hope he is on good behaviour."

Kitty chuckled and got their bags, holding Imara's out to her. "He will be fine. Cats are on the farm all the time. They live in the barn."

"He isn't actually a cat, though, and he hasn't had any large prey to chase for a while."

Kitty paused. "How big?"

Imara sighed. "I shouldn't have said anything."

"Is he dangerous?"

"Only if I am threatened, otherwise, he is a pussycat."

"Good. He will be fine here then. There isn't anything to harm him or you at the farm. Well, unless you try and milk the bull. Then, you get what you deserve." Kitty laughed.

Imara winced. "I will try not to milk anything while I am here. I think it is just a safer practice."

Kitty grinned and led the way to the big house. A black flash streaked across the green in the distance, and Imara's mind was filled with giggles. At least he was already having a good time.

The door to the main house opened, and a man approached them, wiping his hands on a dishtowel and sporting a smear of flour on his cheek. "You made excellent time."

Kitty hugged him. "Nice to see you, too, Dad. This is Imara Mirrin. Imara, this is my dad, Andrew Deegle."

Imara stepped forward and extended her hand. The handshake was warm and firm, Andrew's calluses were heavy enough to hurt, but he watched his grip.

She smiled. "I am pleased to meet you, Mr. Deegle."

"Andy, please. I am delighted to meet you as well. Kitigan doesn't make many friends."

Kitty wiggled her fingers with their multitude of rings. "I'm too sparkly."

Imara laughed. "I think it is your propensity to tell folks you can see the future. It either repulses or intrigues."

Andy asked, "What did it do for you?"

"It made me relax. I hadn't met anyone else with a properly weird talent until she showed up." She chuckled.

"Kitty keeps it interesting without having to discuss her talent all the time, once she knew I wasn't going to pester her for a reading."

Andy looked at her. "You have really never wanted to see your future?"

Imara shrugged. "Nope. My past is past, and my future will decide itself. No sense rushing the identification of trauma or joy."

"That is a very mature attitude."

She wrinkled her nose. "Not really. I just hate most surprises and knowing that they were coming would make the anticipation worse."

"No worries around here. The worst thing to anticipate is a stray sheep." He inclined his head. "Consider yourself at home."

Kitty shifted from foot to foot. "Can I show her to the guestroom?"

Andy shook his head. "Given that she has a familiar, I have pulled out our newest acquisition."

There was an ear-shattering squeal from Kitty, she grabbed Imara's hand and hauled her around the far side of the house where a micro house was perched with connections to water and power.

"It was on order when I started the term. It is even cuter than I imagined."

"It's a tiny house."

"That it is. Come on. I have been dying to see inside." Kitty opened the door, and Imara followed her into the building.

The space was well organized. A small desk against the wall had a padded stool tucked under it, the bed was in a loft, and the kitchen had regular-sized appliances.

"This place is nice. Is that a quilt?" Imara climbed the ladder to check the bed. She tucked her bag next to the mattress and ran a hand over the patchwork fabric. "It's lovely."

"My mother made it. She makes and sells stuff on the internet, and this is one of her crafts." Kitty stood on the ladder and looked over the object that Imara was stroking.

"It's amazing. I have seen this kinda thing online, but never up close." The geometric patterns wove one piece into the other, and the stitching that held them together added texture and strength. A symphony in blue and purple, and she got to sleep under it that night.

Imara looked to Kitty, "Will they mind Mr. E up here?"

"Of course not. That is one reason they offered you privacy. Mages with familiars are more sensitive to strange environments. This one is all yours while you are here, but you can still eat with us in the main house."

Imara smiled. "Can I see the rest of the property?"

"Sure. Did you want to ride horses? It will make it easier."

Excitement stirred. "I haven't ridden a horse before."

"This is an excellent time to start. The horses won't tell a soul if you are a little stiff."

Imara approached the ladder, and when Kitty moved back, she climbed down to the main floor. "Lead the way. My humiliation awaits."

"I won't tell if you don't tell my parents that I tried to make lightning using my own energy. In hindsight, it was a very stupid move."

"You are not wrong."

Imara grinned as Kitty huffed and led the way out of the tiny structure and across the yard toward the large barn.

"So, you ride horses a lot?"

"Sure. There is no better way to get around this kind of terrain. They can fuel themselves if they need it."

Imara couldn't argue. The scent of hay and animals came to her on the wind as they reached the barn.

"I will go in and see who needs exercise. You can wait out here if you like."

"No, I would like to see how this is done. I imagine it is different in reality than it is on television."

Kitty shrugged and hauled the door open. "Not really. Sure, there are a few more bits to attach to the horses, but the key is to make everything comfortable and secure for horse and rider."

They walked into the dim interior, and Kitty headed for a

shed in the rear of the building. Imara followed, passing stalls where curious heads poked over their doors, giving her a long look. Imara inclined her head formally and kept following the other human in the building.

"So, how do you tell who needs exercise?"

Kitty grinned. "We don't ask them if that is what you are getting at. We check the schedule. Every time we take a horse out, we make a note of the date and duration, as well as anything awkward on the ride. It helps the vets as well. We can track an illness in the animals if we have to, back to the day it happened. Sometimes, it is even naturally occurring plants that cause an issue."

"Oh."

Kitty blushed. "Sorry. I am just excited to have a visitor with me. You wouldn't believe some of the views we are going to ride through."

"Gotcha. I get the same way talking about the dead. It is exciting but only from a certain angle." Imara grinned. "Ignore me. I am eager to learn how to do this."

"In that case, let me pick a good mount for you, and then, you can carry the tack to the stall."

"Yes, ma'am. I am throwing myself on your mercy."

"Good plan. I have your comfort for the rest of the day at my discretion." She checked a clipboard on the wall and looked down the line of stalls. "I think that Bright Bell is a good choice for you. He is friendly and good-natured, as well as an excellent trail horse. He can find his way home on his own. All you need to do is hang on."

"Great. That's encouraging."

"It should be. Some of these ladies or gentlemen would dump you in a ravine and run off giggling or the horsy equivalent."

That was a warning as much as encouragement. Kitty picked her own mount and then, they were into the tack room to get the leather straps and saddles that would hold them in place.

Imara watched the process in amazement as Kitty tucked, buckled, strapped, and tugged at the leather until their horses were standing and ready for them.

The instructions of how to lead Bright Bell out and into the yard were a blur as Imara focused on the huge creature that she was holding by a flimsy strap. It seemed friendly enough and nudged her lightly.

"He likes you. That's a good thing."

"Oh. Good."

"Are you ready to get on?"

Imara inhaled and exhaled slowly. "Yup."

"Good. Gather the reins in your left hand, keep them firm but loose, so they don't pull his head. Left foot into the stirrup, hand on the pommel, and haul yourself up while bringing your right leg over. He is a patient horse, so take your time. He can hold you."

Imara looked at the satiny grey hide and the calm brown eyes. She nodded, arranged the reins, and used all of her yoga practice to get her foot high enough to reach the stirrup. The grip on the saddle and heaving herself upward was done in a controlled rush. A few seconds later, she was blinking in surprise at her new point of view. She stroked Bright Bell's neck and whispered, "Thanks."

He shifted slightly, and she let her hips move with him. She was going to be sore tomorrow, but this was another experience to add to her collection.

Kitty got up onto her mount gracefully, and she turned the chestnut horse and walked back to Imara. "Slip your right foot into the stirrup, if he increases his pace, use the stirrups to get your butt off the saddle or be jolted into bits, but otherwise, let me guide and he will follow. You just have to look at the scenery."

Imara remained calm while her ride started moving. She hoped that Mr. E was having fun in the fields. She was on her own little journey of exhilaration; she just didn't have another life waiting if something went wrong.

Chapter Seven

The view was amazing. No matter which way she turned, Imara saw beauty and life.

Kitty rode ahead of her, and her ease in the saddle was apparent. Aside from envy, Imara had a few things she needed to ask, so she steeled herself and made her move. It took a bit of goading, but Imara got Bright Bell to draw even with Kitty's mount.

"So, Kitty, who did you need me to work with?"

Kitty looked confused. "What?"

"The spectre."

"Oh. It's a long story, but the end of it is my grandfather."

"I need a bit more information, please."

Kitty sighed. "Twenty years ago, my grandfather passed, and my grandmother didn't take it well. She was an orb seer, just like my father and me, so she began to stare into the future. She took the master orb that my dad had made and poured her energy into it. In that orb, she saw my grandfather holding her hand once again. Ever since, she spends her days looking five minutes into the future, looking for him."

"Oh damn."

"Right, so you see the problem."

"Did you put your grandfather to rest as a mage?"

"We did. I mean, I was a child, but my mother says that his gravesite is properly cared for."

Imara sighed. "I will have to talk to your parents about his effects. I can use one of the retaining stones and his link to your grandmother to bring him out, but only if the connection is strong on all counts."

Kitty looked hopeful. "You actually think you can do it?"

"If the proper rituals were engaged in when he passed, yes. It is easy." Imara had a thought. "You were right about the Mage Guides. They are eager to have me volunteer by taking a tour through a cemetery in order to talk to some spectres."

Kitty smirked. "Thought so. It is a neglected area of mage-craft just because we can't get anyone to show us around. It is always depicted as creepy, just because it is unknown."

Bright Bell stiffened under her, and Imara looked around to see what had gotten his attention.

"Damn. Dad said they had moved in, but I was hoping that they weren't this far to the edge of their territory yet." Kitty's mood shifted suddenly as she stared at the brush in the valley below.

"Is something here?"

"A new werewolf pack split and left their elders and are now running around on the fifty acres to the west of our property line." She grimaced. "It is nowhere near enough space for them, but it is what was available."

Imara stared at the edge of the treeline, and within it, she could see the flicker of shadows and flash of silver fur. "Don't those trees abut your property line?"

"The first row on our side is the windbreak."

The horses shifted restlessly. Kitty got her mount under control, but Imara had to focus as Bright Bell got nervous. "Easy, dude."

"We had better turn back."

Kitty had no sooner mentioned it than a howl broke free of the woods and a rush of dark fur came toward them.

Bright Bell reared and tossed his head before turning and bolting toward the barn. Imara's grip on the saddle kept her in place during the jarring sprint, but a glance back showed that the wolves were waiting on the ridge, defending what they considered to be their territory. This required investigation as soon as she got her butt of the leather that was being pounded into it.

Kitty and her mount beat them to the barn, and she held Bright Bell while Imara slithered off with the grace of a bag of pudding.

"You go and grab a hot shower. I will take care of the

horses."

She nodded and headed for the tiny house with the intent of contacting Argus. If anyone knew what was going on and what could be done about werewolves encroaching on territories, it would be another shifter.

When she dragged herself out of the shower, wrapped in a towel, the flashing light on her phone told her that Argus was up.

She called him and smiled at the rumble of his voice.

"What have you gotten yourself into, Imara?"

"Nothing. Just a little light territorial encroachment by a pack on a local farmer. I want to know what I am able to do to defend the space."

"Can't the farmer do it? He has the right."

"I don't think so. He is mainly a seer, and his daughter is still in school with me."

She could almost sense his brain heating up while he worked out what he would say next.

"Technically, they are responsible for their defense, but if they offer you a legal foothold for yourself or your power, you can act on their behalf."

"Wow. It is like you are a seer yourself. I have that very setup, or will by the end of the evening. So, I am allowed to defend this place?"

"By any means necessary. Call me if things escalate beyond posturing. I may not be able to come, but I can get a local XIA detachment to send someone out."

"I will."

"And Imara? Take care of yourself. This could get dangerous very quickly."

"I will. Thanks for the consultation, Argus. I owe you dinner when I get home."

"You don't cook."

"But you are a very brave soul. I am sure that I can figure something out." She grinned, her soul bubbling a little as it always did when she talked to him.

"Make sure that Mr. E is nearby if you want to do anything really stupid. He knows his job."

"Yes, Agent Argus."

"I mean it. I worry about you." His tone was low.

"I know. I don't mean to get into trouble, but it seems to seek me out."

"Well, at least you are lucky."

She smirked. "Of course, I am. I met you, didn't I?"

His laugh was wry. "Yeah, you did, and I am willing to pay the price for the association. Be on guard but be cautious. I am going to look into the pack that has moved in and see if I can get you any more information."

"I await your update. Have a good shift. Don't let the boys eat too many tacos. You know that trolls have delicate digestion."

"Don't remind me. Have a fun evening. I should have details in a few hours."

Imara smiled and disconnected the call. They didn't say goodbye, just like they didn't need to say hello. Their communication was just one long conversation interrupted by time. Nothing could, or would, separate them. Part of her had realized it the moment that they met.

She got dressed in fresh clothing and went in search of Kitty. Mr. E sauntered up to her, and she lifted him to put him on her shoulder.

"Dude, you smell like sheep."

I was making friends. They are very friendly sheep.

She rolled her eyes and found Kitty in the barn, brushing Bright Bell and soothing him. The horse was still quivering with upset.

Let me speak to him.

Imara approached and cleared her throat. "Mr. E is going to chat with Bright Bell."

The kitten walked from her shoulder to the top of the stall door.

Kitty paused in her ministrations when the horse visibly calmed. "What is he saying?"

"I have no idea. He is speaking via his kitten side, so I am not privy to it. It isn't anything bad though. Bright Bell looks calmer already."

The horse in question moved forward and pressed his long nose to Imara's shoulder. He nipped gently at her sleeve, and she stroked his head.

"Well, whatever he said worked. All of the horses are relaxed and at ease." Andy's voice was low and calm. "Ladies, time to wash up for dinner."

Kitty nodded, and Imara finished petting Bright Bell as her friend exited the stall.

Mr. E hopped back onto her shoulder, and they left the barn where the animals were diving into their dinners and went to find their own.

The family dinner table was something that Imara had heard of but never experienced firsthand. Meals at the hall were generally had around the table in the library or in the common room.

Dishes were set around the table, and everyone had a place. Kitty's mother showed her the seat that was set aside for guests. "Here you go, just call out if anything is out of your reach."

"I will. Thank you. It smells wonderful."

"Thank you. It is delightful to have a friend of Kitigan's here at the farm."

"It has been fun so far. Thank you for having me." She went through the rituals that Bara had drummed into her. "Oh, I am May, by the way."

"Pleased to meet you, May. Your daughter has been an excellent study partner."

Kitty came in, shaking her hands. "Don't listen to that. Imara is an amazing and natural mage. Anyone near her gets better by simple proximity."

"Can you get your grandmother?"

"She is washing up. Is she any better?" Kitty looked worried.

"She is as she has been."

Imara cleared her throat. "I have some questions to ask about her husband, if I may."

May looked at her for a moment. "After dinner is soon

enough when my mother-in-law has resumed her watch on the future."

Imara nodded, and when the elder Deegle appeared, she introduced herself to the vague and unfocused woman.

Dinner conversation was polite and centred around the class that Kitty and Imara were taking. Weather was a large concern on the farm.

When the grandmother rose and headed back to her attic room, Imara sighed, "All right. I hate to ask, but what measures were taken when Mr. Deegle passed away? Was his spectre stone generated? Are there any artifacts to anchor him? Where is he buried?"

May looked confused, but Andy cleared his throat. "We have the spectre stone, but we didn't anchor it."

Imara made a face. "Right. Okay."

"We have enough personal effects to fill a room. This entire property was his selection. They moved here, and May and I moved in with them when we married. The land was perfect for both our family needs."

"Would you mind having his spectre around?" It was an important question, and she watched them carefully.

Andy nodded his head slowly. "I would like to be able to speak with him again."

May asked the pertinent question, "Would the spectre outlast Anna? I couldn't bear it if she lost him again."

Imara smiled. "I can anchor him to the land and give you directions for his slow dissolve after she passes. If you choose to keep him, he can be a permanent guardian."

Kitty blinked. "You talk about him like he's a dog."

Imara rubbed her jaw. "His soul is gone; this is a copy of his emotion and intellect. He knows he's dead, but I can give him enough energy to keep him solid when he wants to be. His spirit can roam this land and watch over it if you like. It would just involve a lot of rock and some planted trees."

Andy stared at her. "It is that easy?"

"Well, if you are a Death Keeper, yes. The primary issue is the generating site. Where do you want to keep him and talk to him directly?"

Andy got up from the table, and he returned in a moment with a map. He moved dishes aside and opened it up. "Here. We always meant to install the stone here, but it is so expensive to get a private installation."

"Right. I am going to need a hammer, chisel, the spectre stone, and a bunch of pebbles or river rocks. The trees can be planted later."

May asked, "Do you need it by midnight?"

"Well, I would like to head to bed before eleven, so the sooner, the better. Time isn't a factor, and we could do it tomorrow morning if you wanted. I just thought that having him here tonight would be a good start."

The Deegles shot out in different directions, and Imara prepared another plate for Mr. E.

Why are you doing this? It will take a lot of energy.

"They are in pain. An entire family is in pain, and I can fix it. That doesn't cost me anything but slight dizziness and a few hours of focus. I will be fine in the morning, and I can send them powered items as they need it."

They are mages, and hundreds of families can't afford what you are about to do, are you going to do it for all of them?

"The ones that I meet face to face, sure. Just imagine, we can come back here for maintenance and you can chase more sheep."

Point taken. Focus. You are going to connect some very rusty dots. This I have got to see.

With that encouragement, she started the inner chant that would focus the energy she needed to wake the spectre stone and bind it to the rock. She was going to need another meal when it was over or maybe just some pie.

Chapter Eight

The box was carved with designs, and she could feel the magic humming inside it. It was a holding box, and the glyphs were designed to keep the consciousness as fresh as the day that the deceased passed on. It was a bit unpleasant to think of it in such terms, but the spectre she was going to be releasing was not the original man. It was a copy.

The Deegles were waiting for her. She could hear the tapping in the rock to prime the hole. She would do most of the work, but a niche to start with was always appreciated.

Imara looked down at her robes. Packing them had been a whim based on what Kitty had mentioned. Now, Imara realized that they were at least two inches too short. She had grown since she started as apprentice.

Are you ready for this?

"Yeah. I have done this before."

I thought you had to be a master before you activated a spectre.

"Only if the family is watching. This isn't a first for me."

Well, well. The more I live in the modern age, the more I learn. Are you ready?

"Stop asking that. Yes. I am ready. Here we go."

She opened the door with the box held carefully in her left hand. Leaving the small house was symbolic. It was a neutral site that had nothing to do with the family. There were no ties for the spectre to attach to, so it was the safest place to start from, just in case she activated him early. It wasn't going to happen, but protocol meant that someone had been stupid at some point.

She crossed the yard with Mr. E at her side, heading up slope from the house and against the trees, geographically in the centre of the property.

The family was waiting, even the grandmother was standing with her burned-out orbs on her fingers, around her neck, and held in her hands.

Andy was standing with the hammer and chisel in his hands.

Imara smiled, "Please set the tools down."

He nodded nervously and set the tools at the base of the stone that held the chisel marks.

"Does anyone here not wish to see the spectre of the deceased?"

The family looked at each other, and they shook their heads. Andy cleared his throat. "We are in agreement. We want as much of him as we can have."

"Very well. I will let you know when you can speak to him. Please, allow me to work without interruption."

They nodded again and stepped back. The grandmother was watching her with fascination, so Imara smiled to her before she picked up the implements and set to work.

The first strike took her an inch into the hard rock. The second made the cavity she needed. With care and reverence, she opened the box and removed the stone that carried the residue of the man who was beloved by those around her.

Imara took the glowing gem and rammed it into the cavity in the stone. The rock melted as she focused on joining the stone and the gem together.

When her hand felt the burn, she pulled her palm away. Now, it was time to do her part as a Death Keeper.

She whispered to him, drawing him out, calling him to the objects he had left behind. She appealed to his love and the wedding ring that was sitting on velvet within the box.

It took an hour to pull the consciousness from the stone, but when she felt him release into the bedrock around her, she stood back and smiled.

"Anderson Morden Deegle, you are requested to join us."

The spectre emerged from the stone and took form. Anna gasped and sobbed, May had tears in her eyes, and so did her husband. Kitty was simply in shock.

"Death Keeper, how did you come to be here?" Anderson Deegle turned his head. He was still transparent, but his voice came through.

"I am a student who shares a weather magic class with your granddaughter, Kitigan. She is an adult now, and as I was here for a weekend off, I am repaying my hosts with your rejuvenation."

He nodded. "What about when you leave? How quickly will I fade?"

"You won't. I will plant power nodes around the property tomorrow, and you will be able to walk the farm again, even hold Anna's hand again if you wish."

"Anna." The longing in the voice was obvious.

"Yes, she is waiting for you. She has seen this moment and has spent twenty years waiting for it."

He looked around and spotted his wife. "Anna."

Tears filled her eyes, and she dropped the glass in the grass. "Anderson. Is it really you?"

Imara poured her death magic into him, turning the translucent body into something far more solid.

"Anna." The spectre reached for her and then paused.

Anna didn't hesitate, she held his hands, and when she felt the solid warmth of him, she sobbed and threw herself against him.

Imara looked to Kitty. "Did you get those rocks I asked for?"

Kitty nodded, and her gaze darted around until she found what she was looking for. She moved past Imara and grabbed a large pail from next to the stone. "Here they are."

"Thanks. I am going to take these back to the tiny house. In the morning, if you are up to it, we can take another ride and anchor Anderson to the property. He can then come and go as he pleases or wherever you please. He will be able to reach the edges of your property."

Andy was hugging the spectre of his father, and the joyful and tearful reunion was heartwarming.

"Yeah, you introduce yourself to your grandfather. I have to have a nap with rocks next to me. Ah, the life of a Death

Keeper is so glamorous."

Grinning but tired, Imara headed back to her tiny sanctu-
ary.

Mr. E trotted along on his little legs, keeping up with her
tired steps.

I thought that enhancing spectres didn't exhaust you.

"It doesn't, but fusing and raising one does. Tomorrow
will be easy in comparison. All I need tonight is a good
night's sleep."

It was as if she was casting a curse.

The howl brought her out of bed in a heartbeat. Imara
rolled to the floor and sat blinking as she fought to figure out
where she was.

The huffing and growling around the tiny house warned
her that the wolves were in her territory.

Those little bastards. Do you want me to hurt them?

Imara spoke silently, "No, I want to take care of this myself. They are young, not homicidal."

The door to the roof opened from the upper loft, and she
slid out, removing her nightgown as she did. She gathered
her focus and launched herself from the roof, shifting form
as she fell.

The first wolf that had her full vulture weight went to the
ground with a grunt. She pecked and pulled, tearing a strip
off his neck. Another launch and she got the second wolf.

The third moved so that she was on the ground and
couldn't launch. Imara wasn't having any of that, so she
shifted and jumped at the bugger, pinning him to the ground
as her form slowly became fully human.

"Naughty fellas. This isn't your property, and it sure as
fuck isn't your territory. If you come back here, I will be
much less polite."

She levered herself off the wolf, and he and her two victims ran back to their territory.

Imara stretched, and when she heard a small cough, she
turned to see the family staring at her. Kitty was bright pink
and pale at the same time.

Imara grinned. "I will get back to bed."

Andy raised his brows, "I didn't know you were a shapeshifter."

"Last term. Top of my class. It isn't a glamorous shape, but I am definitely comfortable as a vulture. The nudity is literally par for the course."

He nodded and herded the ladies back into the house. May turned back. "Thank you. I dread to think of what they would have done to us."

"Just peed on you. That is their big move. My tearing a strip off them will follow them into their human form. It is one of the annoying little bits of etiquette that you have to learn when you change shape."

Kitty looked as if she wanted to ask a question, but she was tucked inside the house.

Imara opened the door of the tiny house and returned to bed. Mr. E had pulled her nightgown off the roof, and he was using it as a cat bed.

She was tired enough that she didn't really care.

Over breakfast the questions started.

"How do you learn to change shape?"

Imara cocked her head at Kitty. "You study for it. Not everyone makes it, and many are stuck in forms that would haunt your nightmares."

Kitty shuddered.

Imara slathered some butter on her bread and tore the bread apart to dunk in her egg yolk.

May cleared her throat. "How is it that you have such a variety of skills at so young an age?"

Imara smiled. "That one is easy. I had nothing to do but focus on my future, so when I was given access to magic, I dove into it with my entire being. For my ultimate goal, I need to get through college with a degree as fast as I can. I have set my sights on courses that offer multiple credits because of their difficulty and that included the shapeshifting course."

Kitty blinked, "Is that how you met your boyfriend?"

"No. We were in an ethics course. He was taking it for work, and for me, it is a requirement to getting my magical consulting license."

May asked, "Consulting?"

"Yeah, I want to be a spectral consultant. Since Death Keepers are so few and far between and I am already a registered member of their guild, it is just a matter of getting the Mage Guild to accept me as a commercial member and I am on my way."

"You would do things like you did last night?"

"Like wrestle wolves naked? Not usually, but I could and would pull a few more coherent thoughts out of the spectres, no matter how old."

The family nodded and paused when Anna came in with Anderson at her side. They both were glowing with happiness, and it wasn't in Imara's nature to ask why.

Kitty, however, hissed, "Can they do *that?*"

Imara grinned. "It takes a lot of effort on his part, but yeah, they can."

Andy chuckled. "It was how he died. They had a great sex life right until the last."

Anna smiled, focused, and in the moment. "And it is back."

Imara blushed at the hot look that the grandmother was giving the spectre, twenty years her junior.

The worst thing was the reciprocation. He was seeing her as she was, and he obviously thought she was hot.

The eternal bond of love had never taken physical form for her before. She wondered if she and Argus would still be looking at each other with that intensity when they were old enough to retire? She really hoped so.

Chapter Nine

"**S**o, what are we going to do about the wolves?" Kitty asked it as if she was solely responsible for carrying out a hit. They were out on the ridge where the wolves had made their run the day before.

"We are going to keep planting these stones. Once they are in place, Anderson can keep them out."

"Why is my mom calling the local arborists?"

Imara knelt at the first site she had identified as a good point of support. "Because on their own, these stones act as a battery for your grandfather. With the trees living and carrying the signal, it is like Wi-Fi. He can appear and act within several hundred feet of one of those trees."

"So, in theory, he is the ultimate watchman."

"Yes. Spectres love being useful. The majority of degradation happens when they have nothing to do. They just let their energies float back into the aether or whatever you want to call it."

Bright Bell was nearby and waiting patiently with his reins on the ground. Imara smiled at the picture he made with Mr. E perching on the saddle. After the first ride, he wasn't letting her out on her own again. She didn't mind. He obviously had more experience with horses than she did.

Humming to herself, Imara dug a hole a foot deep and as narrow as she could make it. When it was ready, she dropped in one of the rocks, covered it up, and sighted for the next target.

"Okay. Off we go."

"Is that it? You don't have to chant or cast a spell?"

"No, proximity to me has charged them, and it will keep him running as long as you need him, or until the energy fades after I die."

"Oh. Wow."

Imara got back on her horse, and they started the slow amble to the next site. "Does the future you see stop being possible because you aren't paying attention or you haven't cast a spell?"

"Um, no."

"Same difference. It is just what happens around me. It was freaky at first, but I am simply used to it now."

Kitty grinned, and she checked the map. "I have the next one."

"Be my guest." Imara watched as Kitty urged her horse to a faster pace to get to the next site.

It went fairly briskly after that. They hopscotched around the property until it buzzed with spectral energy. There were less than a dozen sites to go when Anderson appeared in front of them.

"Kitigan, you and Imara are needed at the house. The XIA are here."

Imara looked to Kitty and shrugged. "I think we are on our way. We should be there in five minutes."

He nodded and winked at his granddaughter. "See you shortly."

Kitty looked at Imara wide-eyed. "What do you think they want?"

"I am guessing they are reporting a shifter-on-shifter attack from last night. Or they are complaining about the spectre on your property. In the latter case, I filed the registration this morning after I brushed my teeth and before breakfast, and if it is the former . . . I am not a shapeshifter by nature." To be sure, she sent a text to Argus asking for his advice. It was after noon, and he was an early riser for his evening shifts, so there was a chance he would get back to her.

You will be fine. You have done nothing wrong.

"I know, but I still like to have my facts straight as for what I am and am not allowed to do."

It is a habit that has served you well. I have your back if needed.

Kitty was tense and curious. Imara had to guess she didn't

run into the XIA that frequently.

They rode in silence, and the collection of vehicles in the yard was visible when they were still a few minutes out.

"Oh, look. A parade."

"How can you make jokes? You could be in trouble."

"Could be, but I haven't done anything that isn't allowed by their own regulations. I checked."

Their horses ambled right into the collection of irate wolves and the black-garbed XIA representatives.

The shifter officer took point. "Which of you is the shifter?"

Imara leaned on the pommel of the saddle and raised her brows. "I am not a shifter, but I am a mage who passed the course with one form."

"I am putting you under arrest for assault of a minor."

She looked over at the smug teens, two of whom were wearing bandages on their necks. "I really don't think so."

The man snarled. "Get off that horse."

"Sure, but I am still not under arrest. By shifter community standards, a non-shifter is within their rights to defend themselves with non-lethal force. They came into my territory and tried to mark it as their own, so I marked them. It isn't anything that won't heal and is definitely something that my shape does naturally."

The teens looked a little nervous.

The agent backed off slightly. "What do you mean?"

"I mean that I was offered the tiny house over there as my home while I was visiting, and as such, when howling and milling wolves circled it at night, putting on my beast and letting them know what I thought of them was within my rights."

The agent turned to Andy. "Did you give her the house?"

"For the extent of her stay and anytime she wishes to use it. That is her home and her property whenever she is here."

The agent got a little frustrated. His teammate came forward and pushed him back with a gentle shove. "Apologies, miss, but we have to look into this."

She inclined her head to the fey. "I am guessing that their

complaint was that I either used magic or attacked them unprovoked?"

"And that you attacked them while they were in human form."

She snorted. "I can prove that one right now." She lifted the edge of her t-shirt where a criss-cross hatch mark of wolf claw residue was raised in red on her skin. "Last time I checked, toes didn't grow that close together on a human form."

All of the males in the area with the exception of Andy and Anderson were staring at her pale skin marked with red welts.

"And, miss, if I may, what is your beast?"

She grinned. "Gryphon vulture."

The wolf officer paled and whirled on what appeared to be his relatives. He began speaking rapidly, growling and cursing them out for being cowardly little pups who didn't deserve to be sneaking around on their own territory.

The parents of the youngsters were shocked. One mother spluttered, "But what about the sexual assault?"

Imara paused, stunned. "The what?"

The woman stiffened her spine and glared at her. "The sexual assault. Henry said you were all over him and he had to fight you off."

Imara grunted. "Right. Of course. Did he also mention that in shifted form I am a *fucking bird?* He was coming in for attack, so I had to shift to defend myself. If you would like to examine the residue outside the tiny house, the claw and footprints tell the tale. I mean, unless you have a way to change shape with your clothing on, and you can fight off an attacker without touching them. It was his claws that made the marks on my abdomen. I don't think I left any on him."

The mother blinked. "Can I see the site?"

Imara looked at the elf and cocked her head. "Care to come with?"

"I believe it would be wise. Jerry doesn't seem quite himself today."

Imara nodded and walked toward the tiny house with her

micro-entourage and Mr. E at her side.

"You seem very well possessed for a woman your age."

"Um, thanks, I guess. I have had a lot of practice." Her phone pinged.

What are the names of the agents?

"Can I ask the names of your team?"

"I am Noro, there is also Agent Wells and Agent Atrico."

"Cool, just a moment." She keyed in the names and sent them.

She was walking them through the events from the roof to the ground when Argus pinged back. *Stay away from Noro. He's a perv.*

Funny, he doesn't look pervy.

He has a girl in every town, sometimes two.

Jealous?

Hell no. I can wait.

"Who are you texting? You have an amazing expression on your face." Agent Noro was right beside her, his silky hair sliding over his shoulder and the scent of wild flowers riding along with it.

"My boyfriend. He's concerned and a bit frustrated that he can't smooth this over."

"Ah, a pity." Noro gave her a long, slow look via his rich purple eyes.

"Not really. I usually do pretty well on my own." She smiled. "Now, what is your verdict on the situation?"

"Well, I can taste the blood and magic of the shifters here, as well as the marks of your claws. What I can also sense is a spectre in the area, and there isn't a registration on file."

She blinked. "There isn't? Huh. Check again."

He raised one pale brow and checked his database. The new entry was marked in hot purple. Imara could see it over his shoulder.

"Master Mirrin. My apologies for not giving you your title."

She wrinkled her nose. "He was my qualifier. It is difficult to find a stored situation that hasn't been installed."

"I don't understand."

"I was an apprentice authorized to make spectres last night, and with my fifth installation behind me, I am now a Master."

"Ah. Congratulations. Would you like to celebrate?"

She grinned. "No."

He blinked and leaned back. "No?"

"Correct. I have chosen my mate, and you are not him. I choose not to dabble."

"That is . . . unusual."

She shrugged. "That is my personal choice. Respect it."

Noro looked more intrigued than perturbed. "I certainly do, but should our paths cross again, I will definitely be checking to make sure that you have not engaged in your prerogative of changing your mind."

The mother was looking at the traces of the scuffle, and she was getting angry. With a brisk nod to Imara, she headed back to the group.

Imara watched her stance and winced. "From previous observation, that pose means that someone is going to get it."

The hand that slapped the young, un-injured man across the face was wielded with righteous indignation. The man stumbled and went down on one knee while his mother grabbed him by the back of his neck and shook him with a lot more power than a human mother would have mustered.

The adult males let her rave on about how her son had not only risked his own life but the lives of mages and seers who had been nothing but polite neighbours.

She hissed at him, and the young male grovelled, begging for forgiveness from Andy.

"I am sorry that I brought my pack to your door. Please forgive me." He had his head bowed, but the rest of him was standing tall.

"You did not assault me or insult me. You owe your words to my guest." Andy extended his hand toward Imara.

The resentment in the young man's gaze should have scalded, but Imara looked at him with what she hoped was an impassive expression.

He turned his head and didn't step toward her, but she let out a sharp yip that made the assembled werewolves jump. He stared at her and walked to her, kneeling in front of her.

"I am sorry for infringing on your territory. It was wrong, it was stupid, and I am deeply sorry for any injury I caused or that my pack caused you."

"Sorry that you saw me naked?"

He looked up and flashed a quick grin. "No, but if there is anything I can do to make up for the injuries, I would be happy to oblige."

She cocked her head. "Are you serious?"

He nodded. "I am. We overstepped our territory, and it will not happen again."

Imara looked to May. "Are the trees on the way?"

May caught on quickly. "They will be here within the hour."

Imara then turned to Noro, "The charges of assault and trespassing will be dropped if they work it off. We have trees to plant, and the more hands to the task the better."

The father cleared his throat. "We were not charging for the assault."

Agent Noro nodded. "She has it right. There is nothing to charge her with. She was perfectly within her rights to act as she did and well within her rights to kill the pack."

The adults paled. Henry's mother stepped forward, "Thank you, miss, for not doing more than you did. They are young, they are stupid, and they are learning. You will have them until your task is complete, and anytime you need extra labour around the farm, call on them. They will work for nothing more than meals, but they do eat a lot."

May nodded. "We will manage the meals, even after Imara and Kit return to school."

Imara reached down and took Henry's hand. She pulled him to his feet, and the tension was broken. The pack members introduced themselves to the Deegles, and everyone was neighbourly.

"So, Agent Noro, I am free to go?"

The elf glided over to her and inclined his head. "You are.

Thank you for your cooperation. My partner will apologize to you at a later time; he has ego and pack standing to contend with."

"A brutal combination."

"Are you sure you will not join me for a meal, perhaps coffee?"

"No. I am good. Thanks though." She winked and scooped up Mr. E.

"This boyfriend of yours is a lucky man to have you so focused on him."

"Yeah, he's nearly as lucky as I am." She nodded to the assembled and headed for Bright Bell. There were stones to bury, and if the trees were on the way, the sooner she got the anchors set, the sooner Anderson would have his lands to roam again.

With unlimited labour on a guilt trip, there was no time left to lose.

Chapter Ten

Kitty was still gasping and giggling about the morning's events. "I can't believe it. You faced down an entire wolf pack."

"Exams are worse. This was just a standard neighbour dispute. The new guys were trying to see how far they could push. If not for your invitation, your family would have dealt with it, I am sure."

"Not as quickly and someone might have gotten hurt."

Imara smiled and patted the soil over the last stone. With the barrier in place, she powered it up. It was enough to last Anderson a few years of free wandering and a light top up could be done remotely.

"No one was hurt. I am a little scuffed up, and Mr. E has confiscated my favourite nightgown, so a few losses on my side, but nothing I can't survive."

Kitty got on her horse and waited with Bright Bell. When Imara was back in the saddle, they headed back to the farm with their hands covered in soil and sweat on their backs.

"So, was Agent Noro really flirting with you?"

Imara chuckled. "The fey don't flirt. For a nearly ageless species, they are shockingly direct. If they want you, they let you know."

"You said no?"

"I did. He isn't my type, and the lithe body type isn't my preference. I like a guy who looks like he can rescue you from danger and you get that feeling in the first glance." She smiled softly.

"Your face is doing that thing again. I can hardly wait to meet your guy."

Imara laughed. "Fine. I will ask him to go out for dinner or lunch with us on his day off."

They were back at the farmstead in a few minutes, and Kitty asked one more question, "So, is he really an XIA agent?"

"Yeah. We met in class."

"That is so cool. Back in a few minutes. These guys have gotten quite a workout today."

Imara headed to the hosepipe outside the barn, and she scrubbed her hands before pressing the wet skin to the back of her neck.

"You were working on something." The older male from the pack was next to her, and she left the stand and the barrel that caught the over pours.

"I was. Just wrapping up one project before the trees get here."

"They just arrived. The ladies are arranging lunch, and when the boys have earned it, they will eat."

"Great. With cooperation, we should be done in two hours. It's a good thing that your guys can dig."

He paused and blinked. "You mean the wolves?"

"Yup. They transgressed, so they need to make themselves useful. At each tree, we need a hole and then the tree planted and filled in."

"Do you know how many trees were ordered?"

Imara smiled, "Enough for our purposes. The sooner we start, the sooner we finish. Don't worry; the soil is soft. I have already dug the initial holes, and the trees go in to the left or right. If I can do it with my pathetic human hands, you wolves should be able to manage it."

His skin darkened with embarrassment. "Ah, right."

She laughed and walked over to the driveway where the process of unloading was happening.

The quantity of trees was staggering, but then, the same quantity of rocks took a lot less space.

Andy asked her, "Can you explain what we are doing with these?"

Imara stood up on a bench, and she clapped her hands. "Right. Ladies and gentlemen. We are working to plant a security ring around the property. The beasts will be repelled by it, and the humans will be reminded of the barrier."

She made eye contact with everyone for a moment, keeping her gaze calm. "This morning, Kitty and I went around and buried stones with a power signature. The only person that they matter to lives on this property. Taking or removing them from their resting places will not benefit anyone unless you want a spectre in your room."

Henry raised his hand. "What is a spectre?"

"A physical manifestation of a deceased mage, containing his power and intellect."

Anderson stepped forward. "I am a spectre."

Anna smiled at him, her mind appearing to have righted itself overnight. "He really is. He died twenty years ago, and here he stands today."

The wolves still didn't seem to understand.

Imara looked to Anderson, "May I?"

He nodded.

With a slight alteration of her energy flow, he went from solid to transparent. With a few steps, he walked to the young wolf and passed his hand through him.

When he stepped back, she powered him up.

He extended his hand to the young man, and they shook on it.

"Holy shit. How did you do that?"

Imara sighed and pinched the bridge of her nose. "I am a Death Keeper. It is what I do. It comes as easy to me as the fur form does to you. Now, who is ready to plant some trees?"

Kitty raised her hand. "I am!"

May nodded, "A few of us will stay here and prepare lunch. You have fun."

Imara looked around and found her shovel. "Oh, we will."

A quad was rigged with a trailer and delivered the trees to the sites. All Imara and the others had to do was trail after and dig holes.

The rush of binding the tree to the stone was powerful. She hadn't done it in ages, but she wanted to do more. It was the strange mix of life and death that made it so heady.

They had completed the first thirty trees when she heard the quad approaching again. A glance over her shoulder made her freeze in place. She stood with her hands grimy and everything else coated in sweat.

The rider dismounted and walked over to her, tipping up her chin for a kiss. "Hiya, Imara. I thought you could use a hand."

She went up on her toes without touching him with her grubby hands. When the kiss was over, she sank slowly to her heels. "Afternoon, Argus. You have a day off?"

"I was called because of a rogue Master Death Keeper threatening a young pack. I was on the road when you were texting me and laughing my ass off at the reports that Noro was filing."

She wrinkled her nose. "Did he call my judgment into question?"

"He definitely did. Apparently, you rebuffed his phenomenal attractiveness. That was according to him, not in the official file."

She blushed. "Right. Good. Well, not good but yeesh. He was persistent."

Argus pressed his forehead to hers. "You were unreasonably attached to your chosen mate. It baffled him. I, however, had a very different reaction."

"I am guessing you did, and as much fun as this is, not only are we not getting closer to lunch, but we are also the focus of many curious gazes."

He chuckled and straightened. "Right. What do you want me to do?"

"Dig holes next to the small holes I made earlier, put in a tree and go to the next one."

She flinched when his uniform shirt came sailing her way, and she tried not to look like she was looking as his footwear, socks and then pants and underwear were left on the quad.

His shift into his gryphon was like watching liquid gold filling a mold. He flew to the next site, and with two claw swipes, he had made a deep hole in the rich soil. Imara got on the quad and followed him with the pack scampering after.

As they filled the fifth hole that Argus had created, Henry looked at her with a grin. "So, that is your boyfriend?"

She blushed and kept working. "Yes."

"You don't share his scent."

"We are waiting until I finish school. I need to focus to get my degree, and after that, we have all the time we need. He's a slow-aging shifter, and my family lives into their nineties."

"You have planned this out."

"Of course. I have one life, and I don't want to waste it. My teen years were skewed because of circumstances beyond my control, but now that I am all grown up, I can pick and choose what I become and what I do."

Henry glanced at the figure of the gryphon flying above the trees, seeking the next sight. "He's what you want to do with your life."

"Part of it." She grinned and looked back at Henry. "The fun part of it."

He laughed, and they trudged off to the next gouged site. It wasn't a bad way to spend the morning.

Chapter Eleven

She was sitting with her hip pressed to Argus's when her phone went off. Imara rose from the bench and wandered off for some quiet. The occasional howl that broke from the pack was making everyone laugh.

"Hello?"

"Hello, Apprentice Death Keeper Mirrin? This is Mage Guide Leader Severance. I am just calling to confirm the visit to the spectral event for Monday night."

Imara blinked. "Of course. If you send me the list of names, I will make sure that the relatives of the girls are aware and ready for our visit."

"That will be wonderful. Thank you so much."

"I will meet you at the rest site. See you on Monday at seven in the evening. I will explain what Death Keepers do, and then, we will all go into the site. Those who are scared can hang back, but if any of the parents wish to come along, I am willing to work with their family spectres."

"That is amazing. We will see you there."

Imara hung up and sighed. Before she could forget, she put the information in her phone. "Damn, almost forgot about that."

Once she had secured the appointment, she returned to the table and snagged a passing slice of pie.

"You look like you saw a ghost, and for you, that is saying something." Argus murmured it in her ear.

"I was just reminded that I am volunteering with the Mage Guides on Monday night."

His shoulders started shaking. "You are going through with it?"

"I am. The more folks learn about Death Keepers, the more it will be a developing branch of study. It is the fear of death that stops folk from using the wisdom of passed mages."

Argus grinned. "You are practicing right now."

"Hell yes, I have to face nine Mage Guides on Monday night. It is a miracle I am not drinking." She stabbed the pie savagely.

Down the table, Mr. E was eating the pie that had been made for him alone, and the pack was cheering him on.

"Is he really eating an entire pie?"

Imara grabbed a second slice and got munching. "Yup. I have no idea where he gets it from."

Argus laughed again.

Imara looked around and kept eating until there was nothing more than crumbs left in the pie plate in front of her. She never could resist pie.

After the sun started to sink, Andy got up and thanked them all for helping them plant. The regular farm hands agreed that the help had been welcome, since they didn't have to do anything.

Imara joined the others in cheering and applauding their host's generosity. She did it lightly because her hands were raw from the digging.

"I hope this can become a fast friendship between our two properties. It was a bumpy start, but the Deegles stand ready to help with all of your seer needs. Oh, and dairy and wool."

The pack applauded and let out yips of agreement.

Kitty came over to Imara. "You get separate thanks later. Tomorrow, my dad is firing up the glass works, and you are going to get some custom pieces."

Imara smiled and yawned. "Sorry to be a party pooper, but I think I am going to have to turn in. It has been a tiring day."

"No worries. We will see you in the morning."

Imara turned to Argus. "I am sorry you came all this way, but I am beat."

"I loved helping out. Should you get calls for brute labour more often, I would love to find a way to be there." He wrapped his arm around her shoulder and gave her a hug.

"You used your other form."

He shrugged. "I was making a point. You have to with some of the new packs. It is a matter of strength."

"And you got to play in the dirt."

Argus snickered, "That too."

She groaned and flexed her hands, glancing over the crowd. "When did Noro and his guys get here?"

"While we were planting. It isn't often that we get to take part in rather enjoyable community activity."

"Do you know them?"

He chuckled. "Yeah, we train together on an annual basis. The wolf is a hot head, Noro is a tramp, and their undead member only moves when he has to. He should be pulling up in an hour or so."

"I don't think I am going to make it. I have to finish binding the trees, and then, I am going to be done for the night."

"What does that entail?"

She smiled softly. "Come with me."

Imara paused and checked in with Kitty, letting her know that she was turning in for the night.

"So soon? Grandpa was going to play his violin."

"I am sure I will be able to hear it. I am just a little tired, and I have one more task to do. I will see you in the morning."

Kitty nodded, but there was a frown between her brows.

Argus was waiting. She took him by the hand, leading him behind the house and to the spectre stone.

"What are you doing?"

"The most secret part of my job. Since you are law enforcement, I thought this would be educational for you." She breathed deeply and placed her hands on the stone.

Argus watched as her body tensed. Light began to glow under her palms, and slowly, Imara took on the same glow.

Her breathing increased in speed, and the glow got brighter. When the light was blinding, she dug her fingertips into the stone, and the switch was flipped.

Light coursed out in a spoke pattern, streaking out to all edges of the property. As one, the trees lit up. All the new, small, wavy saplings thickened and became heavy and mature as the light burned within them.

She was aging the trees.

"Holy shit." He whispered it softly as the display continued. The family and pack gathered behind him to watch.

Slowly, the light faded, and she pulled what was left back into the stone. From the stone, it seeped back into her skin.

There was something about her posture that alerted him. He rushed forward and caught her as she fell.

Imara smiled. "There, now, he can last until all the trees are gone. If he wants to go earlier, they can just let me know."

Her lids were fluttering, and her pulse was beating fast in her neck.

"You need help."

She muttered softly. "I need sleep. If one freaking wolf scratches around my door tonight, I am going to use lightning."

"I will pass along the message." He lifted her higher and walked past the stunned audience.

Andy Deegle nodded. The Althos pack master nodded as well. No one was going to wake her up until she wanted to wake up.

Mr. E trotted along next to him, relaxed and casual. It made Argus feel considerably better. If her familiar wasn't worried, she was just tired.

The tiny house was ridiculously cute. Climbing the ladder to the sleeping loft wasn't easy, but once he had her in bed, he wasn't sure if he should help her out of her clothing.

May Deegle cleared her throat from the main floor. "I will take it from here, Agent."

He nodded. "Oh, thank you. That wasn't a conversation I wanted to have with her after the fact."

"I know. Shoo."

From the unconscious woman on the bed, he heard the

distinct, "Night, Argus."

He grinned and headed down the ladder. "Good night, Imara. Good work today."

Her eyes opened slightly, she slowly raised one thumb before she closed her eyes and relaxed.

Argus left the tiny house, and May headed up the ladder to help Imara get ready for bed.

May helped Imara out of her grimy clothing and shoes. "Imara, how can we repay you? Not only have you become one of Kitty's few friends, but you have also given consistently and selflessly. What can we do for you?"

Imara mumbled, "More pie, and do you know a tailor?"

May smiled at the young lady as she settled into bed. "What do you need a tailor for?"

"New robes. Upgrade and I got taller. They don't match anymore." She rubbed her nose in the quilt. "And quilts. I love the quilts."

May stroked the dark hair from her forehead. "I think that something can be done. You are a Master now?"

"Master Death Keeper. That's me." It was her last utterance; she fell back and was snoring gently in seconds.

May nodded and left the woman to her rest.

Once outside the tiny house, she grabbed Kitty and hauled her to the edge of the gathering. "Do you know her size?"

"Sure, me plus three inches and thirty pounds. She's a solid, tall size twelve."

"Excellent. Fire up the embroidery machine and get the patterns for Death Keepers from the internet. I need them coded as quickly as you can manage it."

"Why?"

"We are making her a present. I am heading into town and shaking up your aunty April."

May turned to her husband and let out a sharp whistle. The keys to the truck flew through the air in seconds. "Thanks, Honey."

She got into the car and headed into town. Having her mother-in-law restored to sanity and her father-in-law back to help work the farm was a gift that she had never imagined. The least she could do was use her family's fabric shop to outfit the Death Keeper appropriately. Anna could make the pie.

Imara woke up feeling itchy. The sweat from the day before was fused on her skin. She could vaguely remember being tucked into bed, but now, she wanted a shower, a glass of water, and breakfast.

Her arms could barely hold her as she headed down the ladder. The shower helped, warming her muscles and getting rid of the dirt and sweat. She was nearly human when she left her small house with Mr. E pattering along beside her.

"Did you stay out long after I passed out?"

No, I curled up next to you, occasionally licking salt off your wrist. I am a cat after all.

She scooped him up and softly mashed his ears until he purred. "You are a kitten, and don't you forget it."

The scent of coffee was in the air, and when she headed into the farmhouse, it was Anderson who was making it. Around the room, it looked as if a fabric bomb had gone off and taken the Deegles and the pack with them.

"They couldn't decide on a colour, so they made you one in brown, one in grey, and one in black." Anderson grinned.

"One what?"

"What did you ask for before you went to sleep?" He hinted.

"Pie?" It was a safe guess.

He chuckled. "I believe you are entitled to your Master's robes. That was what you mentioned to May, and she was the right person to talk to. My daughter-in-law is a champion seamstress who used to win every county fair with her needlework. She shifted to quilting after I died, but this was a chance she couldn't resist. That new machine of hers was chugging along all night."

Tears started to sting her eyes. "They made me robes?"

"Three different styles. Kitty got the patterns and made the sewing machine recognize them. Digitizing, I think they said. Everyone else was measuring, sewing, and checking the fit."

"How did they check the fit?"

"Anna noted that the pack alpha was the same size as you but one inch shorter. After that she was used for all pinning and assembly."

"Why is everyone lying around like the dead?"

"Well, it does take a contribution of living energy for the enchanting of the robes. With three sets of robes, everyone donated some energy. I don't know of many others who will be wearing power from seers, fey, shifters, and two undead."

She blushed. "The XIA donated as well?"

"They have great community spirit, especially your fella. He only has eyes for you, you know."

She smiled. "I know. The feeling is mutual. Only two more terms and a license and I can do something about it."

Anderson raised his brows. "Marriage license?"

"No, business magic license. I am going to make my natural skill for the dead pay."

"Speaking of that, what did you do? I feel almost alive again."

She flexed her fingers and took the cup of coffee that he held out to her. "Ah, well, the saplings were given a taste of age. It was a division of power. I gave them some of you, and as you live here, your presence will be fed by their strong, vigorous lives. It is like a battery and a solar panel. They will charge you continuously, but you can also instantly appear at any point near a tree. If there is a disturbance, you can be there in a blink. If there is a lost lamb, missing calf, or a wild animal, you can be there in a heartbeat."

"What about Anna?"

She brushed the hair from her face and sighed, "I have primed the standing stone that you are embedded in. When she passes, either you can fade away, or I can set her in the stone as well. She can share the energy lines, and you two can exist here in any physical memory you have. You can both appear young again, or you can remain the doting grandparents."

"Speaking of which, what kind of woman is my granddaughter?"

Imara smiled. "She is a wonderful woman, good heart, strong magic, and willing to embrace whatever comes her way. She is the kind of woman to give you the shirt off her back in a blizzard and then pretend she isn't cold." She summed it up. "She is a very good friend."

"Good. She was a kind child, but I have not known her for twenty years."

"You know her now. Learn who she is now, and it is definitely a person worth knowing." She looked around. "Should I be here?"

He chuckled. "I was going to tend the animals and saw movement. Thought you could use the coffee."

"What time is it?"

"Five. Dawn was ten minutes ago."

"Oh, hell. I am going back to bed." She didn't know when Mr. E had made it to her shoulder, but she reached up to pet him. "Did you want to come along, or do you want to use our last hours here to chase sheep."

He was off her shoulder and at the door in seconds.

She opened the door, and the dark streak disappeared. "I hope he doesn't hurt them or himself."

Anderson took her empty cup. "He won't. He's riding them."

The shock that ripped through her was followed by a bubbling laughter that wouldn't be contained. She sprinted out of the farmhouse, ran into the tiny house, and let the laughter loose.

When the mirth had faded, she checked the charge on her phone and tiptoed out of her small temporary home, heading for the sheep paddock. This was worthy of a photo.

Chapter Twelve

Kitty begged, "You have to send me a copy of that."
Mr. E let out a low growl.

"Um, I really don't think he wants me to share it. This image of the kitty riding along on the head of your ram will have to remain a myth or legend."

She stroked the embroidery of the grey Death Keeper robes.

Kitty glanced over without swerving. "Do you really like them?"

"I love them. They are gorgeous and far better than what I had in mind. I am humbled by the effort that your family and the pack put into it."

"I think we have been given adjunct pack status. Now that everything is out in the open and a community has been forged, they are going to be nice and reliable neighbours." There was smug confidence in her tone.

"I still can't thank you enough for these robes. At least I will look somewhat official tomorrow night."

"I really want to see you give that talk to the Guides."

"You just got to witness the practice version. I am just wondering if I can make it plain-spoken enough to get it through to the kids."

"I am sure that you will be fine. What do you think Eckoak is going to have for us tomorrow?"

"With my luck, something involving precipitation." Imara grinned.

"Oh lord, not snow. I really hate snow." Kitty grumbled.

"Ladies, today we are working on snow. You have to combine wind, cold air, water, and cloud density. When you make seven snowflakes, you can go."

Imara wrinkled her nose and looked at the black fabric on the ground around her. Kitty was across the practice area and on the same type of cover.

Imara smiled. "Last one to do it buys the burgers."

The challenge was on.

Rain, sleet, fog, they all came easy. Snow was more delicate.

Imara stood still and raised her hands as if lifting the cold air mass to the cloud cover she had managed. She pushed it up slowly, and the thick fog swirled. It moved in a slow twist, and soon, a single white object fluttered to the ground. Imara ignored it and kept going, using up the fog until the ground around her was covered with snow.

"Mirrin, you are dismissed. Go get some hot chocolate. I set up a carafe in the antechamber."

Imara was shivering and she nodded, heading off to the promise of hot sugar.

When she cupped the hot mug in her hands, she returned to the classroom and watched as Kitty found the move that worked for her. She used cold air into a rain cloud, but the result was the same.

One by one, small flakes separated from the cloud mass and drifted down to the black flooring.

"Good job, Deegle. Get your hot chocolate, and see you at the next class."

Kitty stumbled off the practice area, and Imara caught her, helping her out and to her own cup of hot chocolate.

"How long were we working on that?"

"Four hours?"

"Damn. That was intense. Do you wonder what our marks are?"

"Nope. This is pass or fail. Anything else is just annoying."

Imara waited until they had both finished their beverages before she got her bag and Mr. E.

"Come on, Kitty, you are buying lunch."

"Yes, ma'am." Kitty laughed as they headed up on the lift.

Out in the sun, Kitty asked a question that she had obviously been mulling over. "So, you really aren't sleeping with

Argus?"

"No, I am really not. We agree that he is mine and I am his, but no shenanigans of that nature until after I have my commercial magic license."

"Why wait? Why not just jump him after school is done?"

"Because of the contamination testing."

Kitty looked blank. "What?"

"If they feel you have been compromised by someone who isn't a mage, they can deny your license. It doesn't matter if he or she isn't an influence on you, they still can show up as a contamination of your magic. Having a lover from the extra-natural population who isn't a mage is enough of a factor to deny the initial license. After that, it doesn't matter."

Kitty blinked. "I didn't know that."

"They don't advertise it, but the Death Keepers have a lot of notes regarding membership in the Mage Guild. If you want, I can show you some of the early documentation. Reegar has it in his library."

"That would be wonderful. I confess that I saw those tomes and I started drooling."

Imara laughed. "It happens to us all."

They headed off and had their lunch, with Kitty only mentioning dealing with the Mage Guides twice.

The day was definitely not over.

Imara came out of the change room at the spectre repository, and she was wearing her new Master's robes. The charcoal-coloured fabric was embroidered with dark pewter designs that denoted her rank and her occupation.

Master Wylkinson was manning the desk, and he whistled softly when she emerged with Mr. E on her shoulder. "Those are some great robes."

"Thank you. They were a gift from a friend." She turned and looked toward the door. Lights were beginning to enter the parking lot, and there were quite a few more than she was expecting.

"Are you all right to handle the crowd?"

"I am. Do you have a map of whom I can disturb?"

"All the alert spectres are eager to have visitors. Those who are not alert are indifferent." He shrugged, paused, and cleared his throat. "May I watch?"

"Oh, of course. I am just going to go out and greet the troupe."

"Wait a moment until their Guild Master has them under control. Once they are attentive and focused, make your entrance."

She took one of the staffs with the lamp, and she waited in the shadows of the doorway. When the Guide Master had gathered forty people, Imara verified that her watch was correct, and she stepped out with her hood up.

The crowd stirred nervously when she approached, but when she lifted her chin and smiled in the friendliest manner she could manage, a few of the parents exhaled in relief.

"Guide Master, allow me to introduce myself. I am Master Death Keeper, Imara Mirrin. The local Death Keeper, Master Wylkinson, has allowed me to take you on an exploration of his grounds, and we will be able to meet a few of your ancestors in the process."

She looked to the serious little girls in front, all wearing their little uniforms with the blaze of fire on their shoulder. "Guides, how many of you are a little nervous about being here tonight?"

A few small hands went up.

"Good. Being honest is important. Now, who knows what a spectre is?"

One girl shot her hand into the air and answered before Imara could call on her. "They are the souls of dead mages."

"That is a common thought. What spectres are is an imprint of the magic left behind when there is no mage to control it. I will give you an example. Guides, who among you have a computer with photos on it?"

Eight of the nine girls raised their hands.

"Well, what happens if your computer breaks down? What happens to the files?"

One of the girls raised her hand.

"Yes?"

"My brother knocked a soda into the family computer, and we had to send it away to be fixed, but the information was gone. We got the pictures back, though."

Imara smiled. "Excellent example. In this case, the mage's body is the computer. It holds all the memory of everything it has ever done. When it was broken, the memory was gone, but the cloud and other information storage sites were able to help you put the data back together. Right?"

The little girl nodded.

"That is what a spectre is. It isn't the original; it is a log of all the information and experiences. It can't make a new opinion, and it can't change personalities. It is just a copy of the old information." She nodded toward the stones in the distance. "They are not scary; they are the information printed into magic. No more, no less. Now, as for Death Keepers, what we do is we talk to the spectres, and using our magic, we can take those copies and let them inch into our current world. We can let strangers talk to them, let their families talk to them, and we wake them up so that they don't end when their soul has passed."

One of the girls had her hand up.

"Yes?"

"My grandpa died last year, and he is here. Can he talk to me?"

"Yes. If you want him to. That is another part of the job of the Death Keeper. If you don't want to talk to the spectre, we can make them stop."

The little girl nodded with wide eyes.

"Now, as part of the introduction to Death Keepers, I will explain the clothing."

She extended her arms. "As far back as mage records go, Death Keepers have worn the long robes in the repositories. The spectres expect us to look like this, so it makes communication easier. You know that Guild Officers dress like Guild Officers, and bakers dress like bakers. You expect a uniform and you need to see it. As I have mentioned, spectres are not capable of learning on their own, this is one of the reasons for the uniform. Now, the staff and the lamp.

That one is easy, can anyone guess?"

One of the girls shot her hand up. "You work in the dark?"

"That is correct. While you can address a spectre during the day, they are harder to see. The magic of the Death Keepers makes the spectres glow, and when they glow, we can see them. Night makes it easier to see them."

She looked to the adults, "Now, does anyone have any questions before we go for our little walk?"

One of the fathers looked at her with a grim expression. "Why are you called Death Keepers if the spectres aren't souls?"

"Because the spectres are removed after death. They can't be pulled while someone is alive by the average Death Keeper. Also, in the old days, the distinction was as fuzzy as it is today. No one made a distinction between a ghost and a spectre. Ghosts are trapped souls; spectres are chatty magic exclusive to mages."

A woman blurted her question, "Why is it so expensive?"

Imara had been waiting for that question. "Since so few mages have themselves tested for death affinity, it is an in-demand occupation. The spell work required is taxing, and few Death Keepers can comfortably create a spectre or a holding stone. It is a draining process that needs more respect. Nocturnal vultures is a common epithet, but we show up night after night and let folks talk to loved ones, recover everything from family spells to favourite recipes. We keep the dead company and comfort the living. That is why it is so expensive; you are literally buying a portion of our lives." She smiled brightly. "Now, let's go on into the repository, and I will explain the security features."

Two hours of the gathered Guides and their families talking to the spectres and even the Guide Master tearing up as she spoke to her great-grandmother left Imara tired. Mr. E purred against her neck, and he kept her calm while she shook hands with all of the visitors and got a surprise hug from the Guide Master.

When the cars were gone, she turned back to Master

Wylkinson. "Thank you for that. If we can manage one recruit out of that batch, I would be over the moon."

He was staring at her. "Do you want a job here? Seriously. You can have my job. Those spectres are more alive than they have been in decades."

She rubbed at her forehead and headed back to the office. "Nope. I have my own plan, and it doesn't involve working nights all the time."

"What is your plan?"

"Spectral consulting. I will gladly come here and supercharge your facility, but the guild will have to pay." She grimaced and put the lamp back in its holder.

Master Wylkinson paused for a moment, and then, he smiled. "When you open your office, send me your card. This is a service I would gladly charge folks extra for."

She laughed. "I will. Should be late next year if the Mage Guild grants me the license."

"I look forward to the card in the mail, or if you want to bring more Mage Guides here, you can come anytime." He bowed.

She sighed. "You think I did okay?"

"I think that you made Death Keeping accessible and understandable. The spectres you bolstered were delighted for the added energy, and their families have made appointments to return in the next few days."

"Good. The effect should last anywhere from a week to a month."

"Thanks. I am sorry I was so rude on the phone."

She smiled and pulled her hood back. "No problem. We usually work with the dead, after all."

He laughed and extended his hand. "It is a situation I will change the moment you are available again."

Imara grinned and shook his hand. All in all, it was a good night for her reference page.

Chapter Thirteen

Imara blinked at the command, and then, she looked to see if Kitty had heard what she had.

"Don't just stand there, I want you to go topside and clear up the thunderstorm without affecting the surrounding area."

"Um, Professor Eckoak, that is a little beyond us."

"Really? You two have separately created weather systems; together, you should be able to take down a storm without wrecking the local weather system. Go on up and give it a shot."

"We can work together?" Kitty's eyes were hopeful.

"Of course. I don't want you to die. If you two can't manage it, you fail. Well, you will be given a barely passing grade, but you won't pass with flying colours. For that, I need a rainbow."

Imara looked to Kitty, and they headed to the lift. Mr. E sat up from his bath time and blinked. *You are leaving?*

"We are going to break up the storm up top. Are you coming?"

This I have got to see and possibly offer an opinion on.

Imara extended her hand, and he ran up her arm, settling on her shoulder. She grabbed her bag, and she and Kitty stood close on the lift.

Kitty lifted her hands and created a dry bubble around them. "This is going to be tricky."

"No kidding. First, we have to contain it and then—"

Do you need to contain it? Check the local weather.

Imara grabbed her phone and looked for the local information. "Holy shit."

"What?"

"Our instructor built this storm, just for us. The

245

surrounding areas are clear and sunny. All we have to do is unravel this carefully, and it should fall apart."

Kitty exhaled slowly. "That is something. So, we just have to contain and dismantle weather magic. No problem."

"Right. So, sorry, but we need to get a feel for the temperature."

Mr. E hid in her hair as the wind lashed at them and the heat in the air was apparent.

Imara pulled a solid bubble of warm air around them. "Well, that was fun. Okay, so high humidity, low pressure, and minimal precipitation. If we use cold, we are going to have a tornado. So, thoughts?"

Kitty frowned and looked around. "I know you are going to hate me, but how about lightning? It will drain some of the pressure system and cause a cascading reaction through the cloud layer. I think tearing the sky a new one might be what we need."

"I am willing, but we are going to have to ground it far enough away from us that we won't get zapped."

"I can take the statue on the far side of the field; you can take the one outside that parking structure." Kitty bit her lip.

Imara looked around and saw her distant target. "Right, well, I am going to drop the bubble, are you ready?"

"Yup." Kitty flexed her fingers. "Up from the bottom, right?"

"You got it. Mr. E, hold on." She dropped the air bubble.

The wind hit her, and she staggered. As soon as she could, she focused on calling heat down from the clouds while pushing energy up through the distant statue.

Lightning crackled in a jolt that made her jump. She pushed and did it again, and again, draining the clouds of the magic that powered them.

Behind her, she heard matching crackling and booming, and the sky began to show through. They kept it up, draining the sky of magic until a rainbow arched over the administration building.

Imara sat heavily on the grass, and she looked to see Kitty kneeling with a stunned expression on her face. "Did we do it?"

Eckoak appeared from the lift and looked at the sign of their efforts. "Took you long enough. You should have been able to drain it with four strikes, but well done, ladies. You pass. High marks. Ninety-three percent for the both of you."

The grumpy dryad left them, and they were stuck staring at each other.

Kitty started laughing, then Imara followed suit. They sat in the grass with the sun beaming down on them, revelling in the fact that they hadn't killed anyone.

Mirrin Deepford looked out her office window and saw the rainbow. "Thank goodness."

Eckoak appeared in the chair next to the desk. "No kidding. I thought they were going to fry each other."

"And yet you let them try to break the sky, Koki."

Eckoak shrugged. "They needed to learn. They still think that it was magic in the sky and not natural energy. I believe that I will save that little informational tidbit for their post-class briefing."

"You didn't build that storm?"

"Nope. I had it blown in by another weather mage overnight. They managed to burst it and keep it from travelling, which is all I was after. You have a good kid there. Makes me almost wish I had reproduced myself."

Mirrin laughed. "That is a frightening thought. Where are the girls now?"

"The women are laughing their asses off in the meadow over the classroom. All that power has a somewhat euphoric effect. It's why most weather mages are so damned cheerful."

Mirrin looked to her friend and shrugged. "Glad you are in a good mood then."

Eckoak waved her hands. "Give me your computer; I need to enter in their marks, so I can get the hell out of Dodge."

"I thought you were writing a post-class report."

"I am coming back." Eckoak sighed in exasperation. She

grabbed the laptop, logged in, and her fingers flew in a rapid blur that was hard to watch.

Mirrin smiled and cocked her head. "Where did you learn to type?"

"It was a misspent youth. I still prefer the Dvorak keyboard, but this is fine." She typed for a few minutes, saved her work, and then logged out.

"There, Mirrin, you daughter's grades are final. You can breathe now."

"She succeeds or fails on her own. I am not using any clout to get her a passing grade."

Eckoak stood and stretched. "You don't have to, she's your daughter. Lucky too. It was like she could figure out everything and then used hand signals to pass the information on to Deegle."

"It isn't cheating."

"No, but it is a little weird. Ah, well, I will see you in a few weeks before you get all crazy with the next term."

Mirrin rubbed her neck and then smiled. "Thanks for teaching this course."

"You are welcome. It was fun to see what your genetics can do in a proper receptacle. She's impressive, and I get the feeling that she is destined for surprising things."

"She wants to open a consulting business."

"She will be good at it. If she teams up with the Deegle girl, she might even go further with it than she can imagine."

Mirrin sighed. "I don't think she imagines much. She wants stability and is willing to do what she can to achieve it. That is what the whirlwind of courses is all about."

"Whatever. I tried to be nice, and you disagreed with me. See you in a few weeks. Good day, Chancellor."

Mirrin stared at the spot where the dryad had been, and she leaned back in her chair. "Further than she can imagine, huh? I am looking forward to seeing it."

Bara was waiting when they got back. "So, how was your weather class?"

"Pretty good. I think we just had a surprise exam."

Bara frowned. "Really? I had a present for Mr. E. I think he would enjoy it."

Present?

"You can still give it to him."

Bara grinned and headed into the kitchen area. When she returned, she held out some tiny objects, and Mr. E wasted no time in putting on the tiny yellow galoshes and standing up on his hind feet. The bright miniscule umbrella set off his black fur.

Imara snuck her phone out and took another picture.

You have to stop doing that. It was hard to take him seriously as he pranced around like an itty-bitty bear in his little boots.

Imara tried to fight her laughter, she really did, but instead of fighting it, she created a miniscule raincloud above Mr. E's head, and he stomped around, completely dry.

When her giggles had faded, she dissipated the cloud and licked her fingers.

Bara stared at her. "Did you just make it rain indoors?"

"I think so. His boots look wet, so I am guessing I did."

"Wow. That's . . . wow. Is it complicated?"

"Is what complicated?" She burst into giggles again. "Damn, I think I am high on magic."

Reegar appeared and gave her a long look. "Weather magic. Have you been using lightning?"

She nodded and went off into giggles as Mr. E tried to pull his little boots off.

"Magic, ozone, nitrogen, and oxygen. It will wear off in an hour or two. Just stay away from your kitten and you will be fine. Maybe follow your friend's example and sleep it off."

Imara sighed. "Boring! I am going to help Mr. E get his boots off, and then, I am going to braid his hair."

She lunged, and all hell broke loose.

"I am fine now. You can untie me." Imara sighed.

"Oh, no. I am not falling for that one again." Bara scowled and pulled her still sticky hair away from her face.

"Listen, I didn't know I could make it rain soda. I am sorry." She tried to put her sincerity into her voice. "I am very, very sorry, Bara."

She looked down at her feet, "You, too, Mr. E. I am really sorry."

His fur was all matted, and he was giving her a homicidal glare. *You are going to owe me for this.*

She didn't know what he meant until he moved behind her and the ropes were shredded. She flexed her wrists and got to her feet.

Bara was shocked. "Why did he let you go?"

Imara wrinkled her nose. "I stopped laughing at him. He knew it had worn off."

She ran the water until it was warm to the touch and got a clean cloth. She filled a basin with warm water and sat at the table. Mr. E came up to her, and he stepped into it.

Imara dipped the cloth in the water and squeezed it out, blotting the soda out of his fur an inch at a time.

"It is a good thing that you are this size. It makes it easier to undo this."

Bara sat at the table. "I am next."

"I am not going to wash all of you."

Bara snorted, "I just don't want to touch any of my stuff on the way to the shower. You will pick up my clothing, hang up my towel, and close the door after me."

"Yes, ma'am." She continued to get the sticky residue out of her kitten for another ten minutes.

When he was dry and curled up in a clean, dry towel, she went to act as Bara's butler for a few minutes.

After she was finished cleaning up the floor from the impromptu soda storm, she sat in exhaustion and looked at Reegar. He was sitting near the library with a book in his hands. "So, power drunk?"

"Apparently. My instructor didn't mention it."

"Eckoak is not very forthcoming with mundane bits of information."

"You have that right." She leaned back and tried to relax tense muscles.

"What is your next insane course?" He raised his brows.
"Just a little bit of stealth magic. Nothing serious."
Reegar jumped to his feet and headed into the library. He came back to the table and dropped a stack of books three feet high on the wood. "Read these and then tell me it isn't serious. Can't you take another course?"

She frowned. "What do you mean? Stealth magic is just like enchanted hide and seek, right?"

"Start reading. If you still want to take the course after you finish them, I will help you all I can." He left her alone.

Not one to ignore assistance when it was offered, Imara started reading the stack of tomes, and by the third, there was a nauseated feeling in her brain.

By the fifth book, she was shaking. Stealth magic wasn't quite what she thought it was when she chose it for its high credit load.

I will help as well. I was a master of most of the skills of assassination and concealment. It is how I was able to make it into the homes of so many demon-contaminated mages. His little nose and wide eyes peeped out of the towel, at odds with his subject matter. *The key to stealth magic is to calm your soul before beginning anything. You already have mastery of that move from your work with the spectres. If you wish to do it, I will help you through it.*

Reegar returned. "So? What do you think so far?"

"I am petrified, but I am going to do it. Mr. E says he has used the magic before, and I trust him."

Reegar heaved a sigh. "Well, in that case, read these."

He beckoned, and a stack of books came floating toward the desk. "These are on practical exercises and means to strengthen the reflexes you will need. Your gentlemen caller will be able to help you with the physical assault aspects."

She wrinkled her nose. "Is that really necessary?"

"It is if you want to come out of the course whole in mind and body. How did you even get in?" He growled it.

"I had a recommendation from my domestic magic instructor. She said I had a natural talent for assassination. I thought she was being funny."

Reegar closed his eyes and covered them with his hands. Imara got the feeling that if he wasn't already dead, he would have wished it on himself. When he sat up, he took a deep breath to steady his nerves, and he looked at her. "Right, the first thing you need to know is the art of being still."

She smiled and focused. After an hour of lectures, she came to one important discovery, if she acted like Mr. E, everything would become easy. It was as terrifying as it was encouraging, and she tried to find a middle ground.

Two more terms and she would be out on her own. What was she going to do without Reegar and Bara?

Kitty groaned and clutched her head on the sofa. "What happened?"

"You got caught in a storm. Go back to sleep." Imara grinned and fished out her phone to order pizza. She had just gotten through one of the toughest courses at Depford College, her friends were with her, and one of the toughest courses at the college was looming. She really needed a celebration.

You had to celebrate the small stuff, or the big stuff could pull you under.

Stealth Magic 401
The Hellkitten Chronicles Book 4

VIOLA GRACE

Stealth Magic 401

THE HELLKITTEN CHRONICLES

Stealing an ancient artifact is a strange test, but going up against her family and the law adds a new level of difficulty.

Imara wants nothing more than to find a different course, but stealth magic gives her the credits she needs to stay on track, and there aren't any other options rearing their heads.

Stealth Magic is not what she thought it would be, and the idea of breaking into a home to rob an ancient artifact for her final exam was a little daunting. Luckily, Imara has friends who are going to help her through training, some old and some new.

Through some work with the XIA, she finds a tutor for her training and a place to do it. Ritual Space offers her a welcome, and the inhabitants set themselves to the monumental task of her training. The exam is getting closer and time is a factor.

Mr. E just likes chasing the enchanted bunnies of Ritual Space.

Chapter One

Doing push-ups in the living space with forty pounds of books on her back was not the way she wanted to be caught by Argus.

"You are supposed to read them."

She kept going through her set, and muttered through clenched teeth, "I know, but I got bored with that, so I am trying osmosis."

Argus crouched next to her, and she caught a very distinct lungful of the warm scent that made her cuddle with him at every opportunity. "You know that your kitten is on top of the books?"

She grunted and shoved upward again. "I suspected. I keep getting snickers in my brain, and I am definitely not laughing."

She finished her set and collapsed on the rug, sending tomes of magic and her kitten to the floor.

"So, how is the physical training going?"

She muttered against the wool fibres, "Fantastic. Give me five minutes, and I will be ready to head out with you."

He chuckled. "You look half dead."

"I will wake the other half, I promise." She pushed herself upright and gave him a quick kiss. Before he could make a grab for her, she jumped to her feet and headed up the stairs.

A magic wave scrubbed her skin clean while she peeled off her exercise clothing and yanked on her date-night outfit. Her domestic magic course had not gone to waste.

Jeans and a lace-up shirt were just the things, and as she headed back downstairs, her familiar jumped onto her shoulder with a determined bit of claw work.

You are not leaving without me.

She sighed. *Eventually, I am going to want to be alone*

with Argus.

Not until you have graduated.

Spoilsport.

They are your rules; I am just making sure that you adhere to them.

She made a face and kept going as if she didn't have a fluffy chaperone on her shoulder. He was right, they were her rules. She had decided early on that no man was worth interrupting her education, but every now and then, when she and Argus were cuddled and watching a movie, she wanted to try to have it both ways.

"Okay, ready."

Argus smiled brightly, his appreciation glowing in his eyes. "This is going to be the best undercover operation I have ever been on."

She grinned and linked her arm with his. "Shall we? I have never been to a carnival before."

Mr. E wriggled with excitement. He was up for it as well.

"Never?" Argus's shock was apparent.

"Nope. How many times do I have to tell you that I have been sheltered by choice?" She waved at Reegar on their way out.

"I suppose it still seems peculiar to me. I apologize." His smile said he wasn't particularly contrite.

They walked to his SUV, and he tucked her inside. She buckled up, and Mr. E jumped onto the dashboard.

Argus got behind the wheel and buckled in. "He really loves to pretend he is driving."

"Yes. It is one of his favourite parts of modern life."

He started the vehicle and started the long drive to the carnival outside Redbird City.

"Thank you for doing this, by the way."

She smiled. "The XIA is compensating me for my time via the Death Keepers. My rise to Master is really paying off."

He grinned as they went around the on-ramp toward the city. "How did the last mage guide tour go?"

Imara smiled and leaned back. "I am getting the hang of it. The repositories and memorial gardens are lining up to get me in, and the mage guides are doing the same."

"Is that good?"

"It is very lucrative. It means that I will be able to afford a decent set of furniture when I open my office."

"You charge for taking the kids to the repositories?"

She wrinkled her nose. "No, the mage guides don't pay. The repositories pay the Death Keepers guild for my services and the rise in recruitment. There are teens taking the initial exams to determine aptitude for being Death Keepers because of the tours. Apparently, I make the tours *less creepy*."

He laughed.

"So, how are the guys? Are they upset that they aren't with us?"

"Oh, they are going to be there, but it would look a little odd if we all arrived in the same vehicle."

Imara nodded. "Makes sense, so shall I be all giddy or fawn all over you?"

"Just have fun. When you have fun, your face lights up, and everyone around you catches your joy."

She blushed so hard she felt like her shirt melted.

Mr. E was asleep on the dash, and his snoring distracted them both. He had a mature man's snort in a tiny kitten's body.

"Are Ivor and Lio going to be here?"

"Eventually. They will be arriving the moment that the sunset is firmly entrenched."

She smiled. "Right. Good. Sorry, but I am imagining them together on a carousel."

Argus chuckled. "No, not a carousel. They are far more inclined to ride a roller coaster."

"I am imagining Ivar eating a toffee apple."

Argus snorted, and they kept the conversation light while they drove the distance to the carnival. She paused and stared once. "Is that really Ritual Space?"

"It is. Adrea is a charming woman who will not suffer anyone to abuse her property. She runs the place with an iron grip, and it is refreshing to know that she will uphold the law."

Imara looked at the structure of the fencing that would keep any standard mage from climbing over it for a peek. "That is serious fencing."

"It is. Few folks are stupid enough to try and get in. The rabbits are always on guard."

She widened her eyes with delight. "Rabbits?"

"Bunnies. The story goes that folks brought them in for fertility rituals, but the bunnies escaped before they could be sacrificed. They fled through the grounds and have absorbed the magic of all the improperly executed spells."

"Wow. Do they have a leader?"

He chuckled. "They actually do. Aside from Adrea, they answer to a bunny named Blueberry."

"Wow. Good to know the chain of command if I ever need to go there."

"As you are in mage training, you probably will, at one point or another."

She grinned and looked back over her shoulder at the main entrance. "Maybe."

The rest of the ride was her holding his hand as they approached the carnival with its visible structures in the distance getting larger by the minute.

Mr. E tucked himself behind her hair as they got in line at the entrance.

She looked around her in amazement. Being raised in Sakenta City, she didn't have much experience with magical races, but time with Argus, Lio, and Ivor was helping considerably.

The smells of the carnival were amazing. Popcorn, sugar, deep-fried everything, and the chemical tang of toilets designed for crowds.

Argus paid for their entry tickets as well as a giant wad of ride tickets.

Imara linked her arm with his and nudged him with her hip. "So, where are we off to first?"

"Did you want to play some games? Go on some rides? Get a snack? I would recommend the last two in that order, by the way."

She chuckled. "I am expecting a proper meal after this."

"Of course. Now, do you want to try your hand at a ring toss, or maybe darts at a balloon?"

She wrinkled her nose and checked her pocket, pulling out a few bills. "I think that the hoop toss is about my speed."

"Hoop toss it is."

She smiled politely at the young man at the booth and said, "I would like to try, please."

He was bored, and he handed her three rings in exchange for two dollars. She glanced up at the wall of toys and then down at the pegs.

She looked at the ring, noted its imperfections, held it lightly, and threw it at the bottles in the centre of the booth. It sailed over the red-banded bottles and snagged on the black.

"Winner!"

She frowned. "What about my other two tosses?"

He raised his hands and stepped back. She focused again and struck the second and then the third black rings. Lights and sirens went off. The teen was screaming, "Winner!"

Imara blinked rapidly and looked at the barker. "What can I pick?"

He reached up and was going to give her the lion, but she held up her hand. "The black panther, please."

The youngster grabbed the medium-sized toy with fluffy fur and huge green eyes.

"Thank you." She smiled brightly and turned to Argus. Her date was bent over, laughing.

She linked her arm with his and dragged him over to the darts. "I have something for Mr. E, now something for you."

It was another round of precision and checking the weighted darts, but she walked away with a lovely fluffy griffin for Argus, and he was still strangling himself with amusement.

"Those are fun. Now can we try a ride?"

He looked at his griffin and grinned. "Yes, of course. What do you want to do?"

She cocked her head up at the swings and wrinkled her nose. "I can already fly, so why not one of those ones that goes around backward?"

And so, they walked amongst the other folks out for a fun afternoon and drifted down toward the ride that let out a siren and then swirled backward on a loop.

She looked around and then she got excited. "Can we go on that one instead?"

Argus looked down at her with his golden eyes resigned. "Are you sure?"

"Yes. Yes, I am."

And with her heroic and charming companion resigned, they got in line for the spinning teacups.

All Imara remembered of the ride was laughter flashed with a feeling of being rather ill.

She leaned against Argus and made a face. "That was a mistake."

"Yes, but it is one that you needed to make for yourself. Are you up for the haunted house?"

She looked at him with her eyes narrowed. "Does it mean we have to pass the food stall?"

"No. It is in the other direction."

"Excellent. Nothing like some fun and festive ghosts."

They got to the line, and she leaned against Argus. He wrapped his arms around her and ran his hands up and down her spine like they were a normal couple.

When they were fourth from the front of the line, he lifted her chin on his knuckles. "Feeling better?"

"Yeah. Who knew that those little cups would make me and Mr. E so queasy?"

Her kitten was clinging to the side of the panther she had won, between it and her body. He was still looking a little woozy.

"They are famous for it, but you need to rack up these experiences for yourself."

She smiled. "Yeah, thanks for that. At least this one just goes around and tries to scare us."

"Yes, but a lot of couples use it as an excuse to make out."

"Is that a suggestion?" Her cheeks got pink, she could feel it.

He smiled slyly. "Merely a commentary."

Imara could feel the pull of a spectre, but it was hard to pin it down. There was shielding in the way.

"I am going to feel so protected with you next to me, surrounded by all that metal."

He kept an arm around her and gave her shoulder a squeeze to let her know he was catching on.

The line moved forward, and the couple ahead of them got into the car. Imara watched the attendant lock them in with a snug-fitting bar, and she leaned her head against Argus. If he was snug, she should be able to get out if she needed to.

Their car came around, and she kept the stuffed animal and Mr. E between her and the bar.

Argus also slid his arm in between them and flexed as the bar came down. The result was that as the car started moving, Imara had room to spare.

She cuddled up to Argus and smiled into the darkness, "Now, let's see what we can see."

The shadows flexed and twisted around them, and Imara looked around curiously. She had never been in a haunted house before. She looked forward to being frightened.

Chapter Two

Imara ignored the flopping synthetic mummies, the flashes of crimson light, and puffs of smoke-filled air. There was something in the ride that was adding to the creepy ambience, and she had only touched something similar once before.

Her senses went on the alert, looking for the accumulation stone.

When spectres began to lunge out at her, she knew she was close. Argus was flinching, but he didn't break character.

As a spectre of an old woman lunged at her, she screamed and burrowed close to Argus, curling her legs up and onto the seat. She pressed her familiar and the panther onto Argus's lap, and when they were under the mount for the stone, she lunged upward and captured it. The spectres ceased immediately, and she resumed her seat next to Argus.

"What was that?"

She whimpered. "Sorry I am so jumpy. The ghosts scared me."

Mr. E climbed into her lap, and she pulled the panther in to cover him as they went from dim light and loud noises to red sunset and thronging crowds.

The mechanism unlatched the restraint, and Argus left the car, taking her hand as he kept his griffin under his other arm.

He kept his arm around her as they walked down the steps. The attendant looked at her with a frown. "Is she okay?"

"It's her first carnival, and we started with the teacups. She's enjoying the novelty."

The attendant laughed; they headed back to the midway

at a slow and steady pace.

Argus asked casually, "What did you catch?"

"A stone that shouldn't exist."

"Really? That is fascinating."

"Are they following us?"

"Oh, yes. We are going to make the exit before they catch up though, or we would if you fainted."

She smiled and stumbled. He picked her up and carried her through the exit, with folks murmuring in their wake.

Out in the lot, he kept walking toward his vehicle, but the multiple feet scraping on gravel proved that they had, indeed, been followed.

"Put the lady down and hand over the stone."

Argus turned with her in his arms, and he looked at the humans who were demanding the stone. "I am sorry. I don't know what you are referring to."

"Your lady friend grabbed a stone in the haunted house. We need it back. It is a vital component of our operation."

Imara looked them over and didn't see a Death Keeper in the bunch. She murmured to Argus, "They can't carry it."

"Why not?"

"Not Death Keepers. It isn't a soul stone; it is an accumulation of dying spectres. By themselves they are powerless, but together, they are a deadly force."

The leader of the men, a surly fellow, shouted, "Enough. Hand over the stone."

Imara kept her hand clenched, and she shook her head. "No. It's fucking dangerous."

Argus slid her to her feet, and Mr. E crept to her shoulder.

She stood with her hands at her sides. "I am not going to give up this stone. I don't want your deaths on my hands."

The guys blinked, and their spokesman said, "What the hell are you talking about?"

"You didn't put this in place. It was done for you by someone who specializes in death. This stone was getting stronger with each screaming client, and soon, the mages would have been strong enough to do more than gather stray energy, and the people they would feed off are those who are close to it at a fixed proximity."

The men looked at each other, and in the next heartbeat, full darkness fell. The XIA agents moved silently, and when the head of the thugs said, "Fuck it," and charged, the extranaturals moved in and took over.

Argus lunged forward, but he dropped his griffin. Imara bent to pick it up, and one of the thugs tackled her.

She went down to the gravel with a thud. Mr. E went flying.

A grubby hand scrabbled at her wrist, but she didn't open her hand. No one was getting that stone.

A low growl got the idiot's attention, and Imara's hellkitten had morphed into a hellcat once again. His eyes glowed with rich flames, and he grabbed the man clawing at her by the back of his shirt, flicking him away toward the parked cars.

He stood next to her while she got back to her feet. When she was standing and had the stuffies in her custody once again, she leaned on him and watched the zip-tying of the thugs from the haunted house.

Argus came up to her after glancing warily at Mr. E. "Are you all right?"

"Yes. I think so. I have a grip on the stone, and that is what matters."

"Imara, your hand is turning black."

She nodded. "I thought so. I am using my life force to wrap around the stone. It consumes me much more slowly than it does normal humans or other mages."

"Consumes?"

Mr. E's giant head lapped at her fist, and she opened it slightly. A moment later and her skin felt like skin again.

"What happened? Mr. E, what did you do?"

Her familiar looked at her with a smug demeanour, and he shrank back down into his normal fuzzy form.

Don't worry; I can regurgitate it when we get to a safe storage area.

Imara flexed her hand and ignored the kitten climbing her thigh, dangled from her shirt, and continued up her arm.

When he was settled against the back of her neck, she turned to Argus. "Well, he has it. So, now, we need a place to safely store it."

"Can't we take it to a repository?"

"No. This thing is dangerous. Degraded spectres are worn down to the basic compulsions. They want freedom, power, and life again. They can't have the life, and it makes them angry, so they take what they can. They have no intellect; they can't be reasoned with. They are formless ghouls. Creepy fuckers."

He blinked. "Right. Well, where do you suggest?"

"A Death Keeper made this, so until we figure out who that was, it needs to be safe from interference."

Lio came forward and offered, "Why don't you contact Ritual Space? They might have some sort of facility for storing powerful artifacts."

Argus pulled out his phone and dialled. "Good evening, Madam Adrea. My name is Agent Argus Dencroft with the XIA, and I need your help."

Imara got a slight smile as Argus went into detail on the phone.

Why are you so happy?

He asked for help.

Her kitten snorted and rubbed his head against her neck.

Argus turned to her and extended his phone. "She wants to talk to you."

Imara took the phone. "Hello?"

"Hello, I am Adrea from Ritual Space. Who am I talking to and what do you have that needs our special brand of concealment?"

"My name is Imara Mirrin, I am a Master Death Keeper and a student at Depford College. The object that we need secure storage for is an accumulation stone. Some idiot Death Keeper has fused nearly a dozen faded spectres into one stone. This makes it an excellent power source for a weak mage, and it makes it a deadly weapon in the wrong hands. Until I can unravel and disperse the spectres, I need a safe place to put the stone."

"Can you do that?"

"Oh, yes. I have an affinity for the dead."

"How long will it take?"

"Well, provided that it goes smoothly, I should be able to disperse the mages in about eight weeks. I am a student, after all. It is a bit out of the way for me, but I can make it there once a week at your convenience."

"Have Argus bring you in. I look forward to seeing what you can do."

Imara smiled, though Adrea couldn't see her. "Thank you."

She hung up and smiled at Argus. "We are good."

"Really?"

"Yes, she will help us."

"How long can Mr. E hold that thing?"

"Two hours, tops. So, please, let's get out of here."

Lio called out, "What do we charge them with?"

Imara answered, "Possession and use of an uncontained artifact of mass destruction."

Argus whistled and looked at Mr. E. "Right. Well, we had better get it somewhere safer. Get in the car, and I will get you to safety."

She nodded and looked out at the sea of dark SUVs. "Um. Give me a hint."

He walked up to one of the vehicles and opened the door. She hopped up and settled into the seat, buckling up and keeping her stuffed animals at her feet. Her live buddy she kept against her and kept a hand on as they left the carnival parking lot and headed back to the highway.

Her fuzzy buddy's body temperature was lowering. His normally warm little tummy was approaching her skin temperature.

Ritual space was less than half an hour away. They would have plenty of time.

"So, what was going on with your hand, precisely?"

She flexed her fingers. "It was dying slowly. It's an emergency response that I learned from Thomins. He was the one who offered me an apprenticeship, and he eventually pushed through my journeyman papers with the guild."

"A good man."

She snorted. "A man who liked to have someone to do the bulk of the maintenance on the spectre stones. He was a good friend, though, in as much of a friend as I had in those days."

Imara continued, "He taught me to block energy from my limbs in case of a thirsty spectre."

"Have you run into one of these before?"

She nodded. "Once. Death Keepers are given bonuses for clearing shattered and worn spectres from their memorial gardens or repositories. A friend of Thomins was filling in for a few hours while Thomins got some dental work finished up, and he took a stone out and showed it to me. I can only describe it as horrific. He had cleared out his fading section to make room for more spectres and stuffed the remaining traces of passed mages into the stone in his hand."

"Let me guess, Thomins came in."

"He did and beat the shit out of his friend. His friend dropped the stone, and I picked it up . . ." She trailed off, trapped in the memory.

"What happened?"

"The strongest of the spectres was leeching power from the weaker ones. They were all still there, the stronger roaring, the weaker screaming. The stronger one grabbed hold of me and tried to pull my energy out through the contact point. Thomins slapped it out of my hand, put it in a pouch, and called the authorities."

She rubbed her hand in memory. "When the guild officers were gone with Thomins' buddy, he started showing me how to defend myself against an accumulation stone."

"Does it always threaten your limbs?"

She looked at him and reached out to pat his hand. "Only when there are other targets that the stone could choose. Contact with me revs them up, and pulling in extranatural energy is very easy for them. It is why Death Keepers were created as a branch of the Mage Guild. We are needed if folks don't want embedded spectre stones to be draining life left and right out of all who pass."

"Deadly jewellery."

"Very."

He grabbed her hand and kissed the inside of her palm. "I am glad you made it out, fingers intact."

"Me too."

She kept tight to Mr. E, feeding him what she could via their connection. Her eyes scanned the horizon and watched for the first signs of Ritual Space. When the lights of the parking lot flickered in the distance, she nearly cried. Keeping her Death Keeper face on was the key to getting through this, but inside, she was sobbing with relief.

When she got out of the car, she stepped toward the gateway, just in time to watch it swing open.

"Imara? Welcome to Ritual Space. I am Adrea Morrigan, this is Officer Hyl Luning."

"This is Agent Argus Dencroft. Oh, and this is Mr. E, my familiar, and currently the fading containment of the stone."

Adrea smiled; her snow-white hair and bright blue eyes glowed in the limited light. "Come this way, and we will find you a gateway to safe storage."

Imara smiled gratefully. "Thank you. Mr. E, cough it up."

She set him on the white gravel, and she supported him while he went through the standard feline retching noises before the crystal fell. Imara grabbed it and scooped her familiar up. "Lead the way."

Adrea led them through the gateway, and Imara could feel the magic in everything around her. There was an outburst of life, and nothing could suppress it. "Wow."

Adrea smiled. "Thank you. It has been the work of generations to keep it this invigorated. I am sorry; I made an assumption. Is this your first time here?"

"Yes. No apologies necessary."

A white and blue flash appeared in front of them. Adrea nodded and crouched to pet him. "This is Blueberry. He is effectively my butler. He will lead you to the position he deems safest for the stone."

"Don't you want . . ."

"No, I don't want to know where it is. Just follow the blue rabbit." Adrea winked. "I will put a kettle on."

Imara turned to Argus, gave him a thumbs-up and headed off in search of the bunny.

Chapter Three

Walking through the brush and into the shadows, she followed Blueberry until he led her to a gateway.

"Holy heck." She stepped through the wall between worlds and looked around at a pocket dimension filled with benches of stone and archways of energy.

The bunny hopped up on the bench and chattered at the arc.

Imara stepped forward and settled the stone into place. The energy in the archway grabbed it and held it in mid-air. The power had the signature of inert gel. The stone would get no purchase there. There was no power for it to consume.

Imara reached out and withdrew her power from the stone, filtering it through Mr. E until they were both back to normal strength.

Well done, Mage.

"Thank you. Now, I hope that bunny is willing to lead us back."

The blue and white escort waggled his puff of a tail and hopped out of the building, leading the way.

Imara followed the rabbit and waited for Mr. E to ask to be on his own four feet. He seemed content to ride along in her arms.

After the shadows and trees, they stepped out amongst berry bushes. A barely visible path led her to a backyard where Adrea was sitting with the two men, a tray of cookies, and a pot of tea. The entire area was illuminated by lanterns that were not attached to anything.

Argus got to his feet and came to her. "Imara, you have been gone for hours. Are you all right?"

She blinked. "I thought it was just a few minutes."

Adrea winced. "Sorry. I forgot to regulate the temporal

energy in that area. You lost a few hours."

She checked her watch, and it did, indeed, show that it was nearly midnight. "Damn."

Argus stayed next to her as she went to have a seat. Adrea poured her some tea, so Imara grabbed a cookie.

Adrea smiled and asked, "So, you are at Depford College?"

Imara swallowed her mouthful of chocolate chip cookie, and she mumbled, "I am in accelerated general studies."

Hyl smiled. "What does that entail?"

Argus grinned. "Taking a bunch of mindboggling courses to add skills that most mages can't manage."

Imara ignored his words but patted his leg. "I am taking a number of high-credit courses to get a mage degree as quickly as I can so I can open my own spectral consulting agency."

Hyl nodded. "Nice. What is your next course?"

She glanced at Argus and then looked back to Hyl. "Stealth Magic."

Hyl looked shocked and amused. He pulled a card out of his pocket, wrote something on the back, and handed it to her. "When they ask you if you have a tutor, say yes."

Adrea looked between the two of them. "Is there something I should know?"

Argus was looking suspiciously at the business card. "Why does she need you?"

He informed the group of them. "Stealth Magic is a difficult course. On the first day, you are going to be offered a tutor. Once you have that tutor, you will need six to eight weeks of intensive training to work your body, your spells, and your nerve. On the last day of actual class, you will be given your assignment. It usually entails breaking and entering into the house of a prime family to retrieve an easily identifiable heirloom. You bring it to your instructor, and you pass."

Imara's eyes bugged out. "Are students arrested?"

"All the time, but if they have their course assignment sheet with them, they are usually just dismissed, as long as they are caught on the date of the exam."

Imara ran her left hand through her hair. "Shit. It is too late to cancel the course."

Adrea lifted her hand. "If you have a secure space, I can link a temporary gateway to you. You can come and go for training. Hyl lives here, so he is here more often than not."

Hyl smiled. "Not many women pass the course. It would be my honour to help you through it."

Argus looked at the gathered folk. "I can help as well."

Imara looked to Hyl and took in the silence of his figure. He had training, and she guessed that some of his assignments ended in death.

"Argus, you are distracting as hell when you are around me. It is wonderful when we are together, but I can't imagine concentrating when you are next to me. Also, I can't work out at the college if I am understanding Hyl correctly. This is a very competitive course, right?"

He nodded. "I took it years ago, but I can't imagine that it has changed much."

Imara stroked Mr. E and looked around. "Thank you. I will take you up on that offer."

Adrea grinned and clapped her hands. "Excellent. When do you start?"

She bit her lip. "My course starts in thirty-nine hours."

Adrea nodded. "Good. I will lay in some extra supplies."

Hyl chuckled. "It isn't a tea party."

Can I go and play with the rabbits?

Imara looked down at a sheepish Mr. E. *Don't chase them. They are not food.*

I know. They glow with power. The damned kitten wants to play.

She set him down, and he went bounding over to the bunnies on the grass. There was a moment of introduction and then black tumbled around with white and grey.

Adrea blinked. "He is a very fun familiar."

"I know. He isn't fond of being a kitten unless he is standing in a banana cream pie. Perhaps coconut in a pinch."

"Is that good for him?"

"He isn't an actual cat, so yeah, it's fine. He gets a little gassy but is blissed out for days. The bunnies just looked like fun to the beast brain that comes with the fluffy body."

Hyl looked at her. "He won't be able to be with us while you train."

"That is fine, as long as he can run around and play here, he will be fine."

Adrea smiled. "While you are here for training, can you start on that stone? It is weighing the area down."

"Oh, sure. If I can get some pebbles from around here, I could even start taking it apart tonight."

Argus grumbled. "No. Not tonight. You have already changed colour in your extremities; no more spectre manipulation tonight."

Adrea got to her feet. "Right, speaking of pebbles, I will give you something to use to make a portal."

Imara sat in surprise. "Right. I will have to make a portal."

It isn't hard. I can show you the best book.

She glanced at the critters and stifled a laugh as Mr. E rode the much larger Blueberry around the yard and through the gardens.

Argus was chuckling, and Adrea let out a snort when she returned. "That is something I am going to remember."

The way it was said, it was as if the space was going to remember it.

Adrea wrapped an arm around Hyl and leaned forward with her hand extended. "Here you go. Four stones from Ritual Space. Set them out in a box formation, step through a mirror, and you will be here in no time. Only a first level transport chant is needed. From here, I can boot you home."

"And when the training is done, I bring them back?"

Adrea grinned. "If you like. If we get along, you can keep them for visitation purposes."

Imara looked at the small black rocks. "What if someone steals them, tries to break in here?"

"Well, first, you are going to text me to let me know that you are coming. But the stones are also keyed to you and your familiar. No one else can get in on your ticket, so to speak."

Relief flowed through her. "Right. Yes, thank you. That is a relief."

A small paw clawing at her jeans got Imara's attention. Blueberry had a small drawstring bag in his teeth with R and S entwined on it. "Just in case I forget. Thank you, Blueberry. Did you throw Mr. E?"

She looked around, and the kitten in question was napping in a pile of bunnies. That was a lot of fluff.

"He is out for a few minutes. Have some tea. Recover from your evening." Adrea didn't look much older than Imara, but she seemed to have centuries of calm.

Her host poured the tea, and Imara held the delicate cup for a moment, inhaling the herbal scents that were soothing and invigorating at the same time. A first sip said that the tea had the same properties.

Imara drank the tea and felt a tingling down her left arm. The gravel abrasion from the fight was going from angry red to pink as she watched. "Okay. So, healing potion?"

Adrea sat and poured her tea from a different pot. "No, just herbs from Ritual Space. I, myself, can't use any magic. I am just a curator."

Hyl snorted. "Yes, she is a curator of everything you see around you. It all comes when she calls, one way or another."

Argus looked at Imara. "I know that feeling."

She smiled brightly at him. "I text. I don't call."

The group laughed, and Imara finished her tea.

Imara sighed on the ride home. "Sorry that we had to take the detour, but I am delighted that I got a tutor out of it. I had no idea that this course would involve breaking and entering."

"Imara, promise me that you won't be involved in illegal activity."

"I promise. I am only going to engage in the exact requirements of my course."

"Will you quit the course?"

"No. There is nothing comparable for credits."

"Will you promise me you will be safe?"

She smiled. "Always. I have plans, you know."

He chuckled. "Yes, I know."

She stroked Mr. E and pulled tufts of white fluff from his midnight fur. It was a strangely serene drive home.

Reegar was waiting for her when she entered the hall. "Why were you out so long?"

"We found the problem and fixed it, but then, we needed to store it somewhere safe, so we had to go there and time got away from me."

She grimaced at the babble, but it was all accurate.

The hum and click from the floor above indicated that Bara was still awake. "Is she still weaving?"

"She has taken to it. She has started looking into specialized fabrics, but the selection of options is very limited." Reegar pointed to the table nearest the library. "Sit, and I will get you some tea. I want to hear all about it."

She smiled. "Yes, of course. At least you won't balk if I have to do something illegal."

"The test for the stealth magic? Yes, I am aware of it. I have had a few incursions here to try and take my stone from the building. Those were in the days before you arrived, and so I had to resort to poltergeist methods and calling campus security."

"So, you won't mind if I study for the exam?"

He grinned. "You have had an interesting evening if someone outlined the exam for you. Start at the beginning."

She started at the beginning, and just as she reached the fight, Bara came down and pulled up a chair.

The mention of Ritual Space earned her a gasp, and when she detailed the requirements of the exam, Bara sat up with a jolt. "I have just the thing. I am working on an adaptive fabric, and it takes a day just to make a small strip, but I should have enough to cover you in a month."

"And Mr. E?"

She blinked and grinned. The kitten in question was

passed out on a spell book. "Of course. Right, you would take him with you."

"Yeah, he won't train with me, but he will be with me on the day."

"Then, he shall have enough to wrap him as well. This is exciting."

Reegar grinned. "She isn't wrong. Can I do anything?"

"I need to find a level one transport spell. Just enough for me and Mr. E."

Reegar looked at her familiar and smirked. "Would you believe he is sleeping on the book?"

Bara snorted. "So, if it is competitive, what will you do to make them think you are training at the college?"

"Kitigan has been after me to jog with her. I am fairly sure that the schedule can be flexed to accommodate a run in the morning. If I have to go to the gym while they try and do me in, I will just have to go."

Bara nodded. "Right. I think I have a plan for that as well. This really is fun."

Imara shook her head. Four co-conspirators and she hadn't even started the course yet. It was the antithesis of stealth.

Chapter Four

"I am Professor McClairie, and this is Stealth Magic 401. You will learn how to be silent, invisible, and think on your feet, but to do that, you have to train." The professor paced in front of the scant dozen students in front of him.

He raised his hand and waved a sheet of paper. "In my hand, I have a list of the contact information of twelve volunteers who are willing to train you with a goal toward your final exam. They know what will be required."

Imara raised her hand, and he paused.

"Yes?"

"What is the format of the course?"

He gave her a pitying smile. "You will train, you will come back to get your exam information. You will fail, and you will probably cry."

A loud, braying laugh got her attention from across the small space. *Great, another brother.*

"Edgar Demiel, you have the first pick of names." The professor walked over to him and handed him the page. "When you have made your choice, strike it out. Once you have the information, you are dismissed until the next class date where you will get your assignment."

The professor went through the class in no particular order. What rapidly became apparent was that he was saving her for last.

The last student had scribbled on the page, and the professor passed it to her.

"The pickings are slim, but I am sure you will find something to suit you."

"We are allowed tutors from off this list, correct?" She smiled brightly and got to her feet.

He blinked in surprise. "Yes, you are."

She extended the card that Hyl had given her. "He has volunteered to be my tutor."

He looked at the card and paled. "Why would he . . . how would you even meet him?"

"Oh, I had to do some work with the XIA last night, and we ended up at Ritual Space where he makes his home. He admired my attitude, and as he had already passed this course, he offered to train me for it."

The professor made a strangled sound. "What did you do with the XIA?"

"My job. They subcontracted me via the Death Keeper Guild. I was uniquely suited to the situation."

"Death Keeper?"

"Yes, don't you have files on your students?" She clued in, "Or do you only bother with the ones from prime families?" She tutted. "Do your homework, Professor. You missed something."

She took the business card back and nodded politely. "Good day, Professor."

She left the classroom with Mr. E chuckling madly on her shoulder.

Right, she was in it, and her friends were all on board. It was time to get busy with her portal work. Reegar had gotten clearance via the Chancellor's office for transports within the Hall, so she was clear, as soon as she could manage the transport. It was not a method of magic she had even considered. This was not going to be pleasant.

"Did she actually suggest a mirror portal?" Reegar was shocked.

"She did, but she also said she didn't do any magic."

He frowned and paged through the tomes. Mr. E jumped on the table with the small pouch in his teeth.

Imara smiled. "Oh, yeah. She gave me four stones from Ritual Space. Will that help?"

Reegar looked at the pouch as if it held pure gold. "Those are stones from the actual space?"

"Yes."

"Pure and not enchanted?"

"Yes."

He sat back and exhaled. "This is easy. You just need a measuring tape and a wall."

"I don't need a mirror?"

He waved that away. "It is considered to be necessary by the weak, but I find it tacky. It is more dangerous for the mage to use a mirror than just use energy to formulate a door. You are strong enough to do the job without the prop."

She blushed and was going to reply, but across the space, Bara's hand shot into the air. "I have a measuring tape. Three, actually."

"You need to take her height, width at her widest point and the height of her average stride."

Mr. E jumped up and onto her shoulder, sitting with his head high.

Imara grinned and waited for Bara to come back and do the measuring. Her grin faded when she took a look at Bara's fingers. "What the hell is that?"

"Oh, blisters and splinters. The fibre I am working with isn't very friendly."

"Damn. I have a recipe for a healing cream."

She shook her head. "Cream makes my hands softer, and that makes the problem worse. I will toughen up."

While Imara stood there in shock, Bara quickly got her measurements, paused and cocked her head. "Can I use you as a model for my dressmaking class?"

With all Bara had done for her, Imara nodded. "Of course."

"Excellent. I am looking into making a utility belt that is actually useful."

"A utility belt?"

"That fits with a formal gown." Bara smiled. "Here you go. Metric and imperial measurements. Don't mix them up." Bara gave her a fierce look and winked. "Arms out to your sides and hold still."

Ten minutes of precise—and occasionally tickling—measurements later and Imara was free to study the spell.

It was bizarrely easy. She just needed to place the stones out and power them up then speak the name of her destination. It would only work if someone were waiting for her on the other side.

"You should set up the stones on your wall using glue."

She nodded at Reegar. "I will tape them up until the glue holds."

"It isn't necessary. Go into the lab and find the super stick adhesive. It will bond in two seconds, so be quick."

She nodded, gathered the book and got the notes that Bara had left. Mr. E followed her into the lab, and he sat quietly on the counter until she found the adhesive.

What followed was a relatively easy procedure. Measure, mark, measure again with a different pen, and when she was sure, she took out the stones and brushed the adhesive on the back. She wore gloves and ended up having to cut one free when they were all in place. The adhesive was sealed to stop a comical moment, and she took it downstairs.

Are you ready?

"No. I am not ready, but the spell is easy. All I have to do is text her, and we can walk through."

Do it.

She took the number that Adrea had given her, and she entered in the new contact. She sent the first text. *Hi, it's Imara. Can I come through?*

She waited for three minutes, and then, her phone chirped. *Come on over. Dress to sweat. You have one hour to use your portal.*

"Oh, shit. Right."

Imara quickly got an exercise bag together with bottles of water, put on a set of grubby sneakers, and when Mr. E was on her shoulder, she stood in front of the stones and powered them up the same way she offered energy to a spectre. A moment later, she was looking at Ritual Space, and Adrea was sitting and reading a book in her garden.

The scene was so idyllic, Imara hated to ruin it.

Imara stepped through, and after a short moment of disorientation, she settled on the other side with her familiar on her shoulder.

Adrea waved at her. "You made it!"

Imara nodded, and Mr. E was kneading her shoulder. "Yes, Mr. E, you can go play."

He was off her shoulder and bolting after some bunnies who waited for him before leading him into the undergrowth at high speed. Imara could hear him giggling via their connection.

"Hyl will be here within the hour, but he said I should start you on a few things."

There was a stack of books in the centre of the table, and each book had a bookmark hanging through it.

"Each of these has a spell necessary to what you are going to be doing, so he suggested you begin studying until he arrives. Once he does, you are heading to a special section of the space that I have put aside for your training."

Imara sat and pulled one of the books toward her. "I don't know how to thank you two."

"Pass your exam. Hyl says that women are frequently sabotaged in the course, so he wants you to shove it in McClairie's face."

"Ah. Well, that does explain the major dicks in the room." Imara smirked and opened the first book. The spell that he marked was *Surface tension and wall climbing.* It was a good place to start.

By the time Hyl had arrived, she had made it through *Obscuring the scent of magic,* and *Passing through.* She was in the middle of *Pulling shadows* when Hyl walked in and gave Adrea a kiss that turned her bright red.

Hyl lifted his head and smiled at Imara. "Are you ready to work?"

"I am."

"Good. There is a pack under the table, bring the books."

She scrambled to put the books in the pack, and she shifted it to her back, grabbing a bottle of water.

"Where is your familiar?"

"He is off playing with the bunnies."

"Good. It is better that he is occupied. This is going to take a while." Hyl nodded, turned, and jogged off toward the nearest stand of trees.

Imara turned back and smiled at Adrea. "See you later!" Adrea waved her on.

Imara turned her back on her host and ran after her tutor.

Hyl was walking briskly, but no matter how fast Imara ran, she could never quite catch up with him.

The books were excessively heavy, but she just hitched the straps tighter until they moved with every step she took.

She chased him for half an hour before she burst out of the forest path and ended up in an open field with a wide tower in the centre of it. Hyl was standing near the bricked tower.

She ran up to him and paused. "What next?"

"Climb it."

She looked up at the tower and back to him. "Pardon me?"

"I have observed your musculature, you will be able to support yourself, so you have two hours to climb the tower and then, I will help you with your technique."

She stared at him. "You are kidding."

"I am not. You can use any method that you can to get to the second story."

She paused and nodded. "Including the books on my back."

"Correct. I am here if you have questions, but figuring things out for yourself is more useful. We can tweak the technique from there."

It was a challenge she wasn't backing down from. She got the pack settled firmly on her back and stepped forward.

Chapter Five

Imara fell on her ass three times before she used the sticking spell. Once she had placed the spell on her body, she was able to press her body against the wall and use it as a point of grip as she slowly crept upward.

"Well done. You read the books?"

"A few of them." She grunted and pushed up with her foot while reaching with the opposite hand. "The ones that were bookmarked."

"Bookmarked? Huh." Hyl chuckled.

She reached up, and her hand hit open air. She glanced up and exhaled.

"Now for the hard part. Come down slowly. Be sure of your footing."

She didn't nod, she just did as he suggested. Her hands were aching, her toes were cramping, but she still moved down, row by row.

When she hit solid ground, she dropped like a stone. She sat on the ground, her knees splayed, feet curled inside her shoes, and her fingers wrapped inward to stop their raw throbbing.

Hyl looked her over and nodded. "I will be right back."

He went into the tower and emerged a minute later with a thermos flask. He crouched next to her and poured a cup. One look at her hands and he held the cup to her lips. "Drink it. It is the same tea that she gave you the other day but with nettles to help make your skin more durable."

She swallowed and winced at the burn of the tea. The last time it had been cool.

He pulled the cup back. "It has to burn to toughen your skin. How are your hands?"

She flexed them, and the raw and bloody fingertips were

healing over. "Are you sure she doesn't use magic?"

He chuckled. "No. The herbs are grown here, and they have their own magic."

"Do they work outside the space?"

"Sure. Adrea is just getting her online shop ready. The sales will be by invitation only after the purchaser has passed a security check, but yeah, she is going digital."

"Nice. She will sell out in seconds."

Hyl chuckled. "I am not so sure. Most mages have some kind of legal trouble in their histories. If they do, we will find it."

"So, getting caught during my exam would knock me off the list."

"No, but getting caught the day after would."

She pulled her legs up and rested her forearms on her knees. "So, I have one night to finish the exam?"

He grinned. "That is where folks get it wrong. You have twenty-three hours and fifty-nine minutes."

Imara stared at him. "So any time during that day. Oh, wow. That makes things easier and exponentially harder."

"How harder?"

"I don't know what the best time would be. This is going to take some research."

"You will figure it out. That is one point where I can't advise you. All I can do is give you the physical skills to engage in your stealth manoeuvres."

"Right."

He nodded. "Now, do your hands feel better?"

She looked at them and nodded. "They do."

"Good. Now get back up the tower and try to keep it under two hours this time."

She widened her eyes. "It took longer than two hours?"

"Yes, it did. Now, get up and get down in under two hours."

She nodded and grunted as she got to her feet. She faced the tower, summoned the sticking spell, and crawled upward as quickly as she could. This time, her limbs obeyed her, and she was able to move along the stone in what felt like a few minutes.

The moment she got down to the base, she turned to him. "How long?"

"One hour and twenty-two minutes. Very good for a first day."

She groaned. "It felt so fast."

"It will. The thing you have to remember is that you can't depend on your perception of time. You have to move as rapidly as possible to throw off the effects of the spells you will need."

"The sticking spell. It makes me slow."

He grinned. "It does. It keeps you on the wall, but it takes four times your normal speed."

She exhaled and then looked at him. "What else for today?"

"You want to do more?"

"I do."

He nodded. "Right. Back up the tower. When you can get to the top and back down again in five minutes, we can work on the next task."

She looked at the tower and the small smears of blood she had left behind. With a focus on increasing her speed, she muttered the spell, jumped to stick herself to the wall and hauled herself as fast as she could. When she was down, he applauded slowly. "Excellent, but still twenty minutes."

She whirled and climbed the wall for the fourth time, this time without the sticking spell.

She slipped a few times, but it made her faster. She climbed up twenty feet and then lowered herself back down again with careful dexterity.

Hyl grinned and applauded. "Excellent. This time, you are dead on five minutes. Now, let's go and get some food. Adrea is waiting."

Her limbs told her that she had been climbing for days, but Mr. E's perky face when they made it back to the gardens told her that it had barely been any time at all.

He ran up to her and waited until she had shucked the pack off her shoulders before he jumped up and rubbed against her sweaty face with his fuzzy one.

I had a marvellous time. When do we come back?

She looked to Hyl. "When is our second class?"

"Tomorrow will be too soon, but Thursday should be fine."

She scowled. "I don't want to interfere with your work."

Adrea waved that off. "He is assigned as my bodyguard, and he only leaves when I authorize it. I am willing to hang onto him as long as you need him."

Hyl grinned and handed Imara a platter full of sandwiches. "Eat. You need it."

She dropped into her chair with a thud.

Adrea gave her a commiserating look. "Hard, huh?"

"Yeah. Thanks for that tea. I was wondering if I could buy some when you get up and running. A friend is helping me, but the material she is working with is tearing up her skin something awful. I think that tea would be just the thing."

Adrea got to her feet and walked into the house.

Imara blinked at Hyl. "Did I say something wrong?"

"No, just wait."

Adrea came out with a large muslin bag. "Here. I have divided it into doses. Have her drink one when you see her and then another one twelve hours later. You need to do the same, or tomorrow, you won't be able to move."

Imara was eating as if had been days and not hours since she last had a meal.

She cleared her mouth. "Day after tomorrow. Same time as today."

Hyl grinned. "Deal. Just so you can prepare yourself, the tower is getting higher."

She smiled and nodded. "I figured. Well, at least I can practice the spell and work on my technique at the hall."

A half-hour of polite chitchat later, Adrea sent her home.

"Now that I know where your portal is, you can come through anytime. I am opening it so you can get a clear run home."

She confirmed with Hyl, "I leave the books?"

"You leave the books. These are for Ritual Space use

only."

She nodded, grabbed the bag she hadn't used, and ran for the open portal with her familiar on her shoulder. She stumbled into her bedroom. Shower. The shower was her first port of call.

Once she was no longer covered with blood and sweat, she grabbed the muslin bag and took it down to Bara. Without asking her, she made a pot of tea and poured her a cup. "Drink this."

Bara leaned back, suspicious. "Why?"

"Because it will heal you and help toughen your hands without losing dexterity. It is a gift from the owner of Ritual Space."

That was all it took. Bara finished the whole pot, and she sat there shivering and flushing as the effects were all seen in her body. The moment her hands cleared up, she sighed in relief.

"What is that stuff?"

Imara settled at the table. "Herbs from Ritual Space. It's a gift from the owner."

Bara looked at her cup as if she wanted to bronze it. "Have you been there?"

"Yeah, it is where I am training. That is what the portal was for."

Bara looked at her with a wistful look. "When you are done training, can I come, too?"

"I will ask. I think it will be fine."

Bara grinned. "That is definitely something to look forward to."

Imara nodded, gathered the rest of the herb packs, and handed one to Bara. "Drink this in twelve hours. According to Adrea, that should do it."

"I feel so much better; I don't know what another dose could do."

"She's an herbalist, so if she says to drink it, drink it."

Bara took her phone and set the alarm. "There, that should bring me out of my weaving stupor."

Imara chuckled.

"So, what are you doing tonight?"

"I am applying to the Death Keeper Guild for a dozen empty soul stones. I need to keep a promise to Adrea about dealing with the rock I found the other day."

Bara nodded. "Right, well, I feel so much better, I am heading back to the loom."

"Enjoy. Don't forget your phone."

"Yes, Ma'am."

Imara sighed and looked around. There was no sign of Reegar, which was odd. He was always around.

She reached out with magic and located him. Blushing furiously, she withdrew. Liirick was in town, and they were engaged in a private moment.

Mr. E hopped up onto the table and stretched. *I could have told you that.*

She scratched his chin. "Did you have fun with the bunnies?"

We told jokes for the first six hours, and then, they brought me to Adrea for a snack. She kept me busy for an hour, and then, we went to play again.

She frowned. "What? We weren't there that long."

Well, I am a cat, my observation of the time period could have been skewed.

I hope so. She checked the time and date on her phone and sighed in relief. She was right where and when she was supposed to be, but she didn't put it past Ritual Space to knock time around . . . again.

With nothing do to and no one to talk to, she sent the email to the Death Keepers, and then, she went to look for spells that might be useful while she was breaking into a magical building full of people. Some kind of bladder control might be in order.

Hyl was peeling an apple with a knife. "Do the warm-up."

She nodded and scaled the six stories of smooth brick, and then, she worked her way back down. They were in week three of her six weeks of training, and this was now an experience she was used to.

When she was standing at the base of the tower again, she caught her breath. "Now what?"

He smiled. "Inside the building, I have hidden a valuable object. Once you retrieve it, you will have to find your way out of the building again. It will not be easy. Go."

She nodded and used the door-opening spell that she had already practiced. So far, he had left her chocolate, a glass of water, and a happy kitten on a post-it note.

Imara moved through the rooms as quickly as she could until she found the valuable object. She scooped Mr. E up from the basket where he had been sleeping, and she turned to the doorway she had entered by. The wall sealed, and there was no trace of a doorway.

She winced. She had been afraid that this was that spell. She held the still-sleeping Mr. E tight to her chest, and she cast the *pass-through* spell. She stepped through the one wall, and all other walls were solid again.

She turned and looked around her, orienting herself to the tower she was in. She approached her chosen wall and passed through it, waiting until she was on the other side before she gasped. The air was fresh, and the green grass stroked her ankles.

Hyl applauded as he approached her. "Well done. The shortest distance was through the outer wall. The only problem lies in if you are on an upper floor, so that is where we will practice next."

Mr. E disappeared from her arms, and she ran around to the point where she could sense him, and she climbed the wall before entering via the window. She grabbed him and was planning to go back out the window, but it had paved itself over.

His sleep wasn't normal, so she made an executive decision. She stepped to the wall, placed them within it and used the molecular resistance to drop them to the main floor. When she felt solid ground beneath her feet, she forged forward along the line of the wall until she was outside.

Hyl nodded. "Right. Enough of that for today. Time for lunch."

She smiled and breathed deeply. "In a moment. Emotion and spell casting don't mix."

Mr. E started to squirm in her arms, and Hyl nodded. "Right. Sorry, but it was necessary to see how you would do with a living being."

She nodded. "I understand. It is also why I have the weight on my back the whole time."

He shook his head. "You will see what a difference that makes when you are done with your training. If it makes you feel better, there are only two exercises left, and they can both be combined. Drawing shadows and hiding traces of your presence. After what you have been doing, they are mainly mental exercises. Once those are mastered, you can continue to come here to practice, but you won't need me anymore."

"Can I practice now? It is only two weeks to my exam."

"Well, you are filthy, sweaty, exhausted, and reeking of magic. If you can walk back to the garden without being besieged by bunnies, I will consider you graduated."

Imara looked at the sleepy kitten in her arms, and she nodded. "You are on."

Chapter Six

Running the two spells together was difficult, and it meant she had to move slowly through the woods, careful to measure her steps. She might be in shadow with no scent of man or magic, but her footsteps still made noise.

Hyl was sitting with Adrea in the middle of a pool of light. Imara whispered for help to the space, and the lanterns dimmed. She stepped to the side and approached the chair she normally sat in, facing the herb gardens and the rioting rabbits. The moment she touched the chair, the spells dissipated.

Adrea laughed at Hyl's expression. "Hooray! You spooked him. How did you get the lamps to dim enough to give you cover?"

"I asked. You have told me enough about Ritual Space over the last few weeks to know that as long as what I wanted wouldn't affect you, it might just help me."

Hyl poured her a cup of tea. "I consider you a very successful student. Well done, Imara."

Adrea raised her cup. "Well done, Imara."

She blushed and looked down at her grubby hands. "Thanks. I still need to practice."

"And I am glad of the company."

Hyl chortled. "I am sure that Argus will be happy if you can spend a few more days with him."

Imara waved her hand through the air. "He knows what I am focused on. While he is right for me, I might not be right for him. If he changes his inclination, I won't hold it against him."

Adrea quirked her lips. "That is why you have kept it to a friendship."

"Until I can afford for it to be more, yes."

Hyl whistled. "You really do have a plan."

"Yes, and I am very lucky to meet the right people at the right time." She cupped her teacup in her hands, and she sipped slowly. For once, she wasn't served from a separate pot.

Adrea looked at Hyl, and her expression softened. "To meeting the right people at the right time."

They all toasted with their teacups over the table. Mr. E snorted into consciousness and stretched.

The talked softly of friends and families and how it was a great thing that you could at least choose one.

She scratched under Mr. E's chin as they entered her room. She glanced back at the portal a moment before it closed. "I am guessing I won't have it much longer."

I would not be so sure about that.

"Technically, it would be dangerous for them to leave those stones with me."

True, but it is Adrea's choice. Her space, her choices.

She put him on the bed and grabbed her clothing for after her shower. "How do you think I did?"

I think that I only learned of your actions through your mind. You did very well. Hyl is a good teacher. He got the physical into your muscle memory and then moved on to the strategy.

"I know. I got lucky."

His chuckle was in her mind while she headed for her shower.

Kitty was waiting in the common room when Imara came down. "Ready for coffee and gossip?"

Imara checked her watch and blinked in surprise. The sky was still light, though she felt like she had been at Ritual Space most of the day. "Of course. Sorry. I lost track of time."

"You look exhausted. Even Mr. E looks sleepy."

"I will get some coffee and be right as rain. Are we walking?"

"Yes. It's a wonderful night."

"Great." Imara smiled. "I need some fresh, normal air."

"I can't guarantee normal, but it is definitely fresh. Get a coat."

Imara patted herself down to make sure she had her wallet, beckoned to her familiar, and then slipped on a loose poncho. Mr. E popped his head out the neck hole, and he got comfy.

"Okay, ready."

Kitty smiled and linked arms with her, hauling her out of the hall and down the street.

The restaurant was busy, but ordering quickly meant that they had time to chat while they waited for their food. Mr. E had his usual fans, so he sat at the edge of the table and let people stroke his chin.

"Okay, Imara, what have you been up to?"

Imara shrugged. "Working out, getting ready for the class exam. How about you?"

"My apiary is twelve feet tall, and I don't have the nerve to harvest the honey for testing." Kitty looked abashed.

Imara looked at her. "Do you need help? We could do it tonight."

Kitty looked at her with adoration. "Really? That would be wonderful."

"Sure. Let's just fortify ourselves first and then get the boxes for the frames and a ladder. We will get the honey out of the hive tonight ... before they know what has happened."

Kitty sighed. "I have missed hanging out with you."

"Yeah, I am getting that a lot, but this course load is heavy. It is one class, but it takes all my time."

"I know. It just sucks. I only found you a few months ago. It is just that I want to hang out more."

Imara nodded. "I feel the same. So, tonight, we will make up for lost time."

"You still look exhausted."

"I can sleep in tomorrow." She toasted Kitty with a cup of coffee and took a swig of the hot brew. Their night was set.

Kitty spent the rest of the dinner explaining the technique

for harvesting the honey with minimal interference with the bees.

They paid for dinner and Mr. E's dessert and headed over to the agricultural centre.

It felt just like the days that Imara had spent with the Deegle family. With the equipment and protective gear, they crept out to the apiary, and Kitty had not been kidding. The stack of boxes was actually twelve feet high, so Imara made sure that she had a box to catch the first rounds of frames with honey.

Imara was going to remove the frames and lower them one by one to Kitigan's gloved hands.

Imara removed the lid of the hive and pried off the inner cover. There were next to no bees near her as they were down keeping the brood warm, or so Kitty had promised.

She pried up the edges of the box and lifted it. The weight wasn't bad at all, considering her recent training, so she tucked it on one hip and moved down the ladder.

Kitty was staring. "How can you lift it so easily?"

"I told you, I have been working out."

She went back up the ladder and took down the next box the same way, shaking out a few bees and going down the ladder again.

The next level was the final one that she needed the ladder for, and the trolley that Kitty had grabbed took the hive boxes easily.

"How many more until I get to the excluder?"

"Just two."

Each level had more bees on it, but she shook off the slightly more agitated inhabitants and kept working her way down to the excluder.

The stack of brood boxes was chest high when she finished robbing them. Several bees were cruising around, but they didn't move far from the original hive.

Kitty handed her the empties, and Imara set them in place, evening out the frame spacing before putting the next on top. The cover and lid went in place, making the entire tower nine feet tall and ridiculous.

Imara descended the ladder and shook her head. "You are going to have to do this yourself, you know."

"I know. I am just afraid of getting stung. These little bastards pack a punch."

"Please, they are ladies." Imara laughed and carried the ladder to the equipment shed.

Kitty trundled the boxes into the lab, and Imara followed when the single-use gear was stowed.

In the lab, they prepped the equipment, removed their protective gear and began harvesting two hundred sixty pounds of honey with magical properties.

"What are you going to do with all this?" Imara stared at the settling vat that contained it all.

"Study it, try different enchantments, that sort of thing."

Imara didn't want to ask, but something made her. "Can I have a litre of it?"

"Sure. Let me get you a jar. What do you want it for?"

Imara rubbed her forehead. "I don't know yet. I just feel that I need it."

"Good enough."

The jar of honey was produced; Kitty made her notes on her records' chart, and Imara started yawning.

Kitty looked around and saw the clock. "Good lord, I have kept you all night."

Mr. E was snoring softly against her neck. Nothing woke him.

"It's fine. It was fun. What are you going to do with the extra bees?"

"They are nearing the end of their life cycle. Why? Do you have an idea?"

"I will make a call, and if you need a place for them to go and sniff flowers all the year-round. I know just the spot."

Kitty smiled. "I will think it over."

"Good. I am going to head back to Reegar Hall. It has been a very long day."

"Thanks for coming out, Imara. I appreciate it."

Imara was turning to leave when she had a thought. "If you know anyone who is giving away a bike, let me know. I think it is another thing that will come in handy."

"Will do, now shoo!" Kitty grinned and waved her off.

Imara nodded and headed out the door. There were only a few security vehicles on campus, and her calm and even stride didn't raise their suspicions.

It took her twenty-five minutes to get to the hall, and she peeled off her wrap with a sigh, stumbling through the hall and up the steps until she got to her room. Changing her clothing was going to take too much effort, so she just dropped onto her bed.

Bara rubbed her shoulder. "Imara, come on. I have my exam in two hours, and I need to make final adjustments on the gown.

Imara sat up, and she flung her arms wide.

"Damn. Okay. Come with me, and I will do what I have to so you can get back to bed. Are you still ready to be my model?"

Imara nodded.

"Good. Now stay there, I will get the gown."

Imara was on autopilot as she was stripped, stuffed into eveningwear, and pinned.

"Wow, you have been working out. Impressive. This is going to look fantastic."

Imara nodded, and when the gown was gone, she thudded back into bed.

Imara woke fully in a strange environment with Bara fussing with her hair. Bara grinned. "There you are. Mr. E was willing to drive you on autopilot all day, but he was gravitating to ordering his own pizza, so I was hoping you would come to."

"I am so sorry."

"You have been burning the candle at both ends. I get it. Now, we are up next, walk with your head high with an expression that everyone is beneath you but amuses you."

Imara smirked. "That is my normal expression."

"I know. Down the runway, turn, and back up. No

drama."

"Nothing dramatic. Got it." And so, barely awake, she walked up the steps, waited for the announcement of Bara's name, and she walked down the runway, wondering why the hell they had made it so long. At the end, she caught a look at what had to be her father, but this was a drama-free zone, so she kept walking back to the rear of the stage.

Bara's hug nearly crushed bones.

They waited backstage until the scores were announced, and when Bara was declared, "Ninety-eight," Imara was hauled onto the stage once again.

There was applause, she took a bow, and she had to wait for Bara's return after her fellow students applauded her because Imara had no idea where she was.

Mr. E rubbed against her ankles, so Imara reached down and picked him up. The population around her made cooing noises, and since he had driven her there, she offered him up for caresses and cuddles.

The party that Bara had planned was extensive, but Imara only had to be there for the first twenty minutes. She scampered upstairs and checked the calendar. She hadn't missed it. Tomorrow, she would get her exam assignment and the rest of the time would be used for preparing her assault on whatever hall she was assigned.

Imara looked at the engraved document, and she looked back up at Professor McClairie. "You are joking."

"I am not. That is your assignment." He raised his voice. "Guard your assignments well, as your fellow students can find you, foil you, and use their skills to work against you."

Edgar Demiel was still sneering at her, and Imara had no idea why. She had his ancestral home on her card. *Demiel Hall,* on the twenty-seventh. It was the last place she wanted to be.

When the professor finished reading out the rules of their exam, she stood up. Another card dropped in front of her, and when she looked up, Edgar was out the door.

She didn't look at the card until she was home, and Mr. E

was fighting to cackle. It was hard with a kitten's face.

"What the hell?"

Reegar stepped over to her and looked over her shoulder. "You have been invited to a birthday party."

"It is my father's birthday party and an introduction to my first niece. This is . . . something is . . . damn it is the same day as the exam."

She huffed and sat down for a moment before Hyl's advice ran through her head. "It has to be that day but not during the day."

Bara looked up from where she was sewing together the wraps that would keep Imara from being glaringly visible during her adventure. "What does that mean?"

"That means that I am going to be doing a lot of night work, but this is all going to work out in the end."

Reegar grinned, Bara gave her a thumbs-up, and Mr. E stretched before going back to sleep on his favourite book. Now that the Death Keepers had taken off with the spectres from the accumulation stone, everything was finally coming together.

She might be able to master stealth magic with just a little help from her friends.

Chapter Seven

Imara had given up on telling herself that she was an idiot. She already knew it. Mr. E was wrapped in the same fabric that she was, and it appeared that Bara's weaving work was paying off. They were nearly invisible.

Demiel Hall was exactly where the map had shown her it would be. The magical sensors were at the edges of the property, and it was with a slow and casual motion that she walked past them, waiting for the alarm.

Hyl had been confident. She just had to act like she belonged there, and the grounds would accept her.

She moved calmly to the house and used her fingers and toes in the brick and stone to pull herself upward. Mr. E was sensibly using her for transport.

When they made it to the second floor, she closed her eyes and looked for what she knew had to be there. A spectre stuck its head out and spoke.

"Should I alert the family?"

The words were faint, and Imara gripped the wall with her left hand and extended her right. The spectre ran her hand through Imara's and smiled. "A daughter of the Demiels? Well, well, what do you want here?"

Imara whispered, "The crystal. Just for three hours."

"Well, your timing is impeccable. They have been preparing to put traps in the chamber, but they won't put them in place until the morning."

Imara nodded and spoke low, "Can you open the window?"

"I can turn off the whole security system, but why should I?"

"I can give you enough power to let you take physical form when you want for a year."

Her ancestor grinned. "Deal. Do you want me to bring you the crystal?"

"Can you?"

"I can, I will give it to you now, child, and put it back when you bring it. Your soul does not shine with greed."

The ancestor disappeared for a moment. Imara hung on and felt the panic begin to take hold. The window opened, and the crystal fell the few feet into Imara's hand. She slipped a little of her energy into the crystal and felt the response.

She wrinkled her nose, and she waited. The slight ripple of shadow gave her what she needed, and when the weight returned to her shoulder, she took the crystal and headed down to the ground.

The bicycle was where she had hidden it, tucked in the shadows.

Now, it was time for the most dangerous part of the evening. She rode over to Professor McClairie's home and cast an assessment spell. The professor was asleep in the study, main floor, rear.

She went to the back of the building and sent Mr. E a signal.

She stepped back against the building as her kitten gave a strangled yowl. The professor came out warily and looked around. With their wraps still on, they looked like bent landscape. If they didn't move, they were unseeable.

"Professor McClairie? I have completed my exam."

The face turned toward her with shock and his fist raised. "Who is it?"

She carefully parted her mask. "Mirrin, sir. I have my assignment, and I wish to register completion of my project."

"Show me the assignment."

She reached into the wraps and found the page that she had guarded with her life. "Here."

"The Lieth crystal, at Demiel Hall. Where is it?"

She extended the crystal to him, and the moment he touched the glowing blue crystal, it dulled.

"Well, Mirrin, this is a fail. This isn't the crystal."

Mr. E started hacking up a hairball, and the genuine crystal slid out of his throat and onto the grass.

Imara reached down and picked up the crystal, wiping it off on the grass before handing it over.

"Is it still wet?"

"No, he isn't really physical, so that sound was just for fun."

Mr. E was busy putting his mask back in place, and he soon disappeared.

The professor examined it, and he nodded. "You have done it."

A flash went off, and he blinked. "What was that?"

"A record that I finished in case you wake up thinking this is a dream."

"Oh, right. Why are you here now?"

"Ah, I wanted to return the crystal to the hall before anyone notices it is gone. Since they are so eager to set me up, I thought that I shouldn't let them panic. Plus, I have to go to a party there tonight, and all eyes will be on me. Breaking in before dawn to complete the assignment will be difficult, but if I leave now, I can manage it."

He grinned and handed her the crystal. "I normally just return it via a spell, but I like your idea. If you survive to attend class tomorrow, let me know how the party was."

She mentally cursed as much as she could manage, but she took the original and the dummy crystal, nodded her head, and Mr. E hopped on for a ride.

So, we could have just handed it over?

Yes. She got back on her bike and pedalled as fast as she could as the night crept on toward dawn.

I think I am going to do a pass-through.

Are you in a good state of mind?

Yes. Can you show me where to go?

So, you will carry me?

Of course.

This is getting exciting.

I have been learning, may as well use it.

She pulled up and tucked her vehicle deep into the bushes

where she had set it before and saw the security vehicle patrolling the area.

Her heart pounded heavily, but when it continued past her hiding spot, she noted that it was a simple set of human mages behind the wheel.

Bara said this clothing could take a shift. He looked at her.

I am trusting that she was right. Did you want to eat the crystals again?

Sure. It will be easier for you to get us through, and I will deposit them back in the chest. Side by side.

She set down the crystals and shielded them with her body while he swallowed them.

She exhaled and nodded in personal determination. *Let's go.*

Imara held still and felt her body melt and twist. When her contortions ceased, she flexed her wings and gave a few practice flaps. She was ready to fly.

I will snag you in the open.

I will try not to run.

She took a few steps and pushed down with magic as her wings propelled her upward.

A few heavy beats and she was high enough to get into open space. She climbed to about sixty feet, wheeled, and went looking for her familiar.

She found him by scent, not by sight. Imara dove down and grabbed him carefully, keeping her claws wide to snag him before she carried him up and over the peak of the hall.

Down to the third chimney. The northeast space.

Got it. Going pass-through.

Ready when you are.

Her wings thrashed the air as she cast the spell, and when she felt it working, she dropped through the roof using her flying magic to keep her from moving too quickly.

The layers of the building were exposed to her, but having trained for this, she was ready for it.

Next chamber down.

Got it.

She came through into a huge horde of magical artifacts. She dropped her kitten and hovered in the space, not touching down. The pass-through spell only worked on objects that she touched, but since her kitten was part of her body, she could scoop him up and carry him away later.

Mr. E moved like a professional. He climbed over a few displays until he reached a box that was open and tempting.

He did his hairball hack silently and brought up the genuine stone. Next to it, he brought out the fake. Just to let them know that their subterfuge had been discovered.

He finished with the deposit, and he pushed the lid closed with his little paws.

Imara kept herself in place, and when he jumped for her, she caught him, carrying him right out through the wall and into the night.

The security officers were near her bike, so she turned toward home and flew steadily.

The night was beautiful, and the dawn was pinking the edges of the sky. The stars mixed in with the lightening sky were gorgeous.

When she saw Reegar Hall, she headed to the familiar rooftop. The XIA vehicle down in the lot did make her nervous, but she wasn't doing anything wrong. Well, not *now* anyway.

She dropped Mr. E off, banked, wheeled, and landed on her own, down on one knee. She stood and pulled the wrappings from her face and hands. Mr. E was tucked up under her arm, and she headed to her room.

She heard voices downstairs but ignored them in favour of getting to her room and stripping off the wrappings, getting a normal outfit of underwear, jeans and a sweatshirt in place, just as Reegar knocked on the door.

"Imara, there are XIA agents downstairs."

She paused. "Argus?"

"No. Not Argus."

"What do they want?" She pulled her sneakers on.

"A Death Keeper."

"Oh. That I can help with. Be right down."

Mr. E finished his disrobing, and he hopped on her shoulder. *Not without me.*

"Right. Not without you."

She finished getting dressed, combed her hair, and flipped it over her shoulder, catching Mr. E in the face.

He dug his little claws into her skin, and she left her room to head downstairs.

The agents were not ones she had met before, but she had seen them that night at the carnival.

"Hello."

"Death Keeper Imara Mirrin?" The elf was polite, but there was tension around his eyes and lips.

She inclined her head. "Yes, yes, I am."

"I am Iofer, this is Morgig and Henry. We have been sent to ask you to assist us in a matter involving a spectre."

She scowled. "I thought that was the Mage Guild's issue."

"That is the problem. Please, come with us."

If he didn't have panic in his eyes, she would have turned to Reegar for help. But, as it was, she paused and sent a quick notice to Argus.

A moment later, she got a thumbs-up, two hearts, and a black cat.

"Gentlemen, I am yours for the day, but I have an event this evening. I need to be home for that."

Iofer blinked, and she could swear that his ears flapped a little. "Of course. Right, well, this way, then. Time is of the essence."

She nodded and waved toward the door. "After you."

The elf, the goblin, and the troll wearing sunglasses surrounded her and escorted her to their vehicle.

The moment she was inside, she was urged to buckle up, and as the click locked her in, the SUV took off.

"We are going to use a mobile transport, Ms. Mirrin. Please relax and don't fight the magic."

Imara nodded and sat back against the polished seat. Next to her, the troll took some gulping breaths, and she reached out and held his hand while they were surrounded by magic and pulled through space.

The moment they stopped, Henry opened the door and threw up.

She unbuckled and got out. "Now, will someone tell me what I am supposed to do?"

Feel it, Imara. There is one of those stones here . . . and it isn't good.

She extended her senses and found the stone. "Aww, shit."

The lot where they had stopped was outside a Mage Guild office, and as she ran toward the pull of magic, Iofer, Morgig and a still-green Henry surrounded her to give her a mobile escort.

The underground parking lot was filled with panicked guild officers. The XIA pushed them aside and showed her the problem.

"What do you want me to do with it when I get it out?"

One of the officers asked, "Who are you?"

She scowled at him. "A Death Keeper. Who are you?"

He was elbowed aside, his golden good looks ignored by those around him.

"We need the stone contained by whatever means you can arrange."

She nodded and looked down at the woman who had a dozen dead mages trying to take over her body.

Her right hand was clenched, and the flickers of power were running through her.

"What is her name?"

"Officer Corral."

Imara sighed. "Her first name."

The older officer crouched next to Imara. "Etta. Her name is Etta. She has two brothers, a sister, and is the fourth generation to be an officer. She was cleaning out and bagging evidence from this vehicle, and she touched the stone. The Death Keepers recommended you."

She nodded. "Right. Not many of them would like to do this."

Mr. E, get to safety.

You need me.

You can take the overspill. I don't want you taken over. If these guys are aggressive, I am going to have to drain them. That will be messy.

"If I could get a little more space, please. This will throw off a bit of power."

The crowd shuffled back a few inches, but Imara didn't care. She was where she needed to be with her kitten out of touching range.

"Etta, my name is Imara. I am here to help."

She frantically shook her head, but Imara placed her hand over the hand clutched to Etta's chest. The dynamic of power shifted rapidly, and the heat from the stone localized.

"Let go of it, Etta. Push the spirits out of you and give me the stone. This is what I am trained for. I will be fine."

Etta's eyes resumed a beautiful cornflower blue. "Don't. Don't, it hurts!"

"I know." Imara took Etta's hand and turned it over. She was using all of her concentration to subdue the spectral energy, but she needed to keep Etta calm.

She smiled and said softly, "When she is free, pull her out of the way. I am going to need to bleed off some power."

She glanced around her quickly, and the XIA were ready to take action. It appeared that Etta was on their team.

"Okay, I am taking it in three, two, one . . ." She eased the stone free of the mage, and the world went white.

Chapter Eight

The roar of her hellcat brought her back, and she looked down at those gathered. *Fuck.* She was hovering.

You are ours now. You will be our limbs, our eyes, our touch.

Fuck you and your little dead brains. You are going to discover something surprising right about now.

She vented the power through the large feline version of Mr. E. He scrubbed the power and dumped the clean energy back into Etta, who was being held by Iofer a few feet away.

What? What are you doing? We will be free!

You will return to the wave. Congratulations.

Once Etta was returned to stable, Imara topped up the XIA with the spectral energy, and then, she let the rest power off through the open doors of the car park and out into the surrounding flora and fauna.

The scrubbed energy was powerful, but Imara didn't give anyone else a drop of it. She took the last remnant of twelve mages and left only a vague murmur of their energies so she could identify them later.

With a smile, she made a small kissy noise, and Mr. E shrank and hopped back on her shoulder. "Okay, so how am I getting home?"

Iofer held Etta close, and she was sobbing onto his shoulder. "We will take you back, but it is a four-hour drive."

She nodded. "Right."

The older man who appeared to be in charge said, "What just happened here?"

Imara blinked. "Which city am I in?"

"Leobrad Municipality. Where are you from?"

She sighed and rubbed her head with the hand not holding the deadly crystal. "Depford College."

His eyes widened. "How did they find you?"

She wrinkled her nose. "Do you have a vial or some kind of containment for the crystal?"

"No. I don't want that thing in my guild."

She fought the urge to sigh. "Right. Well, can someone get me a coffee, two sugars, two creams? This has been a long fucking night."

The gathered might of the Leobrad guild offices stared at her.

She sighed and used her free hand to scroll through her phone for Adrea's number.

"Ritual space, Adrea speaking."

"Hiya, Adrea. This is Imara."

"Oh, hi! How did your exam go?"

"Pretty good, are you willing to take on another stone? I have one here in my hand, and no one wants to take it on."

"Sure? When?"

"Three hours if I can get a lift." She looked around, and none of the mages would meet her gaze. "Just a moment."

She looked at the guy in charge. "Can someone take me to the transport station, at least?"

A shadow fell across the door to the garage. "We'll take you home." The voice was feminine and amused.

Mr. E bristled. *Demon magic.*

Not truly. Check it again. It is much a demon as you are an actual cat. If they are willing to give me a ride, I will take it.

I . . .

Hold your objections until we can get home. Then you can give me your assessment.

Yes, Imara.

She could feel him sulking against her neck.

"I will take that ride, please."

She turned to Iofer. "She will be fine. I will send you a report as to the construction of this particular stone by the weekend. I am going to have to pull the spectres apart, and that takes time."

"Thank you, Ms. Mirrin. I am sorry that we can't take you

back, but this crew was heading that way anyway, and they answered while you were floating."

"How long was I floating?"

Iofer blinked. "About an hour."

"Dammit. Thanks. Have Etta contact me if there are any side effects beyond trauma. Contact a counsellor for that."

She kept her fist closed over the stone but tried to keep it relaxed. Mr. E was not going to be in the mood to swallow this one for storage.

She walked toward the female shadow and smiled. "Hiya, I am Imara Mirrin, stranded Death Keeper."

The other woman smiled and extended her hand, "I am Benny, blended mage and our Mage Guild's contribution to my XIA team."

Imara felt tremendous power in the woman's hand, and the eyes that she looked into were stamped with fey energy.

When they approached the vehicle, the guys were out and leaning against it. They all had the excellent physical tone that most of the XIA sported, and their gazes on Benny were possessive.

"Oh, this isn't going to be an uncomfortable ride at all," Imara muttered.

Benny chuckled. "I will sit between you and Tremble. Smith is driving, and Argyle will be co-piloting."

"Thanks. My familiar is named Mr. E, and he is a little touchy right now."

Benny chuckled, and she nodded for the guys to get in the vehicle. "Demon hunter?"

"Me? No."

"No, your familiar. He has the look of an inherited familiar, and those tend to be folks who displeased the Mage Guild. His bristling when he identified me is a pretty good sign that he doesn't like mages with demon blood."

The other three settled in the vehicle, Benny slid into the centre of the back seat, and Imara got in, closing the door awkwardly before settling in. Not being able to use her hand was difficult, but letting that power go in this small space with the shifter, the fey, and the vampire wearing shades, was not a great idea.

Buckle up.

"I can't buckle up without my hand."

Benny smiled. "I will give you a hand with that."

A moment later, after the stranger had leaned over her and tucked her in, they were on their way.

"How did you know about my familiar?"

"One of my best friends is a hellhound. She is locked into her servitude, and she was born into it. I am guessing that he is a generated one, which makes him an ancient mage, which makes him one of the demon hunters. Everybody else just went from spectre to flecks of energy."

"You . . . you have studied."

The elf, Tremble, leaned over. "Her family is in possession of the largest library of spells and magical lore in the country."

She blinked. "You are Beneficia Ganger?"

Benny beamed. "That's the one. You have done some studying yourself."

"Oh, wow. I read a book by one of your ancestors. It helped me solve a problem."

"Really? Which one?"

"Lenora Ganger."

"Oh, that's my mom. She's older than she looks." Benny smiled. "Was it a textbook?"

"Oh. No. It was a romance and a diary rolled into one."

Smith was the shifter; he looked back at her in the mirror and grinned. "I think Benny might be willing to trade you for that one. It doesn't seem that she has it."

"It isn't mine to trade."

Benny smiled. "To whom does it belong?"

"The owner of Reegar Hall. That is where I live."

Benny's expression was shocked. "I used to visit Reegar Hall. I don't remember who owned it, though."

"Technically, the college owns it, but Reegar is the spectre of the hall. It is his support, and it keeps him going."

Tremble piped up, "He was mourned by one of my clan."

"Liirick?"

Tremble nodded. "How did you know?"

"He comes by, and he and Reegar knock boots now and then. Mostly, when he is doing speaking engagements at the college."

Tremble looked around Benny in astonishment. "How is that possible?"

Imara wrinkled her nose. "I am a Death Keeper. My passive talent is boosting the presence of the spectres. Reegar is as solid as he wants to be."

Argyle turned around in his seat, and he gave her a piercing look with his red gaze. "Are you single?"

"No. I have a boyfriend."

Benny grinned. "Do tell. We have a long drive before we get to the college."

"Oh, can we stop at Ritual Space? I have to drop this off." She held up her closed fist.

Smith nodded. "Wherever you need to go. Iofer says that you saved their teammate." Smith grinned before he turned back to driving. "And we can go very fast."

The acceleration to the interstate was very tangible.

Benny turned to her again. "So, tell me about your fella or lady, and then, let me know what is clenched in your hand and why is it turning black?"

Imara sighed. "I am holding the spectral amalgamation of seventeen mages who were not pleasant men. There has been a rash of these kinds of stones recently. The right combination of faded spectres can make an incredibly powerful talisman, but this one is just dangerous."

"And why is your hand turning black?"

She grumbled, "It is trying to take power from me, so I have to deaden the area for containment. It will be fine, I hope."

Benny frowned. "Well, while we rocket down the highway, I am going to return to the topic I am interested in. How did you meet your boyfriend?"

Imara wrinkled her nose. "We met in class."

"Aww, did he help you with your homework?" Argyle had a strange singsong to his voice.

"No, he helped me with a skeevy instructor, and I helped him with his homework." She smirked and checked the stone. There was a little leakage, so she had to change her technique. Argyle was getting influenced.

She pulled in the energy she needed to contain the stone and let the band of black form around her wrist. She watched the vampire shake his head to clear it.

Benny raised her brows. "What was that?"

"Leakage. The technically undead are more susceptible. Sorry, Argyle. I have it now."

Mr. E crept down her arm. *Let me have it. This is doing damage to you.*

Are you okay with the occupants of the vehicle?

Yes. My investigations indicate that their link to the demon king who spawned them has been severed. It is a daring and complicated move. I must say, I am impressed, now give me the stone before it hurts you.

Thank you. If it gives you trouble, I will take it back.

"My familiar is going to take the stone. There is going to be a bit of a release of power, and then, things should be fine." She watched the kitten crouch over the stone, and when he gave her a slight nod, she opened her hand.

A slight flare of energy and the pulse of power shut off. The colour started to return to her hand immediately.

"Thanks, Mr. E." She smiled, and he walked over to her lap and curled up.

"Wow. Is he seriously a kitten?" Benny's fingers were flexing.

"Yes, but wait until he has hacked up the stone before you try and pet him. He has warmed to the demon influence in you and your men, but he isn't a fan in general."

Tremble laughed. "He picked up on that?"

"Your connection? No, your posture on your vehicle did. You were all equal, and all fixated on Benny's walk. That indicated intimacy."

Smith nodded. "Body language is key. What do you and your boyfriend do for private time?"

She smirked. "We find a public place and go to a movie or

something. No sex until I finish college. Mr. E is willing to enforce it."

The entire group was shocked. Imara laughed, and Mr. E started purring. It was interesting. She had never murdered a conversation before.

Chapter Nine

They made the three-hour trip to Ritual Space in ninety minutes. Mr. E was growing cool with his efforts to contain the spectres, and she wanted to get it out of him.

Adrea came out to the parking area with a smile that turned into delight. "Benny!"

Benny passed Tremble and hugged Adrea.

Imara undid her seatbelt and carefully carried Mr. E to the proprietor of Ritual Space. "Hi, Adrea."

Adrea came forward and hugged her as well, her white hair swinging around her face. "Not again. Okay, come this way."

"If Blueberry is in, he can lead me to the stones."

"Of course. I will see you when everything is contained."

Imara nodded and clutched her limp familiar to her as she entered the space. Blueberry was waiting, and he hopped ahead of her at a good pace, leaving her to stride after him and into the space between realities where it was safe to store this sort of spirit.

Blueberry sat next to the open gateway on his hind legs, and his expression indicated that he was willing to wait.

Imara set Mr. E down on the wide stone bench, and she tickled him. He kicked his legs and opened his eyes.

"Hack it up."

She petted his fur and held him as he started hacking. For a moment, it seemed that it wouldn't come up, but then, the small crystal dropped to the stone.

She sighed and picked up Mr. E with one hand while placing the stone into the arc above the bench.

"Right. Gentlemen, I want the bossiest of you to come out now." She sent a trickle of power into the stone, and a torso formed above the containment band.

"I don't need to talk to a lowly mage."

"I am not just a mage, but keep insulting me. I will just do this."

She grabbed his energy and tore it apart, shredding it into particles so small that they were only good for blending with the next wave.

Sighing, she spoke to the stone. "I will return, I will question all of you, and I want to know who you are. If you give me a satisfactory answer, I will put you into a soul stone and give you a second life as a rejuvenated spectre. Think it over."

She turned and cuddled her kitten while following the bunny down the trail that only existed when she was moving to that pocket between worlds.

Blueberry led her to the rear patio where the garden was flourishing, and some small tables had been assembled so that Adrea could serve tea. The XIA team was sitting around and eating scones.

"Imara, are you done?"

She nodded. "For today. I will still have to come back to conduct interviews."

"Aside from the one you dispersed."

"Yeah, that. He was just an asshole."

Benny blinked. "You destroyed a spectre?"

"Sure. It's not tricky." Imara sat in the empty seat that was waiting for her.

Adrea patted her on the shoulder. "Don't be smug."

Imara blinked. "It isn't being smug. Anyone with magical skills can tear apart a spectre. Being a Death Keeper just means I can tear it up really, really small."

Benny laughed. "Fair enough. So, you have been here before?"

Adrea snorted. "Every two days for the last six weeks. Hyl has been tutoring her for her class."

Smith looked at her in genuine surprise. "*Hyl* has been tutoring you?"

"Yes." She petted Mr. E with one hand while sipping her tea with the other.

Argyle was sitting in the shade, but he asked, "What is your class?"

"Stealth Magic. He taught me how to move and a few spells to assist in my final project, which—thankfully—was completed."

Tremble arched his pale brows. "Did you pass?"

"I completed the exam. That is a pass."

She checked her phone and smiled at the text from Argus.

Etta is doing well, Iofer is worshiping the very idea of you, and his team has pledged allegiance to you. Are you home?

She texted back. *Ritual Space. Had to drop off the annoying item.*

Benny smiled. "The boyfriend. I can tell by your expression."

"Yeah. He was just checking in."

Adrea rolled her eyes. "He checks in a lot. I swear, I was almost hoping for a crime spree just to stop her phone from going off."

The XIA officers looked at each other in surprise.

Smith asked, "Crime spree?"

Adrea grinned. "Didn't she tell you? She is dating Argus. He has been hanging around here with annoying frequency while she was training, though he did bring excellent ice cream every time, so that says something."

Imara started to blush. "I like sugar after a lot of magic expenditure."

Smith was still staring. "Argus? *Our* Argus?"

Imara grinned. "Technically, I have dibs on him, but that particular claiming is still six months or so away. I have to get my accreditation from the Mage Guild to be a commercial mage, but I inherited a building from a friend of mine, so my offices are set. No romantic entanglements until I have my professional life in place."

Benny stared. "How old are you?"

"Twenty. I will still be twenty by the time I graduate."

"How did you and Argus meet?"

Imara chuckled. "I told you. I met him in class. Ethics

class. He had to take a course for work, and he helped me out with my shape shifting course."

Benny was enthralled. "You can shape shift?"

"Yeah. I passed the class."

Smith challenged, "What is your beast?"

"You are going to laugh."

Smith held up a hand. "I promise to try not to."

"Griffin vulture."

Mr. E perked up at the cacophony of laughter that surrounded them. *What is going on?*

I said something funny. Are you okay?

He was very strong.

He is a celestial smear now.

Good. When can we go home?

I am hoping that we will be on our way shortly.

Adrea settled and smiled. "This quartet had their bonding ceremony here. It was just after I had taken over and a nice way to start my life in this place. You might want to consider it when you and Argus want to tie the knot."

"There is no proposal in the air."

Adrea snorted. "I would have to be blind to miss the bonding with you two; now, eat two scones with cream and jam, and I will let you go. Until then, no one is going to make a move for the door."

Imara looked, and the other four were frozen in time. "I hate it when you do that."

"There is no other way for you to gain the skills you did. You got six months' worth of training in six weeks. I had to slow time here to achieve it. And it was fun. Mostly fun." Adrea winked and waved at her to load up the scones. "I wasn't kidding. Two scones with cream and jam. Go. And then, I will let them loose."

Imara put some clotted cream on a plate for Mr. E and set up her two scones. One was blackberry and one strawberry, both had cream.

She chewed her way through them with deliberation, and when the final bite was in her mouth, the other four were released from time.

Mr. E was sitting on the table and enjoying his cream, and the others looked a little disconcerted at her jam-stained face.

Benny blinked. "Did we miss something?"

"Nope. Just Adrea throwing her weight around."

Adrea crossed her arms. "Imara doesn't eat properly, and she burns a lot of energy. She's the seventh child of a seventh child twice over. She's got so much luck, it is dizzying."

"Love you, too, Addy." After wiping her lips, she blew Adrea a kiss.

"I can give you a ride home, Imara." Argus's voice was behind her.

She turned her head, and he set his hand on her shoulder. "That would be great. Mr. E isn't really comfortable."

Argus looked over her shoulder at her familiar. "Aw, he looks exhausted."

Smith cleared his throat. "Argus, when were you going to mention your lady friend here?"

Argus squeezed her shoulder. "When it was any of your business, Smith. Argyle, Tremble, Benny, nice to see you all."

Smith winced. "Right. Got it. Imara is an incredible choice. She deserves better than you."

"Yes, I am aware, but she keeps saying that she got lucky."

"I did. Well, this has been fun, but I have to grab my kitten and go. We both need a bit of rest before I get to meet my family tonight."

That got everyone except Adrea curious.

Imara held up her hand. "Too long to explain. If we ever meet again, I am sure I will be happy to fill you in."

She got up and cuddled a sleepy Mr. E against her chest. "Lovely to meet you. Have to run. Have a great day, and thanks for the ride."

Argus put his arm around her, and he supported her very tired self out to his vehicle.

"So, everybody else is off shift?"

"Yeah, lucky for you I don't need much sleep. You look haggard but lovely."

She laughed softly and buckled in with Mr. E on her lap. She poured a bit of energy into him, and he sat up, stretching.

"Thanks, Argus. I want nothing more than my own bed. I have to brace for my family party this evening."

"Do you need me there?"

"No, but be braced for a call if the Mage Guild can't manage it. I am pretty sure that there is going to be a riot by midnight."

She slumped over and leaned against his shoulder.

"You sound like you have had a long day. What happened with Iofer?"

"They came by the house and asked for my help. They used an emergency transport spell that spit us out in their home city. I am guessing that it was their mage component that had touched the stone, the stone started using living energy to propel the spirits, and she went down. I don't know how long she had been there, but those mages were useless.

"Anyway, I get there, I take possession of the stone, get it contained, bleed off the extra energy and give it back to the XIA team members. From there, I was looking for a ride home. The XIA agents couldn't manage it with their wounded member, the Mage Guild didn't want to come near me because I had arrived with the extranaturals. Benny and her team came in just at the right time."

"They are a solid unit. I don't know what their assignment was, but I am glad that they were there."

"As am I. I will get you home in one piece. Just rest. I will wake you when Bara is glaring at me out of the window."

"Thanks, Argus. It has been a hectic few hours."

"I gathered as much, but when Iofer sent out the call for help, I knew you could manage the job. Glad you made it, now sleep."

She breathed in, breathed out, and the world went warmly dark.

Low voices surrounded her, and she was carried and settled down on the couch in the common room. She opened her eyes just enough to see Reegar, Bara, and Argus, and she could feel Mr. E.

"Wake me at six, so I can get ready for the party."

Reegar frowned. "You need a healer."

"That can wait until tomorrow. Today, I just need some rest."

Argus sat next to her, holding her hand, and the other two disappeared.

She opened her eyes a little wider and sighed. "Thanks for getting me home."

"No problem. I am happy to have been there." He stroked her cheek.

"I still have to write that report on the spectres. Someone seems to be looking for something, and they aren't waiting for the dissipated ones anymore. They are grabbing some really strong spectres and smashing them together. That isn't good."

"I know. I have learned that much from you."

She sniffed. "Do I smell food?"

"It has been decided that you will get more of a boost from a large infusion of food than simple rest."

She groaned. "Everybody is trying to feed me today."

"Adrea?"

"Yeah, and she paused time to do it. That is one scary lady when she wants you to eat a scone."

He chuckled and gave her a light kiss. "There are a bunch of scary ladies out there; you just have to find their triggers. Apparently, Adrea's is knowing that you need food after magic."

"Why do folks fuss over me?"

Reegar came into her field of view with a tray in his hands. "Because you are young, and you are fearless. It makes us worry."

Argus nodded and helped her sit up.

"Oh, this isn't for her. Mr. E looks a little weak, so we defrosted a pie. Imara's food is still on the stove."

Mr. E perked up and looked around. Reegar reached between them and scooped up the fluffy familiar, setting him on the tray, on the coffee table, next to the pie. It didn't take long before the familiar and the pie became one.

Imara talked quietly with Argus and Bara while the kitten romped in the dessert; when her food arrived, it did wonders for her sense of reality and connectivity to the universe.

Bara finally asked, "How did the fabric work? I got it out of your room."

Imara raised her thumb. "It was excellent. It should give you the grade you were looking for as well."

Argus asked, "What fabric?"

Bara smiled. "It was a speciality wrap that could be worn while shifting. I am trying to find a way to make it in something larger than a five-inch strip."

"Can't you stitch it together?"

Bara sighed. "No. That is the problem."

Imara smiled and felt the ripple of relief that she didn't have to tell Argus what she was actually using it for. He was in law enforcement, and until she was officially invited into the home of Desmond Demiel, she had committed a crime.

No pressure.

Chapter Ten

Formal clothing was easy when you had someone still majoring in textiles under your roof. The gown that Bara had prepared for her took her breath away. Long, silky panels of black and blue wrapped in a five-inch wide belt studded with jet beads. The gown made her feel very adult, and it matched with her black Death Keeper robes.

The invitation to her father's birthday and her niece's family blessing had mentioned wearing honours. She was wearing her honours. The embroidery that Kitigan's family had created was stunning. All she needed was a staff, and she would be at home in any formal death-related setting.

Imara tucked her phone into the pocket in her belt and looked at Mr. E. "How do I look?"

Excellent. I will be on guard this evening. You know they are going to try and trip you up.

She nodded. "I know. At least I have confirmation from my instructor that I passed with ninety-percent in the stealth magic course. Phone, email and the photo. It was nice of Argus to make him make those calls."

You have the photo?

"On my phone and two copies printed. Bara has one copy and Reegar the other. Both are locked up and in a stasis field."

Do you feel paranoid?

She nodded. "Yes, but I am going to see family. From my research, that is an appropriate feeling."

He snickered and jumped to the shoulder of her robes. She had her invitation, the gift for the baby, she had her familiar, and she had her formalwear. She was ready to face the part of her family that had thrown her away.

A deep exhalation and she walked down to Kitigan's car.

She was her designated driver for the evening, and her vehicle was new and a nice SUV.

"So, Imara, when you want to leave, call me. If anything goes weird, call me. If Mr. E hacks up a hairball, call me."

Mr. E lifted his head and made a cute noise.

"I promise. If I don't get furious and fly home, I will definitely call you."

"Good. Now, get in the car." Kitty held the door open and made sure that the robes and the dress were safe and tidy.

The rest of the drive was basically silent with the exception of Imara making one call.

"Are you ready?"

The voice on the other end said, "I don't sleep."

She ended the call and tucked her phone back into her belt. "Whoo."

"It will be fine. Everyone will be fine."

Imara glanced over. "My family is going to hate me."

Kitty chuckled. "They already hate you."

"This is true. Thanks for that." Imara grinned, and she relaxed and petted Mr. E the entire way to Demiel Hall.

"Call me when you want to leave. I will just be around the corner at that donut shop. I brought some homework with me, so don't rush it." Kitty grinned as she pulled into the circular drive in front of the wide and ancient hall.

"Will do. Happy studying." She opened her door and slid onto the crunchy black gravel.

Mr. E popped up and perched proudly on her shoulder. *I am going to be on alert tonight.*

Thanks. Me too.

With her back braced and her robes hanging straight, she walked up to the double doors, and they were swung open by two trolls in uniform.

She smiled and inclined her head. "Good evening. I am here for the party."

One of the trolls extended his hand, and she produced the invitation. He peered down and inclined his head. "Go through to the ballroom."

She patted his hand and smiled. "Thank you. I think that

is the most polite thing I will hear this evening."

He looked surprised, and he gave her a slow, toothy smile. "Welcome, Death Keeper."

She nodded and remembered that that is what she was here. She was a powerful mage invited to an event. That was all.

The huge archway in front of her was glowing with light. She tucked her invitation into her belt and walked through the security spell.

A human butler stood by and held out his hand for the invitation. She pulled it smoothly from her belt and handed it to him.

He frowned, looked at her robes, and then announced her to the room of strange but rather familiar faces in the room. "Master Death Keeper, Imara Mirrin Deepford-Smythe."

Technically, it was her name, though Imara Mirrin was acceptable for legal purposes.

The man who had to be her father strode forward. He glared down at her but didn't speak.

A young woman came to his side and clung to him. "Didn't they take your coat at the door?"

Imara raised her brows. "This is my formal garb, just as every man here is wearing his own master's robes."

She blinked and frowned. "They don't look the same."

"They would not be. I am not a master mage."

That seemed to satisfy her. "That's it. What do you do?"

Imara inclined her head. "This and that."

"What are you doing, calling yourself a Death Keeper? Their branch of the guild is exceptionally strict. Wearing those robes could get you bound by law." Desmond was trying to intimidate her.

"I am aware of that. It is why I proudly wear the rank earned by hundreds of hours of work with spectres. There are four in this building alone, are there not?"

He blinked. "You can't be serious."

"I can. If you are my father, happy birthday, by the way."

The young woman jolted. She might be four or five years older than Imara, but her attitude was much younger.

He extended his hand in greeting, and she knew it was to test her power.

She extended her hand, and their grip generated blue and crimson lightning throughout the room.

He released her and smiled. "It is a pleasure to finally meet you, daughter."

"And you as well, Master Demiel. Now, may I bring out the spectres and have them join the party?"

He shrugged, and the doubt was still in him. "As you like. Your brothers are here and will introduce themselves and their wives. You are welcome at Demiel Hall."

She nodded. "Thank you for your welcome; now, let the deceased join us."

She powered up the spectres to the point where they appeared solid, and they began to migrate toward the party.

Luken smiled at her and came over. "Come on, let me introduce you."

She leaned toward him. "I hope it gets less tense."

"Probably won't. Let's start with the baby. She's friendly."

Imara laughed and walked with her twin to meet her oldest brother, his wife, and their new baby.

The baby was genuinely a newborn. "She's adorable."

Her brother, Michael, and his wife, Hannah, watched her for a moment, and then, Hannah seemed to act on impulse and handed the baby over.

Imara blinked and cradled the little one with the pink cheeks and rich blue eyes of a new baby. "Well, I am not technically your aunt due to fun family stuff, but every baby deserves a present."

Imara cradled the baby with one arm and reached into the belt with the other hand, sticking her fingers into the pocket specially made for this purpose. With a light touch, she brushed a tiny smudge across the forehead and then the back of each tiny fist. "Congratulations on the magic, little one."

Hannah smiled and whispered, "Imara."

"What?"

"Her name is Imara Rose. We call her Rosie for short, but

Michael felt this was right."

Imara grinned as the smudges disappeared and the baby's bright blue eyes got a little brighter. "In that case, this is a very good gift."

Hannah asked, "What was that stuff?"

Imara chuckled. "Dirt from the site of the last local wave of magic. It will give her a grounding when it comes to learning and the ability to call on nature for what she needs. Perhaps we can get another family member through the sky breaking course."

Luken groaned. "Don't tell me you got in."

"I did. It was a fun course but hard as hell. You were never doing what you thought you were until you suddenly got it right."

One of her nearest brothers walked over. "How did you get in?"

Luken made the introductions. "Edmund, this is Imara, Imara, Edmund. His twin is Edgar."

Imara reached out for Edmund's hand, but he didn't take it.

"How did you get in?"

"I passed the aptitude test. It was as simple as that. If you didn't get in, then the course would have killed you."

Michael was frowning. "Edmund, why are you being rude?"

He hissed. "She doesn't belong here. She's stringing everybody along, making them think she is a true mage, a true talent, but we all know she was eighth. She is unlucky."

Luken looked at Edmund. "Are you nuts? You know the truth."

"Dad says it's a lie. She was eighth. There was no doubt in his mind."

Imara pinched the bridge of her nose. "Right. And he wasn't in the room for any of the deliveries. Oh, and on my birth certificate, it lists my birth as a minute earlier. Oh, and our mother says I was seventh. For someone supposed to be unlucky, I do tend to be in the right place at the right time to help those around me. If you want to argue that, feel free, but you had better bring backup."

Edmund flushed and spun around, stalking over to their father.

She looked to Luken. "Is there anyone else I can alienate while I am here?"

She handed the baby back to her mother after stroking her cheek one more time. "Bye, Rosie."

Her married brothers were all fairly calm; it was the three in school that were tense. Michael, Alexander, and Desmond Jr. were all fine. They had achieved their Master status and were relaxed. Edmund, Richard and supposedly Edgar were all tense. Luken wasn't, but he was lucky. That explained that.

The spectres came to her, and they all smiled and spoke favourably. Lord Demiel, Lady Demiel, and their two children, Halos and Nyxos, had been spectres since a plague had swept them away over a hundred and fifty years earlier.

Desmond came over. "Who are these folk? How did they get in?"

Imara blinked. "They are the spectres of Demiel Hall. They have been here the entire time."

He paused, and Edmund shifted eagerly behind him.

Lord Demiel stood between them. Imara glanced over her shoulder and nearly choked. The portrait of Lord Demiel was right behind him.

"Tell me something that only my ancestor would know."

Lord Demiel looked offended, but he leaned forward and whispered in Desmond's ear. Whatever he said made Desmond stand upright immediately.

"I . . . I thought you spectres too weak to speak."

"We were. This Death Keeper of Demiel blood offered us her energy, and now, we can interact with the world again. Well, we can interact with the world within these walls. She is exceptionally powerful. You should be proud as it is your blood in her veins. She is clever."

Desmond turned to Imara. "You may leave now."

She nodded and turned to the spectres. "I offer you a physical presence for a month or two."

Lady Demiel smiled. "We will take it."

"The house is yours." Imara smiled at the few friendly siblings she had, and she left the same way she had come while the spectres exclaimed at their physical presence. That was going to mess with her father and his bride for a while.

The power sparked as she left, and she grinned. The building was being warded against her. They needed her physical presence to drop a barrier against her. She had had to be invited in, so she could be locked out.

She patted each of the trolls on the hand as she left, and Mr. E started to purr the instant her feet stepped on the walkway.

She fished out her phone and dialled Kitty. "Hello, Kitty. I am done here."

"Great. I will be there in a minute."

"I am walking toward the donut shop, so don't rush. I think I need time to clear my head."

"Excellent. I am still getting into my car." Kitty chuckled. "See ya soon."

The call ended, and Imara kept walking until she was off the grounds and onto the road.

You handled that well.

She chuckled. "We know why I was invited, so it is nice to have that confirmation. They think they have what they need, so they booted me out. It rings a bell."

You didn't remember the first time.

"Ah, you know that I got to read it out in black and white. Mom wasn't even allowed to keep me because of that contract."

And that was in the past, and you are now an adult with a cooler head for your situation. You still have luck, friends, and a mom who is just getting to know you.

She grinned and kept walking. "I know. I am not bitter. I am feeling better now that I am away from them. That is one toxic atmosphere. At least Michael and Hannah seem pretty normal, and Rosie is a cutie."

She is very cute. If you see her when she is older, I sense tail pulling in my future.

Imara giggled until Kitty pulled up next to her and rolled down the window. "Hey, little lady, going my way?"

"Kitty, I am going to give you such a butt kicking." She walked around and got in on the passenger side.

When she was buckled up and Mr. E was on the dashboard, she sat back and sighed. "Home, Jeeves."

"Yes, madam." Kitty put the vehicle in drive, and the trip home began.

Imara could hardly wait to see what had happened at Reegar Hall while she had been gone.

Chapter Eleven

Imara got out of the car with a groan, and Mr. E perched on her shoulder. Kitty grabbed her books and headed off to finish her homework elsewhere.

When Imara came through the doors, she paused and blinked. "Wow, this is a little more active than I thought it would be."

Edgar Demiel was tied up on the floor and gagged. Bara was baking cookies, and Reegar was going through a pile of books that had been spilled to the floor.

The security officers were taking a statement from Bara while she baked to calm down.

Imara checked her watch, and she nodded. A quick photo and an email later and she introduced herself to the security officers.

Reegar growled, "Get him out of here."

Imara nodded. "Good evening, officers. I see there has been an intrusion."

Bara sniffled. "It was horrible, Imara. I heard a noise upstairs, and that guy was there, tangled in my loom. He ruined three weeks of weaving! I am never going to get my ninety-five percent in that class now."

Imara kept her face concerned. Bara's drama courses were paying off.

The security officers kept making notes. One asked, "Who are you, miss?"

"I am Imara Mirrin."

"Do you know who this man is?"

She looked at Edgar and bit her lip. "I think he is in one of my classes. I haven't been formally introduced, but I am pretty sure we are related."

The officers looked confused by that. "What is his name?"

"His last name is Demiel."

Both officers lowered their notepads. She gave them a bland look. "And I am Imara Mirrin Deepford-Smythe Demiel. He broke into my house, and I don't know what he wanted. I will assist Mage Reegar with pressing charges for any broken materials, and compensation should be issued to Bara for the destruction of her weaving project. It does look good on him, doesn't it?"

Edgar was flushed and furious, writhing from side to side. The notebooks came back up. "What did he try and take?"

Reegar scowled. "He was rifling through my books."

One of the officers thought to ask, "What class were you in with him?"

"Stealth Magic. Don't worry; his deadline was forty-five minutes ago." She smiled and inclined her head.

The officers had tensed, and then, they smiled at each other with a smug air.

Imara knew that Edgar was going to fail the course, but she also knew he would get off without any consequences. Her checks on Demiel history showed that they were primarily bullies who liked to throw money around.

Just as they were hauling Edgar to his feet, with the gag still in place, the door opened, and Hyl arrived. He smiled at Imara and paused to stare at her brother. "What is this?"

Bara sobbed and set the cookie batter down with a thud. "Hebrokeinandwreckedmyprojectandtoreitupandthrew-booksaroun-dandnowtheyaregoingtolethimgobecauseheisaDemiel."

Hyl grabbed Edgar by the shoulder, his Mage Guild uniform neat and tidy, and his eyes twinkling. "Did he use magic to break in?"

Reegar nodded. "He did. He used a spell to break through the glass, but he still managed to do a lot of manual damage."

"Using magic during the commission of a crime is a serious offense."

He pulled the gag from Edgar's mouth. "Did you use magic in the commission of a crime?"

"It was my assignment. I had to!" Edgar was nearly foaming with fury. "She has a stone stolen from my house! Check her!"

Mr. E jumped down, so Imara could remove her robes and hand them to Hyl. There was no way that anything could have been hidden in her gown. She undid her belt and handed it to him.

He checked everything, handed it to the security officers to check, and he looked to Edgar. "So, that is one lie."

"It was her assignment! She had to! Ask her! She was at Demiel Hall tonight. She had to have stolen it, or she is going to fail."

Hyl raised his brows at Imara. "Were you at the hall tonight?"

"I was. I was surrounded at all times and left promptly at midnight when requested. It was a little cold blooded of them actually."

He nodded. "You have completed your courses?"

"I have. I have emails, a voicemail, and a photo indicating that my course is complete and was complete before this evening."

Hyl grinned. "Excellent. Well, I will take this young mage and have him up on charges of magic outside of scholastic purpose."

Edgar's eyes were wild. "It was an assignment."

Hyl looked at him blandly. "It was stealth magic. What sounds stealthy to you about your actions this evening?"

Imara watched as her tutor left her hall with the officers trying to figure out how to get on the guild's good side.

Bara started to scoop out the cookies, and she grinned over at Imara. "How was your family?"

"Half nice, half horrible. What kind of cookies?"

"Chocolate and peanut butter. I kept some of the dough without chocolate for Mr. E. He looks like he has been hard at work keeping you calm."

Mr. E jumped on the table and perched up like a prairie dog. Bara made tiny balls of dough for him and set it out on a plate.

Reegar sighed. "You were right; he is after the demon codex."

Mr. E paused and looked over at Reegar.

Imara moved forward and petted her familiar. "It is a book belonging to Reegar. Part of his collection, but I am fairly sure that Edgar would not bring it back after stealing it. That book in the hands of the Demiels is a nightmare."

He calmed and continued consuming his treat.

A call brought Kitty over for a post-mortem of the evening and some cookies.

They all sat around the table while Reegar continued to work on the dents and dings his books had taken.

Kitty munched a cookie and smiled. "So. What is your general impression of your family?"

"They are half good, half bad, and not to be trusted. I think I will stick with my mom's side. Her folk are broke, but they have character." She looked at Bara. "I mean, aside from Luken. He's great."

Bara raised her cup of hot cocoa in a toast. "To Luken!"

Kitty and Imara followed suit. "To Luken."

They all sipped hot cocoa and sat back at two in the morning.

"When do you go to your final class?"

"Tomorrow morning."

Bara frowned. "You need to get some rest. You have had a stressful couple of days."

"Yes, ma'am. See you in the morning."

Mr. E ran ahead of her, up the stairs and into her room. Her wards were still in place against members of her own bloodline, and she dropped to her bed, trying to ignore all of the insults she had absorbed that night.

Don't worry. You are still beloved by your family. Your true family and that gathering is expanding daily.

Thanks, little dude. Sorry you are saddled with me when I am all weepy.

I have had worse mages to deal with. I am truly enjoying myself for the first time in centuries. Keep doing what you

are doing and get some sleep.
Imara did as she was told.

The tiny class was a sullen and sombre place. Professor McClairie looked them over. "I told you when this term began that stealth magic is a difficult skill to learn. It is nearly impossible to get the skills together in one short term. Out of the ten of you, only one student managed to exhibit the skills and technique necessary for a passing grade."
Imara was shocked.
"This is not an unusual occurrence, but it was surprising that the student I thought least likely to succeed found the most success. And the object that was drawn was removed, presented and then returned. Unlike most of you, this student took the day of the event literally. The assignment was completed before dawn."
Her classmates were looking like they had been struck with hammers. One asked, "You can do that?"
The professor nodded. "The day begins one minute after midnight."
The professor had folders in his hand, and he went through the students and handed them out. Imara read her name, opened the folder, and her shoulders slumped in relief at the passing grade. Over ninety percent was nothing to sneer at.
Edgar was sitting at the far end of the room, and he got to his feet, stalking toward her. Mr. E hopped off her shoulder and landed on the folder.
He was nearly in front of her when the professor stepped in front of him. "You didn't manage it, Edgar. Get over it. Enroll again next term, and if you display any emotional development, I will consider it. Right now, you are a pathetic rich brat."
Edgar snarled and pulled his fist back. Imara blinked, she hadn't thought that he was the bully in the family, but it seemed that the twins were both assholes.
The professor caught the fist, and he clenched his fingers. Edgar grunted and then began to whine as he was forced to

his knees.

"I didn't care for Desmond when he tried and failed this course, and I don't care for you. I know you only took this course to attack your sister here, but it is a shortsighted plan. Get your own path in life. Following orders puts you in unpleasant situations and deprives you of self-sufficiency."

Imara gathered her things and tried to leave, but they were blocking her exit.

Edgar looked over at her with anger in his expression. "She ruined everything."

Imara piped up, "If you are referring to your mother, *our* mother, she was going to leave the moment that she fulfilled the contract. Desmond is an ass."

"You grew up with her!"

She rolled her eyes. "Not this again. I grew up in a group home. I just met my mother, *our* mother, after I arrived here at college. The contract didn't let her keep me. Read it if you don't believe it. No issue of the Demiel line was to remain in her custody. So, she stuck me in a series of orphanages and homes run by her extended family. I grew up knowing that I was alone and that I was not allowed to be with my family. I tried to go and meet you all on your terms, and you tried to break into my fucking home while I was with your twin. He doesn't know how you cock your head when you are getting mad, by the way. He can't fake being you."

He scowled. "I don't believe you."

"Ask her. She will take a call from you. Read the contract. It is available online at the mage contract archive."

Edgar blinked, and she saw the abandoned toddler in his expression. He would have been two when Mirrin left.

"Or don't. Just don't consider me a threat. I won't consider you at all." She climbed on a desk and slithered behind her brother and the professor. She was out the door with her familiar and on her way home in seconds.

She slapped the folder on the table, and Reegar came by to take a look. "Excellent. That is one of the highest scores I have seen."

"You have seen others?"

"Of course. Stealth magic is a hard skill to learn, but a few have an actual knack for it. The hardest part is the professor keeping track of all the temporal trackers that he has out. McClairie is a master at temporal magic."

"Wait, there was a tracker on me?"

"Yes, it is in the notecard he gave that outlined your assignment. It tracked your every move, marked the acquisition of the artifact and, also, marked its return."

She stared at him. "You knew?"

"Yes. I thought it would make you nervous to know about it. It doesn't matter anyway. It is a standard tracking spell."

Imara sighed and looked at her marks, the credits and knew that there was only one class that would give her the credits she needed to finish quickly.

"What are you thinking?"

"My next course. There is only one thing it can be, but it is going to be really dangerous."

I can handle it. I mastered welding after all.

She wrinkled her nose at him. "Spell Crafting 501. I have managed soul casting, shape shifting, sky breaking and now stealth magic, along with business and ethics courses. So, if I can get spell crafting under my belt, I will be able to get a broad-spectrum magic license. I will have way more skills than I need, but I will qualify for an immediate license. It is that, or they have to kill me."

Reegar grinned. "You have a fascinating career path in mind."

"Yeah. I know. But it just feels right. When it feels right, it feels right."

"What will you do for staff?"

She grinned. "I think that I will pick people with skills I can use, but any of my friends are welcome for work experience when they graduate."

Imara sat back and looked at Reegar. There was no one better to ask. "So, what do I need to know about writing spells?"

Reegar beckoned, and a stack of books began to pile up

on the table. More and more came in a huge cascade. "Start here."

She blinked. "Do I have to lift them? I can do that now."

He laughed, and she smiled as she prepared to take on the skills that would set her free to live her own life for the first time.

Don't be scared of the future. I will be with you every step of the way.

Imara laughed. "Riding on my shoulder and eating my snacks."

That is what a familiar is for.

Grinning, she pulled the first tome in front of her and started to read while her other hand finished the registration for the next term. It took three hours for the confirmation to come back, but her path was set. She was going to learn how to craft a spell.

It had better be a good one.

Spell Crafting 501
The Hellkitten Chronicles Book 5

VIOLA GRACE

Spell Crafting 501

THE HELLKITTEN CHRONICLES

The final classes have begun, and the only thing standing in Imara's way is an ancient and deadly enemy . . . of her kitten.

Imara's life is going according to her plans. She has her boyfriend, her kitten, and is about to earn her degree in Magecraft and graduate. Once she has that degree, she has the right to request an application for a commercial magic license. It is the goal she has been working toward all along.

A shadow begins to haunt her during the day and stalk her when she is away from the college. She doesn't know what it wants, but it follows her with a purpose she can't fathom until she finds the identity of her stalker.

By the time she learns that it is Mr. E the stalker is after and not her, the trap has already closed.

Chapter One

Imara took inventory of the magical-items cupboard for the fifth time. She worked to get every herb, powder, and weird liquid committed to memory.

No Mage has all their herbs committed to memory. You are going to burn your nose out. Mr. E was sitting on the counter amid the bottles and cleaning his paws. It wouldn't be so odd, but he was wiping them with a tiny hanky that she didn't remember giving to him.

She put the bottles carefully back in the cupboard. "My nose is fine. I just want to be careful with my studies. I have to do half the work in class, so it is going to be difficult to do things with someone watching."

Yes. I can imagine. You do your best work with the dead. Why are you taking this course again?

Imara looked over at him. "Short time, high credit."

Ah. Right. I saw the application for commercial magic in your room. Everything is filled out but the date of application.

She made a face as she kept loading the cupboard. "Sue me for being positive. I am hoping that I don't have to tear it up and go back to the college board for a full course load next semester."

I don't want to stay around here any longer than I need to. What can I do to help?

"Well, I have two days before the classes start, and each evening, I have tours of the local mage repositories with mage guides and members of the XIA. I hope I can tell them apart." She smiled slightly. "They are delighted to have access to the spectres via their cooperation with the Mage Guild or the Death Keeper's guild."

The mage guides? They are getting really advanced. He

smirked. *You do have much more of an affinity with the other Death Keepers than with mages. Those who work with the dead are rather easygoing.*

Imara closed the glass door and latched it. "That is because we are the conversational superstars of the night."

To be fair, you are competing with the dead.

"I am not competing with the dead; I am competing with the sentient magic of the dead. There is a vast difference." She wrinkled her nose and picked him up, tucking him up on her shoulder and walking down the hall toward the common space.

Reegar was sitting and reading a tome that he had probably memorized, and Bara was sitting on the couch with her feet up, embroidering a sash.

Imara went to the kitchen and got a cup of coffee.

Bara called out, "Another late night coming up?"

Imara walked out of the kitchen and over to the loveseat that she called her own. "Yeah."

Bara gave her a quirked look. "Is it worth it?"

Imara sipped at her coffee and then replied, "It is. I am introducing people to a skill set and resource that has dwindled dramatically. Nine families that I have dealt with have now put spectres in their wills. It benefits us and their heirs."

"Don't you feel weird selling services to the dead?"

Imara sighed. "I am not selling anything. I just demonstrate how useful it would be if their children's and grandchildren's essences remain available for consultation."

Bara blinked. "I don't see the purpose."

Imara leaned back. "I am primarily called on when there is an unresolved legal matter or an event regarding a property. Not everyone passes with a copy of their will in their hands, but the settings for a spectre can kick in automatically, and their mind can be consulted the next day."

Bara whistled. "That makes a lot of sense."

"Thank you. The repositories set the spectre stones in a larger obelisk, and that provides the power of projection for the consciousness."

Bara grinned. "Now I don't have to take a tour."

Imara snorted. "You never had to. It is just like what I did for Reegar. He is powered up and able to interact as if he were still living."

"Aside from being confined to the hall."

Imara wrinkled her nose. "There are options for that, but the hall is acting as the obelisk. There are so many objects of power here that they are making his projection easy. I healed his fading spectre, and he is doing the rest."

Reegar snorted from his corner. "I can hear you, you know."

Bara laughed. "We know. It is definitely nice to actually see you now and not just feel you lurking about."

Reegar looked up with a smile on his dapper features. "I just wanted you to know that I was here and I was paying attention. No frolicking or odd behaviour in my home."

Bara grinned and returned her attention to her embroidery. "I know, and I had no intention of doing anything else other than studying."

Imara chuckled. "With a mind like yours, I am amazed that you aren't entering the Mage Guild's research and development department."

"Organized research isn't for me. I much prefer to gain skill after skill and simply hoard them." Bara looked up and winked.

"I respect your choice and enjoy your talents." She finished her coffee and checked the time.

Reegar flicked a look at her. "Are you going to wait for Argus?"

"No, he is picking me up for tomorrow's tour. Tonight, it is the mage guides again. Different group and different memorial garden." She got to her feet.

Bara asked, "What is the difference between a repository and a memorial garden?"

Imara smirked and headed for her room, yelling out, "The tax base."

She heard the snort as she walked up the stairs to her room, one hand absently holding on to Mr. E. It was time to get changed into her robes and get into her car for the hour's drive to the small town near Redbird City. The highway was the easiest part of that night's excursion. The mage guides she was meeting with were all under the age of ten. They were confident enough to ask questions and young enough to not have a grasp of the adult world. It made conversations with the spectres a little wearing. Keeping spectres from using foul language was sometimes an uphill battle.

Imara settled her robes on and around Mr. E, and she smiled. She loved her job.

After an hour of driving with the radio blasting and Mr. E singing along with the rock ballads that she found, she turned off the noise and pulled into the parking lot outside of the Redbird City Garden of Spectral Retirement. Imara kept herself from smiling as she got out of her car, and Mr. E perched on her shoulder. That was a very grand way of saying *this way to talking rocks*.

Imara hadn't been to this facility before, so she made sure that Mr. E was tucked in before she walked to the welcome building.

The first thing she saw was the flicker of a screen in the back corner of the room, and she investigated. The staffer was sitting in the corner and sleeping. Her chest was rising and falling slowly, so it was almost difficult deciding to wake her.

Let me do it. Mr. E's words were loud in her head.

Imara shrugged and let him down, holding her hand out so he could simply walk down her arm. He hopped lightly to the desk and sat in front of the flickering screen.

She was about to ask what he was going to do when he opened his little mouth and yowled loud enough to make the lights flicker.

The woman screamed, tilted back, and thudded to the ground before she scrambled to her feet with her hair wild and her eyes white in her dark features.

"What the hell was that?"

Mr. E sat licking his paws like a normal kitten. Only Imara could hear his inner guffaws.

"My familiar wished to wake you, miss. I am Master Imara. I will be leading the tour tonight."

The woman blinked. "That's tonight?"

"It is. I have confirmed with the mage guides. They will be here in half an hour. Just tell me which zones would have the most friendly spectres, please." Imara smiled.

"Uh . . . I don't really know." The woman straightened the chair and sat down. "I am just keeping the chair warm. The actual Death Keeper went to a concert in town and told me that nothing was happening tonight."

Imara winced. "Right. I am going to go for a quick tour. If the mage guides arrive, stand with your back straight, fold your hands in front of you like this."

She demonstrated, and the woman stood and mimicked her.

"Excellent. Tell them that Master Imara will be here shortly and show them the video in the visitor's centre. It is already primed for the visit."

The woman looked over, and she frowned. "That ass."

Imara grinned. "Yeah, he knew we were coming. What is your name, by the way?"

"Connie. Thanks for being cool with this."

Imara winked. "Make sure that he gives you the share of the four hundred dollars that the guild is paying him for the tour."

Connie stared at her, and something strange happened. A flicker of magic ran across her skin. Imara blinked several times as the woman's skin went granulated and then smoothed back into the medium brown of her normal tone.

Imara paused and then said, "I am just going to check the gardens, looking for something that won't curse in front of the kids."

Connie blinked. "They do that?"

"They have all the bad and good habits of their human lives, without the soul. It can make for some exciting conversations."

Imara held her hand out, and Mr. E made a phenomenal leap from the desk to her bicep, and then, he curled around her neck once again.

Connie looked like she didn't know what to do, so she turned off her screen and was straightening items in the entry room when Imara went through the warded doorway and into the gardens.

She let a short wave of spectral energy out and walked toward the bank of elder stones that she could feel in the distance.

Imara walked along for a few minutes and found the spot that had a sign indicating that it was *The Garden of Repose.*

She walked into the shadowed darkness, and she spoke, "Is there anyone here who wants to speak to a group of mage guides? I will be bringing the girls this way in a few minutes if you are willing to be polite and informative."

A few flickers of energy formed into spectres, so she powered them up.

"What are you, miss?"

The woman was wearing ancient robes, and her eyes were focusing on Imara.

"I am a Death Keeper. I just happen to be very good at my job."

The woman smiled slightly. "I will speak to your young ladies."

"Who are you, Madam?"

"Magus Elder Reetha Nakura. I passed over three hundred years ago."

"I am Master Imara Mirrin. Death Keeper and tour guide when necessary. I can also rejuvenate spectres. I have an affinity for the dead."

The woman bowed. "I will await your tour eagerly. How long will I remain visible to the living?"

"How long do you wish to be? I can make you transparent for the time being and then introduce the girls to you as you solidify."

The elder quirked her lips. "That sounds like more fun than I have had in decades."

"How many others are here?" Imara could feel nine, but they were all very faint.

"Seven. All masters like myself."

Imara kept her face emotionless. "Excellent. I look forward to bringing them here."

She withdrew the power she had donated to the elder and the others. She bowed to the empty space, and she walked out.

She kept her shiver of dread until she was away from their sphere of influence.

"Well, the kids don't need that."

Mr. E shivered a little. "Do you think she recognized me?"

"Someone in there did. There were nine signatures aside from the elder. She wanted me to bring them all out, and that means there were two people in there she didn't want me to know about. I am going to a weak target, not a faded one."

She hunted around and found something suitable. An instructional mage who had died one hundred forty years ago, but she was the last of her line. No one visited. She was happy for the company and the promise of letting her magic drain into silence.

With her willing participant in the demonstration charged and waiting, Imara returned to the welcome centre. It was time to lecture the little ones.

Chapter Two

Instead of little ones, a group of teenagers was there with a harried-looking guide leader and two adult women. Imara grinned. "Benny!"

Benny Ganger came forward and shook Imara's hand. "When I heard who was doing the tour, I had to come. This is my best buddy, Freddy. Freddy, this is Imara, the Death Keeper."

Freddy extended her hand, and when Imara took it, she read generations of suffering and torment embodied in the soul of the woman.

Mr. E moved in a blur and sniffed at Freddy's hand. Instead of growling at the taste of the demon magic, he rubbed his head against her knuckles while perching on Imara's wrist.

Hellhound. There was pity in his voice.

Don't you despise magic from the demon zone? she asked him softly.

No, I despise demons and those who traffic with them. Hellhounds are mages bound to draw on the demon zone energy at the will of other mages. She's a slave.

Imara looked at Freddy's face, but the other woman was exclaiming how cute Mr. E was.

"He's adorable!"

Imara released Freddy's hand and scooped up her familiar. "He really is. Would you like to hold him?"

Freddy nearly snatched him away and proceeded to murmur to him and cuddle him.

Imara ignored the black thoughts coming her way, and she turned to Benny. "So, you are just here for the tour?"

"Yes, and to keep these ladies on track." Benny jerked her head at the teens who were paying more attention to them than the video screen.

"Well, in that case, we should start the show." She beckoned, Mr. E squirmed free from Freddy's kisses, and was back on her shoulder in a bound.

Imara stepped toward the Guide Master, and she introduced herself to Sandy Dale. Once that was done, she turned to the back door, grabbed a staff and lantern before she offered a polite, "If you wish to speak to the dead, please follow me."

The teens scrambled up off the floor and were at her heels a moment later.

She paused near the door to the gardens. "The doors here are warded. No spectres can pass through without the help of a Death Keeper."

She turned and addressed them, giving them the basics of what it meant to be a Death Keeper.

A young woman put up her hand. "Isn't it all the same guild?"

Imara smiled. "No. Death Keepers answer to their own guild before the Mage Guild is allowed near them. It is a specialized position, and the Death Keepers can override a Mage Guild decision. There aren't enough folk with a talent for death."

A young woman with blue and green stripes in her hair asked, "Why do we even need Death Keepers?"

"We will figure that out tonight. Now, follow me and we will wake the spectres."

She fired up the staff and walked through the wards, waiting for her group to step through the glowing glyphs and join her on the other side.

Imara stifled laughter as some rushed, some jumped, and a few closed their eyes and took one giant step. When Benny, Freddy, and Sandy were all on the correct side, Imara continued her lecture.

"When a mage has prepared for their spectre to be generated, they are sent to the crystal at the moment of death. In that moment, their magic transfers instead of simply disappearing into the ether. A copy of what they know, how they know it, and all of their personal memories are placed in the crystal. That crystal is then taken and secured to an obelisk, statue, or headstone of the deceased's choosing."

She led them to the recent portion of the memorial garden. "The spectres here are awake, conscious, and able to speak to me normally, and you, if I boost their situation a little."

"Why can you speak to them all the time?"

"I am a Death Keeper. Speaking to the dead is what comes naturally." She walked slowly to the nearest monuments, and she activated the spectres to full energy.

The girls gasped as the spectres approached, but when they paused and looked at Imara, she inclined her head. "Thank you. These young ladies are mage guides, and I would like you to speak politely with them or not at all."

The spectres nodded.

The mage guides looked confused.

"You are welcome to ask them anything. They know how they lived and how they died and are not shy about anything in between."

With that stated, the bravest of the girls went first, and she spoke to one of the spectres who was a mage that specialized in investment banking.

Benny came up next to her. "There aren't a lot of high guild spectres."

"No. They are kept at a separate facility until they fade. They are dangerous until they get to the fading point. Then, and only then, are they retired to one of these places to slowly bleed off."

Benny chuckled. "I should take notes."

"Why?"

"Because my XIA team and I are coming back tomorrow night for the same tour."

Imara laughed, but Benny was serious.

After fifteen minutes, she faded the spectres back to their normal states.

The girls drifted toward her, and they were all remarkably enthusiastic.

"Now, for a demonstration of what a Death Keeper can actually achieve, we are going to meet a Mage who passed on over one hundred and forty years ago."

She led them past the aging stones and to the section where the instructional mage waited. Imara powered her to full physicality and smiled as the woman touched the stone her crystal was embedded in.

The guides gasped in shock, and the woman gave Imara a wry look. "Thank you, Death Keeper. You have made my last night honourable."

"Thank you, Mage. You are giving these guides a night to remember. Ladies, ask her what you will. Mage Echoheart used to be an instructor, so she can offer you help in a variety of subjects."

The mage blushed.

The Guides rushed forward to ask questions, and Imara hung back.

Freddy pushed up next to her and whispered, "I have seen Death Keepers work before, but I have never seen them make a solid spectre."

"You have seen it now. We all have different talents. This just happens to be mine." Imara stood with her lantern lit, and the darkness pushed back from the gathering.

She had her own question to ask. "Freddy, you are a hellhound?"

Freddy jolted. "I know Benny didn't tell you."

"No. Not by name, but now, I know she was referring to you when she mentioned a friend who was an obligated familiar."

"Yeah, that is me. I found out when I was young. Any moment I can be hauled across the world where my mage is. Lately, she has been using me in familiar battles with other mages. It sucks."

"She makes you fight?"

"She bets on me. I have always had a strong draw to the demon zone energy, and it gives me multiple forms."

Imara reached up and stroked Mr. E's fuzzy head. "Yeah, I know something about that. If there is any way I can intercede with your mage, let me know."

Freddy looked at her in surprise. "You would do that?"

"Of course. You are a friend of a friend. I will help you any way I can but, please, understand that my skills are limited."

Mr. E snorted on her shoulder.

Imara smiled. "That said, I do have a knack for getting lucky with things." She reached into her robes and withdrew one of her business cards. "Here. They can get in touch with me around the clock."

Freddy looked at the card in surprise. "You have an answering service?"

"Yeah. I am in classes a lot, so if it is urgent, they put the call through. I am free most evenings, though, if you just wanted to get together to discuss stuff. I mean, I know you probably know more about your situation than I do, but I am willing to talk or listen."

"Thanks." Freddy looked bemused. "How old are you, anyway?"

"Does it matter?"

"No, I suppose it doesn't. Thanks for this." Freddy opened the small purse she was carrying and tucked the card inside.

"You are welcome."

Freddy blushed. "This is going to sound weird, but can I hold onto your kitten for a while?"

Imara checked with Mr. E, and as he was fine with it, she reached up and handed her familiar over.

Freddy cuddled the kitten and whispered to him, pausing to hear his answers as he nodded and purred.

Imara watched the mage guides interacting with the spectre, and she smiled at the enthusiasm of both parties.

Benny moved close. "Why is she solid?"

"Because I gave her what she needed to become solid."

"That easy?"

"For me, but that is what I do. My body projects spectral energy, and I passively wake those that I am around. I can also focus it."

Benny blinked. "That . . . so that is how you did the trick with the stone?"

"Yeah, I kept draining the energy, and it was burning my skin, so I had to put energy into it, and that just led to a weird cycle. Thanks again for the ride to Ritual Space."

"No problem. It was nice to have another girl in the car." Benny grinned and then whispered, "What is Freddy doing?"

"Having a conversation with another familiar. I am afraid that I don't have clearance to listen in."

Benny nodded. "Right. Of course. How long are you going to let the kids keep getting spell techniques from the instructor?"

"She isn't giving them all the techniques. Each is missing a piece. If they try a spell, it won't come to anything. No flash, no bang, no nothing."

The guide master gave her a nod, and she stepped forward. "Ladies, please thank the Master Mage for her time."

The guides filed up to the spectre and gave her bows of respect. The spectre nodded in return and had a smile on her face.

When the guides were filing back toward the welcome centre, Imara looked to the mage. "So, do you still want to fade right now?"

The woman shook her head. "The guide master said she will bring the girls back in a few weeks for a follow-up presentation about what they learned. I want to be here for that."

Imara smiled. "Then, I will leave you a little less solid than you are now but still able to generate a hug if you want to."

"Thank you, Master Imara. Is Mirrin your family name?"

Imara touched the woman's shoulder and thinned the spectre's density slightly. "It is all the family who would claim me. Enjoy your waking hours. Talk to the other spectres. Your range extends to most of the corners of the gardens, so simply contemplate magic in all its forms."

"You are surprisingly wise for one so young."

"I have had good teachers."

The mage smiled. "That is all that I ever wished for my

students. I wished that they thought of me as a good teacher."

Imara grinned. "I think that you underestimate your impact. Do you remember a mage named Reegar?"

The woman paused. "I do. He was cranky, irritable, and never followed instructions."

"His spectre remembers you fondly as the best teacher he ever had." Imara smiled.

The mage gasped and tears formed in the spectre's eyes. "Thank you."

Imara inclined her head, and she walked back to the welcome centre where the last of the group was passing through the wards. The moment that Imara passed through, she felt a pressure on the magic around her. She turned to focus on the energy, but it was gone.

The shiver that ran up her spine remained active as she turned and thanked the mage guides for coming.

Sandy made sure that they all gave proper thanks to Imara.

When the young women were gone, Freddy turned to Imara. "Here you go. Thanks for letting me talk to him. Not all mages would have."

"He sometimes needs to let off a little steam as well. He was not truly impressed with the body he got stuck with."

Freddy nodded. "I totally get that. I am a hellhound, but I also take on a chihuahua form. It is humiliating, but it gives my mage a leg up when she puts me in a fight. No one expects the second form."

"That would be an effective weapon. Does the fighting hurt?"

Benny sighed. "Join us down the road at the all-night café, and Freddy can fill you in."

Freddy nodded. "Please. You look like you could use a cup of coffee."

Imara consulted Mr. E, and he was in the mood for a pie. "We are in. I just have to finish up here, and I will meet you there. It is to the left of the exit, correct?"

Benny gave her a thumbs-up. "See you in a few minutes."

Imara looked around and found Connie skulking in one of the rear offices.

"Connie, I am leaving. Feel free to resume your videos or homework or whatever."

Connie looked around and then focused on her. Imara knew that look. This woman's name was not Connie.

"Um, great. Thanks."

Imara smiled and said, "I will just lock up when I leave. I know it can be creepy to be working alone at night."

"What? Lock up? You don't have to."

"Oh, I insist." Imara turned and walked swiftly to the door. She exited, made sure that the door was closed behind her, and then, she activated the Death Keeper warding that would only allow their kind to come and go.

Did you just lock her in there?

I did. I will make a call before we get to the café and have someone come in to check on her. I don't know where the regularly assigned keeper is, but they will be needed on duty tomorrow.

Mr. E was chuckling, but then, he was watching the door to the welcome centre.

She is trying to get through the wards with a chair.

Fascinating. That isn't going to work.

She doesn't appear to know that.

Imara got into her vehicle and opened her phone. A few minutes of chatting to the dispatch office, letting them know that there was an incursion into their territory and then she was off in search of pie and a cup of coffee. Oh, and a slice of pie for herself.

Chapter Three

The café was bright, cheerful, and filled with non-humans. Imara paused at the door, identified where Benny and Freddy were, and headed toward them.

Benny looked at Imara, looked around, and grinned. "You found us all right."

"Yes. Sorry I was late. Administrative issue."

"Have a seat." Freddy scooted over to the side so that Imara could take up the empty space.

She sat and set Mr. E down on the table. "This place is really jumping."

Benny smirked. "The side effect of a nocturnal lifestyle. Are you all right with so many non-humans around you?"

Imara nodded. "Yes. It is just a shock after the college. You almost forget that anyone else exists."

Freddy agreed. "It was like that when I was taking journalism. Everybody was either a mage or a human. It was a relief to get over to Benny's house for a touch of the extranatural. Her family never disappointed."

Benny grinned. "I am still getting used to my dad having days where he is looking human. It is quite a change."

"What did he look like other times?"

Benny snickered as the waitress poured the coffee. "A demon. He was an incubus, and I am amazed that my parents never had more children than just little old me, but that was not in the cards."

"Is your mom human?" Imara took her cup of coffee and added cream and sugar.

"She looks human. That is enough for most folks. Her line has wolves, vampires, fey, and there is rumour of a troll."

It was apparent that Benny was proud of her heritage. There was no reason not to be.

The server came around again, so Imara ordered a slice and a whole coconut cream pie.

Freddy asked, "Are you hungry?"

"Mr. E has a sweet tooth. He also likes to chase bubbles. Jumping into the occasional pie isn't doing him any harm." Imara scratched him behind his ears.

Benny and Freddy were eating something more substantial.

It appeared that they hadn't quite gotten the idea of Mr. E and his appetite because when the pie and the slice arrived, they squealed in delight when he leaped into the centre of the pie and started eating his way out.

The laughter from the other patrons around them told Imara that Mr. E had an audience. She ate her pie, and he ate his while Benny and Freddy played with him, putting globs of whipping cream on his nose to watch him lick it off.

Mr. E didn't mind. He was going to get all that cream anyway.

Imara sipped at her coffee, and as she sat in the good humour and giggles that flowed around her, she checked her phone, and the intruder was in custody. The message from the guild was clear. The Death Keeper who was supposed to be on duty was missing.

Imara sighed and returned to her coffee.

Benny glanced at her. "Bad news?"

"The woman in the welcome centre wasn't a Death Keeper. She was a stand-in or a thief. I don't know which one. I do know that the actual keeper who was supposed to be on duty is missing."

Benny looked concerned. "Do you know them?"

Imara shook her head. "No. We don't usually socialize. The only Death Keeper I had met before I joined the college was my master in Sakenta City."

Freddy blinked. "You don't have guild meetings?"

"No. There aren't enough of us. There are barely enough to man the memorial gardens. That is why they are so far from cities, though that is where most of their population comes from. They have to increase their access while increasing their distance from population centres."

Benny blinked. "That is . . . weird. So, you don't have to go to class?"

"No. This is on-the-job training. If you have a talent for it, you have a talent for it. That is all."

Imara finished her coffee and looked at her kitten. He was sitting in an empty pie plate and beginning the laborious process of getting all the coconut and whipped cream off his black fuzz.

Freddy sat back. "Dang. If I had known that, I might have tried for it."

Benny smiled. "You aren't suited to it. You are firmly on the side of life at all times."

Imara glanced from one to the other, and she could almost visualize the spiritual tie between them. "You have been friends for a very long time."

Freddy wrinkled her nose. "Don't put it that way."

"Sorry. I meant that I can see the link between you."

Benny smirked. "Freddy became my friend in kindergarten. She has been defending me against those who would think harshly of me for my entire life. She is an amazing bully repellent."

Imara grinned. "I can see why. She is a force of will."

Freddy grimaced. "I have to be when I can be. I could be summoned by my mage at any moment, and that tension drives me nuts. It is not something that makes me sleep easy."

Imara nodded, and she reached out to stroke Mr. E's clean, damp fur. "I understand."

Freddy smiled. "If it makes you feel better, he doesn't care that you are bound to him. He is exceptionally impressed with your skills and your determination. He is honoured to be your familiar."

"Good. I am honoured to be his mage, so it works out well." Imara smiled.

Benny laughed, "Well, I get the pleasure of your company twice this week. Tomorrow, three XIA teams will be with us, including my own."

"Oh. Wonderful. It will be nice to see your mates again." Freddy spluttered. "Really? You just say it like that?"

Imara blinked. "She is not human, and she has shifters in her circle, so she has mates, not husbands. Partners, if you will."

Benny grinned, and her eyes glowed. "So, you know that too."

Imara wrinkled her nose. "Your magic isn't human magic. It isn't standard mage magic. I knew it when I first met you."

Benny nodded. "It makes sense, considering your talent. I mean, you know about some of my ancestries."

"Yes, I do. It makes sense now." She grinned.

Freddy snorted. "So, Imara, what are you doing for the rest of the night?"

"I am heading home, getting some more studying in for my final course and then getting some sleep."

Freddy blinked. "You are still in school?"

"I am finishing my qualifiers at Depford College. When I have this last course done, I will be able to get my commercial magic license."

Freddy whistled. "Wow. That is a hard rating to get."

"I know. That is why I went for it in this way. I have taken every high-credit course I could find in order to make this go as fast as I could, and there is only one left to go. Not many folks get through the course or even try it, but I am confident that I can get it done and gain some insight while I am doing it."

Benny looked up from her fries. "What is the course?"

"Spell crafting."

Freddy cackled. "She should meet Minnie."

Benny finished her food. "You know, I think you are right. What are you doing right now, Imara?"

She blinked. "Uh, wiping the last of the whipping cream from my cat?"

"Come with us to the city, and we will introduce you to a friend of ours." Benny winked. "If we are lucky, we might meet her dragon."

"A dragon?" Imara blinked.

"Oh, I do love those mythical shifters. They get me all tingly. Benny occasionally works with a gryphon, and he sets my hellhound on fire." Freddy sighed wistfully.

Imara smiled. "You don't say."

Benny chuckled. "Imara has met him a time or two. She understands."

"I do, I really do." Imara chuckled.

Benny grinned. "Wonderful. Freddy, you be her co-pilot, and I will lead the way. If we get lost, you can tell her where we are headed."

Freddy nodded. "Will do."

The server slid their bills in front of them, and Benny grabbed them all. "I have got this."

Imara scowled. "I can get my own."

Benny shook her head. "It is my pleasure to get you the pie and coffee. The XIA owes you a lot more than that."

"I get paid. I get paid quite a bit. I wish folks would let me spend my money." Imara snorted as Benny handed the server the cash.

Benny grinned. "We are going to a shop next. You can spend your money there."

They were on their way when Imara asked Freddy, "Who are we going to meet?"

"Our friend Minerva. She is in town from Corudet City and working on taking inventory at an herb shop. She's a master mage and an excellent judge of character. Also, she is married to a dragon. It's a sweet story."

"It sounds like it. Do you have a romantic attachment?"

Freddy smiled. "Aside from drooling over the gryphon with the dreamy eyes? Nope. I can't. I have to be available to my mage."

"That sucks." She kept her vision on the red sports car that Benny was driving.

"It does. So, do you know any available mages who don't have familiars?"

Imara scratched Mr. E's ears. "No. I don't socialize much, but I could ask my mother. What are your criteria?"

"Seriously? It has to be a human mage or I would have asked Benny's family. I can't get my family to ask around. We are bound by a geas. No call for help is allowed from us to another mage unless they approach us first."

"So, because I asked, you can tell me?"

Freddy nodded. "Correct."

After a few minutes of chitchat, they pulled into the parking lot of Sawberry's Magical Supply. The door said CLOSED, but there was light inside.

Benny got out of her car, and she beckoned for them to come to the door. Imara shrugged and got out of her car. Freddy followed, and soon, they were at the door where Benny was texting frantically.

A moment after she finished the texting, the door opened. A tall woman, who radiated power, was standing at the entrance. "Come in. I have some tea brewing."

Benny reached out and hugged the heavily pregnant woman. "Minerva. It is so good to see you again."

The energy that Minerva was exuding was far more than the average master mage. To Imara's senses, it was nearer to the power of a sun.

Freddy hugged the woman next, and then, it was Imara's turn to greet her. She inclined her head. "Pardon my lack of hug."

Minerva smiled slightly. "Thank you, and you are pardoned. I am Minerva."

"Imara."

"Death Keeper?"

"Yes. It pays for schooling."

Minerva cocked her head. "Deity in the bloodlines?"

Imara shook her head. "Not that I know of."

"Huh. Well, please come in. I am guessing that you are the reason that they came to visit."

"I am. I am taking a spell crafting course at Depford College, and they immediately thought of you."

Minerva nodded. "That would do it. Please, come in and have a seat. I am in the process of purchasing this shop, so I am doing inventory. The wards dissuade anyone who wants to nag me, and it sends them off to the next shop."

The interior of the shop was neat and tidy for the most part, but the scent of herbs and the feel of magic were heavy in the air.

The woman walked slowly to the circle of comfy chairs, and she lowered herself into one of the seats. "Someone else pour, please."

Benny sat and took the pot into her very competent hands. "Here. When are you due?"

Minerva chuckled. "By human standards, three weeks ago. By dragon standards, I still have two months to go."

Imara asked, "So he is really a dragon?"

She sighed and inhaled the fumes from the teacup that Benny handed her. "He really is. Zemuel has his territory in Corudet City, but I have decided that my child needs more than just his empire in its life. This shop will give me a reason to come visit as well as an outlet for the child to work when it is of age."

Freddy grinned. "Nothing like looking ahead . . . way ahead."

Imara smiled softly. "It is good that you are planning for their life. Even if things change, it is alterations to an existing design."

Minerva looked at Imara and grinned. "I like you. So, I am going to give you the best advice I can. When you get assignments to make spells and potions, look at the ingredients and think of what they mean to *you*. The meaning in your mind will determine the end result, no matter the dictates in the spell book. If you think of sunny days when you see a sunflower, it will make the spell brighter and happier. If you look at a lily and remember a funeral, it will darken and mute the effect of the spell. You have to put all of your focus in it and realize that there is no incorrect spell, just an undesired result. By concentrating on the ingredients, you can guess at what the spell will achieve or what it won't."

That made so much sense; it explained why the strongest magical sensing strips that she had ever made were made with her favourite paper. "Thank you. That explains a lot."

"You are welcome. Is that your familiar?"

Mr. E crept out from behind Imara's collar.

"It is. While I regret the shape I chose for him, I regret nothing else."

Minerva smiled as the kitten crept closer.

"Eadric the Hellborn. I never thought to see you walking free." The deep, rumbling voice came from a corner where Imara would have sworn there was no one.

The kitten sat on Imara's arm with deep formality, and he bowed.

"Imara, this is Zemuel. Zemuel, you remember my friends Benny and Freddy."

He chuckled. "Of course. Now, beloved, you need to return to our home to rest. This flitting around in portals isn't good for you."

In a moment, Imara felt the tremendous power of the dragon's mind weighing down on Mr. E. He met the pressure and returned it calmly and directly. Their conversation was short, but it was obvious that they were friends of a sort.

Minerva snorted. "I can rest for a day after I have the baby."

He stepped forward, and Imara was struck by the size of him. Minerva was a tall woman, but Zemuel was a huge man. He was easily over seven feet tall, and the air of power that he wore was casual as if it didn't matter to him.

"Eadric, what are you doing wearing that ridiculous form?"

Mr. E answered him on his personal frequency, and the dragon shifted his gaze to Imara. "You are one of those from the demon-mage families?"

She cocked her head. "Genetically, yes. The Deepford-Smythe line is mine. I have not looked into the ancestors that were killed."

That seemed to surprise him. "Why not?"

"I am not close to either side of my family, so I don't concern myself with the past. I can't do anything about it."

Mr. E perched on her forearm and looked smug.

Zemuel raised his brows and actually looked closely at

her. "You have the air of death about you."

She quirked her lips. "I live at a college. Some of those folks don't bathe. Sorry."

Minerva barked a laugh. "I like her."

Zemuel sighed, and the communication between him and Mr. E continued for a moment. The dragon snorted, and a shot of fire was exhaled. "Fine. I will leave her alone."

Minerva's eyes went wide. "That is one impressive kitten."

Mr. E stood and fluffed his fur out a little before looking at her with big eyes and a soft *murp.*

Imara smiled. "He loves compliments."

Zemuel crossed his arms over his chest. "He always did."

Mr. E hissed.

Imara yawned. "Apologies."

Benny grinned at her. "Long day?"

"Yeah. Prepping for classes takes a lot out of me."

Freddy gave her a commiserating look. "Maybe you should head home."

Minerva hissed. "Not until she has had something to keep her alert for the drive. Give me a minute."

Minerva got to her feet with alarming speed and made her way across the shop. Zemuel was behind her, ready to catch her if his posture was any indication.

Minerva grabbed the wheeled ladder and slid it over to wherever she was targeting, and then, she began climbing. Minerva was muttering as she found a drawer and began to paw through it until she found what she was looking for. "Aha!"

She turned her head to Zemuel and murmured, "Coming down."

He held out his arms and caught her when she jumped off the ladder. He didn't stagger, but his knees bent slightly.

When he carried her back to them, she held her hand out toward Imara. "Here you go. It is a clarity stone. It will keep you alert. It is warded against detection, but I wouldn't recommend that you take it to class."

Imara smiled and took the tiny glass pebble. "Thank you,

but I wouldn't take it to class. Mr. E would eat it if I tried to cheat. He doesn't need more clarity."

He crept up to her shoulder and purred happily against her neck.

She slipped the stone into her robe pocket and inclined her head. "It has been pleasant to meet all of you, but I had best get back to the college. I have to get my supply list together for the course."

Freddy smiled. "I thought you would have it already."

"I would have, but they won't give it to us until the day before the class."

She bowed low and paused when Zemuel shifted Minerva in his arms, and he held out a card. "Here. Call us if you need us."

She reached out and took it. The card was heavy with magic. "Um, thank you."

Minerva grinned. "Let me know if you need any supplies. I can get them for you fresh and inexpensive."

Imara smiled. "Thanks again. Good evening and take it easy. That baby needs a bit of rest."

The room erupted in hugs and laughter, so Imara took that moment to escape and head for her vehicle.

Time to get home and check her email for the shopping list she needed for her course. She would apply what Minerva had told her in the class and see what following her associates could generate.

Chapter Four

She carefully put the stone in her storage cupboard in the lab and went through the list that she had gotten in her email.

You sure that you don't want to take that with you? Mr. E idly batted around the cap from an empty herb bottle.

"I am sure. This is just a quick trip, a light lecture, and then, we are on our way home again. Sorry, buddy. No pie tonight."

He sighed but hopped onto her shoulder. *Too bad. It was tasty.*

"And it was squishing through your paws for an hour. Gross."

He chuckled in her mind as she grabbed her robes from the hook near the door.

She waved goodbye to Reegar and Bara and headed out the door. Time to talk to the dead . . . again.

The Death Keeper at the welcome centre was attentive, helpful, and had the necessary magic to do the job. He was deferential to her and got out of her way when she led the three XIA teams into the gardens.

This evening was different from the previous night. She was there to wake a dead suspect in a murder and get a confession from him.

She walked up to the stone, and she tapped the obelisk politely. "Excuse me, Mage Neffling. I have some folk here who would like to speak with you."

She was holding back her energy to stop other spectres from rising. She offered a bit to his spectre, and he took it.

One moment there was a vague glow on his obelisk, and the next, he was standing in full regalia with a sneer on his features. He wasn't handsome, but he wasn't ugly.

Imara nodded to Benny, "I am not part of this investigation, so I will stay off to one side. He can't make contact with you; he will be fine as long as you need to talk to him."

She faded to one side and let the agents of the XIA gather and speak with a killer who had been dead for the better part of a century.

While keeping her energy in, she opened her senses, focusing on the shadowy, fading garden. There were still nine spectres moving, but they were excited by something. She pulled her senses back in, but just as she was nearly closed off, something cruised just out of her sensory area.

She asked Mr. E, *Did you feel that?*

Yes, and it wasn't good. That was ancient and evil.

Where did it come from? She went to open her senses again.

Don't. Don't open yourself to it. You are strong but nowhere near strong enough to take that on.

I hate to say this, but I agree with you.

The XIA members were engrossed in the stories being told by the spectre, and they hadn't noticed whatever it was that had cruised by the edge of the memorial garden. The thing was gone now, so she would just hold the information until it was appropriate.

The questioning took over two hours, but finally, the questions had been answered, and the XIA was satisfied.

Benny turned to her, and she smiled. "So, another pie?"

"No. I was wrong on my timeline. My first class is two days away, but I want to spend time doing more research. It is my last class, and I don't want to blow it."

Benny nodded. "Fair enough. Thanks for this, by the way."

"Not a problem. The money is already in my account."

When she had escorted them to the front door of the welcome centre, she turned to Argus. "Did you learn what you needed to know?"

"Yes, and I got to see you in action. My heart is yours. You are a wonder to behold."

She blushed and quickly kissed him on the lips. "Go and have pie with your team. I have to get back home and think about how fast I can blow through this course."

"Good luck and well done. He told us everything."

"I am glad. It also proves that spectres can still be useful after their bodies are gone."

He hugged her and walked her to her car. Once she was tucked in, he closed her door and walked to his SUV with the other team members laughing and elbowing each other.

Benny's team was on the way to pie when Imara pulled onto the highway. They were on their way to the café, but Imara had to head home.

She was heading toward her turnoff when she saw a flash of midnight green.

The car crunched as it was struck and flipped into a rapid roll that had Imara holding her breath and trying to gain access to her location.

She wanted to scream, but her thoughts were shorted by the sudden thud of her head into the window glass.

She heard a hiss next to her, but a roar from Mr. E's hellcat form seemed to freak out the attacker. There was a rumble of growling and hissing, but when Imara touched her head, she felt the ribbon of blood that was wrecking her robes.

She was lying upside down with light blazing into the side of her car, but she didn't know what was casting that light.

"Imara! Imara, stay still." Argus was concerned. How sweet.

She didn't turn her head to look, but she croaked, "I am seat belted in. I am not going anywhere right now. Where is Mr. E? Can someone find my cat? Please." Tears started to run up and over her forehead.

One of Argus's team said he would follow the crash through the woods.

There was a low growl, and a cranky Argus pulled the door to her driver's side away. He reached in, and his claws severed the seatbelt, catching her in his arms. He eased her out of the car, and he asked her over and over if her arms or legs could move. Once she wiggled everything to his satisfaction, he gave her a tight hug.

She looked up at him and caressed his cheek. "Something hit me."

"We know. We can see it; we can smell it. It was big and serpentine."

"Well. Shit."

The vampire brought Mr. E back. His hair was matted in places, but he was in one piece.

Imara, I am so sorry that you were targeted.

So, I was a target. That is what it felt like.

I wish I could say it was the last time.

I got lucky in that I was able to wound it, but it will be back. Her kind is always fixated.

What is she?

Argus lifted his head, and he sniffed. "Lamia."

"What?"

"She is part woman, part snake, and known for being particularly hostile when she believes she has been wronged."

"I guess I pissed someone off."

"I guess. I am taking you to the hospital."

She leaned against his shoulder and cuddled her kitten. "Sounds like a fabulous idea."

He got to his feet and carried her and Mr. E to the rear seat of the SUV. His team surrounded them, and soon, they were on their way to the hospital in Redbird City.

It was amazing how fast you were seen when three heavily muscled and body-armoured men carried you into the emergency room.

She was scanned, probed, and a healer came up to her, wrapping her abused skull in gauze soaked in herbs and magic.

Mr. E was curled in her elbow, and Argus held her other hand.

"You were exceptionally lucky; your car is totalled, but

you only have the small cut on your forehead." Argus smiled. "I have filed the report with your insurance agency."

Imara lifted a hand to her head. Mr. E was already healing her. "Huh. Did they catch whatever hit my car?"

"No, but we have some serpentine samples at the lab."

She sighed and swung her legs to one side. "I don't suppose I could get a ride home?"

"They want to keep you for another day."

She glared at him. "I want to be home."

He squeezed her hand. "I will check with the doctor. If he says you can go, I will take you home."

She smiled and nodded. "Thanks. I will stay here."

"So will I." He lifted his hand and jerked his head.

Imara carefully turned in time to see Lio leaving the doorway. Ivar was still standing guard.

"They are still here?"

"They are hoping that when you graduate, you are willing to join our team."

She wrinkled her nose. "I am not going to join the team the way that Benny has."

He winked. "Good. I am not up for sharing you. We want you for your magic."

Imara nodded carefully. "I know. I promise to make you a priority, but I am not going to cruise around with you every night. There are folk who want to talk to the dead, and they are willing to pay for it."

"Do you have to do that at night?"

She grinned. "Thanks for asking. No, it doesn't have to be at night, but it is easier to see the spectres after dark. They glow."

He grinned. "I don't know why I never asked that question before."

"Most folks just think that spectres are like ghosts. That they need the person seeing them to let down their mental defenses, usually via fatigue."

"Have you met a ghost?"

She grimaced. "Several. They are generally unpleasant and unhappy with their situation."

She tried to get out of the exam bed, but he tightened his grip on her hand.

"Stay where you are until the doctor releases you."

He's right you know. You could have been killed and then where would I be? Getting the stink-eye from a kitten made it all the more profound.

She scratched Mr. E behind the ears. "I am not trying to hasten your next job. Sorry for the close call, and Argus, thanks for pulling me out of the wreck."

He lifted her hand to his lips. "You gave me a heart attack when your car flipped like that."

"My heart had some unusual activity in that moment as well." She felt her fingers shaking in his grip. "How messed up was my car?"

Ivar muttered from the doorway, "I am amazed you are upright. The roof was crushed into the back of the driver's seat."

She shivered again, but this time, Argus held her hand in both of his, and he pressed his forehead to the back of her wrist.

"You are fine. You survived, and you will continue to be well, or I will station a watch outside Reegar Hall."

She chuckled and bent her head to his, pressing the un-lacerated part of her forehead against his hair. They remained like that until Lio returned with the doctor.

She blinked slowly as she straightened and got a good look at him. The third eye that he sported told her one thing that she hadn't noticed earlier. She was at an extranatural hospital.

"Well, you have had a nasty knock on the head; we were going to give you stitches, but the wound started sealing itself. Your familiar is very powerful and adorable." The doctor smiled. He removed her bandage and nodded. "You have some bruising, but it is healing."

She sighed. "Good. So, I can go home?"

"I would prefer that you remain under observation tonight."

She gave him a serious look. "I would rather be home. I

can arrange to have someone wake me up on the hour if necessary."

He frowned and glanced at Argus. "Will you be there?"

Argus shook his head. "No, but she does have housemates who would do that for her."

The doctor nodded. "I want you to go to a medical centre tomorrow and get a full workup. I will give you the tests I need run to close your file."

"What happens if I don't get the tests run?"

"I notify the XIA, they notify the Mage Guild, and they will put a mark in your file regarding lack of concern for your own safety."

Imara gave him a dark look. "They talked about me while I was in for scans."

The doctor looked smug. "They are chatty as hell when they are worried."

"Fine. Medical check tomorrow to confirm that I am healed."

"Excellent. In that case, I will fill out the discharge form, and you can be on your way."

She nodded and smiled until he left, and then, she made a face.

Argus laughed and asked, "What was that expression about?"

She cuddled Mr. E. "Never ask a woman to be excited about discharge."

It was Ivar that caught the reference first, and he snorted and then hooted with laughter. Lio caught on next, and Argus just gave her a look that said she should be embarrassed by the pun.

Imara didn't care what they thought. She got to go home that night, and a few hours earlier that had not been a sure thing.

Chapter Five

The XIA had driven her to Ritual Space where Hyl and Adrea had sent her home. Reegar had popped in like clockwork every hour until noon, and her medical scans were completed and sent to the hospital she had attended the night before. Since her tasks were complete, it was time to meet Kitty for a late lunch.

It took longer to walk to the café than it would have to drive to it, but when she met with Kitty, she didn't mention the accident. Kitty's news was extremely exciting.

"They want my bees!" She leaned forward and whispered it while the server was busy with their coffee.

"Really? Who?"

Kitty smiled. "The Mage Guild. They looked at the trials of our honey, and now, they want the bees."

"*Our honey?*"

"Mine and the bees." She grinned.

"Interesting. What are they going to do with them?"

Kitty shrugged. "I don't know. I expect they will be transported somewhere to live out their lives making magical honey."

"I hope that you are right. At least you got an excellent mark."

"I truly did. We used a split up at the farm to start our own hive. They are thriving."

Imara smiled as the server returned with their coffee. "Thank goodness. You worked hard with them; you deserve to have a portion of your efforts as a reward."

Kitty smiled and then she paused. "Are you all right? You seem a little dull today."

"Wow. That is direct."

"Did something happen?"

Imara wrinkled her nose. "Yes, I wrecked my car. Totalled it. Flipped it right over. I am fine, but it was a bit of a shock."

"When?"

"Last night."

Kitty's eyes went wide, but she kept her questions to herself until the burgers showed up.

Once they were eating, she interspersed her questions with her own consumption, and when she had assured herself that Imara was fine, she seemed to come to some kind of a decision.

"Take my car if you need it."

"You mean the truck?"

"Yeah. If you need it for a job, let me know."

Imara smiled. "Thank you. I think I am going to take a leave from my Death Keeper duties. I want to finish this last course strong."

"Smart."

Imara acted as she thought about it. "In fact . . . there, I have sent the text to the guild hall. They will spread the news."

She set her cell phone aside and gave Kitty her full attention. "How is the family?"

"I can't believe the change in grandma. She blushes, she flirts with grandpa's spectre, and they disappear for hours on end. It is so sweet."

Imara laughed. "They were definitely very much in love. How are your orbs?"

"My father and mother are letting me take the count down to five."

"That is progress."

"Yes. They still want me to be able to know what is coming but are not as worried about my ability to deal with shocks and surprises."

Imara smiled. "I think you have proven that you can handle yourself."

"I try, but I always seem to fall short. Master Reegar offered me a place at Reegar Hall when you have left." The last came out in a rush.

The laughter was genuine. "Your family agreed?"

"They did. Since he has you as a reference, there was no need for them to worry."

"They mentioned that they talked to me?"

"Of course."

Imara sighed. She had hoped to keep her interference behind the scenes, but now that it was out, she was glad that Reegar and Bara would have someone else to call family.

"Are you looking forward to it?"

"I am. I think we are all going to miss you, so it will be nice to have all of us together."

The expression on Kitigan's face was happy but sweetly sad at the same time.

"Don't get ahead of yourself. I haven't left yet. One term to go."

Kitty grinned. "I am glad of it. Hopefully, we can get together a few more times. Will you be graduating?"

"I am going to be finishing out of season. I would rather just throw a small party and have friends, Luken, and my mom in attendance."

"That sounds nice. Any particular venue?"

"It would have to be Reegar Hall if Reegar wanted to be there, or Ritual Space if he didn't. That is if I pass my class. I am going to try my best, but it does take weird turns once you start aiming for a position in the Mage Guild."

Kitty nodded soberly. "I wish you nothing but the best."

"I hope your wish isn't needed."

Kitty raised her coffee in a salute. "So do I."

Imara called Argus and left a message, telling him that she was fine and she was starting classes the next day. He could call her or text her in the evening. She headed to bed and went over her applications to the guild and for her magic license.

Mr. E murmured, *Where do you think he is?*

"He is either doing paperwork or thinking about it. I think he's mad about my accident."

He is not mad. He was worried. I was furious. That

creature was trying to kill you.

"I can't be sure of that."

I can. It said so.

She linked with his memory and saw the altercation. Nearly twenty feet of coils, some pale limbs but the face was in shadow. Imara heard the hiss, "She will die, and you will be vulnerable."

Imara blinked as her vision returned to the room around her. "Huh. So, it wants to kill me, but you are what it is after. Why?"

I killed a lot of people. Perhaps this is a relative.

"Really? You killed a lamia's family?"

He paused. *I thought it was a naga.*

"Not enough heads."

There was a demon who had a lamia as a lover. I killed him. She got away.

"That lacked foresight."

Yes, it did. I am sorry she came after you.

Imara rubbed her forehead where the cut had been. "So am I. I am in no mood to play with a nearly immortal shifter."

Are you all right?

"My head still hurts. I don't recover from a cracked skull like I should."

He pushed himself up against her arm, and he sent her extra energy. The burst helped the ache, but it didn't dissipate it completely.

"Thank you."

It didn't help, did it?

"It helped a bit."

He leaned against her and shared the warmth of his little body. The gentle touch helped her more than the shared energy.

She set her paperwork aside and flicked off the light. "Just one more course."

Maybe you should see the doctors again.

"I will think about it after class. For now, I just want to get some sleep and get to class tomorrow morning."

I will be with you. I always loved spell work.
She chuckled. "I know."
As Imara fell asleep, she watched Mr. E's memories of spell work like a movie, and the power and enthusiasm that she felt gave her hope for the following day.

"I am Master Mage Midian. I will be learning what you know about crafting a spell and using the ingredients on your list. This is a master-level class, and if you feel that your skills are not up to it, I would suggest you leave now."
Imara looked around and only saw three other students.
"I also do not encourage the use of familiars, as when you need to craft a spell, you might not have access to your companion. Please, place all of the creatures in the holding area behind the curtain. I am not cruel enough to keep them from you entirely." Midian nodded.
Imara went and carried Mr. E to a nice basket behind a curtain. "Here you go, dude. Enjoy your nap."
I wish that I could have played.
"I know." She scratched his chin and headed back to the class. Two of the other students also stowed their familiars. One had an owl, the other had a ferret.
She returned to her workstation and kept her hands at her sides.
"We are a small group, so I would ask you to introduce yourselves." Master Midian paused by Imara's station. "You first."
"I am Imara Mirrin, Master Death Keeper."
"Really?"
"Yes, Master Midian. I gained Master status several months ago."
"What do you do for fun?"
Imara cocked her head. "I go out with friends; I do some consulting work."
"Consulting? For whom?" The master kept her face pleasant.
"The Mage Guild and the XIA. Occasionally, I take tours of mage guides around memorial gardens to introduce them

to the possibility of working with the dead."

Master Midian nodded with an impressed grimace and moved to the next student.

Carlos Roderick was a ninth generation mage, and he wanted to take the spell crafting course in order to gain a skill that none of his family could master.

Libirak Nolthin wanted to learn how to make spells that could benefit the world.

Margo Pograth was a mage guide leader, and she wanted to set a good example for those who looked to her as a role model.

Imara suddenly wished she could change her answer.

"Excellent. Now, in front of you is a box, and inside of that box is a series of ingredients. I want you to use all of them, and anything you wish that you brought from your list."

The master walked back to her desk. "You have two hours, and you can use any of the tomes in the room, as well as all the equipment. You can begin now."

Imara stepped forward and opened the box. Her lips quirked when she took in the sight of the contents. She bent and got her notebook out, clicked her pencil, and got to work.

Class was now in session.

Chapter Six

Imara slowly stirred the beaker with a glass rod. All of the ingredients from the box had been noted and were now suspended in the liquid.

The scramble to get started had been stilted. The stops and starts of the other students were distracting, but it was their darting looks as they tried to guess what the other ones were up to that made Imara angry.

She inhaled the floral scents from her box, and she relaxed. It was time to add an ingredient from her own collection.

She stared at her supplies for ten minutes before she closed her eyes and reached out. When she saw what she had selected, she knew what her spell was for.

Imara jotted down the final ingredient and measured out ten flakes before dropping them into the beaker.

The liquid inside the beaker turned a soft and gentle green, so she put a strainer and a new bottle down and slowly poured the mixture into it.

When she was done, she broke down her station and washed up. She glanced at Master Midian, and it triggered the short brunette into jumping to her feet.

"Well, Master Mirrin, what have you made for me?"

Imara looked at the other students who were still deep in their preparation process. "I have created a potion with an interesting effect."

The master brought out a small silver cup. "What is the result?"

"Well, the box contained different flowers, which all had something to do with love. Some were obsessive love, some were love of self, and others were love from afar, and others were lost love. The potion is designed to lessen the effects of love and to ease the pain."

Midian nodded and took the vial from Imara's desk, pouring a measure into the silver cup. A bright streak of energy came out of the cup, and Midian grinned. "What was your ingredient from the list?"

Imara bit her lip for a moment. "Oatmeal flakes."

Midian cackled. "Gentle fibre for moving emotions through. Why did you make it into a potion?"

"The flower petals were all fresh and soft. Smashing them would have just been a work of violence they didn't deserve."

Midian looked thoughtful. "Well, your spell does what you say it does, so you are dismissed. I will see you this afternoon for the second class."

Imara blinked. "That's it?"

"That's it. This afternoon we will discuss your final exam. You are going to have eight weeks to prepare it, but you will have to make the same spell with the same result three times."

Imara grabbed her bags, collected Mr. E, and walked out of the class while the others were trying to speed their efforts. "That was definitely odd."

Mr. E rode proudly on her shoulder. *I knew you had a knack for this. I could feel that you have an awareness of the ingredients. It is an intensely important part of the art of crafting magic.*

"Thanks. It just felt like the thing to do. Minerva was right. You need to let the ingredients tell you what they want and let your experience with them guide the magic."

Lucky that you met her then.

Imara smiled. "I would say so."

She was carrying on this conversation while she crossed the quad. A few of the newer students gave her strange looks, but they probably couldn't see Mr. E on her shoulder.

"I think I have to buy a new car."

That is sudden.

"Not really. Not since I saw the wreck of the car from your angle."

Ah. Maybe one of the big ones like Argus drives?

"No. That is way too expensive. I need something new so that it will at least have airbags that go off. You can help me shop online, and we will see if someone can take us around on the weekend for test drives."

You need a driver to find a car?

"Yes, it is one of the great ironies of the universe." She chuckled.

Very strange.

"Yeah, but in the modern era, I can look up something online before I go see it. It cuts down on all the running around."

Are you looking because Kitty offered you her truck?

"No, I am looking because I realized that I can't even drive across the college for a quick bite for lunch."

Ah, you feel confined.

"Hobbled. Yes."

She entered Reegar Hall and headed for the fridge.

Reegar appeared at her side and walked with her. "How was your class?"

"It was good. It was weird though. I didn't use any tomes. I just did what Minerva said to do. I listened to the ingredients."

"Minerva?"

"Yes. She is a friend of a friend. She is also in the process of purchasing one of the herbal supply shops in Redbird City."

"I knew a Minerva. Tall woman. Exceptionally smart with a weird aura."

"That does sound like her."

She put together a sandwich and made another one for Mr. E. She brought everything to the table and sat down.

Reegar poured her a glass of iced tea and brought it over. "So, tell me what you got."

She blinked. "You know the format?"

"I do. I was part of the crew that invented the course. It has been the same for the last seven decades."

She took a bite of her sandwich and swallowed. "Flowers. It was flowers."

"Oh, what kind of flowers?"

"Sunflowers, narcissus, roses, white roses, yellow roses, and gardenias." She kept eating and spoke between the pauses.

"What did you do with them? Love spell?" Reegar was grinning.

"No. We had to use one of our listed ingredients, so I used oatmeal."

Reegar stared at her, and then, he whispered, "Genius. Letting love pass."

"Right. According to the silver cup, the spell works."

"Did you try it?"

"No, I don't have any love that I want to turn into a memory." She finished her sandwich.

"Why did you choose oatmeal?"

She sat back and sipped at her iced tea. "When I was a child, I wandered into a patch of poisoned oak. My skin burned, and the only thing that helped was oatmeal baths. I see flakes of oats, and I see comfort. There is nothing better than comfort after the love brought on by obsession or self-involvement. Also, it binds stuff and carries it away without harm."

"Wow. You know a lot about oatmeal."

She smiled. "I like it."

Mr. E finished his sandwich and curled into a ball on the plate. *Wake me when we have to go back to class.*

"Is Midian teaching your course?"

"Yes, she is."

"She's good. Fair and direct. Just what you need. There is nothing subjective in her class. Did she give you study aids?"

"No. This is a lab course. It is full days for a week and then once a week until the end of the course."

"So, why are you home?"

"Lunch break. I have to head back in half an hour."

"Ah. Well, in that case, I will keep meals ready for you."

She smiled. "Thanks. I would not have been able to get this far without your help."

Reegar put his hand on her shoulder. "Sure, you would. It

just wouldn't have been as fun."

She laughed. "Fun. That is a word for it."

He chuckled. "Life in our world is odd. I know it is a jolt from Sakenta, but you are adapting well. Think of this as a transition between here and Redbird City."

"A halfway house."

"Precisely."

She looked around. "It is a very nice halfway house."

"Thank you. And thank you for letting me keep my home under control."

"Where are the other students who are supposed to be moving in?"

He waved his hand. "They will wait until you no longer need privacy and support."

She sighed. "I hate to think I am depriving someone else of this shelter."

"Don't. Kitigan is moving in next term, and she will need your advice long distance."

Imara chuckled. "She told me. I think she will be fine here, but you are going to have to make room for her bees."

He quirked his brows. "I didn't know about them."

"She doesn't know about them, but I was watching them when we did the harvesting. She is their queen. I just don't know how to tell her that. She's letting the guild take her bees and their honey."

"Huh. Then, how are they going to come here?"

Imara grinned. "They are going to follow her."

"You are sure?"

"I looked up bee behaviour, and it is definitely something that will happen. There is too much magic tying them together."

"Ah. Yeah, those things can't be broken. Well, not without one party losing their lives."

She shivered. "That isn't worth thinking about."

"No, but stupider things have happened with less reason."

Imara nodded. "Right. Life is complicated."

"More and more as you live in it." Reegar smiled. "You will get used to it. You are simply reaching the end of one goal. You need to find another."

"What?"

"You heard me. Your focus has been on attaining your license, but that is nearly within your grasp. You need to look wider. Find a new focus and gain a new purpose. Your consulting business is passive. You need a goal to reach for."

Mr. E looked up from his plate. *He is not wrong.*

"How would I even start finding something else?"

"There are counselling services offered by the college. You also might want to speak with the XIA or the Mage Guild and ask if they have any programs or if the can use your services on a more regular basis."

"Oh. Right. I forgot about that."

"Or even possibly run your own garden of rest. You are a master now. You can prime and create spectres. There are many options open to you. You are smart. Once you finish with today's class, get out a corkboard and start planning. Figure out what your options are and then start making a decision."

She nodded. "Thanks for the pep talk. It is helping."

Imara's headache faded, and she smiled. "Do you want to come back to class with me, Mr. E?"

No. I am fine here. I will see you after class. He yawned, got up, turned around, and sat back down on the plate.

She made a face and headed back to class. She had a lot to think about, and the walk would do her good.

Chapter Seven

"Well, we have lost Mr. Nolthin. It appears that the idea of improvisation was too much for him. We lose a lot of students on the first day, so I am very pleased to see that you have returned and that you have abided by my rules to keep your familiars out of the lab."

Mage Midian smiled and paced back and forth in front of her class. "Now, we are getting down to the details of the course."

Midian slammed her hand on the nearest lab station. "For the next five days, you will be in here all day, every day or for at least six hours if other courses interfere. I hope none of you are stupid enough to have additional courses this term."

Imara kept herself quiet and paid attention.

"After the next five days, you will have the following seven weeks to prepare a single spell. That spell will have to be what the books consider to be a *great* spell. The spell will have to be powerful, exotic, and here is the fun part . . . you must execute it equally three times. You will be allowed to keep one example of your spell, one will be executed in a protected space, and one will be kept in the archives."

Margo asked, "What ingredients can we use?"

"Anything you wish as long as you have enough for three spells. You can use any materials, any containers, any combination of the above, but it has to be an original spell. We will test the result against all known spells, and if you have come up with an original spell, you are fast-tracked to Master Mage status. If it is a derivative but mostly original spell, you will qualify for Senior Journeyman Mage status. A copied spell is an automatic fail."

Imara nodded.

"On the wall behind my desk is the largest collection of

how-to guides for writing spells that we have located. Know your ingredients. Have fun."

Imara asked, "How are our days to be structured? Will we receive one box of ingredients per class?"

Mage Midian smiled slightly. "You can have as many boxes of ingredients as you can manage. Practice is key in mastering your ingredients."

Imara nodded. "Do you wish us to provide you with notes as to our ingredients, recipes, and the spells?"

"Yes. I would like a copy of everything you hand in."

The students nodded, and Midian looked at them with an expectant air. "Well, the new boxes are on your workstations; you have two hours, ten minutes to create a spell from the contents within. If you find something poisonous, feel free to do something creative with it."

Imara looked over and found the box on her station. She opened the box and lined up the ingredients in even rows.

A quick glance at the other tables showed her that they all got different contents. No two boxes were the same.

Imara's ingredients were dry herbs and minerals. She got her notebook out and started to make notes as she started with the lapis lazuli and a mortar and pestle.

Sweat dripped into the mortar containing the multicoloured sand comprised of herbs, flowers, and rocks. The sweat activated a tiny cascade in the mortar, so Imara called it quits.

Now came the tricky part. She took a piece of obsidian from her own collection, and she centred it above the mortar. The sand gathered around it and sank deep.

Imara watched and murmured a low, wordless chant over the work, coaxing the desert storm into the obsidian.

She watched as it began to swirl and twist, pulling the ingredients down into the stone. The obsidian was shiny, and the storm of sand was visible inside the glass.

Imara lifted the stone out of the mortar, and she set it on a soft chamois. Midian was at her station before Imara could wash out her mortar.

"So, what do we have now?"

Imara smiled. "I think it is a desert storm."

"Not very useful." Midian looked at it and frowned.

"I am working through some personal issues, so this reflects my current state of mind."

"Ah. Well, let's see if it is what you think it is." The mage picked up the stone and eased it into her silver cup.

The roar of wind that spiralled out of the cup accompanied the whirl of light.

"Well, you have definitely created a solid spell here. This is a concealment spell mixed with a sandstorm. Well done. Partial marks as you didn't know about the other half of your spell, but good start, Death Keeper Mirrin."

Imara sighed. "Thank you."

"Clean up and go home. You look wiped out."

Imara nodded. "Halfway there."

She finished up, watched that the master was putting her stone in one of three boxes near the window, Imara guessed that it was what would become her collection.

Midian smiled slightly, and another box appeared on Imara's desk. With a glance at the clock, Imara opened the box and started her next spell.

She paused and smelled each of the items and smiled. That was what she was creating, a spell to ease laughter into the world. Since scent had tipped her off, she was making a concentrated oil to become a vapour.

It was going to be a rush to finish in time, but she knew what to do. All that studying of techniques was finally paying off.

She focused on laughter as she bruised the plants and set them into a decoction flask. They swirled around in a bright solution of purified water and saffron.

While the flame did its work to heat the herbs and release the oils, Imara worked to clean up after her previous spell.

She knew when it began to drip the oil through the small still, that she had created a flight spell. It was a dangerous spell as the euphoria that it created was not an amazing combination for the power of flight.

She kept her thoughts on the spell as she recorded the ingredients and her technique.

When she had a sixteenth of an ounce of oil, she poured the oil into a tiny vial, and she capped it. She took the rest of the herbs off the flame and disposed of them.

Midian had been checking on Carlos, but she changed direction when Imara was washing up.

"What do you have now?"

Imara looked at the clock. She had five minutes to spare. "Icarus oil."

Midian blinked. "What?"

"A levitation potion that elicits elevated mood as well as the physical side effect." She handed over the vial.

Once again, the silver cup came out, and when a drop struck the bottom, the energy in the cup sent a cascade of golds and yellows skyward with enough force to jar the cup from the mage's hand.

Master Midian stared at the cup. "You didn't make a lot."

"No, it is dangerous. I considered it unwise to make more."

Midian nodded. "Huh. So, you are concerned with the welfare of those around you?"

"Of course. I would never want to be responsible for someone getting injured, or high, for that matter."

"And yet, you made the oil."

"It was what the ingredients wanted to be today."

"Interesting. I will see you tomorrow morning. I am working on some strange combinations that I think you can do justice to."

Imara swallowed, but her stomach filled with lead. "I look forward to it."

"Don't lie. It doesn't suit you. Dismissed for the day. See all three of you tomorrow."

The ingredients, spells, and paraphernalia disappeared from every workstation.

Margo blinked. "I was nearly done."

Carlos patted her on the shoulder. "I don't think she cares."

Midian smiled brightly. "I don't care. In your careers, if you are creating spells, or executing them, there is a time limit involved. The only time in this course that you are not held to a time limit is your final exam. It is your creation, take your time. Now . . . get out."

Imara nodded and left with the other two.

Carlos asked, "You come from a long line of spell crafters?"

"I have no idea. I was fostered." She smiled brightly. "But, I do have supportive friends that have helped me to study and get my head in the right place."

Margo asked, "How could you study for this?"

"You have to focus on each ingredient and how it makes you feel. What do *you* associate with it? When you know that, you know what to do with it."

Carlos stopped. "You are joking."

"I am not. Crafting a spell is more about the mage and less about the ingredients. It makes things predictable if you work it from that angle. If you are in the mood tonight, and you have a space where you live, enchant some of your favourite spices and see what happens when you add them to bread or even just flour."

Margo snorted. "I am not even going to waste my time." She stalked past them and exited through the main doors into bright daylight.

Carlos nodded. "I don't think that kind of experiment is a waste. So, I just focus on the ingredients?"

"Focus on the way they make you feel and add magic to the mix. The rest works itself out."

He nodded. "Thanks for the tip. Can I buy you a coffee?"

They had emerged from the magic lab building and were on their way to the quad. Across the way, she saw a familiar figure. "Another time, perhaps."

She stepped away from him, and she began to jog toward the familiar figure of Argus as he was moving in her direction.

When she got to him, she shocked him by throwing her arms around his neck and pulling him down to her for a kiss, in full view of the assembled and curious students.

When she pulled back, he smiled at her with a foolish grin. "What was that for?"

"I have missed you, and I am going to be a hellish bitch for a week, so you are going to need to be scarce."

He grinned and kept his arms looped around her waist. "How would I notice?"

She punched him in the bicep. "Funny man."

"I thought it was amusing. Rough course?"

"One week of full-day classes, including weekends. I am going to be completely fried." She looped an arm around his waist. "So, what brings you here?"

"I have your insurance cheque for your car and all of your possessions. You keep a really clean car." His admiration was audible.

"It wasn't new or fancy, but it was mine. Now, I have to go looking for another one." She grimaced. "Stupid-whatever-it-was."

"We are still analyzing it, but it appears to be an ancient serpentine shifter."

"Wonderful. Mr. E said it could be a lamia."

"That would be unlikely. They hunt in pairs. This was solitary, so we are guessing some kind of naga."

She wrinkled her nose. "Mr. E fought it, so I am going to trust his guess. As soon as I have a spare minute, I am looking it up as thoroughly as I can."

"I know a few people who can advise you on ancient shifters, but I don't know if they would be willing to travel here to talk to you."

She sighed. "I think I know who you mean, but I am comfortable making that call. Benny should be able to tell me what I need to know."

He nodded. "She is an excellent choice, but I was thinking of her parents. They don't travel much though."

"Ah. Well, I will ask her anyway."

They were slowly making their way toward Reegar Hall.

"What does Reegar think of this course?"

"He knows it is necessary to reaching my goals, but he has

given me some good advice."

"What is that?"

"Now that I have almost achieved a goal I set myself when I was a child, it is time to go looking for new goals and activities to focus on. I am the type of person who needs to drive themselves. Without that drive, I start to lose focus on the moment."

"I see. What is driving your public display of affection?"

She smiled. "There are two factors. The first factor is that the guy in my class was giving me looks that made me a little uncomfortable. I thought it best to nip his intentions in the bud. The second was that you are part of the new plan I need to make, so I thought I would test out public affection. I rather enjoyed it."

His voice got lower. "I did as well. It is probably a good thing that it was in a public place. My beast tried to snap my controls and fly off with you."

She grinned. "I choose my battles wisely."

Chapter Eight

The next week was a blur of calls, spells, potions, enchantments, and hot and ready lunches made by Reegar. Bara was doing Imara's laundry, and she had never felt so cared for in her life.

Master Midian was working them to exhaustion to prove to them the importance of focus and control. Margo tried to make the same spell four times in a row, and it was only when Midian eradicated all of her equipment that she had lifted her head and listened to what the instructor was telling her. She was not cut out for the improvisation of spell crafting.

Carlos, on the other hand, flourished in the class. He worked with his instincts, and his spell work got faster and stronger. The master was impressed and watched him for a few days until it appeared that the change would stick.

Imara had never been so relieved to finish going to class as she was when she finished the spell crafting tutorial. Now, it was all about planning a spell. Reegar made her breakfast and then scowled at her while she ate. "You still don't know?"

She fed Mr. E some of the smoked salmon from her plate. "I still don't know. Nothing I have come up with has felt right, so I am going to ask folks to give me something small, and I will use those objects for the spell, with some additions that I have come across."

"A friendship spell?"

"Sort of. I have written down a few ingredients, but I will have to ask people for them."

He blinked and leaned forward. "Colour me interested. What ingredients?"

Imara sighed and pulled the folded piece of paper out of

her bra, unfolding and straightening it as she went.

"Right. Well, it starts with the hair of a familiar. After that, it gets weirder, the nail of a beast, an empty soul, a moment of joy, the blood of an enemy, the word of a friend, and the will of the caster."

"That is quite the list. What do you think the spell is?"

She looked at the list and the notes she had added to the margins. She would add magic detector strips, a tiny tornado, a leaf from Ritual Space and bind it all with the enchanted honey.

She tapped her finger on the page. "I think it is a spell of need."

"What kind of need?"

"You know, I have no idea." She chuckled. "It just seemed right."

"If it seemed right, get collecting on those ingredients."

"I am going to finish breakfast first. I have a meeting to get to."

He raised his brows. "I didn't know you had a vehicle."

"I don't. I am having a meeting in Ritual Space. It is more convenient for both of us."

"Ah. Well, finish your breakfast and go. You only have a few weeks left before the course is over. Can you hand it in early?"

"I can, but she warned us against it. Mage Midian stated that this was our one chance to create a new spell and that no one benefited from rushing it."

"She isn't wrong. These shelves are full of spells that were rushed and now don't function as they should."

She finished the last caper and took her dish to the sink, washing it before setting it on the drying rack.

"Thanks for breakfast, Reegar. You have been a tremendous friend through all of this."

"I am friend to very few, but I am glad you are among them."

She leaned in and gave him a hug. He stiffened in surprise. She laughed, and Mr. E jumped to her shoulder. He smelled like fish, but it wasn't the worst thing he had smelled like since becoming her familiar. His dietary habits were ridiculous.

She headed back to her room and activated the portal to Ritual Space. She had a brunch date to keep, but she would never turn down breakfast from Reegar. He made the effort, so she was going to eat it. Getting a spectre to do any kind of domestic duty was a miracle in itself.

She sent the text through, and when she got a response, she took the step from her room to the enclosed fun park of magic and nature where mages could learn and spells could be cast with the rest of the world at a safe distance. It was also the place where Imara learned to climb walls and break into buildings. *Ah, good times.*

Adrea was standing near the portal. Benny and Freddy were at her side. Blueberry, the blue-striped bunny rabbit, was at her feet.

Mr. E was wiggling with excitement. *May I go and play?*

Imara silently spoke to him, *Doesn't it lack dignity?*

It is extremely fun.

Fine. Off you go. Enjoy yourself.

Mr. E made a happy murp and ran over to Blueberry. They looked at each other for a long moment, and then, they raced side by side to the garden at the back of the main house.

Adrea smiled. "Now that they are off playing, shall we have a spot of breakfast?"

Freddy's nose twitched. "Sure, but I think someone already had some salmon."

Imara smiled beatifically. "Mr. E. He is mad for it. For an ancient mage, his beast is in control a lot of the time."

Freddy snorted. "I have *so* been there."

Benny grinned. "Nice to see you again. I have gotten that information for you."

"Oh, thank you. I have been working on finding out, but the spell crafting class took all of my time."

"Is it over?"

"Everything but the final. I still have to collect some stuff for that."

Adrea grinned. "Do tell but over breakfast. We just got our blunderberry harvest, and I can't wait for you to taste them."

There was a charming table set for four in the back garden, and the large blue berries sitting on the table surrounded by cream, scones, and small pancakes looked lovely.

Freddy asked the question, "What the hell is a blunderberry?"

"It was supposed to be a blueberry, but the raspberries and blackberries grew into a braided vine with the blueberry, and this was the result. It is a pretty bush, but the fruit is perplexing. Tasty though."

Adrea sat and poured tea all around. "So, what did Imara ask you to look up?"

Benny pulled a chunk of paperwork out of her purse. "Lamias. One trashed her car while she was in it on the highway."

"Oh, the accident."

"Correct."

"I thought they always hunted in pairs." Adrea smiled slightly as she offered fluffy biscuits to everyone.

Freddy split her biscuit and slathered it with the clotted cream. "That changes depending on the reason for the hunt. They mate separately, so if one lost a mate, the other wouldn't go to avenge her companion's mate."

Benny blinked. "She should have just asked you. Yeah, that is what I found out. One hunting alone has a personal vendetta against you or Mr. E."

Imara scooped up some of the berries and put them on top of the cream. "That is what I figured. I just had hoped that most of his enemies were dead."

Benny sighed. "I guess they are not."

"No, I suppose not." Imara bit the dessert, and she had to scramble to suck in all the juice from the exploding berries. Blunderberries were amazing.

The other ladies were all laughing and trying to keep themselves from looking like they had gone face first into the berry bushes.

Slurping and giggles gradually gave way to conversation, and Benny asked the loaded question, "So, what are you doing now?"

"Ah, I am working on my spell crafting course. If you speak to Minerva, please tell her that her advice has been passed on, and my classmate and I are both benefiting. The master mage is a little confused by his sudden competence, but it is going well for him."

Freddy frowned. "Only one classmate is benefiting?"

"Yeah. We started with four students. One dropped out on the first day, and the second wasn't making strides by the lab week. She was encouraged to find another occupation."

Adrea winced. "That is harsh."

"Yes, well, this is a multi-credit course, for higher class levels. You have to have a high average in your previous courses, and at least one recommendation from a faculty member."

Freddy looked impressed. "Who was the faculty member for your recommendation?"

"My stealth magic instructor. He signed the form while laughing."

Adrea grinned. "Hyl still talks about you being a natural assassin."

"He is an excellent teacher."

Benny cocked her head. "What is your final exam in your spell crafting course?"

"I have to make something that hasn't been seen before."

"Do you have an idea of what you want?" Benny sipped her tea.

"I do. Well, I have notes."

"Can I see them?"

Freddy grinned. "Benny was homeschooled when it came to her spell casting knowledge, but there are very few people I would trust to look into your information. Two are sitting at this table, and one is playing house with a dragon."

Imara fished the paper out of her bra and handed it over.

Benny snickered. "I carry everything in there. Let me just

look over this."

Benny looked at the list, glanced at Imara with raised brows a few times, and she folded the page. "We can give you three of the items on the page."

Freddy blinked. "We can?"

"Sure. Adrea can provide three leaves from Ritual Space."

"Of course."

"Freddy can pull out three hairs for the hair of a familiar," Benny smirked.

Freddy blinked. "Hey! I don't give my body parts away easily."

"I know. The thrust of this spell isn't for control over anything, it is for providing for and filling a need."

Adrea cocked her head. "What need?"

Imara answered, "Whatever the caster needs most at the moment."

"Interesting. So, the caster had better be sure of their need."

"Precisely." Imara nodded. "It isn't a spell to be used in haste."

Benny nodded and handed the page back. "I haven't seen anything like it. There are wish-fulfillment spells that come close, but this one uses something else."

Imara nodded. "Exactly. The spell uses ingredients that are enchanted by their very existence. The magic has already been *paid for* so to speak."

Adrea whistled. "That is new."

"And a little vanilla for the scent of cookies." Imara smiled.

The ladies laughed until Freddy paused. "Benny, you said that she could get three ingredients from us. What else?"

"The blood of an enemy." Benny waved her hand. "One of my ancestors arrested Mr. E all those years ago, and I have demon blood in me. Lots of it. That is enough of an enemy in the eyes of her familiar, and it will work for the spell."

Imara blinked tears back. "I was just going to ask Adrea if I could retrieve the empty soul if she didn't mind."

Adrea frowned, "The . . . oh. Is that what that is?"

"Yes. The spectres are gone now, I can remove the stone."

"By all means. Go and get it before you leave."

"Thank you. I didn't want to remove anything from the premises without permission."

Adrea looked bright. "Can I interest you in three blunderberries instead of the leaves?"

"I don't think they would make it for a month without spoiling."

"What about dehydrated ones? The plant won't stop bearing."

"Uh, sure. That will be fine."

"Or the berries and the leaves. Please, please, take the berries!" Adrea clenched her hands together as she pleaded.

She surrendered. "Yes. Yes, of course, I will take as many as you are willing to part with."

Benny snickered. "There is a sucker born every minute."

"Says you. I am going to see if Reegar wants to try planting them outside the hall."

Adrea nodded. "I would be interested in finding out if they grow outside of Ritual Space."

"As would I. Seeing how they would grow within a spectral field would be interesting."

"I think so as well. So, I give you the seeds, and you let me know if they grow."

Imara grinned. "Deal."

Benny cleared her throat. "So, do you want to learn more about the lamia?"

"Please."

"They are creatures of myth and legend. In some cases, they are all said to be one woman who was tricked into murdering her own children, and in others, she was a seductress who lured young men in to their deaths. She can project her vision to find her prey in most legends."

Benny lifted her sheaf of papers. "In the modern era, after the wave, lamia have been sighted in pairs across every continent. There are always two, always female, and they always find each other during their first transformation."

Imara frowned. "Do they have to register?"

"No. They are only recorded if they break the law, just as the rest of the extranaturals are."

Imara nodded. "Thank you. It gives me a place to start. Someone had to have seen them around Mr. E in the past."

"Hopefully. Someone would have acted as a witness against him."

Imara sighed. "I suppose I will just have to make a trip to the archive."

She caught a glimpse of dark fur streaking across the lawn with a bunny in hot pursuit. "Hey, Mr. E, road trip!"

He made an un-kitten-like right angle, and he kept running until he was on her shoulder. *When are we going, and whose car are you going to borrow?*

She quirked her lips. "Car shopping is the next thing on my list."

Freddy nodded. "What are you going to get?"

Imara reached up and scratched Mr. E under the chin. "Something with a big dashboard."

They all laughed at the blissful kitten, and he didn't mind a bit.

Chapter Nine

Imara sat with the counsellor and seer, N'sha, and stared into her brilliant amber eyes as she learned the path her life could take.

"You are exceptionally bright, Ms. Mirrin. You have the opportunity to join the guild at the highest level. While I understand your need to strike out on your own, I urge you to take a more conventional path."

Imara held Mr. E in her lap and stroked him to soothe him and herself at the same time. This was her third meeting with the counsellor, and he was unsettled every time. Frankly, so was she.

"I know that the path isn't one that is normally considered, but it is the one I have chosen. Thank you for the contact information for the Mage Guild enforcement and the XIA. You have helped convince me of the direction I should be looking."

N'sha leaned back. "If you are sure that this is the path you choose, I respect your decision. I do still have some feelers out for more opportunities for you. May I call you if they come in?"

Imara nodded. "Please. That would be very helpful. Any information can be put to use."

"I agree. Well, it has been interesting going over your records. I look forward to seeing you again."

Imara took the hint and got to her feet with Mr. E in her arms. "Have a good day, Counsellor N'sha."

"You as well. You have a bright future. Take care of it."

Imara left and walked through the nearly empty halls of the Brokal Building. Named after Heinrich Brokal, it was famous for not being able to keep inhabitants in its halls. No one liked to stay in his building.

When they were outside the building, she inhaled and exhaled slowly. "I wish I knew how to get that feeling out of the walls."

There is probably a mage who can work the clearance spell, but no one wants to pay for it.

"Right. I forget that magic pays."

You had better count on it. You are about to throw yourself into that realm.

"I know. It is just hard to imagine that a dream I only developed as a frantic escape is coming true."

You have earned this moment. Enjoy it.

She nodded. There was still a week to go, but she had made up her mind. She was going to finish her spell and complete her course. There was no putting it off. This was the spell she had been meant to create.

She got into her light SUV and settled in with Mr. E hopping onto the dashboard. The Brokal Building was on the other side of campus from Reegar Hall, so driving her new car had seemed like the best option.

Mr. E enjoyed the new-car smell. None of his previous mages had driven, and if they had, they certainly hadn't taken him along with them. Imara was happy that she could give him little experiences that he enjoyed. Her happiness was tied to his.

Imara woke up and knew that it was time. After hashing and rehashing what she should use, she knew what she needed. She gathered the ingredients, set up a video camera and went to work.

The notebooks that she needed were next to her, and with precision, she started with her first ingredients across three containers.

The first thing that she added was *soil from her mother's garden*. The soil from the site of the most recent wave.

It was done, she had started. Now to continue with *words from a friend*. Reegar had written the words *You can do this* on three sheets of parchment. She folded them carefully and set them into the three bowls.

The *empty soul* was the shattered spectre crystal from the incident where she first met Benny. When she had finished draining the spectres, the crystal had cracked into three chunks. It had offered itself to her at that moment. She thought of it as the empty soul because it had never held a soul.

The *ties that bind* had been offered by Bara. It was rope that she and Luken had made for this test. Her twin had offered his help, and Bara had put him to work. The rope was cut into three pieces and placed gently in the containers.

The rest of the pieces came together quickly, and by the time the last slip of blunderberry leaf was in, the spell was nearly complete.

She took three matches and lit each group of contents on fire, muttering about blending, binding, and melting together.

Violent purple fire shot upwards with each match touching the ingredients. She focused and murmured encouragement for the fire to give way to liquid.

The blaze turned blue then green, yellow, and finally red before it disappeared and left behind a molten and metallic gold liquid.

The honey from the magic bees was added in minute amounts. The gold liquid began to swirl rapidly, and she took out the final gift from Kitigan's family. Three orbs of seer glass were lined up, and she used the tiny funnel to fill each of them before she corked them.

The one-and-a-half inch orbs were filled with a golden storm of potential. All the love and support that Imara had gotten for this project had humbled her. Argus had even shifted and clipped one of his claws with his beak before snipping the clipping into pieces. She had her piece of a beast.

She held her breath as she transferred the corked spells to velvet-lined, padded boxes.

When the last box was closed, she nearly collapsed. Instead, she put away the ingredients and set them up carefully on the shelves.

Keeping the lab neat was what she needed to stay sane. Once everything was complete, she checked the video and popped the chip.

She looked at the chip and pressed it to her forehead. "Right. Done."

Master Midian had agreed to accept a video as she was out of town until late in the afternoon.

Imara gathered her boxes and notebooks, carrying everything out into the common space, and she settled them quickly into the padded and lined box that Reegar had prepared for the occasion.

The moment that she settled in the chair near the library, she heard shouts.

"Surprise!"

Bara and Luken jumped out from behind the stacks, Reegar simply appeared, and Mr. E crept out from under her chair.

Imara's heart stuttered and then fired up a pounding beat. "Oh! Thank you."

Mr. E crawled up and sat on her lap, purring up a storm. She clutched him, and her pulse immediately slowed to a more normal beat.

Bara chuckled. "You look exhausted."

Reegar nodded. "It is the most trying spell she could make, so she put everything in herself into it."

Luken came up and squeezed her hand. "You did well, sister."

"Thanks, but we don't even know if it works."

Reegar snorted. "You might get partial credit if you misidentified the spell, but you still managed to create something that radiates power. That is a pass no matter the level of it."

Imara looked at him weakly. "Really?"

"Really. I supervised your procedures, and there is no way that any of your mechanics can't be replicated. There was nothing shifty about it. That is what they are looking for."

Imara nodded. "Good."

Bara grinned. "We have cake."

"What time is it?"

Reegar cocked his head. "It is just after four."

She sat up. "What?"

"Yes, you have been working for eight hours without a break. Why?"

"I have to bring the spells to Midian at five."

Bara grimaced. "Have some cake. You need to eat."

Mr. E looked up at her with bright gold eyes. *I made you a present.*

She blinked. "What?"

I made you something to keep your version of the spell on. It is next to Reegar.

Reegar noted where she was looking, and he picked up the box. "Ah, yes. Your familiar made this for you. I confess to being surprised at his dexterity."

Bara smiled. "I helped a little."

Reegar handed her the box, and Imara opened it with curiosity burning in her.

A bracelet made of shining steel with a clasp and a kitten engraved on the back of it was sitting on a bed of black velvet.

"Should I put it on?"

Please. I measured it by hugging your arm while you slept.

She grinned and slipped the band over her wrist. It felt comfortable, and then, she didn't even feel it. She picked him up and got to her feet, walking over to her spells and opening one of the boxes.

"Now, how do I put this on the band?"

Luken piped up, "Just touch your spell to the clasp. It will attach automatically to the nearest link. There are concealment spells on it and comfort spells."

"Thank you, brother, and most of all, thank you, Mr. E."

Her little friend squirmed. *You deserve more from those around you.*

"I have gotten tons of support from friends and family. I am enjoying it for what it is. Affection freely given."

She checked her phone. "Damn. And now I have to run

from this very touching moment."

Reegar reached in and pulled out her private notebook. "No sense in letting the mages get their hands on all copies."

"Right. Well, hopefully, I will be back in an hour or so. Mr. E, you stay here. You know how she feels about familiars."

He sighed and jumped from her arms to the table. *You really like it?*

"I really do. Talk to you soon."

Reegar frowned. "Aren't you going out with Argus tonight?"

"That isn't until eight. I have time."

She lifted the box from the table, inhaled, and said, "Wish me luck!"

Luken grinned. "I did. That is why you were born first."

She snorted and walked out of Reegar Hall, heading for the mage labs.

Midian took the experimental spell and carried it to the testing lab. The lab was designed to mimic a human body and determine the nature of the magic itself.

"Well, Mirrin, this looks good. The spell log is solid, so now, we just have to see what it does or what the potential is."

Imara nodded, and she stood with her fingers woven together tightly. The sacrificial spell was placed on the table, and Midian left the room, placing her hand on the activation glyph and then chanting softly.

The spell shivered, shimmered and then exploded in the room, shattering and rocketing around the space until it gradually faded.

Imara didn't see any change at first. When she looked in, she suddenly noticed that everything was better. The wood was darker, the chair was pristine, the blotter had no stains and was made of a fine-grade leather where it had been rough cardboard before.

Midian smiled slowly. "Excellently done. You will be receiving an invitation to the Mage Guild by the end of the week."

To Imara's shock, Midian extended her hand. Out of reflex, she shook hands with her instructor.

The slight scratch on her finger came when she withdrew her hand. She looked at the pinprick of blood on her finger and then Midian's hand.

The snake ring seemed like something Imara should have seen before.

She stepped back and headed for the door. Midian didn't call out after her.

The main hall was bloated and flexed. The doorway was warped, and it was nearly impossible to figure out the latch to let herself into the fresh air.

The hiss behind her made her turn. To her shock, it was N'sha's torso riding on top of the serpentine lower body. N'sha reared up to tower over her, grinning and exposing fangs dripping with venom.

The shouts coming from the quad told Imara that she wasn't imagining the horror that was slashing at her with claws as deadly as the fangs.

The burn of the claw strike on her right arm sent a shockwave through her limb and left it limp. Imara fell to the ground as the toxin spread. She tried to connect with Mr. E, but there was nothing but fury and frustration on that end.

"Oh, you can't call your little familiar. He is busy with my sister."

Panic and pain turned to worry. "Don't hurt him."

N'sha moved in and leaned over her, her tail snaking around Imara's body and holding her in place. "We can't hurt him, but we can hurt you, and we will."

Paralysis was moving in on her, but there was one thing that she could do. When no one human could help her, she called the spectres. They might not assist her, but it was the only move she had. She gave it everything she could.

Chapter Ten

Mage Reegar watched from the edge of his territory as the lamia hauled Mr. E away before he could run to the side of his mage. Fury and frustration ripped through him as he pounded against the barrier that bound him to Reegar Hall.

Bara and Luken came up behind him, and Bara asked, "What is wrong?"

"The lamia, they have Imara and Mr. E. They are at the mage lab."

Luken was dialling, and he gave a clipped account into the phone, and then, he did it again. "Bara, stay here."

Bara looked at him. "Like hell."

Reegar looked at them both. "Go!"

They ran.

A minute after they ran, he felt a fantastic surge of spectral energy. Reegar took one step after another, and to his determined astonishment, he was running across the lawn and heading for the broadcast point of the energy. Imara had to be there, there was no one else who could do what she did with spectres.

Imara lay in the serpent's coils as she was inflicted with dozens of cuts. Her head remained clear, which was a deviant construct in itself.

N'sha was hissing with delight that Imara had created the spells to bind her familiar when she had made one of the privacy spells. The moment Midian saw it, she knew that it was the spell they had been looking for to bind their enemy.

Imara blinked. She knew the spell. She had made it out of cotton plants, Jell-O powder, the smoke from dry ice, and a dollop of whipped cream. It was a spell of soft silence to give her a moment of privacy from Mr. E when she was on a date with Argus. She had never considered it binding, but the power was in the heart of the mage.

A whisper came to her. "What can I do?"

She blinked. It was Reegar's voice, but he wasn't physical.

She whispered. "I have to set him free. I need to cast the last spell."

"I understand. Prepare to focus."

"It is my world right now."

She could feel the frustration and restriction that Mr. E was wrapped in, and this would make it better.

She watched her right arm lift.

N'sha blinked. "What are you doing?"

"Giving him what he needs."

Her arm was dropped across her chest, the glass shattered and the liquid seeped out. She focused and smiled. "Give him what he needs."

The lamia reared back, but Imara was beyond that. The golden energy lifted her, and it shot off to one side and struck Mr. E in the other lamia's hands.

Imara thought, *Heal his past, mend his soul, brighten his future, give him what he needs.*

The kitten was enveloped in power, and the smothering of their connection disappeared in a blaze of energy.

Imara must have passed out because when she woke up, chaos surrounded her. Argus's gryphon was wrestling with N'sha while Chancellor Deepford-Smythe was pelting the ancient creature with bursts of lightning.

Imara tried to push herself to a kneeling position, but she slipped in her own blood.

A thunderclap of magic struck on the far side of the green space, and Imara watched a strange mage levitate Midian before smashing her to the ground.

Imara gave a silent cheer and watched everything from her hands and knees.

The battles around her weren't hers. She had one fight right now, and that was to stay conscious.

"Imara . . . oh god. Stay still. I have something that might stop the bleeding." Bara appeared at her side, and she started wrapping the wounds.

Imara felt the burn of the slices all over her body as the wrapper tightened against her skin. She exhaled sharply but kept her silent screams to herself. Bara was helping, and she didn't need guilt.

Luken was standing next to her, and Imara could feel the protective shield that he had around her. She teared up. When another set of men came to stand with Luken, she fought a sob. Michael and Alexander Demiel joined their youngest brother, and the wall around her solidified.

Alexander turned from the defenses, and he knelt at her side. "Ah, sister. What did they do to you?"

Imara looked up at him through her exhaustion. "Whatever it was, I didn't like it."

He smiled slightly. "I got my guild status in healing. Can I help you?"

She nodded. "Sure."

"This is going to hurt."

"I expect nothing less."

Alexander chanted, focused and then wrapped her in enough energy to sear her soul. She was lifted off her hands and knees, and the burn along her nerves kept her focused until he set her on her feet.

Imara looked around and said, "Help me over to Midian. I think I can end this."

Bara took her arm. "Which one is Midian?"

Imara pointed to the one on the ground with the other mage. "Her."

They started to move as a unit toward the mage and the slowly writhing lamia.

"Can someone get me a pebble?"

Alexander bent and picked up a handful from a flowerbed that they passed on their way. "Choose one."

Imara looked at the options and grabbed two. Each was round and nearly spherical. She wasn't sure if she was strong enough to do what she was about to attempt twice, but she knew she could do it once.

"How close do we need to get?"

"I need to be within ten feet of her," Imara grunted.

Bara whispered, "Why?"

"She has something I need." Imara kept putting one foot in front of the other, and Alexander took her other arm to help support her. The contact was agony. His healing may have temporarily sealed the wounds, but the venom was still in her bloodstream. It was acid, and it would burn its way out of her. It was just a matter of time.

She felt what she needed the moment she was within range. "Stop here. I can do the rest."

Luken said, "We are not leaving you."

She gave her brother a long look. "Fine. But when we are done here, get me to the other one. She will probably come to us, but just in case, I will need to get to her as well."

He nodded.

She held out one of the stones and took a few slow steps forward.

Midian looked at her, and her eyes widened in shock. "You are still alive?"

"For now. Why?"

"Eadric killed her mate. Revenge was mandated."

"Why now?"

Midian smirked. "We needed to get past his defenses. You handed us the spell. We had to strike today because of your exam."

Imara nodded slightly in understanding. "I was leaving the school."

"This was our chance. So, how will you spend your last few minutes?"

Imara gave her a cold smile. "You won't need to know that."

She held out the hand with the stone in it, and with some concentration and a few murmured words, she ripped Midian's spectre from her and put it in the pebble.

Midian gasped, twitched, and her serpent body faded, leaving only her human form behind.

"What . . . what did you do?"

Imara looked at her in surprise. "You and your sister took mage courses, became masters. I took your magic from you and put it in this pebble. It will explode in a few seconds, but enjoy being human for the rest of your natural, human lifespan."

She looked to Luken. "Please throw the pebble as hard as you can."

Michael grabbed it and hurled it upward. "Luken doesn't have a good pitching arm."

The stone shattered in the air above them in a cloud of bright blue particles.

The scream that heralded the approach of the other lamia was all that Imara needed. She turned and pulled on the magic as hard as she could, breaking the woman free of her shifted body as centuries of magic were crammed into the small rock. She threw the stone upward, and it was still too close when it exploded.

Arms came around her and lifted her up; she heard voices calling her name, but everything around her was dark. At least her family was safe.

She woke several times with lights flaring around her and folk shouting orders. Each time she sought the comfort of Mr. E, he whispered in her thoughts. *Still here, Imara. You lie quiet and let them help you.*

You are pushy for a kitten. I am glad you are all right.

You made sure of that. It was an amazing spell; now, go to sleep and let them heal you.

Bossy kitty.

You bet I am.

She smiled and stopped fighting sleep.

Waking up in a pristine white tent was a surprise. She thought she had been treated at the college medical centre.

The mage from earlier was sitting at her bedside. He was older, had a thick wave of black hair that caressed the back edge of his collar with the rest combed back, a small silver streak was just starting over one temple. His face was slightly dusky with a long, straight nose that was nearly a weapon in itself but managed to make his face—as a whole—rather handsome. The amber eyes made her pause. She knew those eyes.

"Who are you?" Her first words were a little rude, but she meant them.

"My dearest mage, I am amazed you don't recognize me in this form."

She stared at him and blinked. "Mr. E?"

"Please, when I look like this, call me Eadric."

She blinked again. She went to rub her eyes, but an IV confined her hand. She looked up and found a red bag hanging from a pole. "What?"

"Ah, the lamia venom had completely infiltrated your systems, so several complete transfusions were necessary. Your mother was not a match, nor was Luken, oddly enough. Michael and Alexander were matches, as were Lio, Hyl, Kitigan, and several other students who saw your fight and volunteered to be type tested."

She blushed. "They all donated?"

"There was a line of XIA agents being tested. Several of them donated, and their blood was the first rinse to get the venom out of your system. Magic has been used to keep you stable, but everyone was relieved when you began to breathe on your own again."

He reached out and squeezed her free hand.

"So, you are a person now?"

He cocked his head. "I am still your familiar, but you gave me what I needed to fight for our lives. So, now, I have a few more forms. This one included."

She scowled. "Was that what you looked like?"

"It is fairly close. I was older when I was captured, but I think that the small silver streak is a nice touch." He lifted his head, and she burst out into sobs.

He sighed and got up, carefully lifting her out of the bed and setting her on his lap with the IV next to them.

When she finished crying, he whispered, "This is a turn of

events, huh? Normally I am in your lap."

She snickered and leaned against his shoulder. "Are you safe now?"

"As safe as I can be. The pardon has come through from the guild, by the way. You are my last mage."

She gasped and looked up. "Wonderful. How do I set you lose?"

"Oh, I am not getting loose, not until you get a familiar to replace me that is as magnificent as I am. You also have a lot of plans for the future, and I am in them, so it would be rude to have to adjust your trajectory."

She laughed. "Right. Thank you. Are you still a kitten?"

"I can choose the kitten for easy transport, a larger cat when I am on my own, or my hellcat appearance if need be."

"Wow. That must be nice."

He gave her a gentle hug. "It truly is. How are you going to adapt to the scars?"

Imara looked down at the silvery slices that crossed her arm in places, and she shrugged. "I will adapt. They are part of me now, and I don't recall reading about a lot of lamia survivors."

"There are none. They die screaming within a day of their attack. You got lucky that you were close enough to call for help."

She smiled. "I called for Reegar. He would know what I wanted. Where is he, by the way?"

"He's waiting outside with the others. We didn't want to overwhelm you."

The air ruffled the walls of the tent. "Where are we, by the way?"

"Ritual Space. Adrea offered to host your transfusions and recuperation here so that no one could interfere with it."

She wrinkled her nose. "Did you play tag with Blueberry?"

"Of course. He is an excellent companion and wonderful conversationalist. You have introduced me to the most fascinating people." He grinned and gave her another hug.

She sighed and carefully got to her feet, holding the IV pole in one hand. She walked slowly with the soft white gown clinging tightly to her in an ancient toga design. She opened the tent flap and walked out into afternoon sun. Mr. E was behind her and taller than she would have imagined.

A gathering of people was sitting in another marquee, so Imara wandered over to where her friends, family, and intimidating strangers were gathered.

Bara was sitting and holding Luken's hand, or she was holding his.

Imara walked up to her, and she asked the most important question of all. "Was there any of that cake left over? I am pretty sure I passed the exam."

Luken whooped and jumped up, hugging her tight before letting Bara in for her turn.

The next twenty minutes were rounds of tears, hugs, and a sweet kiss from Argus that made her rise up on her toes.

"I didn't know if you would make it." He whispered it against her ear.

"I didn't either."

"I don't want to lose you."

She leaned back and smiled at him. "I will always fight to stay."

"I will have to take that as good enough."

"You will. Just as I have to take your little journeys into homicide and raging trolls as part and parcel of who you are. You have your world, and I am glad it crossed into mine." She stroked his cheek.

Chancellor Mirrin cleared her throat. "Should I be giving some kind of safe-sex speech here?"

Reegar laughed. "It wouldn't do any good. Imara will take care of herself, or she will choose not to. You have little say in the matter. She's a strong person."

Imara hugged Argus and looked at Reegar. "You are still able to roam?"

"Yes, whatever you did went into the bedrock of the college. All of the spectres have a range they hadn't imagined, though only I retain the physical presence."

"You are special."

He grinned and then sobered. "That was dangerous."

"Detonating the spell on my body? Yeah."

"No, facing a lamia."

"Oh, that wasn't a choice. We finished confirming the exam, and then, she shook my hand, and the first venom entered my system. I didn't do anything after that but run as long as I could. I think I made it thirty feet outside the lab before N'sha got me."

Reegar blinked. "Then what happened?"

"I couldn't reach Mr. E, so I called the spectres. You were the only one that showed up, but I know that you knew about the bracelet. If they were after my familiar, all I could do was give him the tools to help himself. I had no idea anyone else would show up."

Argus murmured, "Luken called me."

Mirrin nodded, "And me."

Imara reached out, and Luken came to let her squeeze his hand. "Thank you. I may be pretty flippant about it, but I like being alive."

He grinned. "It was my pleasure. I am just glad that I guessed Argus's number on the first try."

The folks gathered laughed at what they thought was a joke, but Imara looked at Luken and knew the truth. He had simply gotten lucky. It was what he did.

Chapter Eleven

It had been two weeks since she left Ritual Space and returned to the college. Paperwork had become part of everyday life. She had to make out incident reports for the Mage Guild, the XIA, and the Death Keepers. Her manoeuvre of pulling the spectres out of living lamia had caused a lot of fuss.

If it weren't for her injuries, every single one of those governing bodies would have arrested her, but as it was, she simply got a lecture on not doing it again.

Reegar and his lover were off on holiday for a few days, which disappointed Imara. She was about to leave the Hall, and he wasn't even home.

Bara and Luken were on their way to a movie, and Mr. E was engaged in the most disturbing development of all. He was dating her mother.

So that was how Imara found herself free of paperwork with no friends available and Argus over an hour away.

"I guess I could watch a movie." She sat on the couch and turned on the television. Spare time was not something she had had in the last decade.

Her paperwork for a commercial magic license should be confirmed any day now, and then, she needed to make the move to Redbird City.

Imara stared blankly at the screen while she checked off all the boxes for her new occupation. The estate agent had hired a cleaner to go through the rooms and tidy up, a basic bedroom suite and kitchen appliances had been set up upstairs from her offices, and her would-be home was ready.

A tribunal had confirmed that she had passed her course at master's level, and when she knew she had done her best, she had made sure that Carlos was tested on his work as well.

Once she had the license, she would be able to open up a website and wait for clients. She always had the Death Keeper guild for a basic income, but she wanted her own clients.

Her mind went from hopeful to dark in an instant, and she remembered pulling the spectres from the lamias. She stared at her hands, and she shook at the energy that she had been holding in the palm of her hands. She had pulled centuries of magic away from its owners as if they had no true attachment to it. That was terrifying.

She was lost in thought when a pinging rang out. She lifted her head and listened. *Ping.*

Imara got to her feet and walked toward the sound, realizing that it was coming from her room.

She carefully walked into her space, and the doorway to Ritual Space was open and glowing. There was only one person who could open it, so Imara put on some shoes and stepped through, ready to do battle with Adrea's enemies.

"Surprise!" The roar of voices shocked the hell out of Imara, and she fell on her ass the moment that the sound hit her.

Argus came to her rescue and helped her to her feet. There was a huge banner levitating in the air and the words, *Congratulations, Imara* hovered above the crowd.

She looked up at him. "What the hell?"

Reegar and Lee were standing together and smiling. Lee murmured, "You are underdressed. This is a black-tie affair."

A wave of his hand later and she was wearing one of the gowns that Bara had designed for her. Her running shoes were still intact, and that made Imara smile.

Argus offered her his arm, and she took it, walking through the crowd and greeting all the people who came to celebrate something.

"Why are we here?" Imara murmured it.

"Your commercial magic license came in today. Reegar and your mother hid it so that we could still have the graduation party. Everyone here has been part of your journey and part of your fight. That group of XIA officers there offered their blood for you, without knowing you. They only knew of your character via other agents and that was enough to bring them out when they thought they could help."

"They are running through my veins right now." She smiled at them, and they raised cups to her.

"Yes, but I just wanted you to see how many people are excited to see you reach your goals. We all are. You have a community."

She leaned against him and whispered. "I know. The moment that I woke up in the tent, I knew that it had taken tremendous effort to get me back."

"I wish I had been able to help."

"You kept her from slicing me to pieces. That was huge."

"I meant in your recovery."

She laughed. "Of course, you disregard the action and putting your life in danger."

"That is what I do. Your mother wields a wicked lightning blast, by the way."

"Glad to hear it. I didn't know that she was weather trained."

"I think that this is the moment when you can start to learn about your life or, at least, your family before you were born."

Mirrin, with her arm linked with Mr. E's, came toward her. "Imara, please come this way. I have some folk I would like you to meet."

"Certainly. Mother, can you stop cuddling up to my cat?"

Mirrin grinned. "No. You will get used to it. Eadric is charming, caring, and he loves you as much as I do. It is normal for us to be together."

Imara linked arms with her mother and eased her away from a smug Mr. E. "Fine. But if you give me a new brother or sister, expect hairballs."

Mirrin gave a glorious and bright laugh as she and Imara headed to a group of people who were enjoying the beverages and snacks at the party.

"Imara, this is your grandmother and grandfather, Ida and Hector. These are some of your cousins and their children. This is one chunk of the Deepford-Smythe family."

"I am pleased to meet you." She looked around and saw a number of familiar faces. Casually, throughout her life, she had met each person at the table. "I know you."

Ida smiled. "We know you. We have made every effort to meet you and support you across your life. It is a deep relief that you made it this far and are now a Master Mage."

Imara nodded and smiled. "I remember. I remember you all."

One cousin had bought cookies from her at a school bake sale, another had helped her change a flat tire, another picked up her wallet and returned it to her in the store. Her grandparents had been at her first job while she was learning how to energize the spectres.

"You have watched me."

Ida smiled and shook her head. "Oh no. No legally. The Demiels were very strict on your exposure to our side of the family. Legally, we were not allowed to let you know you had any family. By the way, we are having a gathering at the end of next month in Redbird City. You are welcome to attend if you like."

Mirrin gave her a hug. "She might be overwhelmed. I will get her the information and location."

Imara smiled. "I will look into it. I am about to open my own business, so my schedule is currently unknown."

Ida nodded. "I understand. We will keep issuing the invitations, so when you are ready, we will be there."

It was the best thing she could have said. "Thank you."

Ida inclined her head. "We are so proud of what you have done on your own, and we look forward to meeting you properly, but for today, enjoy your party. You have more than earned it."

Mirrin nodded. "They are not wrong."

Imara looked around to see Benny flapping her hands, and so, she excused herself and went to meet Benny to be formally introduced to her parents.

It was part of being the guest of the hour, so Imara went along and met and greeted folk who had been involved in her survival and—in some cases—existence. It was a relief when she could creep away to a corner and simply get her head together.

She was sitting at the table when a lithe black cat jumped up and sat in front of her. She smiled. "You are exceptionally dramatic as a proper cat."

He inclined his head. *Thank you. Are you overwhelmed?*

"Yes. Before I got here, I was alone in the universe with one friend. Now, I am bonded to you, and everybody here has some kind of stake in my life. I know them, they know me, and we like each other. This is . . . not what I was preparing for."

He shifted into his mage form. "I know. I am in your mind, and you are in mine. I know that simply opening yourself up to me was huge. This is overwhelming."

"A little. I am happy about it. So very happy about it."

"I can feel that, too."

She grinned. "You know what I can't get over?"

"What?"

She swatted him on the arm. "My kitten is dating my mom!"

He laughed out loud. "It has been a while for both of us, and we have you in common, so what harm is there?"

Imara grabbed the front of his mage robes and pulled him in. "Stop slipping the privacy wall between us when you and she are making out. It is not a way to keep me sane."

His cheeks blushed, and a moment later, her little kitten was looking up at her, and he let out a little *mew*.

"Oh, you are a manipulative little guy." She picked him up and cuddled him, scratching behind his ears.

The party was in full swing. Her family was talking, the XIA were arm wrestling, her friends were eating blunderberries and trying to figure out what they were tasting, so Imara got up and carried Mr. E along to try and shed some clarity on the flavour.

A white and blue streak went past her feet, and Mr. E was

in the air in the next minute, booting through the crowd and trying to catch the bunny alpha of Ritual Space.

She giggled and walked over to the most formal berry tasting she had ever been a part of.

Imara made coffee the next morning for the survivors of the party who had made it back to Reegar Hall.

Mr. E was asleep in a pie pan that was coated with purple berry juice, Reegar and Lee were cuddled up on a couch. Bara was sleeping sitting up, and Luken was head down on the table. Kitigan was curled up in the library. Mirrin was curled up in a ball on the love seat.

Imara looked at the friends and family around her and doubled the coffee shot. They were going to need it. That had been a ton of blunderberry pie.

She picked Mr. E up, and the pie pan came with him. When he moved his paws, the pan released and hit the table with a clatter.

No one even moved.

She grinned and went to wash off her kitten, glancing at her bracelet and smiling again. "Well, it seems that I am all alone once again."

My eyes are sticky.

"You are getting a bath. You are suffering from blunderberry hangover, just like everyone else."

Why aren't you sleepy? You ate three times as much as Kitty did.

"I know. I guess I just got lucky. What are the odds of that." She grinned as he gave her a silent groan, and as she scrubbed the purple juice from her familiar, she realized that that was exactly what had happened.

The lamia had followed her in a projected form, which accounted for the two extra spectres the day she took the mage guides around the memorial garden. If she had used the fading garden, she would have summoned them into the memorial area, she would have been dead on the spot. Forcing them to hunt her in the open had made them rework their attack, and that had let her get to the point where Imara could summon the help she needed. It had just been luck, instinct, and timing.

With a clean and scrawny familiar, she rubbed him with a fluffy towel until he looked more like a kitten and less like a rat then carried him back downstairs where she was making breakfast for ten. Her studies were done, she had her license, it was now time to get ready to leave the safety of Reegar Hall and step into the world.

She looked at the unconscious friends and family as she made bacon and pancakes. The difference in this move to Redbird City was that she wasn't going to be alone. It was going to take effort to get her grin off her face.

Epilogue

The door needed a slight nudge to get it open, but it opened. Imara looked down at Mr. E, and she nodded. "This is it."

He gave her a polite but attentive gaze from his new height. "It looks to be in good condition."

She grinned. "This is just the exterior door, but I like your enthusiasm."

Imara pushed the door open all the way, and the slightly dry odour of a closed building met her senses. It was mixed with the scent of newly sawn wood, and that scent confused her.

"Who the heck has been doing work here?" Imara let Mr. E in and closed the door behind her newly reshaped familiar.

Mr. E didn't respond, but there was a swish to his tail that said he was up to something. The dark, polished wood of the hall led to the right and left. She wanted to make the left into her office and the right into a conference room. Her application for a building permit was with all of her belongings out in the car.

Her beloved kitty and favourite buddy was heading straight for the office space.

She moved carefully around the corner, and she paused in shock when she saw the sketch from her file in full detail in the space. Everything from the desk, filing cabinets, bookshelves, ritual area, and coffee machine in the corner, were all exactly as she had doodled them.

Mr. E hopped up onto his supervisory stand, and he watched her.

She felt the tears starting to run down her cheeks. Over a decade of planning and here was her office. She had her space, it was paid for, her license to engage in public magic had come through, and she was a Master Death Keeper and had full membership in the Mage Guild.

She sniffled and wiped the tears from her cheeks. "Right. Well, now, I just need the signage and advertising, and we will literally be in business."

He lifted and licked one of his paws. *You might want to check outside.*

Imara turned toward the door, and then, she heard a scrape. There was a whir, and she walked down the entry hallway to the front door, opening it slowly. A cluster of shadows was on the sidewalk, but it was a familiar cluster.

She closed the door, but a scent caught her again. She looked at the door, and it read, *Spectral Consulting, I. Mirrin, Master Death Keeper, Commercial Master Mage.*

When she turned back to the folks who were installing the hanging signboard nine feet over the sidewalk, she grinned at the very decorous but precise signage. The small spectral stone embedded in a corner of the sign gave it the touch that it needed to catch attention.

When the installation crew was done, she smiled as they pulled off their concealing head wraps. Argus smiled ruefully. "We wanted to get it done before you came back out."

She walked up to him and wrapped her arms around him. "I was happy-crying inside, and it freaked Mr. E out, so he decided I needed a distraction. This is amazing. Thank you!"

He held her close, and he sighed happily, as he always did when she cuddled up to him.

Freddy snickered. "You two look so wrong."

Imara looked around Argus, and she grinned. "I know. I am too mature for him, but his age makes up for it."

Freddy chuckled. "I thought that he was energy and life, and you were death, but I suppose your description could be right. You are serious, and he . . . isn't."

Argus turned to look at Freddy over his shoulder. "I am very serious when it comes to Imara."

The woman grinned, and she looked up. "Well, what do you think, Spectral Consultant?"

Imara leaned back and took in the display. Bara and

Luken were standing near the back of the pack, Argus's XIA team was grinning at her, and one of them was still wearing Freddy as an epaulet.

"I think that this is just the way I wanted to see my business start. In the dark with friends being weird and dressing like ninjas."

They looked at her, themselves, and then giggles broke up their serious gathering.

"So, who wants to help me break in the coffeemaker?" Imara laughed.

Freddy winked. "I am more a fan of breaking into the mini bar."

Imara stared. "I have one of those?"

"You have two. Now, you just have to find them." Freddy linked her arm with Imara and hauled her toward the door. Imara looked back over her shoulder, and everyone was slowly trickling toward them.

It was time to get the party started.

Imara sat on her boardroom table and watched the XIA officers smash a piñata with stress balls. Mr. E was the scorekeeper. He chased the balls that rolled under the furniture.

Freddy produced a laptop, and she sat next to Imara. "This was my gift for you."

To Imara's shock, her business had a website, and there were already eighty-five hits and two messages waiting for her.

"When did you do this?"

"I pulled it together with a little help from Argus. It turns out that I am pretty good at web design when I choose to be. See, it even has a calendar so you can black out dates when you need to."

"It doesn't tell folks where I will be, does it?"

"No. It just says that you are unavailable for bookings or consultations."

Imara followed her instructions and got into the messages. To her shock, both were genuine inquiries for her services. "Wow. They are asking about my fees."

"So? The Death Keeper guild had its own fee structure. This is no different. In fact, you can charge more as you have all the credentials and a service that no one on this side of the continent can offer."

Imara blinked slowly. "Right. I keep forgetting about that."

Mr. E bounded up from under the couch with one of the projectiles in his jaws. She knew he was a man in a cat form, but he looked for all the world like a proud hunter.

You are definitely one of a kind, Imara Mirrin Deepford-Smythe Demiel. He set the stress ball down next to her hand. *If the hellhound can help you manage your business efforts, enjoy the assistance. It will give me a break.*

She smiled and stroked his head. "I am taking any help that is offered."

Freddy looked at her and grinned, going into depth on how to manage the website.

When Imara glanced down at Mr. E, he batted the toy with his paw, and it struck the piñata, splitting the pixie wide open and scattering candy everywhere.

The men hooted and dove for it while Imara rubbed Mr. E's head. "Nice shot."

You should see me with opposable thumbs.

She chuckled. "I have. Did you have to hit on my mom?"

Chancellor Mirrin is an attractive woman and nowhere near her prime. We have a date next weekend.

Imara grinned. "Do you?"

Yes, as do you. If Argus gets out of hand, I am only a thought away, but I believe you two would benefit from a lack of my attention.

Argus was crouched over and picking candy carefully from the pile. He walked over to her, kissed her lightly and placed the candy in her hands. It was all her favourites.

"Happy business warming."

She looked up at him in bemusement and whispered, "Thank you."

Freddy looked at them both, and she eased away.

Argus took the spot that had been occupied by the hell-hound, and he whispered, "Are you happy with how things have worked out?"

She smiled. "This is the start of something new, exciting and terrifying. I am delighted with how it turned out."

He frowned. "Even the threats to your life?"

"They brought me into contact with people I never would have met. I would not have spoken to you if the teacher hadn't been such a creep. Once I met you, I was able to help the XIA member possessed by a spectre—"

"Put yourself in the path of a serial killer."

"I made every course with honours."

"And only had to commit a few breaking and entering as well as magical ingress crimes."

She leaned against him. "But those events led me to new friends and learning about what I was capable of. I am so much stronger now that I know who I am and what my family is actually like, which helps me know myself a little better."

"Even if half of them are jerks?"

"Especially because of that. I know that it is in me now, and I can be on guard for it."

He shook his head in astonishment.

"You have the most peculiarly upbeat attitude. It is one of the things that I treasure about you."

She smiled. "I know. It is the hardest thing to maintain, but the most rewarding in the long run."

He chuckled, and she settled against him, watching the rest of the party come up with a new game involving empty and not empty beverage cups on heads, targets for the spongy stress balls. Mr. E was curled up against her other hip, and she was warm and secure for this first night in her new business with her apartment just above it.

Tonight, was the first night of her business, and it marked the start of her actual courtship with Argus. A lot of firsts were taking place in the next few weeks, and Imara could hardly wait to get to them.

At this point, Imara officially joins the plotline of An Obscure Magic. She is going to play a part in the lives of the other characters, and perhaps Mr. E will continue his bizarre flirtation with her mother. I never suspected that Mirrin was a cat lady, but Mr. E knew it all along.

Surrendering Magic
The Hellkitten Chronicles Book 5.5

Surrendering Magic

Hellkitten Chronicles
Book 5.5

VIOLA GRACE

Bara is facing certain madness or a lifetime of frenzied learning. When she is offered a chance to live as a normal person, it requires one thing: surrendering magic.

Bara has lived her life knowing that she is going to have to spend every waking moment learning or go mad, and even though she has a boyfriend, friends, and distant family . . . her future is bleak.

With a family letter, she sees her chance to grasp a future, even without magic in it. She has a chance to step into the human world, and with the blessing of her boyfriend and her friends, she decides to go through the extraction of the cursed magic she was born with.

The next morning starts far too early, and a cat in her room wakes her and urges her to get ready. When she's prepared, they step through a portal and end up in a place Bara wasn't expecting. Ritual Space. Her trials and surrender are going to take place in the safest area in the world. No magic will escape it, and nothing harmful can enter without the consent of the proprietor. It is the safest place to lose herself, so she begins the process of losing everything she had been taught to love and fear.

No pressure.

Chapter One

Bara sat and grinned at the holiday food representing seven countries and six species. Her culinary course had been Luken's favourite. He had gained ten pounds but sensibly worked out to keep himself under control. It just meant he could eat more.

Reegar and Lee were laughing and chatting with their heads lowered. Imara and Argus were trying to pry Mr. E away from the pie, and the chancellor was laughing.

The four newcomers to the hall were each chatting with their guests, and the food was slowly disappearing.

Reegar paused mid-laugh and said, "Oh, Bara. A letter just arrived."

Surprised, she looked at him. "Really?"

"Yes. It has the Wilmington seal on it." Reegar held it up, and it floated across to Bara.

She took the thick parchment envelope and stared at her family crest on one side and her name on the other. There was magic in the parchment.

Bara looked around the table and smiled. "Does anyone mind if I go to the library and read this?"

Imara grabbed the kitten and hauled him into her arms. "Do you want company?"

"No. I think it's okay. I will be right back."

She squeezed Luken's hand and kissed his cheek. They had spent a good portion of the dinner discussing his plans for after graduation, and it had crushed her.

Her love was going to travel the world and enjoy his degree wherever he travelled. Bara was going to be stuck at the college until she completed the entire curriculum and then would have to find a new college with different courses to take. If she could keep her mind working, she could stave off madness. There was nothing like facing congenital insanity to motivate someone to keep their education going.

The paper crackled in her grip as she walked to the library. She followed protocol and set up a protective ward around the desk before she opened the letter.

Dear Bara,

The contents of this letter have been shared with every generation of the Wilmingtons. This is something we all wanted, something we craved, and our actions outlined our choices.

To explain our family heritage, we have to go back to our eldest ancestor. Arthuate Wilmington. He was a mage without focus, and his new family made him want more for him and them. He began to research how he could make the family prosperous and powerful.

This is the point where our family history gets a little dicey. He contacted a demon king. Arthuate tried to strike a deal for his life and his magic, but the demon added the clause that would induce madness if the power ever lay idle. The curse was in the bloodline from that moment onward.

Arthuate felt the urge to learn and read. He began a collection of tomes, and others came to him to have him research through their grimoires and spell books for specific items they could not locate. He made his fortune researching for others, but his wife was shocked by his new focus. Their children were nearly adults, and his eldest began to show signs of the obsession with knowledge.

The demon began to sell obscure spells, and when Arthuate learned of the devastation caused by the actions he had contributed to, Arthuate tried to stop. The demon retaliated, and Arthuate began his descent into madness.

His wife, Moira, looked into the cause of the sudden obsession that was taking over her children, and when she learned why, she was furious. Arthuate was already insensible, and her investigation caused a sudden decline in his health. Her children were researching strange and unusual spellbooks, finding more and more violent spells, so Moira took action. She traded her life to block the flow of knowledge from their bloodline to the demon. Their particular brand of magic could no longer feed him.

This began our family history. We have touched every tome of learning from sea to sea, and that energy simply flows through us.

Two hundred seventy-three years ago, the first one of your ancestors figured out how to break the cycle. Ystine did some research and came across the true source of the curse. It isn't in the blood; it's in the magic. If you are able to surrender every bit of magic that you would ever have, you have a chance at a future. A chance at a life. A normal life, but a life nonetheless.

Think it over. If you choose to break the cycle for yourself actually to choose life over research, solstice night will be the key. Touch a drop of blood to this letter, and guardians will appear to take you to the place you need to be to shed your magic.

If you care to take this path, there are five others who have walked it before you. They laughed, loved, and lived long lives.

Love and hope, your Nanna Gilchretha.

Bara stared at the page. Nanna Gilchretha had died when Bara was four. This was an old letter, but it had a note at the top that it was to be delivered today. Bara dragged in a deep breath. She had to choose by solstice. It was only one day away. It was the reason for the holiday party.

She folded the letter and tucked it into the envelope. Sanity or magic. That was her choice. She opened the wards she had put around herself and walked back to the dining room. Concerned faces turned toward her, and she smiled weakly. "Letter was from my deceased grandmother. It was an offer that will keep me from spending the rest of my life in an institute frantically learning."

Imara asked, "What is the downside?"

Bara sat down and poured herself some wine. "I just have

to surrender my magic."

The entire table froze.

Luken took her hand. He didn't say anything, just held her hand. He was good that way.

Imara set Mr. E down on the table, and the kitten walked over to her and sat on her hand with the letter. The silence at the table was comforting. They were waiting for her to speak.

Bara looked at them all, took a deep breath, and explained. When she finished, everyone was staring at her.

Imara frowned. "Mr. E says he can't feel any demon magic."

Bara smiled. "It wasn't demon magic; it was a paranoia that turned into a family curse. You know, like many other things in our world. The college is full of examples of influence if not collusion. When the head of your bloodline decides on something, it sticks. So, I start feeling itchy in the brain after less than two days away from learning something new."

Luken squeezed her hand, and Mr. E started purring.

Luken said, "I will spend every day finding new things for you to learn so we can stay together."

"So, we can't stay together if I give up my magic?"

Luken smiled. "If you do that, we can find a way for that. Either way, I am happy to have you in my life for as long as you will have me."

Her heart melted. "Is forever taken? I am thinking about forever."

He leaned in and kissed her. Their lips met softly, and the sound of Chancellor Mirren laughing at them slowed their tangle.

They parted, and both of them were blushing. With his mother and sister nearby, as well as her mentor, things were not precisely private.

She held his hand. "Kisses aren't legally binding."

He grinned. "When I first met you, I saw my soul in another body. And then I looked to the side and saw my twin."

Imara cackled. "We know good-quality partners when we

see them."

Mirren smiled. "And we know when it is time to revert things to companions."

Mr. E murped and walked back to Imara.

Bara blinked. "I thought you were going at it pretty heavy."

The chancellor straightened. "We have a few points of difference, and since he is scheduled to continue on as a familiar, it was getting weird for us and for Imara."

Mr. E transformed into his human shape. "It was fun to go on modern dates, but I am not cut out for this particular era."

Bara looked at him. "Gotcha. Be a cat again, or put some pants on."

He grinned and shifted back to his kitten form.

Bara looked at the envelope. "She wrote this when I was a little kid. She knew I would be here one day."

Mr. E mewed at Imara.

Imara said, "She consulted with many forecasters and seers the day you were born. He was around back then with another mage. He met her, sort of. He was an eagle. He hates being eagles."

Luken asked, "Does it happen a lot?"

Mr. E cocked his head.

Imara said, "More than it should."

Bara chuckled. "He makes an excellent kitten or even cat."

He lifted his little chin and looked smug.

Bara grinned. "Well, I have to figure out what I want to do. I mean, I know what I want to do, but it is another thing to say it out loud."

Luken asked, "Do you want to take a walk?"

Bara nodded. "I think I would like some fresh air."

They got up, and Imara started to collect the dishes. The new inhabitants of Reegar Hall had dispersed while she was reading her letter.

They went for a walk, and Luken held her hand.

"Bara, what are you thinking?"

"I want to end the curse, Luken. I want it gone. If that hurts our relationship, I will understand, but surviving is more important to me than living a life that I can't really enjoy. Your father's family hates me enough without adding this to the pile, but I am bracing for it."

He sighed. "My father and half my brothers are certainly stuck in their ways, but as the lucky one on that side of the family, I knew my luck was in action when I first saw you. I am going to stand by on the morning after solstice, and as long as you take my hands, I am there for whatever happens. If I can help, all the better."

Bara smiled. "I think this is something I have to do for myself, but I am going to be looking forward to finishing whatever is happening."

He squeezed her hand, and they kept walking. The moon was high overhead, and she murmured, "I can't believe you are graduating."

"Neither can I, but I am looking forward to the next phase of my life. And you. I am looking forward to being with you until we are both old and grey."

Bara leaned against him and said, "That sounds nice."

"It really does. I have a job lined up and am going to try and be half as successful as Imara." He chuckled.

"Well, with good luck, you can find a man as good as Argus."

He wrapped both of his arms around her and hugged her. "I did. Well, not a man, but a partner with the unique skill of making me feel whole when she's with me."

Bara sighed. "You say the sweetest things. You are going to be good when I come back powerless?"

"I am only going to be good if you come back. If you don't, I am going to come looking, and I am going to bring everything at my disposal."

"So, I will be hunted down by your sister, your mom, and a kitten."

"And the recruiting arm of the Mage's Guild. They are drooling to get me on their team. My brother is a pain in the ass, and I am the star of the Demiel family. I look very good on paper."

"You look very good in person, too." She smiled at him and looked up. A cascade of light streaked across the sky, and she made a wish for all her friends and insane relatives. When a second star fell, she hoped she was doing the right thing.

When the third star passed, she wished herself luck. She was going to need it.

Chapter Two

Bara woke with the stomping of cat feet on her chest. She bolted upright and stared at the unfamiliar feline. "Uh, hello. I am Bara. May I help you?"

The cat darted to the desk and jumped back to the floor with the letter in its teeth. A muffled "meow" came from behind the parchment, and Bara got out of bed, stumbling into the pile of clothes that had been assembled, probably by a cat.

"Oh. Right. I am just going to pee first. Okay?"

The cat sat down, and Bara moved fast. She went to the bathroom, peed, brushed her teeth, and smoothed her hair.

She wished she had brought the clothes in with her. The door opened a few inches, and the fabric was pushed through the opening. Bara shook her head and got dressed as she heard her shoes dragged across the floor.

When the shoes were on, Bara was ready, and the cat meowed, jerking its head for Bara to take the letter. Bara took the hint and picked it up, looking at the new red lettering that had appeared, directing her to open the envelope again.

Dear Bara,

Thank you for making this choice. I hope that the new reality that you seek is all you could imagine. The power won't be removed from you in one piece. It will be eased from you to stop the shock. Each of your little guardians will hold a fifth of your magic until you finally surrender it all.

A trust has been created for those who have taken this step. You will be taken care of. Powerless does not mean alone. Your family will be with you in their own way.

Be strong. You are loved. Good luck, and follow the cats.

Bara blinked and folded the letter. She tucked it into her bra and patted it.

The cat meowed, and Bara looked at the tawny stripes. "Well, hello, guardian."

The cat got up and stretched its head up. It went up on hind legs, and Bara picked it up. A hum filled the air, and the closet door glowed. The kiss of fresh air came to her and curled around her. Birds were chirping, and there were crickets. Bara looked at the portal and took the steps necessary to pass from one area to the next.

The doorway in space closed, and she was left standing in a meadow. The cat in her arms started purring.

"So, is this a purr-for-direction kind of thing?"

The purr picked up strength.

Bara closed her eyes and asked, "How do I get power into you?"

A rustle in the bushes made her tense, and then she gasped as a familiar face with a familiar blue bunny came into view. "Madam Adrea."

"Hello, Bara. Your journey is going to be carried out in Ritual Space. It is my pleasure to host you and to make sure that you are not injured beyond getting sore feet. I am here to keep you alive." Adrea walked toward her, her white hair gleaming in the bright meadow. "They thought it would be best that someone could speak to you instead of purr at you."

Bara blinked. "Oh. Well, thank you."

"You are about to be led to five points in time where your ancestors did exactly what you are about to do, but you will be watching how their lives unfolded after that. I will appear at that point and speak for the passage of time."

"Oh. So, I am actually going to be walking?"

"Oh, yes. Five different environments and on your way to midnight at the North Pole. That is where the beasts will release your magic into the night sky."

"Oh. Wow. Do I start now?"

Adrea nodded. "I would hug you, but I don't want to contaminate this event."

Bara looked down. "Am I dressed right for this?"

"You are. Also, your guardians can't speak to you. They are just guides and receptacles." Adrea smiled. "Oh, and Blueberry will lead you out if you get too lost."

"So, there is a right amount of lost?"

"Of course. That is what Ritual Space is all about."

"How long is this going to take?" Bara swallowed.

Adrea smiled. "As long as you need it to. Today is yours. The space has been rented to assist you in this endeavour. I have checked your family records, and this is where and how the attempts have been made."

"Attempts?"

"You will see." Adrea took a pack from somewhere and handed it to Bara. "Here are supplies for the day. Water, tea, snacks. I am guessing they didn't let you get breakfast."

"They didn't."

"They never do. Okay, you can put your guide and guardian down, and your challenge begins." Adrea's blue eyes sparkled. "Good luck."

Bara set the cat down and put the pack on. The cat jumped back into her arms.

Adrea bowed and gestured toward a path that was blooming into life. Flowers were streaking into the wilderness, and it was an obvious hint. When the flowers nearest to Bara started fading, she realized the path wasn't waiting.

Bara bowed and then walked after the bright flowers. Her journey had begun.

"You know, I have never been one to talk and walk, but this really feels like the moment to do so."

The cat murmured in her arms.

Bara climbed rocks and had to release her companion to suddenly head upward. The cat jumped and twisted upward, climbing level by level and encouraging Bara with small, cute sounds.

Bara hauled herself to the plateau, crawled onto the centre of the stone, and looked around. "Well, looks like this is time for breakfast. The view can't be beat."

She slid the pack off her back and opened it. The thermal flask of tea was the first thing out, and a pack of muffins was the second. "That looks like a solid start."

She crumbled some of the muffins for the cat and ate while looking out at the landscape that was far different from the fenced enclosure she thought she was entering. There were mountains, oceans, meadows, plains, and thick forests leading to a snowy land.

The tea was warm, and she drank a cup before capping the thermos and putting it back in the pack. She put it on her back again and looked at the cat. "Lead on."

The cat took a few steps and sat on a rock. There was a stone with a human hand printed into it. The cat was looking at a cat print on the stone in front of it.

The cat touched its stone, and Bara took the hint. She swallowed and pressed her hand to the stone. Adrea's voice whispered out, "Bara, do you surrender your magic?"

"I will."

"Then, do it. Put your magic into the stone."

Bara felt the cool and rough patches on the stone and pressed her fingers into the groove. Grabbing her own tainted magic was difficult. She usually worked around it. With a bit of focus, she thought of summoning light, and that called the magic. She dropped to the rocks as the connection pulled magic from her.

She closed her eyes as the magic surged out of her, and then the world went cold around her.

The roar of the waves, the salt in the air, and the sand under her. She felt the mist in the air and heard the soft meows beside her as something nudged her hand. A huge tomcat that should never have been able to make such a delicate sound was nudging her hand.

Bara sat up, and the monster tabby looked at her. He let out the softest *mew*.

"So, hello, guide. I am Bara."

The cat purred heavily and bumped her with his head. She was pretty sure it was a him or a very butch female.

"Right. Have to get going."

She pushed herself upright and dusted off the sand, and the cat looked at her and started scampering down the shoreline. Bara followed.

The sun was high and bright. The waves white-capped and pounded against the sand. The cat's trail was getting washed out, and he was disappearing behind the high stones on the beach, so Bara started running. She got behind the stones and stopped. The cat was gone. The prints stopped mid-stride.

"Shit." She looked around and heard a distant meow. A motion on a distant sandbar showed her that the cat had made his way across the waves to the dry spot.

She smiled and got her backpack as high as she could. She looked at the water, thought warm thoughts, and headed to the water, fully clothed. Bara gasped as she stepped into the water and felt around as she went deeper with the waves trying to push her back to shore. She was determined, and the water crept higher and higher until it wrapped her thighs and tried to push her off her feet. Halfway to the sandbank she started swimming.

Swimming in the surf had been Luken's idea. He had taught her to swim, and though there had been a lot of pauses for touching and giggling, she had learned a few things that day, and swimming was one of them.

The large animals under the water bumped her legs, but she kept her focus. Kicked slowly, stroked with her arms, and then walked onto the sandbar. The cat was meowing and rubbing against her, and she rubbed his head. "Nice to see you again, little dude."

He rubbed against her, and she stood up, stretched, and then moved to a set of flat stones slightly raised on the sand.

She staggered to the stones and sat down. She was shivering, and the wind was getting cooler. She took off the pack and reached in. The tea flask was the first thing in her hand, and she drank a cup quickly.

She found a bottle of water in the pack and poured some into her palm for the cat. He had to be thirsty. She held her hand out, and the cat drank and then purred as he rubbed up against her arm.

"Thought that might be helpful. Okay, I am ready if you are."

The guide pranced over to the stone embedded in the sand and put his paw down on the stone. She smiled and brushed sand out of the handprint before she pressed her hand to the stone. Nothing happened, and she remembered sparking flame on her welding torch. Magic surged out of her and left her lightheaded. She sat back and felt magic around her again.

Chapter Three

Bara looked around and sighed. Forest. A black cat that was far fluffier than Mr. E approached her. She bowed and introduced herself. The cat greeted her, and they were on their way into the woods.

She guessed at what was happening. Exertion and memory were letting her magic loose. It was a pretty good method, after all.

Imara, Argus, and Luken were in the meeting centre. Adrea was sitting in a meditative pose, and five crimson stones glowed in front of her. Two of them were flaring bright and hot.

Luken asked, "How is she?"

Imara smiled. "She's fine. The energy is draining."

Adrea nodded. "Our specialists are standing by for the final phase, but she is moving at a pretty good clip. Hyl will call them when he gets up."

Argus said, "I can call them."

"No, they are on a night shift, so they will be getting up when he does. His rising is the alarm clock."

Adrea smiled. "This feels a little like a gameshow."

Imara chuckled. "As long as Bara is winning, it can be whatever she likes."

Adrea nodded. "She is doing well."

The thud of padded paws ripped through the room as a blue rabbit sprinted through the room as the black kitten rode his steed around the meeting room and then back out the door.

Imara was snickering. "He does love that bunny."

Adrea smiled. "Blueberry likes him, too. Oh, she's

climbing the tree."

Bara smelled the sap, felt the bark digging into her hands, and tried to pace her movements to the sway of the tree limbs. There was a platform above her, and she followed the swishing tail of the cat above her as she fought her way skyward.

"You know, going crazy is starting to have a certain appeal right now." She grunted and hauled herself up and onto the platform, slipping as she gripped it and dangling over open space. The sticky sap on her hands helped her pull herself up and onto the wood, gasping and staring up at the canopy.

The cat rubbed up against her and purred.

"Yeah. I get it. It is still really rough. My hands are trashed." She held them up and flexed them. Her skin was raw and chapped, and her fingers barely moved. She sighed. It seemed like that kind of a day. Do a task and feel the pain.

She fought her way to a sitting position and pulled the pack off. She opened it, and the tea flask protruded again, but she looked past it and found a small first aid kit. She found the water bottle and poured some water for the cat in the lid of the tea canister. After that, she rinsed her hands and wrapped them up with gauze. When she finished, she was either wounded or about to box. Her hands felt better, and she would deal with the embedded splinters when this was all over.

She wiggled her fingers and looked at the kitty, who stared at her in concern. The cat had finished the water, and Bara poured some tea into the cup and then dug around and found a sandwich. She took some of the ham and cheese and broke off a piece for the cat.

"You know, I have lived in a dorm with a cat for a while. Things always work out if you pay the cat first." She chuckled and took a bite. She wiggled around and leaned against the tree. The view was amazing, but that was what Ritual Space was all about—the right space for the right purpose. "You know, I am going to miss the side benefits of magic. I really wish Luken was here with me. He would love this."

The cat walked up to her and made a curious sound.

"Oh, Luken is my boyfriend. He's the twin of one of my best friends and a few years younger than me. He keeps telling me that he likes older women and looks at me in a way that I believe him. He says that it was just good luck that I lived in the same hall as his sister, and I believe that, too." She chuckled. "He also has a thing for long red hair, so we are a pretty good match."

The cat lay down and then rolled over happily, paws in the air.

She laughed. "Yeah, that's how I feel about him, too."

The sandwich and mysteriously replenished tea were done, so she packed the containers away.

They moved to the carved marks in the tree trunk, and the paw and the hand were put in place. Bara thought of the first time she had changed the shape of another living thing, and that thought sent the energy coursing into the tree and away from Bara.

She got dizzy again, and when she woke, she was at the edge of an open meadow. The next challenge had begun.

Bara looked around for her guide but couldn't see anything in the tall grasses. Bara focused on the tops of the grasses, and she whistled softly before calling, "Here, kitty, kitty."

She saw a wave in the green and gold stalks and heard a tiny sound. Bara walked forward slowly. "Here, kitty, kitty."

The tiny sound repeated, and she walked forward. It took about ten minutes to find her guide. A tiny golden kitten with a stripy tail. "Oh, hello, sweetie."

She bent and held out her hands, and the kitten walked onto her palms. She picked up the shaking kitten and held it against her chest. "Aw, honey. Come on, we are going to get you fed and warm."

Bara looked around at the meadow, and it seemed to stretch on forever. She checked the wind and sprinted into it, carrying the shaking baby against her chest. Her senses remained on alert, and after ten minutes, she saw a difference in the meadow. A shadow off to the left caused her to redirect her path.

"It looks like there is a dip in this meadow, and we might get some shelter in there. At least enough to warm you up and get you fed. I think I saw another sandwich in there."

She found the shadow and carefully walked down into the depression in the soil. Bara shifted her grip and used a loosely held handful of hair to tell her when she was out of the wind. She shucked the pack off her back and went into it to get some food for the kitten as well as water.

Bara spent five minutes getting the kitten to eat before she sipped her own tea. The tiny little scrap ate eagerly and then purred as it crawled back to her and settled on her lap for a nap. Bara looked at the sun in the sky and stroked the kitten. No one should ever rush a cat nap.

Bara thought about how she felt as she watched the sun descend. She had been taught that she had to feed her magic. Serve it. Keep it satisfied.

Today, she was serving herself, working for herself. She was serving life, and other possibilities were starting to flick through her mind. Going on holiday. A long-term relationship. Maybe kids one day. Studying on her own terms. It was a dream she had tried to fulfill under the confines of the curse, and Magus Reegar had been a tremendous help. Imara had needed help socializing, and it reminded Bara how much fun it was to go out and just see the world for the first time, just like kittens saw it for the first time.

When the little beast in her arms yawned and stretched, the pink tongue curling, Bara smiled. Every day could be new. She was just going to have to learn to live without magic.

She looked around the reddening meadow and saw the magic in nature all around her. If she could just keep this mindset, she might be okay.

The kitten jumped out of her arms and walked ten feet over, and then the tiny mew happened. Bara closed everything up, put on the pack, and walked to follow the sound. The stones with the prints were next to the fuzzball, and the kitten was frolicking wildly. She grinned and knelt next to the human handprint and looked at the kitten.

Ten minutes later, the excited kitten walked over to the stone and mewed. Bara scratched behind its ears and said, "It's okay. We do this together."

The kitten rubbed up against her hand and slowly set its paw in the small print. Bara put her hand in the large print and remembered distance-viewing class when she was in high school. Energy flowed out of her and into the kitten.

The location shifted, and she stood up in shock. She was fucking freezing!

Bara dropped to her knees and looked in the pack. She clawed her way to the bottom and felt something she had been hoping for. Fabric.

She emptied the bag while shivering and shook out the found fabric, wrapping it around herself. "Oh, that's better."

She reloaded the pack and held it to her chest under the wrap.

The air was icy, and so was the ground. Everything was white with the exception of piles of rocks in the distance.

Bara looked around for signs of her next guide, but there was nothing except one small pawprint in the snow. She pressed a hand to the ear that was getting blasted by icy wind and made sure she was headed in the right direction as she followed the mark in the snow.

One-fifth of her magic was still inside her, and it was probably going to be chipped out of her after she froze to death. Maybe one of her arms. That seemed fair.

She staggered forward as the snow and wind pulled and tugged at her, holding the thick fabric around her as she plunged forward. The small, helpless cry got her attention.

"Shit." She looked around and listened for the sad wail again. She turned toward the wind that had carried the sound and then slowly began facing the wind and moving toward the sound.

She remembered Kitigan's warnings about breathing with her mouth open while walking into the wind and kept her head down, breathing through her nose. Every time she heard the noise, she altered her path.

A tower of tumbled rock loomed ahead of her, and Bara pushed onward until she heard the echo of the wail from inside the rock.

She searched along the wall of stone until she felt the sudden opening of the rock under her palm. Stone crumbled away under the pressure from her bandaged hands, and the sound got louder. She was in the right place.

Pushing the pack in front of her, she wedged her way into the darkness until the pack struck open air, and Bara cautiously followed.

Cold, moist air rushed at her as she stepped into the dimness. She squatted and groped inside the pack, getting a strange cylinder in her palm. It was familiar, and she pulled the metal out, touching it and turning on the flashlight that had been provided.

She used the flashlight to check out the inside of the stone pile and heard the wail from further ahead. Bara kept going and kept her mind blank. The creature calling her was going to take the last of her magic, but she was going to keep moving forward. Staying where she was wasn't an option. There was no future for her from this point and time unless she took action. Something was in distress nearby, and she couldn't finish her tasks until she found it.

When the sound began a fever pitch, Bara moved forward as fast as she could while holding the pack. She burst into an open cavern, and an icy pool filled the space. There was a cat on a flat stone in the centre, but it seemed that its tail was frozen in the pool.

"Well, hell. Let me think about this."

She looked at the cat and said, "Be calm. I am working on this."

Humming to herself a little, she looked around the chamber with her flashlight and saw something that might work.

She stepped out onto the ice carefully and felt it bow

under her. It held, but it wasn't happy about it.

"Right. That isn't a great idea."

She finished her thought and crept around until she found bits of wood. She used a flat piece and a stick to make a drill and plucked some of her own hair and fibres from her shirt to make a fire starter. She piled up a bunch of rocks and worked to start a fire. It was just as tricky as she remembered, but Imara had shown her how to do it in the fireplace. Her friend had reiterated that magic was great, but knowing how to do things the human way meant that she would never be without skills or knowledge. She would know how to start with nothing.

She worked until she saw the glowing spark, added the fluffy fibres and then slivers of the wood she gathered, and soon there was a cheerful little blaze. It had taken nearly an hour, but she had the fire. The stones lined up around the edge of the flames, and she grew the fire until a lot of heat filled the space.

Bara used the sleeve of her shirt as she turned the rocks, and when she had one that was hot enough, she picked it up and bowled it across the ice until it stopped near the cat. She paused and held her breath as it slowly sank into the ice and then plopped into the water. It was about a foot from the cat, off to the side. Now, it was time to melt the ice.

"Well, that works."

Bara began to hurl the rocks as fast as she could, and after the sixth, the cat's tail came free. The ice around it had melted.

Bara pressed her blistered and raw hands to the ice and looked at the cat as it scampered across the ice. The cat rubbed its head against her, and Bara nodded. "Right. Tea and then power. Did you want a snack? I might not be able to open it, but I will try."

The cat rubbed up against her, and Bara chuckled and stumbled back to the fading fire.

She opened the pack and found a plastic bag full of tuna. She pried it open and dumped the contents onto a rock.

The cat went berserk on the tuna, and Bara got her

thermos out and drank the last of the tea. She put it all back in the bag and closed the pack as best she could.

The cat looked at her and meowed, walking a few steps toward the hall where she had entered. Bara got to her feet and knew her smile was tired. "Lead on, fuzzy butt."

The cat blinked and got moving.

Bara followed. The last bit of magic to surrender was brewing inside her. Time for an eviction.

Chapter Four

Inside the entrance, the cat turned to the left and led her through a tunnel she hadn't seen or felt on the way in. They walked in the tunnel for ten minutes, twisting left and right. Bara was exhausted. The cat finally made a happy sound, and they walked into a cavern of ice with a set of stones in the centre.

Bara huddled under her wrap and walked to the stone, looking at the cat as it jumped onto the plinth that supported the paw mark.

A voice sounded. "Bara Wilmington, are you willing to remove all traces of magic, to walk the world as a human, and to remember what could have been?"

"That's a little mean, but yes. A future to deal with is better than a future of madness."

"Then, place your hand and surrender your magic."

Bara nodded and pressed her hand to the icy platform, and the cat did the same. She dragged in a deep breath and tried to remember the first time she truly *felt* magic inside her. Bara had been going to visit her grandparents and one of their caregivers. They had made her a popsicle, and then, she had made her own out of frozen fruit.

The memory of her first popsicle was given up with her magic. It rushed out of her, and she slowly swayed as the magic that nature had gifted her with was removed. She dropped to the icy floor. That was it. It was over.

After a minute, she sat up again and looked at the cat. "Right. Now, lead me out of here, guide."

He blinked and cocked his head.

She got to her feet and wrapped herself up. "Come on, kitty. I have a life to live, and I am not going to spend it in this particular cavern."

She looked at the cat, and it led her out. The sky above was dark, and there was only a flick of light in the distance. The cat looked toward that flicker of light.

She nodded. "I am trying. This has been a helluva day."

Imara blinked at the map that Adrea had set up. "She's moving?"

Adrea smiled. "She's moving. One more challenge and we can party. The guests are in place."

Luken stared at the glowing dot and exhaled slowly. "I just want her back safely."

Imara looked at him and smiled. "That is what we want as well, Luken." She looked at the genuine concern and affection on his face as he watched the little dot cross the frozen tundra. Imara had always wanted an actual sister.

Bara felt her lips cracking, and the last of the supplies had been depleted. The pack was empty.

She continued to plot toward the growing light and was emotionally numb when a figure moved to block her.

She paused and blinked. "Huh. Out of the way, jackass."

The demon jolted. "You dare?"

"I dare. Treaty restrictions mean that if I am not of your bloodline, you can't do anything to me without getting put on a death sentence. So, fuck off."

"Do you know who I am?"

"The demon prince Nimyan. Intelligence broker. You have been feeding off my family off and on for centuries." She kept plodding along.

"I can return your magic to you."

"No. You can't. They didn't take it; I surrendered it. My magic is not under your sphere of influence. All you can do is offer me a replacement power of demon energy, and I don't want to have that nasty stuff in my body. So, while I appreciate the offer, fuck off and die."

The wind had ceased, and she continued to plod through the snow. The demon rushed around and tried to block her.

"Bara Wilmington, you are exceptional. I can give you riches, a library, a neverending supply of books."

"Friends? Lovers? Associates? Family? Seriously. No. Absolutely no. I have lived my life with the effect of your assistance hanging over my head. You may not have benefited from the learning, but you aren't going to get back into my family's presence by using me. No."

He clacked his emerald green fingers together. "But what about wealth?"

"I can work for wealth." She walked around him again.

"I can give it to you."

"I don't want anything from you." Bara looked at the growing light that was reaching toward her.

When the clawed hand grabbed her, she was shocked. Stunned. She stared into his serpentine eyes. "Let me go."

"If it is a lover you want, I am very good." He smiled slowly.

"Go away. Let me go."

He smiled cruelly. "As you are determined to reject me, I believe I can persuade you."

She glanced down at his groin and didn't think. She brought her knee up as hard as she could. He stumbled back but didn't go down. She ran, and when the claws drew across her throat, she knew that her choice had the unwanted but necessary effect.

Blood poured down, and she heard the soft *whuff* of a portal. She held a hand to her throat and looked at the demon being held by an elf in an XIA uniform while the rest of his team stood by.

The woman said, "I, Benny of the XIA and Mage Guild, do hereby carry out the death sentence earned by Nimyan. Bye-bye."

Bara was gurgling her own blood as Nimyan burst into flames, screaming and thrashing in the elf's grip before he dropped to the ground in a pile of ash.

Bara saw Benny coming toward her, and then hands on

her throat helped some healing as she started to wheeze air instead of blood into her lungs. Benny murmured, "I have just learned this, but demon wounds are hard to heal. Sorry, we had to wait for him actually to injure you."

Bara whispered, "I know. Demon statutes and regulations were covered in one of my law classes."

The elf came forward and continued the healing. "This is to scrub your blood of demon traces."

She nodded, and when he drew back, she pushed herself up. "I have somewhere I need to be."

Benny said, "You shouldn't be walking. Let us take you back to the meeting room."

Bara started walking. "No, thank you. This isn't done yet."

She looked down and was covered with blood. She kept walking toward what was now obviously the aurora borealis.

The cat with her walked at her side, and as she kept walking, she saw other small figures approaching to walk with her. She swayed, she stumbled, but she was eventually nearly frozen and standing next to a heavy pillar jutting out of the snow.

She grabbed the pillar and hung on. It was warm and gave her feeling back in her hands.

"Well, that's better." She chuckled and looked around.

A woman in soft green appeared and walked toward her. "You are a tough little girl, Bara. None of your ancestors have been able to complete the surrender. Do you understand the purpose?"

"Yes. The influence of the magic is that it wants to be used. I saw what it did to my family members. I never wanted to be like them."

The woman had brown hair. No, it was blonde. No, white. Green. Black. Red. Her eyes were sky blue, and her skin rotated through the same fluctations of skin tone across every species.

Bara knew who she was talking to. "My lady."

"My child. You are very cute. You have two lucky ones at your beck and call, and you don't use them. You had a magic that roared and raged, and you studied fashion design. You had it all at your fingertips and always took the most sensible and considerate choice."

The earth goddess looked at her. "If you could choose power, what would you choose?"

"I wouldn't. Choice is an impulse. I learned to use what I had and will learn to use my human skills in everyday life."

"Of course, you will. You look cold." The woman gestured, and Bara was suddenly warm. She was wearing plush boots, a long dress, and a thick cloak with gloves.

"Thank you."

"I am sorry that your hair lost its fire, but that was a side effect of the surrendering."

Bara pulled a lock of now snow-white hair forward. "Magic made it red?"

"Stress made it white."

"Oh. That tracks."

The woman walked up and linked arms with Bara, and they began walking. "So, it is the solstice, and you have managed to do something that your family has tried to do for centuries. That deserves a present."

"Thank you, but it isn't necessary."

"Well, then, what would you wish out of anything in the world? Not for you, but for anyone."

"I would wish for the madness to be lifted from my family and a lack of interest in learning to be given to those who are suffering from the mania. They have learned enough."

The goddess smiled. "That can be done, but you will have to be the one that does it."

"How?"

"Do you see the lights above you? Radiation reflected by a distance sun. Take it in."

"What?"

"The solstice needs more representation, and I need someone who will not only learn but teach. Take the power of light in winter, and I will tell you what I need from you."

Bara paused and looked back at the cats lined up with the light reflecting off their fur. She looked at the ever-changing goddess and smiled. When she looked up to the gorgeous dance of panels of light, she simply continued the happiness and took them in.

Everything the light had seen, everyone it had touched, it whispered through her mind, thousands upon thousands of years.

Wonder and delight coursed through her regularly, as well as all the children who had gotten their start under the light. It was a heady collection of amazing memories.

She smiled as the light wrapped her and took her away.

Chapter Five

Bara Wilmington, only child of Bart and Agatha, stood before the meeting house, dressed in velvet and fur, and had a book in her hand.

She swallowed and walked to the meeting house and knocked on the door. It swung open, and Luken was there. Tears were in his eyes, but they widened as he saw her.

"Sorry about my hair. Apparently, it's a thing." She smiled and then lost her breath as he crushed her in a hug.

She hugged him back, and there was relieved laughter behind him. He leaned back and kissed her. She kissed him and stroked his cheek. "I am okay. Different. But okay."

Bara looked at him, and he smiled at her. "They took it, but they put something back."

He smiled. "Yeah."

Adrea called out, "Luken, let her in."

He backed up, and the others finally saw her.

Adrea looked at her, blinked, and started laughing.

Imara ran forward and hugged her. "Bara. Love the hair. I am so glad you made it."

Bara hugged her and looked at Adrea. "Who let the demon in?"

Adrea cleared her throat. "That was the space and the landowner. She let him through. You know why."

"It was a test. Every step of the way. I passed, and I got a reward for it." She looked at Luken. "It means I am going to have some travel in my future."

He smiled. "Would you like company?"

"I think I would definitely like that."

"What do you need to do?"

"Record how different civilizations spend the longest night of the year and write them in this book. I can move pretty quick, so it will be a whirlwind event . . . every year."

Luken smiled. "I love a family tradition."

Imara said softly, "Speaking of families . . ." She waved her hand at the five soul stones that contained mages. "Some of your guides would like to speak to you. They are very proud."

Out of the gems, the mages' spectres rose. Bara gasped. "I know you. Grandma?"

The woman floated to her. "Bara. I knew you were made for more than studies."

Bara smiled. "I miss you."

"I know, but you visited the repository. I am sorry that I wasn't clearer. Your friend has helped us all focus for today."

"She is excellent that way."

Bara was introduced to a great-great-aunt, two great-great-uncles, and the original ancestor who made the deal. They moved to a corner of the room and chatted about family things until they all felt that they had been heard.

The other four returned to the stones, but her grandma said, "It is cruel of her to give more education to you as your focus."

"I get to learn around the world and have three hundred sixty-four days just to be myself without an agenda."

Her grandmother smiled. "I see. I think I understand. You aren't locked into any one place or just books. You can continue to develop into yourself anywhere."

Bara smiled. "I was going to do it with or without power. I really want to see the world." She looked over to Luken. "With him."

He looked away from Argus and Hyl and smiled at her. She blushed.

"Tell me, Gran. How does my hair look?"

"Well, I miss the red, but the white is rather spectacular. Just like Adrea's." Her grandmother winked.

"It is going to take some getting used to." She smiled. "But it beats the alternative. Gran, thanks for helping me through this."

Her grandmother's spectre reached out and cupped her

cheek. "It was my pleasure. Have a beautiful life, precious girl."

"Rest well, Grandma."

Her grandmother returned to the red glowing stone, and Imara picked it up and set it in her carrying case.

Bara looked at her hands and pulled off the gloves. Healed, but there was a strange sheen to her skin. It glittered like frost.

Luken walked over to her and took her hand in his, kissing the back of it. "It's still you, Bara. The woman that I love."

"The woman who loves you in return."

He wrapped his arms around her and kissed her temple. "Are you ready for a solstice celebration?"

"I thought it was over."

"No. Adrea explained that time moved differently for you. For us, it was only two hours."

Bara stared at him. "You are kidding. It looked like a day but felt like a week." She whispered, "Some parts felt like forever."

"Can you talk about it?"

"Not yet, but it is the first few pages of my book."

He blinked. "Where did the book go?"

"It's in my pack, which is now a leather pouch. It's a bag of holding and has what I need." She smiled. "I checked for you in there a few times, but I don't think I was allowed to pull you out."

He sighed. "I would have been with you if I could."

She smiled at him and said, "I know. So would Imara and Mr. E. Hell, even Magus Reegar would have been in there helping."

"What about the chancellor?"

"She would be checking the rules and seeing if she could call a technicality if I faltered. Like when I dropped twelve feet on the tree. She would have called a time-out."

He blinked. "I think I need to read that book."

"You can't, but I can read it to you."

"What?"

"The book. The book is my history." She smiled. "It starts today."

Luken grinned. "Tonight, the world is reborn, so it's fitting. You are, too."

Imara laughed. "Great. Come on, you two. Adrea said there is another room where the party has been set up." Mr. E was asleep on her shoulder, and Argus held her hand.

They walked toward the double doors that swung open at their approach, and the great room of Reegar Hall was splayed in front of them with holiday decorations and classmates.

Bara's heart pounded, and she looked back through the doors as they closed where Adrea was talking to a woman with long green hair who looked over and smiled at Bara as the doors swung shut.

Reegar's solid spectre came toward her, took her hands, and hugged her. "Little lady, I am so proud of you."

She hugged him back and felt tears on her cheeks. "Thanks. I am very glad to have come through it. How close is it to midnight?"

Reegar leaned back. "Ten minutes to go. Why?"

"I am going to have to step outside."

"Why? It's cold out."

She laughed. "That doesn't bother me anymore. Not cold. Not heat. It all just feels normal."

Reegar leaned back. "How?"

"I gave it all up, and I got something else." She chuckled. "It was something."

Reegar murmured, "Did you feel hollow?"

"No. I felt at peace. The pain in the magic was gone. I gave it up." She smiled. "It was easy since I knew the alternative."

He squeezed her hands. "I am so proud of you."

"Thank you, Magus Reegar. It means a lot."

Friends came up to her and congratulated her, but when the time was right, she just turned and walked out the door to centre herself in the quad. Her friends gathered with her.

Bara felt strangely powerful as she stared up at the night

sky. Her arms lifted, and she threw some of that power toward the sky. Green flared up and out in a sheet. Red followed, and then white rippled in flat panels of light and magic.

The northern lights danced and flickered. Students and teachers spilled out of the dorms and stared up at the sky. They took photos and looked through a telescope, and when it was time to let them fade out, she released the power and let it float away.

She smiled and felt at peace. No frenzy. No compulsion. Just peace.

She turned toward Luken, and he smiled at her and then dropped to one knee. He pulled a ring out of his pocket and looked up at her. "Bara Wilmington, on this first moment of a new day, I wanted to ask you a question."

There was gasping and a lot of women making happy sounds.

Bara looked at her boyfriend and smiled. "What's the question?"

"You are the light of my life, my hope for the future, and I would be honoured if you chose to marry me." He held up the ring. "Imara helped me pick it."

Bara laughed and smiled at the ring carved out of silver and holly leaves. "It's gorgeous. Did you know?"

He grinned. "I got lucky."

She laughed and nodded. "Yes . . . and yes."

He took her hand and slid the ring into place. She leaned down to kiss him, and he got to his feet while Imara could be heard cheering and howling in the background.

They kissed and hugged, and he twirled her around.

Adrea watched with the earth goddess and smiled. "She has no idea what you did, does she?"

Gaia chuckled. "She doesn't care. She has friends, family, and the man she loves. She is young and will live life to the fullest . . . until she figures out that she and her husband are not growing older. They will deal with that and the little demi gods they are going to spawn over the decades. A new goddess of the solstice has been created, and long may she reign."

Adrea nodded and extended her hand. "Chip dip?"

"Yes, please. Is this your aunt's recipe?"

"No. I got it online."

Adrea sat, and they watched the party with Hyl reading a book and Blueberry texting on his phone. In the displayed image, she saw Mr. E on the phone as well. That was hilarious.

The goddess ate the last of the dip and then exited Ritual Space with a graceful hug and a kiss to Adrea's temple. "Be well, Adrea."

"Thank you, Mother. This has been a wonderful day."

"It really has. Solstice has needed a new representative of change and survival, and Bara definitely fits both, and she did it by turning to joy each time. That is very rare." Gaia chuckled. "I made a good one there. I am congratulating myself. Might even go and start life on another world to celebrate."

Adrea nodded. "Have fun."

Gaia disappeared, and Hyl moved up behind Adrea. "So, is she gone?"

Adrea leaned back against him. "As much as she ever is."

"Why did you call on her?"

"I needed to allow a demon into Ritual Space, and she was the only one who could make it happen. I had no idea Bara's recovery would involve that kind of transformation."

"It isn't so different from yours."

"Yeah, but you feel different when it's yourself. For me, it was what had to happen. For her, there were options." She put her hands on Hyl's while leaning back against him.

"She chose. She chose life, she chose a future, and she chose Luken. We will have to send an engagement gift."

"What do you get a new seasonal god who doesn't realize what she is yet?"

Hyl kissed her neck. "A travelling outfit? Nice towels?"

Adrea chuckled. "I will ask the space what it wants to give.

It is excellent at that sort of thing. Hey, where did Benny and the guys go?"

"A death sentence on a demon is a lot of paperwork." He chuckled.

"Ah. Right."

"And you, dearest, have been running five different realms and containing a demon and two goddesses. You need a nap."

Adrea laughed. "I really do."

She collapsed in his arms, and he carried her up to bed, joining her and taking care of her as he had been doing for a few years.

It was an auspicious start to a new year.

About the Author

Viola Grace is a Canadian author who immerses herself in Fantasy, Paranormal, Sci-Fi, and graphic novels (that's new). Writing for a few decades, she has spanned short stories, novellas, novels, and the occasional collaboration with the result being an astonishingly large backlist.

Focusing her work on humour, lightness of spirit, and now and then a heat level to scorch the pages, she leaves the dark and depressing to others. Happily ever afters are guaranteed.

The crafts she has accrued over her lifetime regularly work their way into her books with a variety of results for the characters.

When she's at home, she is usually hiding indoors with felines of various sizes. The bees come in one size, and their speed is usually fast. When she is outdoors, she takes pictures of the stunning skies above her home and the wildness of nature that surrounds her, imagining fantastical worlds hiding in everything around her.

9 781990 635403